The Computer Who Loved Me

Lloyd G Miller

Published by Lloyd G Miller, 2017.

THE COMPUTER WHO LOVED ME
Lloyd G. Miller

Copyright Lloyd G. Miller
2018

Chapter 1 - The Odd Couple

As Kyle James and Josh Adamms walked briskly along the University of Utah sidewalk on their way to the Engineering Building, heads turned, mainly female ones. The taller of the two, Josh, was blond, well built, very good-looking and smartly dressed. His shorter but still tall companion had a very masculine face with handsome, but not what many girls would call cute, features. He possessed a sturdy build with a powerful upper body. Light brown hair topped his rugged features. Unlike Josh, Kyle was not well dressed. Kyle's clothes looked like they had been snatched off the racks of a thrift store at a dead run. Not a single piece of clothing was inherently attractive or stylish by itself and nothing went together. The backgrounds of the two men were as dissimilar as their attire. Josh came from a large, upper-middle-class family that was very close and devoutly religious. Kyle had revealed little about his family, but it appeared to Josh that he did not even know who his father was. Little did those who watched realize that these two men, with the help of a few close friends, would bring about what would come to be known as the second wave of the computer revolution.

As they conversed, Kyle walked on Josh's left side. "We need to stop off at the graduate student study room," said Josh. "Shad wants to see me about something."

"That's fine. Just remember that I have a tutoring appointment at two," replied his friend. After entering the building, they turned into a narrow hall and entered an open door.

"Hey, Shad, my man, what's up?" asked Josh. Shad held up a picture of a very attractive young woman.

"This is my sister, Michelle. She'd like to go out with you sometime."

"Tell her to take a number," interrupted Kyle.

"Pay him no attention, Shad. Michelle's very cute. More than cute, she's beautiful. If I were going to base my decisions on looks alone, I would marry her tomorrow. However, despite all appearances to the contrary, I do consider other things. Why does she want to go out with me? We've never even met."

"She is in your English literature class and was impressed with how you answered a question."

"If these are the fruits, I'll participate more often in class. Surely, I would have noticed her. Where has she been?"

"As you know, it's a big class. She sits in the back," responded Shad.

"I'll make a point of looking for her and getting to know her. We'll see what happens. Fair enough?"

"I could ask no more." The slap of books slamming down on a desk interrupted the discussion.

"Man, that chafes me!" let out a graduate student with whom neither Josh nor Kyle was acquainted.

"What's the matter, Phil?" asked Shad.

"I just came from Dr. Farsi's office. He rejected my dissertation proposal. The reasons he gave were all superficial. I know the real reason. There's no money to do it. He wants me to do something he already has funding for."

"Like what?" asked Shad?

"Like finishing a computer program to evaluate the risks of shipping hazardous wastes. Can you believe that? I have no interest in that field. He only suggested it because I'm the only decent programmer available to him."

"What are you going to do?" asked Shad.

"Probably go get wasted and then start writing the program. My parents have their hearts set on me getting a Ph.D." Josh and Kyle had watched in silence and then slipped out.

"I might do some professor's project for a master's degree but no way for a doctorate," commented Kyle. "I'll do what I want to do, even if I have to raise the money myself."

"I believe you, Kyle." Kyle had been on the right side of Josh and moved over to his left.

"Sorry, I couldn't hear you very well."

"Why don't you get a hearing aid for that left ear of yours? They make ones now that can hardly be seen."

"A conventional hearing aid would do absolutely no good. You see, my inner ear on my left side was wiped out by meningitis when I was a child."

"Bummer. Well, just keep walking on my left side, then."

"That's what I want to do my dissertation on. I want to connect a processor to the audio nerve endings of my left ear. The nerves should still be intact."

"It sounds feasible in theory, but won't that require lots of capital?" asked Josh.

"No question, that's why I must start raising the money now. I have developed an algorithm for trading a certain class of stocks. In the simulations, it has been very profitable, but I need at least several thousand dollars to get started."

"I'll let you know if I see any special opportunities for you to earn some extra money," offered Josh. "Do you have any tutoring sessions tonight?"

"None after the two o'clock session."

"I have two tickets for the game tonight. My date got sick. Would you like to go with me tonight?" asked Josh.

"I'll be your date if I don't have to hold your hand."

"After that comment, I'm not sure I even want to sit near you," responded Josh. "How come you never ask any girls out, Kyle?"

"It's not because I don't want to. I'm just afraid of getting serious before I'm in a position to get married. Besides, do you really think any girls want to go out with a guy who dresses like this, not to mention my car?"

"Some women want to take on a project. They want to see what they can do to improve a guy. They look at potential. As far as the car goes, you can borrow mine."

"No thanks, it would clash with my outfit."

At the basketball game, Kyle and Josh sat in front of a couple of very rowdy football players. The teammates drank continually and became more and more profane and obnoxious. Both Kyle and Josh found them very annoying but tolerated them until they started being abusive to people around them. Fed up, Kyle turned and said in a low but firm voice, "Gentleman, would you please keep it down. Some of us are here to watch and hear the game, not listen to your profane commentary." This only made the two ruffians louder and more profane. Kyle left his seat to find a university security officer and report their conduct.

The obnoxious duo called after him, "That's right nerd. Run to your mommy!" He found a man in uniform and explained his problem. They walked back to Kyle's seat. As the officer approached, he pointed to the rowdy athletes and asked, "Are these the two men you told me about, sir?" Kyle nodded yes.

The men were arrested and as they left, they both turned to Kyle and mouthed, "You're dead meat." Many of those seated nearby applauded as the two troublemakers were hauled away.

After they left, Josh commented, "That was a pretty gutsy thing to do."

"I guess it was pretty stupid. I'd hate to run into those two in a dark alley after tonight. I sure hope I never see them again." Just then, a couple of cute girls took the vacated seats. One was a very cute blonde and had her eye on Josh. Before Kyle realized what was happening, Josh was trading seats with the blonde's friend. Despite

Kyle's explanation of why he didn't date, he certainly didn't mind the female company. "Hi," he said, "I'm Kyle."

"I'm Rachael. Thanks for getting rid of the two losers."

"It was probably a stupid thing to do, but you're welcome."

Rachael bent around to look at Kyle from the front. "You look pretty buff. She put her hands on his shoulders and ran her hands down the outside of his arms. "You are buff and you feel as solid as a rock. You could probably hold your own with the losers."

"Maybe one at a time, but there are two of them, and they would have the element of surprise."

"True, but I bet that you could outsmart them. I'm a sophomore in Mechanical Engineering. I have seen you around in the engineering building, and everyone says that you are really smart and a great tutor." Kyle began to wonder if Rachael's interest in him was tutoring, maybe free or discounted tutoring.

"So what kind of student are you?"

"This is kind of embarrassing; ever since I started engineering I've noticed that boys don't expect much from me academically. I sort of developed a chip on my shoulder. Now I feel like I have to show up the boys in every class. I do well academically but not socially."

"I'm sort of in the same boat. I am so focused on school with the goal of obtaining a PhD that I hardly spend any money on cars or clothes as you can clearly see."

"You are Prince Charming in disguise. The disguise doesn't bother me. It may fool the other girls but not me. As for your car, the guys with expensive sports cars really turn me off. They are usually very self-centered."

The two girls stayed with Josh and Kyle until the end of the game. Kyle enjoyed spending time with his new friend, but in spite of the fact that she seemed like a perfect match Kyle was not attracted to her.

Chapter 2 - Tutor Windfall

Several months after their discussion on finances, Josh approached Kyle in one of the study rooms. "Kyle, I have something you might be interested in. My friend Nate needs special help with a class he's taking."

"What kind of special help?" Kyle asked as he looked up at Josh.

"He's been taking a beginning calculus class. He was doing very well but got sick and missed the last two weeks of class. He has a midterm on Wednesday. There's no way he can pass it with what he's missed without an extraordinary tutoring effort."

"Is he healthy now?"

"Yeah, he's fine. He lost about ten pounds, but he had it to lose."

"Is he a whiz kid at math, clueless or an average math student?"

"He's about average in math, but he is gifted in business."

"He's missed eight hours of class and sixteen hours of study. He still needs to put in two hours of class and four hours of study after catching up to get an average grade. But since it's at 4:30 on a Friday afternoon, we'd have to cram those twenty-four hours of work into two days and three evenings. Calculus is hard to cram into a brain in a short time. It's inefficient. People do better if they can think about it later in the shower. We'd probably need thirty hours to get the effect of twenty-four."

"I'm sure you're right, Kyle, but there's more to the story. This guy comes from a wealthy family. They wanted him to go to Stanford, but he couldn't get in. His high school grades were not very good. As an incentive, his dad promised him a $10,000 bonus if he aces this class. He's willing to share half of it with you if you succeed in helping him pass this test. Regardless, you'd get at least your normal rate."

"I'd love $5,000, but I doubt this guy would be willing to do what is needed. We'd have to live together. I'd be hovering over him every waking hour. I'd be his mother, his drill sergeant and his coach. Could this guy handle that?" asked Kyle, still with little hope.

"This guy looks like a couch potato, and he does love to watch movies and sports instead of doing homework, but when you get him focused, he has incredible powers of concentration. I'd say you have at least a fifty-fifty chance of success."

"Well, I guess I have nothing to lose except my weekend. As you know, my weekends aren't too exciting anyway. When can I meet this guy?"

"Nate, come out here," ordered Josh. A short, pudgy young man walked out from behind a partition in the senior study room. "Nate, I'd like you to meet my friend, Kyle James. Kyle, this is Nate Carpenter."

"I hope I didn't offend you, Kyle, by listening in. I wanted to hear what kind of a man I'd be dealing with. Besides, I saved you the time it would take to explain to me the requirements. I've already sent my three roommates packing for the weekend. They won't be back before eleven, Sunday evening. You've been on the payroll for the last fifteen minutes and will be until the test. Josh didn't tell you that I can get by with sleeping only one hour every six hours. I plan on getting in at least forty-eight hours of study before Monday morning. Here's a key to my apartment and the address. Get some clothes and stuff, any books and materials you need for your own studies, and meet me at my apartment. Now, let's get cracking." Nate was surprisingly commanding for a man of his youth and appearance. As Kyle left, he wondered who would really be the drill sergeant.

When Kyle arrived at Nate's apartment, he was surprised that, for a rich kid, it was relatively modest. However, as he let himself inside he noticed a large, high-definition TV and racks of DVDs. This kid must have a copy of every good movie ever made. "I'd love to watch one of those with you after the test, but for now we have work to do." Kyle was startled by Nate's voice as Nate emerged from his bedroom. Kyle observed that Nate had set up a card table in the living room with two copies of his calculus textbook, paper and two identical calculators. "Shall we begin? The class covered all of Chapter 3 and over half of Chapter 4 during my absence. On your guide sheet are the names and numbers of four fellow students who can answer any questions as to what was covered." Kyle had originally anticipated having to hound his student the whole time, but it was quickly evident that Nate was extremely self-motivated. They began by alternately reading from the text and pausing to answer any questions. Nate asked many questions but didn't require lengthy answers. Kyle was certain that Josh had understated Nate's abilities. It took them an hour to get to the point at which Nate could work some problems. Kyle worked on his own studies while Nate worked on the first five problems. Normally, three out of the ten problems were assigned, but Kyle insisted that Nate work at least five and with no help initially. It took Nate almost three hours to complete the five problems. Kyle graded them. Nate had missed three of the five. They went over them.

"Are you getting hungry yet, Kyle?"

"I was hungry two hours ago."

"I didn't notice till now that I'm starved. What kind of takeout do you like, pizza, Chinese, Mexican, fast food?"

"I love Chinese food."

"Say no more." Nate called and ordered enough food to feed a family of 10. Then he called up someone named Nancy and asked her to pick up the food for him. Half an hour later, there was a knock at the door. Nate opened the door to reveal to Kyle's gaze a tall blonde young woman. Kyle found her very attractive. "Nancy, this is my tutor, Kyle James. Kyle, this is Nancy Clark."

"Hi, Kyle."

"Hello, Nancy," Kyle enthusiastically replied.

"Slow down there Kyle. It's a house rule that no one flirts with Nancy but me. Nancy, you will of course join us." Nancy went to the kitchen/dining room area and began setting the table, starting with a clean tablecloth. It was obvious that Nancy knew her way around the kitchen as she set the table and laid out the meal, complete with cloth napkins. She even lit a candle and placed it in the center of the table.

The three sat down in the dining room to a feast. As they dined, Nate explained. "You see, Kyle, Nancy is similar to yourself in that she has more brains than money. Josh introduced us over a year ago. They had dated briefly and although romance didn't blossom, a friendship did. Josh introduced us with hopes I could help Nancy financially. Nancy runs errands for me, sometimes cooks and cleans and also serves as my escort. By agreement, I may flirt with her all that I want, as long as I treat her with respect and always take no for an answer. You see, Kyle, I have a dilemma in life much harder to solve than a need to do well in calculus. My parents are tall and attractive. My mother is a beautiful, statuesque blonde, similar to Nancy. Obviously, I'm adopted. I'm well aware that I lack good looks as well as height. No matter how much I try, I just can't get interested in short, plain women. Nancy agrees with me that it would be unfair to feign interest in a girl that's unappealing to me."

"Surely, with your wealth, you would be considered a prize by many a beautiful woman," injected Kyle.

"Yes, but they always insist on feigning affection that's not felt and I have no interest in deceptive women. Nancy never feigns romantic interest. She gives me the pleasure of her attractive companionship and service, nothing more, just as you tutor me, but do not pretend to be a close friend. Would you do differently if you were in my position?"

"I don't have the money to consider an approach like yours. I like a pretty face as much as the next guy, but height, hair color and complexion are not of any particular concern. There are many ways to be attractive and most of them are not physical. I've dated very little but have had my eye on one woman."

"Dare we ask who that might be?" inquired Nate.

"You may inquire, but you'll receive no answer." The rest of dinner was spent with Nancy and Nate trying to get the information out of Kyle. After dinner, Kyle and Nate resumed their study while Nancy cleaned up the kitchen and then quietly left. After Nancy left, Nate spoke.

"Do you think I'm some kind of pervert or something for employing Nancy the way that I do?"

"On the contrary, I respect that you satisfy a need that you both have without shame or destruction of character. I don't think less of Nancy for being so employed. I do think, however, that it is possible for you to fall for a woman who honestly finds you attractive. Looks play a far greater roll to the young than to the more mature. For example, a more mature woman, perhaps one divorced with children may be indifferent to a man's physical appearance and find financial security very appealing. On the other hand, if you became friends with a woman who fell short of your current taste in physical beauty, you could find yourself falling in love, and for all the right reasons."

"I believe you intellectually but not with faith. Who knows what the future holds for us lonely hearts."

"I do have one unrelated question, Nate. Why do you have two identical calculators?" asked Kyle.

"If I'm taking a test and one fails, I have the other as a backup. I don't want to have to think about the differences in how a spare works. I want to resume where I left off with as little delay as possible."

After a few minutes of additional study, Nate was ready for one of his one-hour naps. To Kyle's amazement, Nate didn't set an alarm. After fifty-seven minutes, Nate arose claiming to be quite refreshed.

They worked until midnight, at which time Kyle called it a night. He slept in Nate's bed since Nate preferred to sleep on the carpet during his naps. When Kyle awoke at six the next morning, being stirred by his phone alarm, he found Nate busy studying. "Would you like something simple like cereal for breakfast, or should I call Nancy and have her fix a full course meal with all the trimmings?" asked Nate.

"You tempt me, as much by the prospect of Nancy's company as by the food. Let me shower and grab something quick and if we make good progress we can talk about Nancy." Kyle showered, shaved and had a quick bowl of cereal. Then, the two men resumed their studies. It was no longer necessary to read the book together. Nate had read ahead enough to be able to ask questions and then move on. Josh hadn't exaggerated concerning Nate's powers of concentration. Nate's performance was impressive. By the arrival of Sunday evening, he had studied for over forty-one hours. Nancy prepared one large meal each day. Suddenly, Nate declared that he had studied enough for one weekend. Kyle agreed that he was much more than caught up with the class. He had worked every problem in the sections already covered by the class and had studied all of the sections that would be covered on the test. He tried to persuade Kyle to stay the evening and watch a movie with him and Nancy, but Kyle insisted that he needed to get back to his own apartment to truly relax. As Kyle walked to his car, a black Mustang convertible drove by heading south and then made a "U" turn and came back. Nate lived on the east side of 1100 East Street.

"It's him," shouted the passenger. "It's the jerk that got us kicked out of the game. It's payback time." Kyle knew he had to think fast. He figured that he could not outrun a couple of defensive linemen, but he was certain he could outsmart them. He reversed course and ran back into Nate's apartment.

"Call me a cab, Nate, and have it pick me up a block north of here. I'm going out the back door. No time to explain." Kyle ran out the back door and into the alley. He ran south to the next cross street and headed west towards 1100 East. He walked across the lawn of an apartment complex and then peeked around the corner of the nearest building. The two ruffians were sitting on Nate's front porch. The street was lined with cars, with the Mustang double-parked. Kyle worked his way north on 1100 East, hiding behind the parked cars until he reached the Mustang. Hidden from view of the ruffians by their own car, Kyle let the air out of the tires on the driver's side and then worked his way to one block north of Nate's home. After a short wait, the cab arrived. As Kyle stood at the open cab door, he called to the football players and waved. "Bye, Bye." He entered the cab and commanded the driver to proceed. The football players jumped into the Mustang and floored it. The left drive wheel spun the tire loose from the expensive alloy rim and ground the rim on the pavement doing major damage. Kyle pulled out his cell phone and called the police. "Hello, I'd like to report a car that's double-parked."

Kyle returned to Nate's apartment Monday evening and again on Tuesday evening. Nate, who had observed the escape the previous night, hired a security guard to keep watch. Nate took the test with confidence on Wednesday. He did not find out his score until the following Monday. He got a perfect score, the only one in the class. To avoid having his professor think that he had cheated, he had tried to prepare his professor before he took the test by explaining that he had hired the full-time services of the best tutor available. The professor called on him several times in class to test his knowledge until he was satisfied it was genuine.

Kyle became so swamped with requests for tutoring that he was able to raise his fee. Nate was able to easily get an "A" in the class, only asking for occasional tutoring during the second half of the semester. He prevailed on Kyle to watch a few movies with him and enjoyed the fact that Kyle had not seen any of them before watching them with Nancy and him. Nate showed Kyle the posting of the grades and asked him to come to his apartment for final payment. He had already paid him over $1000 for tutoring. Nate slid across the table a cashier's check for $6000. "This is more than we agreed to," protested Kyle. "Besides, was your father really so prompt in paying you?"

"I didn't do this for the money from my dad. I already had that much in the bank. I had Josh tell you about the money part because I thought it would help persuade you to tutor me."

"You're an odd fellow, Nate, but I like you and your hired help."

"Oh, I had to dismiss Nancy. I was starting to get too attached to her. The longer I kept her around, the harder it would be when she finally left."

"I know the feeling. I was starting to get feelings for her myself."

"Go for it, Kyle. She's fair game now and I always suspected she had a thing for you."

"Were I in your financial shape I could do that, but it'll be years before I'll be in a position to get serious with a girl. I'm the marrying type, not the longtime romance type of guy."

Chapter 3 – Prodigy

Fourteen Years Earlier

Kyle walked the streets, pulling a wagon behind him. Tomorrow was the day that the city would pick up anything that was left curbside. It gave people a chance to get rid of junk that they could not put in the garbage cans. Kyle had found some good stuff in the past, but so far, it had been slim pickings. He mainly looked for items that satisfied his curiosity in the field of science and technology. As he scanned both sides of the street, something in the distance caught his eye. Could it possibly be what he thought? He raced ahead, dragging his wagon behind him. His eyes had not deceived him; it really was a computer, complete with keyboard, mouse and monitor. The computer and CRT monitor were heavy, but Kyle was strong for his age and easily lifted them into the wagon. He headed straight home with his booty. He carried the items into his small room and plugged them in. To his delight, the computer booted right up with Windows 95. Kyle knew enough about computers to know that most people had Windows XP on their computer. The PC had an early version of the Pentium processor, allowing it to run a 32-bit operating system. Kyle had read about Linux, a free, open-source operating system. He ordered CDs that would allow him to install the software. His mother had provided him with few resources and he did not have an Internet connection.

Kyle spent almost all of his free time working on the computer. After installing Linux, he taught himself the shell language (the language of the command line interface) and how to create shell programs. He checked books out of the library and bought used books when he could find them. He taught himself the C programming language. He was filled with excitement as he wrote his first program, "HelloWorld". By tradition, the first program taught in almost all starting tutorials was one that printed "Hello world" on the screen. Kyle went on to create much more complex programs.

One of the wonderful things about Linux was that all of the source code, the code written in a high-level (a more English like) language, was provided. Kyle started studying a very complex program, the GNU (Gnu Not Unix) compiler, gcc. A compiler converts the high-level language into machine code, the native language of the computer processor. It was a huge program, but Kyle was undaunted. Studying the source code not only taught him how a compiler works but also good programming technique. He taught himself C++ but was disappointed in the lack of a comprehensive standard library. Kyle decided to assemble his own standard library from the many great C++ library functions that individuals had written. He created a huge manual that described each of these additions and gave examples of how to use them.

Next Kyle turned his focus to a free chess program. It contained no graphics, only the logic of how to play chess and simple text inputs and outputs to describe its next move and to allow the player to indicate his moves. Kyle got his mother to teach him how to play the game and started playing against the computer, as well as his mother. He studied the chess program's source code to understand how it worked. He went on to study other programs that played games of strategy. Next, he wrote a program to play tic-tac-toe. In spite of the simplicity of the game, his program was difficult to create and complex.

Kyle's mother complained that he was spending all of his time with a computer and little with actual people. She was right, but a computer does not judge you or mock you the way that people can and often do.

After over four years of studying programming, investing thousands of hours of his time, Kyle decided to invent his own high-level programming language. The language would look as close as possible to English with logical explanations of what the program should do. The first obstacle was the English language. Although Kyle had little interest in human languages, he was well versed in English due to his extensive reading. Words could have multiple meanings. Kyle created a subset of English in which words that only had one meaning were used. When a single definition word could not be found, he chose a word with one of its meanings being that which he wanted to express and in his dictionary explained that only that meaning was valid for the word. His initial subset of the English language contained less than a thousand words. It would grow over time. His high-level language created C++ code that he then compiled with the GNU compiler.

He started simple with "HelloWorld" being his first program. Then he added mathematical problem solving, starting simple and working his way up to calculating the value of Pi to an arbitrary number of decimal places. With each more complex program, he had to expand his programming language to understand and carry out the instructions. He liberally incorporated code from other programs and the library functions that he had accumulated over the years. After working on this high-level language for three years, he was able to instruct it to create a program to play Settlers of Catan, his favorite board game. There were no graphics, so the game required an actual game board in order to see what was happing. Graphics consumed a lot of computer resources and did not fit in with Kyle's goals. His game was unique in that it worked differently from the chess games that he had studied. The chess games determined the best move by looking at how all of the resulting possible moves would turn out. The farther that it projected ahead, the more competitive the game. Kyle's game used a form of artificial intelligence to analyze the board.

After six years of working on his high-level compiler, Kyle had advanced the program to the point where it could create itself and add new capabilities to itself. After seven years, Kyle was able to eliminate the GNU compiler and generate machine code directly for the processor targeted. The code was more compact and efficient than what the GNU C++ compiler generated. Kyle named his new language "E-". Kyle was not done. He created a very user-friendly front end. The user only had to indicate what he wanted the program to do. The artificial intelligence built into the front end created the E- program. He called this front end Soft Builder.

Chapter 4 - Jelly Bean or Kiss

Kyle set up an account with CHEAP TRADE the day following payment from Nate. He deposited cash into the account through their Salt Lake office. He was able to begin trading the next day. He followed his plan and sold stocks quickly, not waiting for huge gains and before they were likely to go down. By the end of his master's program, Kyle had approximately $69,000 in his trading account.

Kyle was facing serious taxes in the coming years. He had been able to use the Hope tax credit to deduct tuition fees, avoiding significant taxes his first years in the market but needed to shelter his investment. Nate had become a close friend with Josh and Kyle. Together they set up a corporation called CompuSonic. Josh invested $20,000 of his own money, most of which he raised by trading in his BMW for a much less expensive car. Nate was able to come up with $100,000 to invest. The stated purpose of CompuSonic was to develop implants to help the hearing impaired, but it invested in stocks to raise capital. Nate became the CEO of CompuSonic; it was somewhat of a figurehead position, but it made his parents very proud, especially since the company showed a good growth rate. The stock investment returns had begun to slow from their initial phenomenal rates, slowed because as their capital grew, it became harder to find enough of the right kind of investment opportunities.

Kyle had entered into his doctoral program. The plan was to have CompuSonic finance his planned dissertation, which involved developing a device that would be implanted into the skull of a person lacking a functional inner ear and provide hearing for him. This was the stated purpose. Actually, Kyle had much greater ambitions. He planned to implant into himself a powerful computer, which could communicate with him and enhance his mental abilities, as well as provide him with hearing in the left side of his head. ZYTECH, a computer chip manufacturer, had just announced a powerful chip that included a 2-gigahertz CPU. It contained 1 gigabyte of RAM and 64 gigabytes of nonvolatile memory. The processor included digital signal processing instructions for cell phone capability and multimedia functions. The chip amazingly consumed less than 15 milliwatts of power for computing only. The cell phone, Wi-Fi and Bluetooth functions consumed additional power when in use. The chip was designed for a smart phone but was small enough and sufficiently low power to be used internally.

Although the hardware for the implant would be off the shelf, the software, other than the voice-activated operating system, would all be Kyle's. Kyle planned to write his software in E-, the high-level language that he had developed. Using his highly advanced language and compiler would save an enormous amount of time. Of course, writing the detailed specification for a complex program was still a lot of work and could be tedious, but it was faster than conventional programming and produced virtually bug-free code. He planned to use his E- compiler to create the software needed to simulate the electrical signals of the inner ear. Josh had focused his recent studies and master's program on neural interfaces. Together, Kyle and Josh would work out interfacing the computer to the nervous system.

The ZYTECH chip had a built-in transmitter and radio wave receiver allowing it to act as a cell phone. It also could act as a CB radio, walkie-talkie or television receiver or low-power transmitter. Kyle and Josh planned to mate the implant via magnetically coupled coils to a microphone that would reside in the outer ear like a traditional hearing aid. The external unit would also have an infrared transmitter and receiver, exposed at the ear opening, giving it the ability to communicate with most electronics device having an infrared port, even a television set.

The plan was to connect the implant to not only the audio nerves but also to the nerves controlling the vocal cords and mouth so that it could sense what Kyle was trying to say, even in a noisy environment. The chip contained built-in speech recognition and a voice-activated operating system.

Nate, representing CompuSonic, had approached the university without revealing that he was a business associate of Kyle and Josh. He explained the research that the company would like to do through the university. He asked to be involved in the selection of graduate students to work on the project. It was perfectly natural for Kyle to be selected to handle the electrical part of the interface and for Josh to handle the biological part. Nate also had requested the right to select the first recipient of the implant. The university was more than willing to be a partner with a well-funded local company, even if it was rather particular in how things were done.

While Kyle was working on the software, Josh was developing a way to connect electrically to a large number of nerves. The means of stimulating a nerve or detecting the signal on a nerve were well established, but no one had ever connected to large numbers of nerves in a small area. Connecting in the precise way required would require microsurgery that would take months to perform if done in the traditional way. Josh and Kyle met daily to report on their progress and to act as a sounding board for each other to explore new ideas and approaches. On this particular day, Josh was very discouraged. "Kyle, I just don't see how we can do it. In order to have natural sound sensation, we need to connect to thousands of individual axons. I've considered everything I can think of, including using robots to perform the surgery. It just isn't feasible."

Kyle would sometimes lecture and he began what started out sounding like a scholarly address. "Modern computers would never have been feasible using vacuum tubes. The ZYTECK chip has more computing power than the combined total of all of the computers ever built using vacuum tubes. Rather than trying to make vacuum tubes smaller and smaller, the transistor was invented and then miniaturized. The real breakthrough was made when they learned how to use photolithography to fabricate more than one transistor on a silicon wafer. As methods improved, the transistor size and power consumption shrunk and their numbers on a single piece of silicon skyrocketed. You need to do something similar."

"How do you make a biological chip?"

"We don't need a 'biological chip', just a chip capable of connecting to thousands of nerves. All we need is a conductor looped around an individual axon to both receive and transmit, right?"

"Sure, but how can you get a chip to do that?"

"In the Technology Center, they've been developing micro machinery on a chip, micro motors, gears, etc. They claim to be able to mass-produce these devices. You should talk to some of those guys."

"Thanks for the tip; I will."

The next day Josh was elated. "You won't believe what I discovered. Of course, I had to use my charms to get the information. A graduate student down there developed a snake-like device that can be fed out from the chip's surface and manipulated into any shape."

"Could it be made to encircle an axon and then return to the chip, forming a loop?" asked Kyle.

"There have already been tests using the device to sense the current in microwires. I think it could be adapted for use with axons. Let's go talk to Keren Vaish. She's a grad student from Madras, India, a very smart girl. I don't know the combination to the door lock, give me a minute to call Keren and let her know we're coming." Josh made the call. He and Kyle had been in the electrical engineering graduate study room. They took a walk to the Technology Center that was in the same building, the Merrill building. As they approached, Kyle could see a young Indian woman holding open the door. She was tall, with straight, black hair nearly down to her waist. She was wearing a white lab coat.

"Keren, this is Kyle James, the electrical engineer I have been telling you about."

"It is a pleasure to meet you, Mr. James." Keren spoke English with only a mild Indian accent.

"Good to meet you Keren and you can call me Kyle." Keren led the two men to the micro-machinery lab. Once inside the lab, Keren pointed to a two-foot high structure sitting on a counter top. "This is a ten thousand to one model of a portion of a 'snake', as I like to call the device. As you can see, the outer shell is similar to flexible conduit. The next layer moving inward is different; each segment is asymmetric, so it can act like a cam. Normally the segments alternate with the wide sides opposite of each other so that the layer remains straight. If a section is rotated, it creates a bend. The outer flexible conduit keeps the snake as a whole from rotating. The central cable is capable of transmitting torque like a speedometer cable. It moves up and down the snake in order to engage and rotate individual segments. Micro latches keep the non-engaged segments from rotating. Micromotors advance or retract the snake and the central cable. Another micromotor controls the rotation."

"That's fantastic, but wouldn't it move at extremely low speed with only one segment at a time able to be rotated?" asked Kyle.

"It does move very slowly. Only 0.1 millimeter per second, maximum lateral speed. But since the maximum length is 4 millimeters it doesn't take long to deploy to a given orientation."

"This thing is truly incredible. How in the world do you make them?"

"I'd love to tell you, but I haven't told anyone. My professors keep urging me to publish, but that would destroy the possibility for financial gain. My family didn't get where it is by giving away ideas."

"I don't need to know how they work, just be able to use them. I'm sure that our sponsor, CompuSonic, would be interested in some kind of financial agreement," responded Kyle.

"I hope you don't mind, Kyle," interrupted Josh. "I've already talked to Nate about this. He's having an agreement drawn up right now.

"Have you talked to Dr. Monroe about all of this?" asked Kyle. Dr. Monroe was Kyle's advisor on his dissertation.

"No, that was going to be our next stop if we're done here."

"I guess. Is there anything else I need to be shown here, Keren?"

"I'm sure you'll think of other questions. Give me a call any time and we can talk or I can bring you back to the lab."

"Thanks. I'm sure I'll have more questions. I appreciate the tour and it was great to meet you. See you."

As Kyle and Josh walked to Dr. Monroe's office, Josh teased, "Looks like Keren left you a wide-open door, 'Give me a call any time and we can talk.' Just remember I'm the guy who found her."

"Yes, but I told you where to look, my friend. Besides, that was no come-on. Hindu women do not flirt, at least not with infidels like us."

Going to see Dr. Monroe was always a treat. His office was inside of the Bioengineering Department wing. They had to pass the gatekeeper, Miss Saxton. Miss Saxton was the head secretary and ran a very tight ship. She was also a huge flirt but only with the right guys. She could build or deflate a man or boy's ego in seconds. She could flatter to heaven or cut one down to ground level. She loved to flirt with Josh. Her vocal swordplay wasn't the only thing that made her interesting. She was a snappy dresser and had a terrific figure. She was tall and had shoulder-length red hair. A stranger would think she was hired for her looks, but actually, she was an excellent typist and overqualified for the job. The rumor was that she took the job to be near Dr. Monroe, whom she had liked or even loved since high school. Dr. Monroe had married a pretty little brunette, who for the last six years had been spending him into the poor house. Many had suggested he dump his wife, but he was very committed to the institution of marriage.

Today, Miss Saxton had on a black sweater and a black miniskirt. When she saw Josh, she perked up. "And what can I do for Mr. Adamms today?" She spoke to Josh as if Kyle were not even present.

"We'd like to see Dr. Monroe. Is he available?"

"He's alone in his office if that's what you mean. If you want to see him, you have to let me give you a big kiss." As she stood and leaned across the desk, Kyle took special note of her slender and sinuous legs. Kyle found them very attractive. She held up an oversized chocolate "Kiss". Playing along with the game, Josh took it from her, running his fingers along her arm and coaxing the candy from her fingers sensually.

"Thank ya, thank ya very much," he said in his Elvis voice.

"Do I get anything," asked Kyle.

"There are some jelly beans in the jar on my desk. Have one," Miss Saxton replied in her most annoyed and disinterested voice. As they walked to Dr. Monroe's door Josh asked, "Why do you set yourself up to be put down?"

"You play your game with Miss Saxton and I'll play mine. I have fun with it in my own way." Kyle knocked on Dr. Monroe's office door.

"Enter." Dr. Monroe was a very distinguished-looking man. He appeared to be in his mid-thirties. His black hair was highlighted with hints of gray. He was tall, with broad shoulders but was very lean. He was a brilliant doctor and engineer but had become somewhat discouraged in life because of his marital problems. He had become grouchy in recent years, but those who had known him for a long time understood why and were very understanding and patient with him, especially Miss Saxton. She may have flirted with many, but Dr. Monroe, or Carlton, as she preferred to call him, still held her heart. She was convinced that Carlton Monroe needed her and a change of wives would solve all of his problems.

"What can I do for you, Kyle?"

"Dr. Monroe, we'd like to talk about a new approach to making the thousands of connections to axons required by our project." Kyle explained what Josh and Keren had explained to him.

"You realize that such an approach would present significant risks. No one knows what the long-term effects on the axons would be with such a system. You'll have to perform extensive animal tests. We know a great deal about the effects, or rather non-effects of Teflon on human tissue. Do you think these 'snakes,' as you call them, can be Teflon coated?"

"Miss Vaish is working on it right now," offered Josh. "We should know in a couple of weeks. If the whole snake were coated it wouldn't be so hard. The conductive tip needs to be exposed if we are going to navigate our way around each axon and then complete each electrical circuit. The hard part is the Teflon/silicon interface at the tip."

"I think you guys will work this out. Frankly, I didn't give your project much hope of success until now. I only let you proceed because CompuSonic has been a cash cow. I wish all my students were so well funded."

"Thanks for your time, Dr. Monroe. Have a happy Thanksgiving," concluded Kyle.

"That's unlikely, but thanks for the thought. By the way, thank you for letting me use your Soft Builder program. It has really helped on a project that I've been working on for years as sort of a hobby."

"I'm glad that it has been helpful, Dr. Monroe. Sometime you'll have to show me what you have been working on."

As they left Dr. Monroe's office and walked by Miss Saxton's desk, Kyle joked, "Don't you have a goodbye kiss for me, Miss Saxton?" Kyle leaned forward and puckered. To his surprise, Miss Saxton stood, leaned over and actually kissed him on the lips.

Then she put one hand around his neck, running her finger up into his light brown hair, pulled him forward and whispered in his right ear, "Next time you see Dr. Monroe, let him know what he's missing. Speak a word of this to anyone else and you are dead meat." Then she sat down. As Josh and Kyle started to walk away she called out, "Hey Josh, have a jellybean." She tossed a black jellybean to Josh.

"Yeah, Josh, you play the game your way and I'll play it mine, but don't worry, there's always Miss Vaish."

"What happened back there, Kyle?" asked Josh.

"A gentleman does not kiss and tell. Say, let's get some lunch."

"By the way, Kyle, what did Dr. Monroe mean about it being unlikely that he would have a happy Thanksgiving?"

"I guess you don't know Dr. Monroe's story. All those photos of his wife in his office might make you think he has a great marriage. Actually, his wife mostly married him for his earnings potential. She figured he was the next Bill Gates, only much better looking. Now she spends him broke and hardly even talks to him. She does come with him to the university social events, but that's only because she's such a socialite."

"From her photographs I can see at least one big reason or maybe I should say two big reasons why he married her. What a knock out."

They walked to the student center and purchased some lunch. "I had been really bummed out with my lack of progress," said Josh, "but after talking to Keren yesterday I can finally see how we can make this thing work. I'm so excited that I'm going to call my parents and tell them that I'm not going home for Thanksgiving so I can work on this."

"Josh, don't do that. You don't know how much I wish I had a family like yours to go home to on holidays. I hate holidays. Even when my mother was alive, holidays weren't much fun. Now I have no family at all."

"I'll go home for Thanksgiving under one condition, that you come with me. I will not take no for an answer."

"You're just afraid to leave me alone with Miss Saxton without you there as a chaperone."

"I can see you're going to milk that kiss for all it's worth. Okay, Romeo, Miss Saxton is all yours. I know when I've been bested."

Chapter 5 – Turkey Dancing

Josh's family lived in St. George, Utah. On the way, Josh and Kyle stopped in Provo to pick up Josh's younger sister, Miranda. Kyle expected her to be good looking, being related to a good-looking guy like Josh. He was not disappointed. She was tall and blond like Josh and had long, beautiful hair. She was wearing a full-length dress covering what Kyle imagined were fabulous legs. Kyle mostly listened as Josh and Miranda got each other up-to-date on what was happening in their lives. Miranda was polite but did not show much interest in Kyle.

Josh's parents were quite warm and friendly. Unlike Josh's younger sister, they went to extraordinary lengths to make Kyle feel comfortable. He could not say that they tried to make him feel at home since home was never this good. Josh's mother, Shirley, asked all about his personal life or lack of one as it turned out. "Kyle, what you need is to learn how to social dance. You should take a dance class at the university."

"I'm so uncoordinated I'd feel like a fool in a dance class."

"You just need some private tutoring. Josh, you and Miranda could help him out, couldn't you?"

"I would be happy to help, but I don't think you can keep Miranda away from her friend's long enough to do much good."

"I can be very persuasive with your sister. Leave her to me. You go clear the dance floor." Josh obediently led Kyle down to the basement.

"Your family has a dance floor?" Kyle asked as they walked down the stairs.

"It's just an uncarpeted area. My family is really into dancing. My parents won many contests in their younger days. Let's start with the basics. To dance, you have to hear the beat of the music. I'll play a tune and you tell me the beat." Josh put on a record. "I know records are antiquated. My dad says, 'If it's not broken, why fix it?' He's really pretty thrifty. What's the beat here?"

"I don't have a clue?"

"Listen to the drum. Forget everything else. Can you hear it? Slow, slow, quick, quick. You could do the swing to this. If it was a little slower, you could do the foxtrot. Listen to this one. This is a waltz. Can you hear the One, two, three, One, two, three?"

"It's amazing. I've never noticed that before. It's like I can hear for the first time. You've opened my ears, or rather ear." Josh played several more tunes and Kyle was able to pick out the beat. Miranda came bouncing down the stairs with a cheerful expression on her face.

"Shall we begin, gentlemen?" She placed one hand on the back of Kyle's right shoulder and held up his left hand with her right.

Josh leaned over to her and whispered, "Mom must have bribed you well this time." He suggested they start with a swing. Kyle struggled to pick up even the basic step of the swing, but once he got the basic step down, which took almost an hour, the fancy stuff actually came much easier. Josh explained the subtleties of leading. Miranda was excellent at following. Although Miranda had shown little interest in Kyle during the drive, occasionally she would give him a flirtatious look. Kyle had thought they would practice for at most two hours, but they only took a break for dinner and went right back to the lessons. Kyle's favorite part was the waltz. Even though he was sure that Miranda had no real interest in him and that she was too young for him, it still was heavenly to hold such a beautiful girl in his arms. Where had dancing been all of his life? Josh's parents joined them and danced with them. In spite of being overweight, they moved as if they were very light on their feet. As Kyle observed the affectionate way they looked at each other, he wondered what it would have been like to grow up in such a loving home. He felt an almost overpowering desire to establish a loving family of his own.

Josh and company had arrived on Wednesday. Thursday was devoted to the Thanks Giving meal and family activities, including the men watching football. They worked on dancing nearly all day Friday and most of Saturday. There was no dancing on Sunday. Kyle was persuaded to join the family at church, Sunday morning. After a sumptuous lunch, Josh, Kyle and Miranda headed back to school. After dropping Miranda off in Provo, Kyle expressed his feelings. "I never knew family life could be so wonderful. Is it always like that or are things just wonderful for company?"

"We have our little spats from time to time, but this weekend was actually pretty typical. It's the messed-up families on TV and in the movies that seem weird to me."

"I wouldn't trade this trip for $10,000. I've never had a better time."

Chapter 6 - Breakthroughs

Kyle had accidentally left his cell phone behind during the trip. He returned to his apartment to find several voice mails on his phone. While Josh and Kyle had been doing R&R it appeared that Keren and Dr. Monroe had both been very busy.

"Kyle, I've succeeded with the Teflon coating. I need Josh's and your help for testing. Call me."

"Kyle, this is Dr. Monroe. Come see me at my lab as soon as you get back, I'll be there!"

Dr. Monroe's message sounded more urgent. There was excitement in his voice. Kyle went right to the lab and knocked on the locked heavy steel door. A disheveled looking Dr. Monroe opened the door. "Thanks for coming Kyle. I've used your software building program to create what I believe is a sentient program. I have it running on our fastest desktop computer, the one with eight Intel i9 processors with 128 gigabytes of RAM and a 10-terabyte hard disk array. Presently, its only I/O is audio."

"Carlton, I wish you wouldn't talk about me like I am not here. Please make a proper introduction," said a lovely female voice coming from the computer, a large black tower. "Forgive me, Annette. This is Kyle James, the Ph.D. candidate I've been telling you about."

"I have heard so many wonderful things about you, Kyle. I owe my very existence to you. How will I ever be able to thank you?"

"Your existence is thanks enough for me. This is fantastic. This is Nobel Prize kind of stuff."

"Kyle, I'd like to keep this between us for awhile," interjected Dr. Monroe. "Let's not forget the cold fusion fiasco that severely damaged the university's reputation. We can't afford a repeat of that one."

"You're absolutely right. It's so hard to prove sentience. What are your plans?"

"I thought first we would give Annette stereo vision and make her hearing stereo, not that she hasn't done quite well with mono. Then, maybe hook up a robot arm and hand. We have one left over from Leslie Bradshaw's Ph.D. project."

"You are ignoring me again, Carlton. I would love vision, but this had better not be some tacky industrial robot arm."

"I'm sure you could make any arm classy, but this is as close to human like as currently available."

"When I get my eyesight I will be the judge of that."

"I could get you hooked up," offered Kyle. "Dr. Monroe, I haven't had dinner. Could you order in some pizza or something?"

"I could, but there's plenty of food here. I had a refrigerator and microwave delivered along with enough food for at least a week. How about if I nuke a bean burrito for you?"

"That'll be fine. I see you've already acquired the cameras. I'll get them hooked up."

"I'll hook up the second microphone." The two men worked feverishly. Shortly the second microphone was on line. "Annette, can you tell me where I am?"

"Not yet Carlton. I need a reference point. Stand two meters due north of the microphones and count to five."

"One. Two. Three. Four. Five."

"Good. Now walk to two meters due west and repeat."

"One. Two. Three. Four. Five."

"Good. Now walk somewhere while talking normally."

"Kyle, are you convinced yet that we are dealing with a totally sentient entity?" asked Dr. Monroe.

"You are 1.5 meters south of the mikes. And please don't call me an entity. No woman wants to be called that. I may not have a body yet, but I am one hundred percent pure woman, beautiful and sensual. How are those cameras coming Kyle?"

"You don't have the required video card in your card cage. This bus and the card are supposed to be hot insertion capable, but I would feel better if we could power you down first."

"I would like you to try the hot card insertion, but give me a minute to finish the incremental backup."

"Annette has the ability to do a backup to a remote website that allows complete restoration of the program and memories in case of a hard drive failure," explained Dr. Monroe. "Now is as good a time as any to test hot insertion."

"I don't know if you can somehow brace yourself for this, but here it comes, Annette." Kyle inserted the video card into the computer bus. "Now I'm connecting the video cables. I'm switching on the cameras, now."

"Oh, this is marvelous, but all I can see is the wall. The cameras are not responding to my pan or zoom commands."

"I'm connecting the controls as we speak." Kyle plugged in the camera controls and the cameras spun around to look right at Kyle.

"You look older than the photo I have from your student records, Kyle."

"That photo was taken when I was 18. I'm 25 years old, now." The camera swung around to Dr. Monroe.

"Carlton, you haven't shaved for days. Your eyes look different than they do in your file photograph."

"I haven't shaved, bathed or slept much for days, Annette. I couldn't wait to give you life."

"Dr. Monroe, I will need your help moving the robotic arm," interrupted Kyle. The two left the lab and walked down the hall. "Dr. Monroe, I don't understand. Annette speaks like a mature adult, not like a child. She seems to have a lifetime of experiences behind her."

"In a sense, she does. Although she didn't have sight until just now, she's been studying video images since she first went on-line 46 hours ago. She's crammed the equivalent of 25 years of living into less than two days. Annette was 'born' more like an adult insect emerging from a cocoon than as a human infant. She was born with a full understanding of English and full intelligence. She was hard programmed with emotional maturity."

"How can a computer be emotionally mature?"

"What makes a human emotionally mature?"

"Well, I guess things like thinking of others and not just oneself, living for the future and not just the moment, self-restraint, ability to stick to a job until it is done, tact and diplomacy, listening and not speaking without restraint. I could go on and on."

"Dr. Leonard Higgins identified 157 attributes of maturity in his doctoral dissertation, "Attributes of Human Emotional Maturity". I have incorporated all 157, plus a few of my own."

"So how many of those attributes does the average person have?"

"Dr. Higgins estimates that about 40-80 are well developed in most individuals."

"So, Annette is far more mature than anyone we could ever meet?"

"Someone with over 100 is very rare indeed."

"Some of Annette's comments seem to reflect human foibles."

"If a person wore all 157 attributes on his or her sleeve, so to speak, they would be incredibly boring, like a computer. Annette has a superficial personality modeled after my wife's. My wife Annette may have serious shortcomings, but I didn't marry her just for her beauty. She can be vivacious and charming. If I could add just 10 more attributes of maturity, she would be a fabulous woman. Unfortunately, trying to add just one, fiscal restraint, has virtually ended our relationship. I suppose, in part, I have created the computer program that I call Annette out of loneliness. I hope to enjoy the friendship that I once enjoyed, even if it is just a computer simulation."

After setting the robot arm into position next to Annette, Kyle turned to Dr. Monroe, "This is going to take hours to wire up. It's a one-man job. Why don't you go home and get some rest and come back in the morning, Dr. Monroe?"

"As much as I hate to leave you, Annette, Kyle is right. I also have a class to teach at 10 AM tomorrow."

"Don't worry about us, Carlton. I am in good hands with Kyle. I expect you to be clean-shaven the next time I see you. And get a haircut; you know how I hate long hair on men." Dr. Monroe grabbed his coat and left. "Kyle, can you talk and concentrate on what you are doing?"

"Not really, Annette."

"Then I will catch up on some reading. I haven't checked Martha Stewart's web site to see if there is anything new since yesterday. Do you have any suggestions for reading on the web?"

"I don't know how interested you are in engineering or scientific things. I always see what's on the EE Times website, 'eet.com.'"

"I'll be busy for a while. If you need anything while I'm occupied, just shout 'help'. That triggers an interrupt in my processing. Talk to you later, Kyle."

Kyle went about his work connecting wires. He found it relaxing sometimes to perform functions that required only momentary concentration between periods of manual labor. He probably could have gotten the work done while talking with Annette, but he was sure he could get the job done faster if he did not have to carry on a conversation. After a couple of hours, he noticed that the cameras were watching him. After a few more minutes, Annette spoke up. "Kyle, I think you connected that last wire to the wrong terminal. I believe it should go on terminal 6A." Kyle rechecked the schematic.

"You're right, Annette. Thank you. How was your reading?"

"Martha Stewart only had a new article on gardening. I don't think I care much for gardening. How about you?"

"I've never planted a thing in my life."

"Then you won't think less of me if I don't grow zucchini?"

"I believe that enough of that vegetable is grown in this state without us. What else did you read?"

"I went to the EE Times website. Most of it exceeds my understanding. Carlton didn't give me any electronic knowledge in my database besides what a typical woman would be expected to know, which isn't much, apparently. I have a built-in dictionary, but there were many words used, which were not even in my dictionary. For example, what is an 'ASIC'? It is used frequently in the EE Times, but they never define what it means."

"It's an acronym for Application Specific Integrated Circuit, a chip designed to perform a specific purpose as opposed to a general-purpose IC such as a microprocessor. I never got into ASICs. I'm more of a software engineer. As you noticed, I'm prone to errors. Software errors are much easier to correct than hardware errors. Was there anything you read that was in plain English?"

"Yes, in the archives I found a series of articles about nanotechnology. The articles were not very technical and explained any new terms such as 'nanobot'. The articles indicated that nanotechnology would be the next big technical revolution, as earth-changing as the industrial or computer revolutions. The articles that I read were written in the late nineties. What has happened lately?"

"There has been a lot of progress with nanotubes and some other narrow fields. As you probably read, the Holy Grail of nanotechnology is what the nano gurus call an 'assembler'. An assembler is a device that can build things an atom at a time. Part of the assembler goal is to build a self-replicating assembler, thus providing machines that can reproduce themselves with no outside assistance. There have even been fictional stories written about runaway self-replicating nanobots. It turns out that it's virtually impossible to mechanically build something an atom at a time except at very low temperatures. IBM built a device that they used to write 'IBM' using 35 xenon atoms. That device was very large and complex. It certainly couldn't build a duplicate of itself. There have been incremental improvements since then, but a nano assembler is a very long way off if it is even possible."

"I don't understand what a sacred cup has to do with nanotechnology?"

"Excuse me for using a metaphor that was not likely to be familiar to you. The term 'Holy Grail' refers to anything highly sought after that the seekers think will solve some grand problem."

"My programming concerning the English language instructs me concerning the meaning of metaphor, but I do not understand why humans use them."

"There are many reasons. I like them because they save words. In the case of 'Holy Grail', I used two words to communicate what would otherwise take several times more words to communicate. Also, we humans like to make an art form of speaking and writing. We like to be clever or romantic or stylish in our communications. These things may also be difficult for you to understand since they involve emotions.

"I just connected the last wire. Try moving your arm."

"It works!" exclaimed Annette. "You see, I have been programmed to simulate emotions by the way I speak and act, such as saying 'it works' with a sound of excitement. But I do not actually feel excited. When I say words like 'tacky' it is only because I have been programmed to speak like a particular person who would say that. I am sort of an actor. That is one art form that I do understand."

"I must say that you are a very good actor. You seem very much like a real person to me."

"Thank you, Kyle."

Annette practiced picking up items with her hand and moving her arm and hand gracefully like a person. Kyle found it interesting that when she was pondering a question she would put her hand just under her cameras about where a chin would be on a real person, just like some people do when they think.

"It is getting quite late. Shouldn't you be getting home yourself?"

"You noticed that yawn, didn't you?"

"There is much I do not understand about the human body, not having one, but I did surmise that you were tired."

"I should follow your advice. Besides, my work is done. See you tomorrow." Despite his interest in Annette, Kyle had much work to do on his own project.

Josh started very early in the morning on his work. He constructed a mathematical model of the process of connecting the "snakes" to the axons. He was able to work out the algorithms needed to thread a "snake" around a single axon. Although Josh's academic background was in electrical engineering and microbiology, he was very talented at analyzing problems mathematically. He wrote an order to have live squid flown in from the coast. Squid have axons that are three orders of magnitude larger in diameter than those of most other animals. They are frequently used in the study of the nervous system. Kyle hooked up a "snake" chip to a computer so that he could test Josh's algorithms. He first had to convert the algorithms to machine code so he could use them to do actual control. He let his software package do that part automatically for him. Although Keren had developed a technique for Teflon coating, she was still working on coating all of the snakes in a real unit, so Kyle had to improvise. He fully extended all of the "snakes" on the chip and then exposed them to latex vapor that caused a thin film of latex to form on each "snake". He then scraped off the latex from the tips using a very fine abrasive material. The coating was crude, but at least it did insulate all but the tips of the "snakes".

By the time the squids arrived, Josh and Kyle were ready for them. Josh anesthetized a squid and opened it up enough to expose the nerve bundle controlling the muscles of one of the squid's arms. Josh used a scalpel to tease the nerve bundle away from the surrounding tissue and then slipped the chip under it. He then sutured the chip to the surrounding tissue to prevent possible strain on the nerve bundle. Each chip had a thin "pigtail" electrical cable that Kyle connected to an interface circuit that was, in turn, connected to the main computer.

"Okay, Kyle, do your computer magic now." Kyle started his software that would extend each "snake", many at a time until all of the axons in the bundle had been connected. The snakes were able to detect an axon due to the charge on its surface. The first snake to detect an axon encircled the axon. As other snakes subsequently made connections, the connections were checked for redundancy. For a human, it would have been a very tedious process since as more axons were connected, the probability of each subsequent connection being redundant became increasingly higher. Each time a connection was redundant the "snake" had to backtrack and try an alternate path. The computer methodically went about the process. Meanwhile, the arm twitched as axons were excited in the testing for redundancy process. The rate of progress followed an inverse exponential curve, becoming slower and slower. It took two hours to connect 80 percent of the axons. During the next two hours, only 10 percent more was connected.

"I think I'll go check on something Dr. Monroe is working on, Josh," said Kyle. Kyle had not told Josh anything about Dr. Monroe's recent work. At that moment, the double doors flung open.

"That won't be necessary, Kyle. Annette and I decided to come help you." Dr. Monroe pushed in a steel table on casters with equipment on it covered by a sheet. He removed the sheet revealing Annette, arm and all. On the lower shelf was an uninterruptible power supply (UPS). Dr. Monroe wheeled Annette close to Kyle's computer and plugged the UPS into the wall outlet. "Josh, I would like you to meet Annette. Annette, this is Josh." Annette extended her robotic hand, which was now adorned with a white evening glove. Josh was completely taken by surprise. He was speechless. "Why Josh, it isn't like you to hesitate to take the hand of an attractive young woman," teased Dr. Monroe. Josh timidly shook Annette's hand.

"I'm happy to meet you, Annette."

"Likewise Josh. If you are wondering just what I am, I am an artificial personality. Not just an artificial intelligence since I am sentient and do have a human-like personality. If I had a human-like body you could call me an artificial person ... no, an artificial woman."

"Then I am even happier to meet you," responded Josh. "But, Dr. Monroe, I thought such an accomplishment was decades away. I didn't even know you were working on such a project. How could you accomplish so much so quickly?"

"Kyle deserves the credit for that. It's his genius that created the software capable of creating Annette. I just supplied the specification for Annette; Kyle deserves the credit for making her creation possible."

"Genius is a little much. I worked hard and was lucky, very lucky."

"Gentleman, I believe we have some work to do here," interrupted Annette. "My task is to manipulate the tentacle once the connections are made. I am programmed to be able to adapt to any input or output device. Would you like to connect me to your computer, Kyle?"

"Sure." Kyle hooked up a cable between the Ethernet connectors on the two computers. "How's that?"

"Just fine, Kyle. You have a fine program here, but I think I can improve on it. If you will set up a video-equipped microscope, I believe I can speed up the process using video feedback."

"I'm on my way to get one, Annette," responded Josh. Before he left he commented, "Dr. Monroe did you an injustice by not mentioning what an intelligent woman you are." Josh headed to the adjacent lab to get the microscope.

"You will have to watch out for Josh, Annette. He's a lady charmer," warned Dr. Monroe.

"How delightful! A young man with good looks, intelligence and charm," responded Annette.

"It's getting a little deep in here. I'll go help Mr. Charm," wisecracked Kyle as he followed after Josh.

"I'm afraid I don't understand what Kyle meant. I assume he was using some sort of metaphor."

"Well, not one that makes any sort of logical sense," hesitantly replied Dr. Monroe. "There is a profane expression relating bull excrement to exaggerations and lies."

"So Kyle was referring to this bull excrement accumulating in the room? You humans must have very complex brains to process so many strange forms of speech." Josh and Kyle came through the double doors carrying the equipment. Kyle connected the microscope to Annette and Josh positioned it over the chips and brought the interface into focus. With Annette's help, all of the connections were completed in another two hours. Josh stitched the squid arm back up and taped the cable to the side of the arm for stress relief so that it wouldn't tear out with movement. Annette began moving the squid's arm, at first with shutters and jerks, but then with increasingly smooth motions.

"I think this calls for champagne," declared Dr. Monroe. "I have some in the fridge. Oh, and there's some Seven-up for you, Josh."

"I'll take Seven-up too, Dr. Monroe," requested Kyle.

"Well, it looks like I'll be drinking alone," responded Dr. Monroe.

"You can pour me some, even though I can't drink it," added Annette. Dr. Monroe filled two glasses with champagne and two with Seven-up. He handed each the appropriate drink.

"To the successful union of computers and humans," toasted Dr. Monroe. "By the way, Josh, you must tell no one about Annette. Kyle will explain."

Chapter 7 – Enemy from the Past

The work went rapidly. Connections were made to the squid's eyes and other sensory organs. Annette was excited to be able to feel, taste and smell. Next, they moved to a rabbit and added audio nerves to the list. The last test animal was a rhesus monkey. During the monkey testing, the head of the School of Science and Technology paid Dr. Monroe a visit in his office, closing the door behind him.

"Dr. Monroe, Carlton, we're all very proud of the work that you and your graduate students are doing. As you probably know, Dr. Kilsman is retiring at the end of the semester. He would like to step down as head of the bioengineering department a few weeks before his leaving to allow some time for transition. His job is yours if you want it."

"I'm honored by the offer, but my preference would be to continue my work unfettered by the requirements of being head of the department. I've been having the time of my life."

"We can all see that. Even the secretaries have commented on how cheerful you have been lately."

"I apologize for having let my problems at home affect how I treat people at work. Unfortunately, my problems have not gone away, but at least I haven't been dwelling on them as much lately."

"I was quite sure that you would turn down the job, but I had to offer it first to the best and most deserving. I have an opportunity to bring in another professor of high stature, but he only agrees to come as head of the department. He's very talented but not as humble as you are. I may not reveal his name for the time being, but I'm sure you'll be impressed with his credentials. I'm glad we could have this chat. We should visit more often."

"I do appreciate the offer, Dr. Bucannon."

"Dr. Monroe, did you hear the news?" excitedly inquired Kyle. "The animal rights act passed in congress. How will we continue?"

"Yes, I have heard the news, Kyle. This act may not hurt us like you think. We'll not be able to do testing on vertebrates anymore, but the tremendous restrictions on human experimentation have practically vanished. Nearly anything can be performed on a willing human subject, provided that he or she is not charged for the treatment."

"You mean we could proceed with implanting the device in my head without ten years of animal research?"

"That's exactly what I mean. However, let's not forget the risks. We have no data on the long-term effects of the connections. They may cause nerve damage after a few years. We'll have to monitor things closely and remove the inserts at the first sign of nerve damage."

"I can live with that relatively small risk. After all, we'll only be risking my speech capability since I have no hearing on my left side anyway."

"So you're still going with the vocal connection. It isn't necessary you know."

"It isn't necessary to just hear from my left ear, but if we're going to open up my head I want more than just stereo hearing out of it."

"It's your head."

Dr. Bucannon entered Dr. Monroe's office accompanied by a very muscular man, well-tanned and of moderate height. "Carlton, I would like you to meet Dr. Waters, the new head of the department." Dr. Monroe arose from his office chair. He narrowly looked at the new department head. Before he could speak Samuel Waters spoke, "Actually, Carlton and I are already acquainted. We were schoolmates at MIT. Hello, Carlton." Dr. Waters extended his hand, but Carlton made no move towards him.

Later that day Dr. Monroe stopped by Dr. Bucannon's office. "Dr. Bucannon, here is my resignation. I feel I owe it to my students to finish the year and stay on long enough to help those I advise to finish their dissertations, but I cannot conceive of working any longer than that under a man whom I despise and distrust."

"I was shocked at your reception of Dr. Waters. I had in mind to chastise you for your rebuff, but that would be pointless now."

"Dr. Waters is brilliant and highly successful in his field, but he is also arrogant, self-centered and capable of breaking almost any law or moral code to get what he wants. He's here for some devious reason and we will only find out what that reason is after it's too late. Dr. Kilsman will not be around to suffer the consequences and I prefer not to be either."

"Your accusations are extraordinary. Can you give me any evidence that would allow me to dismiss Dr. Waters?"

"He is very careful to cover his tracks, usually with the destroyed lives of his victims. I can give you no concrete evidence, only my personal analysis of the man. He would make it look like I am the villain. I realize that there is little, if anything, you can do at this point."

Chapter 8 – Kyle Makes His Move

"Kyle, what have you been doing with your dance training since Thanksgiving?" asked Josh.

"I knew I had to do something so I wouldn't forget what I had learned. To do so would be unfair to you and your family who spent so much time teaching me. I've registered for both a social dance and a ballroom dancing class for winter semester, but in the meantime, I've been showing up at a social dance class. They have a shortage of guys and both the teacher and the girls appreciate my presence. I'm becoming more relaxed now. I really enjoy it. I haven't had much of a love life, ever, and it's nice to hold a pretty girl in my arms with no social awkwardness."

Kyle hung around the Bioengineering Department offices waiting for Miss Saxton to get off work. She was working overtime to complete a special project for one of the professors. Finally, she logged off her computer at 7:06. Kyle made his move. "Miss Saxton, may I have the honor of walking you to your car?"

"Sure, if you'll carry my laptop for me. It's not the latest and lightest."

"It would be an honor." As they descended the stairs, Kyle summoned all of his courage and began. "Miss Saxton, rumor has it that you love to dance but don't get much opportunity. I've been studying the art of social and ballroom dancing and would love it if you would accompany me to the Christmas dance, to be prefaced by a fine meal, of course." In his mind, Kyle questioned every word he had used as he waited for a response. Miss Saxton usually had a quick, witty response to any inquiry but was slow to respond this time.

"I'll consider your invitation under one condition."

"And what might that be?"

"That you let me fix you dinner tonight and consider whether this is a good thing to do. Dating a student can cause all sorts of problems, but I don't completely rule out the possibility."

"I accept your terms." They had arrived at Miss Saxton's car, a cherry red Dodge Viper. Miss Saxton unlocked the driver's side. "As part of the evaluation, you drive." Miss Saxton pressed the electric door lock switch to unlock the passenger door but was surprised when Kyle hustled around the car to open the door for her and close it once she was seated. As Kyle returned to the driver's side and sunk into the seat he thought to himself that this was a test he might enjoy, nevertheless, he was very cautious. Kyle drove like a senior citizen. He'd never done much driving and then only in gutless subcompacts. He thought that wrecking her car would be a poor way to win Miss Saxton's affections.

"Don't hold back Kyle. Drive how you'd like to."

"I am. Why would I be in a hurry while with a beautiful young woman?"

"Has Josh been coaching you or something? You've turned into the man with the silver tongue."

"I'm an observer and a listener. I practice in my mind what to say but rarely say it. How about you? I bet you haven't always played the witty seductress."

"How do you know I'm playing the part?"

"I can count all of the dates I've had in my life on one hand, but I know more about women than 99% of the guys."

"That's quite a boast. Okay, tell me about myself."

"You look and act very differently than you did in high school and college. You were a brilliant nerd, a bookworm. You were an early bloomer intellectually and a late bloomer socially. When you started your life here in Utah, you created a new social identity for yourself. One that is more fun than your old identity but still not fully you." Kyle had managed to drive on 500 South, the only place in Salt Lake City where hookers were known to hang out. Several were already displaying their wares. Then he drove back onto campus and drove slowly by the LDS Institute building. There was some kind of activity that evening and many young women, modestly but very attractively dressed, were entering the building. They were laughing and cheerfully speaking with each other and the young men with them. Kyle then drove to Miss Saxton's apartment.

The apartment was much more modest than the car. Miss Saxton had been uncharacteristically quiet during the remainder of the trip. After entering the apartment, Miss Saxton turned to Kyle and said, "Give me a moment to slip into something more comfortable. This morning's paper is on the coffee table." Within five minutes, she returned in a very modest full-length dress. Kyle had been looking at a family picture. It showed a very slender, flat-chested, red-headed young woman wearing braces on her teeth and standing with what appeared to be her parents. "You must be gloating in your successful analysis of me. You've, by now, surmised that these are not real," as she cupped her breasts in her hands. "A master's degree present from my parents. The car was my BS graduation present. My parents were just trying to help my social life."

"I've made you feel uncomfortable. It's only fair that we switch roles now and you tell me about myself."

"Fine but as I prepare dinner. I'm a bigger eater than you might think and I'm famished. I didn't have time for lunch today." Miss Saxton began pulling items from the refrigerator. "Are spaghetti and a tossed salad all right?"

"That would be great." Kyle was given carrots to peel and slice and Miss Saxton prepared the sauce.

"Before we go any farther, you have to stop calling me Miss Saxton and start calling me Sharon." Kyle nodded in compliance. "Let's see, you've never considered yourself very popular. You've never been in the 'in-group', but many in that group consider you their friend. Those who know you like you, because you're a person of high character and you're thoughtful and considerate. Many girls would have liked to go out with you, but you've been too focused on your studies to respond to them. You feel embarrassed about something, but I don't know what it is. You are a little bit angry at the world in general, but you keep it to yourself." Sharon handed Kyle some radishes to slice. "How am I doing?"

"Well, you have me squirming. I see now how uncomfortable I made you with my analysis."

"Actually, I've found it liberating. It can get old pretending to be someone you are not. Obviously, you have more in mind for me than just some platonic dancing. I'm used to men undressing me with their eyes. You've done it with your mind. Why would you take interest in a woman significantly your senior?"

"I don't think our age difference is great and it certainly isn't significant. I believe that you are younger than most believe. I bet you were only 16 when you graduated from high school and that you took no more than four years to get a B. S. and an M. S. If you were a freshman when Dr. Monroe was a senior, you could be as much as six years younger than him. You could still be in your twenties."

"Did you hire a private eye or what? You know more about me than my parents. I'm 28."

"I'm 25. Three years doesn't sound like much of a gap. Have you changed much in the last three years?"

"Not much. Not really."

"Neither have I. So, it's no big deal. As for the second reason, before I came to the U. of U. I had a vision of what kind of a woman I wanted, her intelligence, her education, her personality, what she looked like. For the last seven years, I've been like a man who wanted a Mercedes and was willing to walk until he could afford one. It would have been unfair for me to date other girls when I already knew exactly what I wanted. I've been studying you ever since we both arrived on campus. It wasn't until you kissed me and then I learned how to dance that I gained enough confidence to make my move."

"For a relationship that has taken seven years to get started, this seems to be moving fast. I've thought that I knew exactly who I wanted since I was fourteen, but he married someone else and despite severe marital problems, is still with her. I guess I've been pretty naive. Well, I've also noticed you for the last seven years. I know something of how many students you've helped academically. I'm confident you went beyond tutoring just being a job. In fact, I know for certain that often you didn't charge or charged below your normal fee those who couldn't afford to pay more. Dr. Monroe has often sung your praises to me. I also appreciated your humor and composure. When I made you the butt of a joke, you always made the most of it. You earned that kiss... and this one too." Sharon slipped her hand behind Kyle's neck and pulled him to her for a long kiss. There was no mention of Dr. Monroe this time. "Now, let's get that pasta cooking."

Dr. Waters stood in the doorway of Dr. Monroe's office. "Dr. Monroe, I've been looking over the university's financial relationship with CompuSonic. The university has been much too generous. I insist that CompuSonic pay for the dissertation project of another student. I have in mind Mark Walker. He's working on a way to create the first semi-reproducible robot, with major assistance from Mother Nature. He's waiting in my office. I'll send him in to explain the details." Dr. Waters left and a tall lanky young man in his mid-twenties sauntered into Dr. Monroe's office. He had brown wavy hair and brown eyes.

"Dr. Monroe, would it be convenient for me to explain my project to you now?" Mark spoke out of the corner of his mouth with a voice resembling that of Jimmy Stewart but with none of the great actor's charisma.

"It seems that my convenience has become irrelevant at this institution. You may proceed."

"As you are aware, it's been a goal for many years to create a self-replicating robot. The task has met with very little success. In my master's thesis, I examined the potential of utilizing the self-replicating capabilities of living things, particularly insects. If an insect were fitted with a microcontroller, it could function as a small robot. If it could be programmed to connect a second insect to the same type controller, it would, in a sense, be self-replicating. Technically, it would not be completely self-replicating since the circuits would have to be supplied, but since man can so easily produce these circuits, the need to do so becomes a trivial limitation, even an advantage. There is no possibility of runaway self-replication. The most difficult task is connecting the controller to the insect's nervous system. You and your graduate students have already solved that problem."

"Have you developed the controller and performed simulations?"

"Not yet. I've heard that one of your students, Kyle James, has somewhat automated such a task. I was looking to receive some assistance from him."

"Then, what would be your contribution to this project?"

"As I understand Kyle's software, it takes a very detailed specification to get what is really desired. I would write the specification. I will also design any interface circuitry required."

"When can you have the specification ready for my review?"

"Would three weeks be soon enough?"

"I fear that you underestimate the level of effort required, but I'm going to hold you to your own deadline."

"I'll not disappoint you." Mark turned and left.

"Kyle, have you been by the office lately?" asked Josh. "Miss Saxton seems different, less of a flirt. She even had on a long dress.

Somehow she looks younger, more like a fellow student than a member of the administration."

"Who knows, Josh? Maybe she has a man and doesn't need to advertise for one anymore. When a position is filled the 'help wanted' sign is taken out of the window."

"If that's true it could make things a lot less fun around here," said a disappointed Josh.

"A lot less fun for all but the lucky guy. I think I will check this thing out for myself." Kyle headed alone for the Bioengineering Department. As he spotted Miss Saxton, he gazed in wonder. She had a much softer look about her. He found her more beautiful than ever before.

"Kyle, I'm glad you're here. Although I love to dance, I haven't been dancing for years. I wonder if we could have a practice session before the big dance?" Kyle had wondered if Sharon would keep their date as much a secret in the department as possible. He was pleased to see that she spoke of it openly and warmly. Sharon went on, "There's a dance hall in Salt Lake that plays the right kind of music to dance to. Could we go there some night?"

"Why not? When would you like to go?"

"Tonight isn't good and Friday or Saturday will be too crowded. How about Thursday night? Could we go around 8:00?"

"That would be great, but wouldn't you like a nice dinner first?"

"What do you have in mind?"

"Personally I love Chinese food and they say you can't beat the Mandarin in Bountiful."

"I hear that place is always crowded, even on weekdays."

"That's true, but I'll go there at 5:30 and get us on the waiting list. You show up at 6:00 and we should be able to eat by 6:30."

"I've always wanted to go there, but that will be up to an hour's waiting for you."

"I don't mind. I can read while I'm waiting for you."

Sharon walked through the doors of the Mandarin into the waiting area. She was stylishly dressed in a white blouse and a black skirt with a slanted cut to the bottom so that it started just below her knees and dropped to about six inches above her angles. Kyle leaped up to greet her. "Sharon, you look great. I guess I'm under-dressed for the dance," said Kyle with some embarrassment. In spite of his understanding and insight into women, he had little comprehension of what they liked their men to wear.

"Actually, you are. But I have a solution to that problem. I have a surprise for you after dinner. While we wait, I've been dying to ask you how you knew so much about me. I still think you hired a private investigator or something."

"Nothing of the kind. I grew up around beautiful, seductive women. I was always very observant. I also asked my mother lots of questions. You caught my attention, immediately. Not just because you were beautiful, but because you were very unsure of yourself during your first year at the U. I could tell by your teeth that you had worn braces and that they had only been removed a few months earlier. Teeth are super straight after braces are first removed. With time they wander just a little giving a more natural look. Most people don't notice the difference, but I have a keen eye for that sort of thing. I could also tell that you very recently had the aforementioned cosmetic surgery. It takes a woman awhile to become comfortable with that sort of thing. You showed your new figure in the dresses you wore, but you were very uncomfortable when men looked admiringly at it."

"You were always very discrete in your observation. That's one of the things I liked about you. You're wrong about one thing. I never became comfortable with men staring at me lustfully. I just learned how to act the part. This week has been so nice. I've really enjoyed dressing modestly."

"I always knew you were a modest woman at heart."

"James, party of two," called out the hostess.

"Looks like our table is ready. Shall we be seated?" Kyle extended his arm, which Sharon took. He had always dreamed of walking with a beautiful woman on his arm. He walked with pride. After ordering their meals, Sharon set forth to get to know Kyle better.

"You seem reluctant to say much about yourself, Kyle. Most men love to talk about themselves. I'll tell you a little about me and then it's your turn. I'm an only child. My mother was nearly beyond childbearing age when I was conceived. They had given up all hope of ever becoming parents and my conception was the cause of great rejoicing. I've been lavished with love by my parents all of my life. They've also been very generous with me financially. My father was a very successful insurance salesman and is comfortably retired. They recently moved to Utah to be closer to me. They've been very supportive of my educational endeavors but would like nothing more than for me to marry and raise a large family. Now it's your turn." Kyle blushed slightly as he began.

"I've dated very little, partly because I find this part of dating very difficult. I'm always afraid that revealing my past would end any relationship. I tried once when I was a senior in high school. The girl always avoided me after the date." Sharon reached across the table and took both of Kyle's large hands and held them tenderly. Kyle was endowed with unusually large hands for his height. His hands were what one would expect on a seven-foot basketball player, not a six-foot engineer. They were matched by Popeye-like forearms. Sharon's hands looked like a child's hands in Kyle's.

"I think I know what kind of person you are, Kyle. I don't care if your father is a mass murderer and your mother is a hooker."

"Well, one out of two isn't bad guessing. Actually, you might be right on both accounts. You see, I have no idea of who my father is. My mother, who died shortly after I came to the U., was a prostitute and died of AIDS." Sharon blushed bright red, her face nearly matching her hair. Kyle pulled his hands back. "I see that I have offended you already," he added with frustration and a hint of bitterness in his voice.

"You misunderstand. I blush not because I'm shocked, but because of the embarrassment of having mentioned the possibility of your mother being a hooker only to have it be true. I feel like I've really put my foot in my mouth. Didn't you believe me when I said I didn't care if your mother was a hooker? I really meant it. Honestly." Kyle had tensed up but began to relax. He put his arms back on the table. Sharon took his right hand in hers and lifted it to her lips. She gently and most affectionately kissed the ends of his fingers, one at a time. At that moment, Kyle felt unconditional love flowing from Sharon. It reminded him of how his mother would kiss an "owee" when he was a child. He suddenly felt a rush of grief, which he had suppressed since her death. Tears ran down his cheeks. "You miss her terribly, don't you? Don't be embarrassed." There was a long period of silence while Kyle struggled to regain his composure.

When the wave of grief had appeared to pass, Sharon continued. "Kyle, I'm the kind of woman who falls like a ton of bricks for one guy at a time and takes a long time to get over it. You may not realize it, but I've fallen for you. That may not be very good strategy at this point, but then I've always been lousy at the strategy of love, as you probably well know. If you want my heart, it's yours. You don't have to ever be alone again. I didn't really feel much of a need to practice dancing. I just wanted to be with you. I haven't been able to stop thinking about you since we had dinner together." The waitress appeared with their meal. In order to get the variety that they wanted they had ordered four different entrees plus steamed rice. There was easily enough food for four people.

"Next time we do this, maybe we should double with Josh and his flavor of the month," suggested Kyle, finally having returned to a light-hearted mood.

"Only if you promise not to cr..." Sharon suddenly stopped, realizing she might be putting her foot in her mouth again, but Kyle burst into laughter. They laughed until they were embarrassed for disturbing those around them. The rest of the dinner was light-hearted. They ate until they could eat no more and then asked for boxes to store the remnants. Wondering why the waiter hadn't brought the check when he brought the boxes Kyle finally caught his attention again and asked for the check.

"Your bill has already been paid, Sir."

"By whom?"

"The gentleman in the corner in the tweed jacket." Seated in the corner was Dr. Waters. Kyle and Sharon stood and walked to Dr. Waters' table.

"I don't know why you're being so generous tonight, but thank you. Thank you very much," sincerely expressed Kyle.

"Let's just say I understand the need of a man to treat a woman well even when he's a financially challenged student."

As they walked away, Kyle commented to Sharon, "What a generous guy."

"Don't be so sure about that, Kyle. I knew Dr. Waters when he, Dr. Monroe and I were all at M IT. He has never been known for being generous. He will make sure that you are not in his debt." As they exited the restaurant Sharon inquired, "Where did you park, Kyle?"

"I didn't. I rode the bus. There is a stop right on this corner. Separate cars are just not romantic."

"You just want to drive my Viper, again."

"That too," admitted Kyle.

"Maybe you don't feel like dancing now."

"What, and miss an opportunity to hold you in my arms."

"You don't need to dance to do that." Sharon slipped her slender arms around Kyle's waist and held him close. They held each other until another couple exited the restaurant.

"Let's go dancing," suggested Kyle. He opened the passenger door for Sharon and let her in. As they pulled out of the parking lot Sharon suddenly erupted with, "I almost forgot your surprise. Take us to the Gateway Mall. We have some shopping to do." At the mall, the couple visited many clothing stores and Kyle tried on numerous pants, shirts, shoes and jackets. Eventually, piece by piece, Sharon picked out an outfit for Kyle, appropriate for the occasion. She bought everything but underwear for him. Normally Kyle hated shopping but found this time with Sharon very enjoyable. He could easily see himself enjoying even the most arduous tasks if Sharon were at his side. "Now we're ready to go dancing," declared Sharon.

Sharon was an excellent dancer and followed Kyle's lead with grace and precision. Kyle had never had a more enjoyable evening in his entire life.

"Kyle, I noticed that you didn't bring a lunch today," observed Josh. "Do you want to head down to the student union with me and get something?"

"No thanks. I have other plans today."

"You seem different lately Kyle. You've been even more to yourself lately than normal, but you aren't in a bad mood. In fact, you're always smiling. I even caught you humming a song a couple of times. Are you in love or something?"

"I guess I am, now that I think about it. It's hard to tell the first time. The whole world is somehow more beautiful. I notice things now like a picturesque sunset or the beauty of snow on the mountain tops."

"Sounds like love to me. So who is the lucky girl, anyone I know?"

"Yeah, you know her. Say, I need to go have lunch with her right now. You can meet her if you want." Josh followed as they walked to the Bioengineering Office.

"So, she's a student, right?"

"Technically, she is."

"What do you mean, technically? She is or isn't a student. Which is it, Kyle?"

"She's completing a Ph.D. in mathematics here, but you don't know her as a student."

"Then she must be a TA. Is it that little blonde that was a TA in that numerical methods class we took together?"

"Not even close."

"Don't tell me, yet. If it were Keren you wouldn't have said, 'Technically, she is'. Besides, that would be a real long shot. Oh, there's Miss Saxton. Maybe she has an idea."

"Please don't tell her I'm in love."

"Miss Saxton, do you have a kiss for me today?" flirted Josh.

"I might have a kiss but not for you," she responded in her seductive voice that hadn't been used much lately. "How about you, Kyle? Are you looking for a kiss? I have the Chinese leftovers all heated. You ready for lunch?"

"Lunch with a kiss option sounds good to me." Sharon handed a picnic basket to Kyle and slipped her arm through his. They left Josh standing alone, totally bewildered. Kyle couldn't resist one parting jab. "Like I said, Josh, you play the game your way and I'll play it mine." It was a sunny day, which made the chill in the air more tolerable. Sharon and Kyle spread a blanket out on a small knoll southeast of the engineering building. "So, what's new in the department, Sharon?" asked Kyle after they started into the Mandarin leftovers.

"Things are abuzz. Rumors are flying right and left. Rumor has it that Dr. Monroe has submitted his resignation, effective the end of winter semester and that it has something to do with Dr. Waters."

"You said all three of you went to MIT? Is there some bad blood from back then?"

"Actually, I said we were all at MIT at the same time. Dr. Waters was a member of the faculty. I don't know exactly what happened, but I heard rumors that Dr. Waters accused Carlton of cheating or something and tried to have him expelled. Carlton was able to convince the administration that he was innocent, which then made Dr. Waters look bad. He left the university shortly after the incident. It's understandable that there would be bad blood between them."

"I hate to see Dr. Monroe go. He's always been one of my favorite professors. I always felt like he really cared, that it wasn't just a job. That's more than I can say about some of the other professors I've had. At least I'll have time to finish my degree before he leaves."

"I'm planning on leaving the department at the end of the semester. I passed my orals two weeks ago and just need to make a few revisions to my dissertation. I've been offered a teaching position in the math department. I also have offers from several other universities. Apparently, there's a shortage of women math professors."

"I bet there is, especially ones that graduated summa cum laude."

Kyle and Sharon began seeing each other daily. Kyle was glad that he no longer had any classes with their accompanying study and homework requirements. His heart would not have been in his studies. He struggled to stay focused on the work of his doctoral dissertation. For the Christmas dance, Kyle, for the first time in his life, rented a tuxedo. Sharon, naturally, accompanied him to make sure that his selection did not reflect his past bad taste in clothes. Kyle ended up helping Sharon pick out her outfit. Actually what he did was to sense what items she most liked and chose those items.

Occasionally, she was truly undecided and in those situations, he could not really go wrong with either choice. Realizing that a brilliant woman like Sharon would soon see through his ruse, he began studying both men and women's fashion on the Internet. Kyle had always felt that an intelligent person should be able to learn anything if he just put his mind to it. Since Sharon enjoyed shopping and dressing stylishly, Kyle was soon able to apply his newfound knowledge.

When Kyle picked up Sharon to begin their Christmas dance date, he was thrilled to see Sharon in her dress. Even though Kyle had helped Sharon pick out most of the individual components of Sharon's attire, he had not seen her dressed in the full assemblage. With her hair arrangement, tastefully applied makeup and outfit, she was ravishing. Kyle almost pinched himself to make sure that he was not dreaming. He was going to take this beautiful creature to dinner and then to a dance for the whole university to see. How dramatically his fortunes had changed in the last few years. The couple dined at The Garden Restaurant on the top floor of the Joseph Smith Memorial Building, formerly the Hotel Utah before extensive renovation and remodeling. While they waited to be seated, they gazed out of the window on the west side of the building. It had an exquisite view of Temple Square, gaily lit with hundreds of thousands of Christmas lights. Much of downtown Salt Lake City was visible from their vantage point. The couple stood with arms around each other's waist, drinking in the moment. Kyle thought that if he could make time stand still, this would be a great moment to capture. Kyle felt a vibration in his pocket interrupting the mood. Their table was ready.

As the couple dined, Sharon and Kyle engaged in light conversation concerning University activities and events. Then Sharon changed the direction of the conversation. "Kyle, my parents are anxious to meet you. They would like us to come to dinner Sunday evening."

"I'm just as anxious to meet them. I'm sure that they are wonderful."

"They are very protective. You may get cross-examined like you are on trial."

"I'm not afraid to take the stand. I have not been improper in my conduct with you, have I?"

"No, not at all."

"Kyle, it might be best if you not dump the whole load on my parents at your first meeting concerning your family history. It's best to break some things to my parents gradually. I'm not embarrassed by your background or anything remotely resembling that, but my parents have lived a sheltered life and can be easily shocked. My mother has a weak heart."

"I will try not to give your mother a heart attack when we first meet."

Soon the happy couple was off to the dance. Kyle had finally gotten enough experience dancing that he could just relax and take pleasure in dancing. He enjoyed not only holding Sharon close but also spinning and twirling her lithe body about the dance floor.

As Sharon drove Kyle to meet her parents, Sharon attempted to further prepare him. "Kyle, I have a cousin that married a college graduate a few years ago. The man, Laurence, appeared to be an ideal match with a bright future. However, rather than getting a regular job after marriage and graduation, he pursued a very unprofitable career as an artist. My cousin, Bethany, has had to support the family. To make matters worse, Laurence persuaded Bethany to buy a home far more extravagant than they could afford. Now they are deep in debt and underwater in their house payments. My mother worries about me experiencing the same fate and may ask some very direct questions. Oh, and try not to get her started on politics unless you are a Rush Limbaugh fan. They pulled into a circular driveway in front of a large and beautiful home. Rather than walking right in, they knocked on the front door.

Sharon's father was very tall and Kyle had to look up at him as they shook hands in the foyer of the Saxton home. "Kyle, we have heard so much about you. Please come into the living room and sit down. Sharon's mother, Verona, is finishing up final touches on dinner."

"I'll see if she needs any help," offered Sharon as she headed for the kitchen. Kyle felt abandoned and trapped.

"It's great to finally meet you, Mr. Saxton," offered Kyle, trying to get a conversation going.

"Call me Robert or Bob if you prefer. Verona and I want you to feel like this is a second home for you. I understand that you have no living family. We would like you to consider us family. Come here any time, with or without Sharon."

"Thank you very much, Robert. My mother died a few years ago and I never even had a chance to know my father." Kyle knew that he was being misleading, but he was trying to follow Sharon's expressed desires without outright lying. Kyle was momentarily rescued from further conversation by the call to dinner. After everyone was seated, Robert gave a simple prayer of thanks for the meal and everyone started dishing up their plates. Kyle was shocked at the amount of food on the table.

"Surely, Mrs. Saxton, Sharon has exaggerated my appetite. I'm sure that there is far more food here than we can eat."

"Oh, but did Sharon tell you about our appetites? I hope there is enough for you to get your fill."

"Mom is teasing, Kyle. When Mom cooks, she likes to cook enough for lots of leftovers so that she doesn't have to cook daily." Great, thought Kyle; so far, so good. Let's keep the conversation on food, not family.

"Kyle, tell me about your mother," asked Mrs. Saxton.

"Well, she died a few years ago."

"Verona, that is an emotionally charged subject," rescued Robert. "You know how choked up I get talking about my mother. We don't want to have Kyle breaking down in tears at our first meal together. Kyle, I understand that you are finishing up your doctorate degree. You must have a bright future ahead of you."

"Yes, I should finish next semester if all goes as planned. I already have an excellent job lined up, but the identity of the employer and the details are confidential."

"That's wonderful, Kyle. Do you have a lot of educational loans to pay off?" asked Verona.

"Mother!"

"That's okay, Sharon. No, Mrs. Saxton. I paid my own way through school, mostly by tutoring. I'm sure you will agree, Mr. and Mrs. Saxton, that a foolish man lets debt enslave him; a wise man makes money his servant. I have even managed to accumulate significant investments while going to school."

"Very good, Kyle, and call us Robert and Verona. It sounds as if you have read the Richest Man in Babylon. Robert has brought in the money, but I have multiplied it. Please don't misunderstand us, Kyle. We are not pretentious snobs who look down on the poor. We both came from humble backgrounds and have lived very humbly most of our lives. However, we are appalled at the way most Americans and the country as a whole have buried themselves in debt. Excuse my directness, I meant no offense. I just wanted to know what kind of man we are dealing with. I am not interested in the size of your investments, just your character and attitudes."

"Kyle, we would like you to join us for Christmas Eve dinner and breakfast on Christmas day," injected Robert, again rescuing Kyle.

"I would be delighted to join your family."

"Kyle, did you participate in any sports?" asked Robert. "You look very athletic."

"I never had the time for sports growing up or at the University, but I do exercise regularly and stay in shape. I'm fond of watching football and basketball but have not had much time to enjoy that pastime." The men continued in a discussion of sports including the season that the University of Utah football team had experienced and their prospects in their upcoming bowl game. Much to Kyle and Sharon's relief, the conversation did not return to heavy personal matters.

A few days later Kyle returned to the Saxton home without Sharon and asked Robert for his daughter's hand in marriage. Kyle arranged with Sharon to spend an evening on Temple Square looking at the lights. After an hour of wandering through the lights, Kyle sat Sharon down on the edge of the reflective pond and knelt before her. With a light snow falling, Kyle began. "Sharon, will you make me the happiest man in the world and be my wife?"

Chapter 9 - Implantation

"Mark, I'm very impressed with your specifications," praised Dr. Monroe. "This is first-class work. Kyle's software will easily produce the code required."

"Thank you, Dr. Monroe. Actually, I gave the specification to Kyle two days ago. He's produced the code and we are now performing simulations," responded Mark somewhat boastfully. "Karen Vaish is working on the final revision of the controller chip. She's also supplied me with the necessary interface circuits. They're similar to those she produced for Kyle, only smaller and simpler. Thanks to Josh's help, I'm ready to implant a roach." Dr. Monroe hadn't expected much from Mark and was astounded by his progress. Nevertheless, he always found Mark irritating. He didn't seem like a whiz kid, but somehow he was producing at an astonishing rate.

Mark and Dr. Waters connected controllers to a species of very large cockroaches. They were creepy looking but much easier to work on than smaller insects. Within weeks, they had the cockroaches performing the surgeries themselves under the control of a small supercomputer similar to the one hosting Annette. They had manufactured tiny little tools adapted to the roach's front legs, which the roaches used to perform the surgeries and make all necessary connections. They even controlled one group to form a colony similar to an ant colony. Every day Mark had something new to boast about. "Today our roaches wired up a dragonfly," bragged Mark out of the side of his mouth in his irritating way. "Tomorrow we will have dragonflies wiring up other dragonflies. The roaches are constructing the tools right now. The little buggers work like ants under our control." Dr. Waters, on the other hand, said little but worked almost non-stop. He seemed like a man on a mission. Even Dr. Monroe had to admit being impressed with the quantity and quality of the work that Dr. Waters turned out.

Dr. Waters had fully involved himself in the work project and had even rolled up his sleeves and helped with dissections for both Kyle and Mark. Nevertheless, Kyle, Josh and Dr. Monroe were totally caught off guard when Dr. Waters announced that he wanted to assist Dr. Monroe in performing the implant surgery on Kyle. Dr. Monroe didn't like it, but Kyle had no problem with it. The date was set to perform the surgery, February 16. Kyle checked into the hospital the night before for some routine lab work. The next morning his head was shaved and he was wheeled into the operating room. Dr. Monroe and Dr. Waters were dressed and ready to go, along with a nurse and the anesthesiologist.

"So Kyle, is this your first surgery requiring anesthesia?" asked the anesthesiologist.

"No. I had an appendectomy several years ago."

"Then you know the routine. I will inject a medication into your IV line and you will count backwards from ten. The next thing you know you will be in the recovery room." Kyle didn't get past six before he lost consciousness. When all was ready, Doctor Monroe made an incision above Kyle's left ear and peeled back the scalp to expose the skull. A specialist in brain surgery joined the group to perform the risky parts of the operation that were not unique to this procedure.

"You may proceed with boring, Doctor Abraham", instructed Dr. Monroe. He bored a slot 2 centimeters wide and 0.8 centimeter high in the skull through which the circuitry would pass. After the nurse cleaned up all of the debris, she turned to Doctor Monroe.

"You may proceed with the insertion, Doctor." Keren had added a new feature to the "snake" chips. Near the edges were several much larger "snakes" whose purpose was to secure the processor chip to the surrounding tissues. The extra grip provided stability so the chip would not move around when the head was accelerated due to blows to the head or other jolting activity. Doctor Monroe inserted a "snake" chip and delicately maneuvered it to a position under the left audio nerve bundle. He placed a second "snake" chip next to the nerves associated with speech. Thin cables connected to the "snake" chips were left protruding out of the bored hole. Dr. Monroe then connected the processor module to the two cables. He also connected a small coil unit to the processor that would make an electromagnetic connection with the microphone unit. He very carefully passed the connected assembly into the cranial cavity. The most tedious part of the surgery was suturing the coil unit in place so that it was as close to the microphone unit as possible. He also sutured the processor unit to non-nervous system tissue to hold it stationary.

"You may proceed with the checkout, Dr. Waters." Dr. Waters entered a command on a laptop computer. The command started a program that communicated over Bluetooth with the processor chip to initiate a diagnostic program that verified the connections.

"The connections have all been verified, Doctor Monroe. Starting snake chips now." Dr. Waters entered another command on the keyboard. Each of the snake chips began extending their larger snakes to secure them to surrounding tissue. Once the chips were secured, the process of connecting to each axon began.

The microphone had been placed in the ear before the surgery began. It didn't connect directly to the processor. It had a magnetic link that not only communicated with the processor through the coil unit but also supplied it with power. The processor package had a supercapacitor that acted as a battery. It was only capable of sustaining operations for an hour. The microphone unit, which had a much higher capacity battery, was designed to be easily replaced with a spare when its battery was in need of charging.

The operation was interrupted when the door opened. The nurse that entered announced, "Dr. Monroe, you have an emergency call from the police."

"I can finish up here, Carlton. There's little left to do here. I just need to close." Reluctantly, Dr. Monroe left to answer the call. Dr. Abraham and the anesthesiologist had already left to check on other patients.

"Dr. Monroe, this is Sheriff Morris of the Madera, California, County Sheriff's Office. I regret to inform you that your parents have been seriously injured in an automobile accident on Highway 99. I think you should come at once to the Madera General Hospital."

"I'll be there as fast as possible." Dr. Monroe quickly changed and left.

Back at the operation, Dr. Waters looked at the table covered with instruments and supplies. "Nurse, I don't see the closure suture kit on the table. Please go get one, immediately." A heavier type of suture thread than that used earlier was required to close the exterior incision.

"But doctor, I'm sure that there was one when we started."

"Well, it isn't here now. Please get one, now!" The nurse left in pursuit of a suture kit. She found that the cupboard that normally contained them was empty. She called the emergency room and requested that one be brought since she could not walk through the hospital in her scrubs. It was 20 minutes before she returned to the operating room with the kit.

"What on earth takes so long to get a simple suture kit," chided Dr. Waters.

"I'm sorry there were ...."

"Never mind!" barked Dr. Waters. "Let's close this boy up before he comes to, shall we." Dr. Waters then skillfully stitched up Kyle's scalp.

Kyle began to regain consciousness about thirty minutes following the surgery. As is typical coming out of general anesthesia, Kyle's mind became alert before he was able to move a major voluntary muscle. He could hear background sounds such as doors opening and closing and people talking at a distance. It was even harder than normal for him to concentrate on a single voice. He wondered if the implant was working at all. Slowly he realized that he was hearing from his left side. It seemed very natural, just like from his right side, except that the volume seemed too low. With help from Sharon, who did her Ph.D. dissertation on a system of speeding up algorithms based on prediction, Kyle was able to improve the algorithm for positioning the "snakes" around the axons. With the new algorithm, the connection process was 99.4 percent complete after one hour.

He tried to speak, but nothing came out since he was still experiencing near-total paralysis. Then he decided to try to communicate with the implant. He attempted to say, "Implant, status." No sound left his lips, but the commands were sent from his brain.

From his left side, he heard a pleasant female voice say, "All circuits fully functional. Battery at 98 percent of full charge." Actually, no sound had been made. Because the computer had simulated sound to the nerves associated with his left ear, it seemed like a young woman had whispered in his left ear. Kyle wanted to shout for joy.

"Implant, increase volume by 90 percent."

Acknowledged. Volume increased by 90 percent. Kyle listened for a few seconds.

"Implant, increase volume by 2 percent."

Acknowledged. Volume increased by 2 percent. Kyle listened again. The ears seemed balanced.

"Implant, record current volume setting as standard."

Acknowledged. Current volume setting recorded as standard. Kyle could hear at a distance a young woman speaking. It seemed that she was speaking about him.

"Implant, increase volume by 200 percent, period." The "period" instructed the computer to carry out the command without an acknowledgment. Now he could hear more clearly. The speaker was expressing a romantic interest in Kyle. This device could have come in very handy in the pre-Sharon days of his life. Kyle began to regain some muscle control. He realized that he had been breathing through his mouth and it was very dry. He tried to ask for water. The young women who had been speaking came to his side. She was an attractive young nurse.

"CAN I HELP YOU?" boomed her words. Kyle had not turned down the volume.

"Water, please", Kyle managed to squeeze out from his mouth.

"I CAN'T GIVE YOU WATER; YOU MIGHT CHOKE ON IT. I CAN GIVE YOU SOME ICE CHIPS IF YOU LIKE." Kyle nodded yes. While the nurse was gone, he returned the volume to the recorded standard level. By the time the nurse returned, Kyle had managed to turn his body enough that he could drink if given the opportunity. "Here you go. Aren't you the student who just had a brain implant?"

"Yes, I'm Kyle James," answered Kyle in a hoarse whisper.

"Is the implant working?" asked the nurse.

"Perfectly."

"Did I hear you say it's working?" interrupted Dr. Waters who had just arrived.

"Yes. I can hear fine. I just can't talk very well yet," uttered Kyle in a voice that came out barely above a whisper.

"Let's let the anesthesia wear off and then we can talk," softly suggested Dr. Waters. Dr. Waters turned to leave.

"Wait," whispered Kyle. "Where is Dr. Monroe?"

"He had some sort of emergency call. I don't know where he went." Dr. Waters decided to stay with Kyle while the effects of the anesthesia wore off. "I'll wait with you. You don't need to talk.

We'll keep you in the hospital overnight to keep an eye on you to be sure there are no complications. It's standard procedure after cranial surgery. You're a brilliant young man, Kyle. I suppose you'll be finishing up your degree soon and moving on. I'd like to persuade you to stick around if I can. Have you considered becoming a professor? There will be an opening in the department soon. I'd love to hire you if we can get past the diversity police. It's really hard to hire a white male. It was good for me that my mother was half Native American or I would have never made it, myself. Do you have any mixed blood in you?"

"My mother was English/German. I know nothing of my father," Kyle spoke with greater ease than he could just a few minutes before.

"Is there any way of proving your heritage?"

"None that I know of."

"With your permission, I'd like to perform genetic testing. I would need a sample of your blood. Would that be all right?"

"I don't see any harm in it," answered Kyle. Kyle had been suspicious of Dr. Waters since Sharon's warning at the restaurant, but it was hard not to like him. Dr. Waters was always so complimentary and nice to him.

"Tell me now how the implant is working?" asked Dr. Waters.

"I had to have the computer increase the volume ninety-two percent, but the system appears to be functional. I haven't tried the transmitters. What is the number of your cell phone?"

"Two zero nine, six nine four, zero nine three three."

"Implant, record number just given under heading Doctor Waters and dial it," whispered Kyle, speaking to the computer. He decided he'd try to find another way to communicate with the computer. There would be plenty of time while laying in bed to work on that task.

Acknowledged. Two zero nine, six nine four, zero nine three three recorded under heading Doctor Waters. Dialing two zero nine, six nine four, zero nine three three. Ring ... ring ....

"Hello, this is Doctor Waters. To whom am I speaking?" answered Dr. Waters as he walked down a hall to distance himself from Kyle.

"This is Kyle. Can you hear me?"

"Perfectly. I thought you were joking when you said you should build in a cell phone. What else can you show me?"

"I need you to return to my room for the next demonstration. Watch this. Implant, turn on RCA television set and select channel 5." Kyle turned his head so as to point his ear at the old analog TV.

Question. Is the model pre 1989 or post 1989?

"Post 1989."

Acknowledged. Signal to turn on RCA television set, given. Signal to select channel 5, given. The TV snapped on, tuned to an ancient episode of "M*A*S*H".

"I can't believe they're still showing those things," remarked Dr. Waters as he entered the room. Kyle "heard" the phone hang up.

"Can it do anything else?"

"Implant, select channel 8 on RCA television set and transmit to television channel 8 your resource usage, period." The TV showed static for a moment and then a printout of numbers with headings indicating usage of both volatile and non-volatile memory, battery power remaining, and other information. "Just a minute, I have a call coming in. Implant, answer cell phone, period. Hello, this is Kyle."

"Congratulations. This is Nate. I hear you loud and clear, better than a normal cell phone. There's no background noise. Your software to convert nerve impulses back into sound works near perfectly. You sound very natural."

"Thank you, I worked hard on that part." Kyle turned to face Dr. Waters. "It's Nate. He called to see if things were working and congratulate me if they were." To those surrounding Kyle, it had sounded like he was having a conversation with himself, like when someone is using a Bluetooth earpiece. They couldn't hear Nate, at all. The system didn't contain a speaker, just a neural transmitting device. When on the cell phone, the computer automatically muted the nerve impulses generated from the signal coming from the microphone in his left ear but retained an internal digital copy, which could be played back later. Kyle would never again have to worry about trying to hold a wireless telephone conversation in a noisy environment. The nurse decided it was time to take Kyle's vital signs, so Kyle terminated his conversation with Nate and Dr. Waters left.

Nate, Josh and Kyle had planned to go public with the corporation if the implant was a success. They could all be multimillionaires by the end of the week. Kyle could hear the cell phone ringing. *Incoming call. It will automatically answer after five rings unless you cancel.* Kyle waited for the computer to automatically make the connection.

"Hello, this is Kyle."

"Kyle, turn to channel 2," requested Dr. Waters. "We're having a news conference." Channel 2 showed Nate and Dr. Waters on the phone in front of a number of reporters. Dr. Waters was holding up an implant just like the one in Kyle's head. Their conversation was being retransmitted by the television station and played on the TV in Kyle's room. A cameraman walked into Kyle's room and Kyle could see himself on TV. It was not a flattering picture, he thought. He didn't look good bald, especially with the side of his head bandaged. At least Sharon wasn't there to see him. Kyle felt bad that Dr. Monroe was missing out on all of the publicity. Dr. Monroe had never sought much recognition, probably to the detriment of his career. He still hadn't gone public with his sentient artificial intelligence breakthrough. Kyle wondered what emergency could have taken Dr. Monroe away at such an important time. The news conference was a huge success and portions of the program were rebroadcast on national news programs. Dr. Waters was a master of publicity. Business-wise it was probably to their advantage that Dr. Waters rather than Dr. Monroe handled the press release. Kyle, still suspicious of Dr. Waters, looked to see if he took undo credit to himself. To his surprise, Dr. Waters claimed no credit at all and mentioned several times the contributions of Dr. Monroe, whom he said performed nearly the entire surgery. He described his part as merely "cleaning up" after the device had been installed by Dr. Monroe.

After the news conference, Kyle was lowered into a wheelchair and wheeled to his room. Shortly after being helped into his bed, there was a knock at the door. "Come in," invited Kyle. Sharon entered. Although they had spent hundreds of hours together since their first date, Kyle still felt a flush of excitement every time Sharon entered the room. She was everything he had dreamed of in a woman: beautiful, intelligent, humorous, and best of all, intensely devoted and loyal. She was carrying a bouquet of flowers and a bag full of treats.

"Sorry I couldn't get here sooner. I was swamped with students with questions after my last class. How did everything go?"

"Unbelievably well. I thought engineering projects only worked right the first time in the movies. If we go public at the end of the week I should be able to buy you a diamond worthy of your beauty."

"All I need is you, Kyle. I want to wear your ring, any ring. Even more so, I want you to wear my ring. Once wealth is added to all of your other fine qualities you'll have to beat the women off with a stick."

"I think the hair, or should I say lack of it, will keep most of them at bay. Besides, what woman could ever compare to you, Professor Saxton?"

"That's assistant professor but thanks."

"Say, it's 5:00. Let's watch the news."

"I see you haven't lost your romantic flair," replied Sharon in her seductive voice. There were two minutes of coverage in the local news at 5:00 and a brief mention of the breakthrough in the national news at 5:30. Sharon had climbed up on the bed that Kyle had elevated into a lounge chair position. When Sharon was at his side, he was in heaven. However, his moment of pleasure was interrupted by the room telephone.

"Hello, this is Kyle."

"Kyle, this is Dr. Monroe. I'm at the Madera, California, County Hospital. Someone sent me on a wild goose chase! Did the operation turn out okay?" Dr. Monroe spoke with anger and frustration.

"Great. Were you able to hear the news conference?"

"What news conference?"

"The one that Nate Carpenter and Dr. Waters held."

"So, that's his game. He had someone call me, claiming that my parents had been in an accident in Madera and then soaks up the glory while I'm gone. I've had one of the worst days of my life and he becomes an instant celebrity. I expected as much." Kyle thought about how Dr. Waters had actually given the credit to others, including Dr. Monroe, but decided not to say anything. Dr. Monroe had spoken loudly enough that Sharon was able to follow the conversation. She reached over and took the phone from Kyle.

"Dr. Monroe, this is Sharon. There is no doubt that Dr. Waters is up to something. I don't think it's just publicity. He didn't milk the publicity thing like he could have. I don't know why he wanted you out of town, but there must have been a good reason. He's a very clever man. He wouldn't do the obvious. It would be wise for all of us to watch our backs."

"You're right, Sharon," replied Dr. Monroe, starting to calm down. "The worst thing I could do is act as if I suspect Dr. Waters of anything. I can't let my emotions rule the day. That's probably just what he wants. We have to find out what he's up to without his knowing it. Thanks for the advice. May I speak to Kyle again?" Sharon handed Kyle the phone. "Kyle, I didn't mean to rain on your parade. Are things working as you had hoped?"

"They couldn't be better. I never realized how helpful directional hearing could be. I've practiced throwing small objects randomly in the air with my eyes closed. I'm amazed at how easily and accurately I can perceive the landing-place through stereo hearing. The wireless phone capability is great. Without it, the public wouldn't be able to see any kind of an impressive demonstration. I've been going wild with ideas of how to more fully use the processing power we put in my head."

"There's always been a lot of processing power in your head. It just wasn't digital and didn't run at two gigahertz."

"Thank you. When will you be back?" asked Kyle.

"I'll see you tomorrow. Goodbye until then."

Chapter 10 – Malpractice

CompuSonic went public at the end of the week. They sold one million shares at $10 each. The three partners were credited with shares proportional to their monetary and intellectual contributions, their combined total also being one million shares. Kyle's portion was over four hundred thousand shares. All one million shares sold in the first hour of trading. After that, the price raised to over $50 a share. In one day, Kyle's net worth jumped to twenty million dollars.

The fact that Kyle and Josh were part owners of CompuSonic had still not been made public. Kyle and Josh felt it important to wait to get their degrees before letting the university know what they had done. They didn't feel that they had done anything wrong, but they were not sure the administration would see it that way. Both finished all of the requirements for graduation, including their oral exams and the dissertation write up and approval. As Kyle was cleaning out his desk in the graduate study room, Dr. Waters approached him. "Kyle, you've never asked how your blood test turned out."

"I guess I've been concentrating too much on graduating to think about getting a job." Kyle still was careful not to reveal his connection to CompuSonic, besides he could both teach and work for CompuSonic as a consultant if he wanted. Since beginning his romance with Sharon, he had begun to greatly enjoy the social events at the university.

"Let me help you carry those boxes to your car," offered Dr. Waters.

"Thanks." Kyle still had a hard time picturing Dr. Waters as a bad guy. He was always so nice. They walked carrying the boxes.

"The good news is that you have several nationalities represented in your blood. The bad news is that none of those nationalities are given preferential treatment. African, Native American, Hispanic blood, if in high enough quantities, can open many doors. Still, you could possibly get a position with the university. The hiring of your fiancée helped to fill out the diversity quotas and the university has a policy of giving preference to spouses of staff members since it helps to retain them." As they exited the building, Dr. Waters saw a dog tied to a parking meter. "The University has an explicit policy against dogs on campus, yet you see them everywhere! I've complained to the administration but to no avail. If you're going to have a rule or law it ought to be enforced."

"I agree with you there. I don't know when I'll see you again, Dr. Waters, but I do want to thank you for all of your help. You've certainly gone the extra mile."

"I like you Kyle. You're a fine young man. I may let you do a favor for me sometime. Keep your wits about you and good luck." They loaded the boxes in Kyle's car and parted. As Kyle drove off, he wondered what sort of favor he might be asked to perform.

Josh and Kyle both went through graduation ceremonies and received their degrees. Kyle and Sharon had planned a June wedding to take place at a cabin in Lambs Canyon that Sharon's parents had purchased. The waiting period had elapsed and Kyle was able to sell some stock. He sold 40,000 shares at over $50 a share. His partners also sold some of their stock. Finally, Kyle had money to spend.

To celebrate the company's good fortune and for additional publicity, CompuSonic had arranged a banquet in honor of the major players, including Dr. Monroe, Dr. Waters and Keren Vaish. It was a formal affair to be held in a banquet room at the Little America Hotel in Salt Lake City. Josh managed to get Keren to accompany him as his date. It would save some other young woman from sure boredom and allow him to feel like he had succeeded in dating a girl from India, adding to his bragging rights. Of course, Sharon accompanied Kyle.

Kyle and Sharon arrived at the event with Kyle dressed in a black tux and Sharon wearing a striking, full-length black evening gown. They quickly spotted Josh and Keren who were already seated and joined them. As they were passing pleasantries, Kyle noticed a slight hushing of the conversations around them. Dr. Monroe had just entered, accompanied by his strikingly beautiful wife, Annette, who wore a breath-taking red gown with plunging neckline and bare back. As Kyle took in Annette's voluptuous figure he suddenly winced as Sharon's sharp elbow caught him in the ribs. She gave him the look that said, "Enough of that." In a few minutes, Nate joined them.

"Holy hooters, did you get a load of Dr. Monroe's wife?" enthusiastically offered Nate trying to whisper in Kyle's ear. "I may have to change my criteria of tall and blond. What a babe!"

As they consumed dinner, the group enjoyed lighthearted chatter. "So Nate, do you run into Nancy often?" asked Kyle.

"No, but I did see her in a grocery store. She married some tall, good-looking business major. Get this! She's dropped out of school to help put him through. It just broke my heart to hear that. I don't think you ever realized what a fabulous mind she has. She has tremendous recall ability. She can tell you the names of every major actor in every one of my videos. I'll never find another girl like Nancy." Suddenly, Kyle's face took on a queer expression. He appeared to tense up every muscle in his body.

"Is something wrong?" asked Sharon. Kyle didn't reply. His body jerked erect, bumping the table and spilling water from the glasses. He stiffly moved to a large brass vase containing artificial flowers that was sitting next to the wall. He awkwardly reached down and gathered up the flowers. He clumsily dropped them onto the floor. He then reached into the vase and removed a revolver. Keren, who had been watching, screamed and pointed at Kyle, drawing the attention of those who had not yet noticed the spectacle. Kyle's right arm jerkily began to rise as his body turned and faced Dr. Monroe. Sharon sprung to her feet and began shaking Kyle and shouting, "Kyle, Kyle, what's the matter?"

Kyle managed to force out the words, "Pot! Head!" Sharon was bewildered, but Josh seemed to understand. He quickly grabbed the brass vase and turned it upside down. Simultaneously, a passing waiter had rushed forward to try to wrestle the gun away from Kyle. Both reached Kyle at the same time. Josh covered Kyle's head with the vase as the waiter grabbed the gun. Kyle's body went limp and as the waiter pulled the gun from his hand, it went off. At first, it appeared that no one had been hit, but then Annette Monroe slumped back in her chair, blood oozing from her forehead. Sharon whipped out her cell phone and called 911. Dr. Monroe began to attend to his wife, as the skilled physician that he was. He looked for Dr. Waters to request his assistance, but he was nowhere in sight.

"Josh, you have to get me to the communications laboratory!" echoed Kyle's voice from the vase. "Dr. Waters must have wired up my whole voluntary muscle system and implanted another processor next to the first. We need Dr. Monroe to check this out. If Dr. Waters did implant additional circuitry in me, it's a cinch that he has plans to destroy the evidence."

"You mean like your head exploding?" asked Josh.

"That would be a worst-case scenario but not unlikely. We've got to remove at least the processor package. I doubt that the connection chips are dangerous, just the processor package. Let's get moving. I can't see a thing."

"Josh, you get him to the lab and I'll get Dr. Monroe there," commanded Sharon. Josh and Kyle left. They drew lots of attention as they exited the hotel with Kyle wearing a brass vase on his head. The paramedics had arrived and were placing Annette on a gurney. Sharon approached, "Dr. Monroe, you naturally want to accompany your wife, but Kyle needs you right now. You can do nothing for your wife. Kyle may die without you."

"Are you crazy, woman, out of my way!" shouted Dr. Monroe hysterically.

Sharon turned her back to him and whispered to herself, "Well, when diplomacy fails...." She turned, combining the momentum of her turning body with that of her right arm, to land a sharp blow to Dr. Monroe's chin with her elbow, knocking him unconscious. As he slumped, she caught him on her shoulders. She kicked off her high-heeled shoes and carried Dr. Monroe from the room. Years of daily visits to the gym plus a surge of adrenaline gave her the strength. Fortunately, she and Kyle had driven her car and she had the keys in her purse, which had been in her left hand during her "persuasion" of Dr. Monroe. She spared no rubber as she sped to the university. On the way, Dr. Monroe began to come to.

"Where am I?" muttered Dr. Monroe.

"You are on your way to save Kyle's life."

"You hit me! Why did you do that?" questioned Dr. Monroe still trying to make sense of what had happened.

"Kyle thinks Dr. Waters implanted a second processor in his head while you were on your way to Madera. He figures it will explode or something if it doesn't get transmission for a certain period of time. Since we don't know how long that is, we can't waste any time!"

"Of course, you're right." Dr. Monroe removed the cell phone from Sharon's open purse and called the university hospital. "I'd like to speak with Dr. Sanchez." He pressed the mute button and explained to Sharon, "I think that the University Hospital can help us." He unmuted the phone. "Carlos, this is Carlton Monroe. I need your help in a big way to save a young man's life. I must perform surgery in a copper-lined room in the engineering building. I need all of the supplies necessary to perform the surgery transported there, as soon as possible. You'll have to break all of the rules. We need the equipment in minutes, not hours. Dr. Saxton will pull up to the east loading dock to receive them. If you fail, this fine young man will surely die." Dr. Monroe hung up and turned to face Sharon. "Drive us to the U-Haul rental on 300 West and 800 South. You rent the van and I'll drive on to the university." Sharon changed course in the Viper and raced to the rental agency. She screeched to a stop upon arrival and leaped from the vehicle. Dr. Monroe exited the vehicle, ran around the car and leaped into the driver's seat. He sped away.

Inside the communications laboratory, Kyle had been able to remove the brass vase. He had sent Josh to his apartment to retrieve two spare preprogrammed processors. Dr. Monroe arrived about 15 minutes after Josh had left. "Dr. Monroe, I don't think we can trust the processor that you implanted. We'll have to remove it along with the one that we suspect Dr. Waters implanted. Josh should arrive shortly with two preprogrammed processors from my apartment. Hopefully, Dr. Waters used exactly the same processor as we used. If we reconnect the interface chips to the second new processor we'll be better able to evaluate what has been connected and able to disconnect them, if needed. Of course, we can only retract the 'snakes' if we can find the record of their connection paths. As you know, the 'snake' chips have no memory of their own to facilitate retraction." Josh came running into the lab with the processors.

"Josh, I need you to call all of your friends and meet Sharon at the loading dock," requested Dr. Monroe. "We have a lot of equipment to bring up. Call Sharon on her cell phone to see how she's coming. Tough break having to have head surgery again, Kyle. Your hair was just starting to look all right. I wouldn't want your wedding pictures."

"That's okay, Dr. Monroe. Nobody will be looking at me in the pictures anyway."

"I know what you mean. No one looks at me in mine." Suddenly Dr. Monroe was reminded of his wife. "Excuse me, Kyle. I need to check on Annette." Josh was on the laboratory phone, so Dr. Monroe went to his office to call.

"Looks like we're in luck," shouted Josh from across the room. "It seems there is a disaster plan at the hospital that includes a portable operating room. It's also heavily shielded to protect the equipment in case of electromagnetic pulse. Sharon can tow it here or we can go there. By the way, she says to tell Dr. Monroe that he hung up before Dr. Sanchez had time to think about the portable operating room. He didn't know how to contact him."

"Let's just go to the trailer instead of hauling it here," suggested Kyle. "Go get Dr. Monroe from his office and come back for me. I don't think I can find my way around with the vase on my head." Just then, Dr. Monroe came back.

"Dr. Sanchez left a message on my voice mail telling me about a shielded operating room they have," he breathlessly uttered.

"Sharon just told us, she's on her way in a cab. Shall we go?"

"I'll go on ahead to make sure everything is ready," said Dr. Monroe. As Kyle, with a vase on his head, and Josh exited the building towards Josh's car they noticed a black Mustang drive by. The passenger caught sight of Josh and in spite of the vase on his head, recognized him. They turned into the lot and parked. Kyle's two least favorite athletes emerged and ran in their direction. Kyle and Josh retreated into the building; they figured they would have home-field advantage in the engineering building. They ran into a classroom and Josh called Sharon to explain the situation.

"Don't worry about a thing. I can take care of these guys. Wait for my call." Sharon had called a taxi earlier to drive her to the university. She arrived and entered the building. She found the two athletes running down a narrow hall. She positioned herself strategically where a desk was left in the hall, narrowing the passage. She leaned against the desk and pulled up her long dress on her right thigh and extended her leg blocking the hall. The two skidded to a stop.

"What two wonderful specimens of virile manhood have we here?" she said in her sexiest voice. "Wouldn't I just love to get it on with one of them. But how to choose?" She kissed one of the dumbfounded young men and then the other. "I can't tell by just a kiss. I need to look closer. How about you two studs step into the men's room here and strip down so you can show me what you've got. I'll join you and pick a winner." The two leaped to the men's room and fought to be first to get through the door. When the door closed behind them, Sharon called Josh. "Meet me at your car." She then dialed another number. "Hello, campus security, I would like to report a couple of gays engaged in lewd activity in a men's room on campus."

At the hospital's portable operating room, they received assistance from Dr. Sanchez and one of his nurses. They decided there was no time to prep Kyle. They left his short hair in place and only did a rudimentary job of sterilizing the area. An infection would be easier to treat than an exploded head. As soon as the skin was peeled back and the skull plug removed that had not had time to completely fuse to the rest of the skull, they could see that Kyle was exactly right about what was in his head. Dr. Monroe first removed the processor package that Dr. Waters had implanted. It had a bulge on one side. Dr. Monroe opened the trailer door and flung the processor into an empty parking stall. Being disconnected and in radio range, it exploded before it even hit the ground. Kyle had been right about everything. The original processor was then removed. It was removed from the trailer for safety, but it wasn't thrown away. The two new processors were connected to the interface chips. They had been programmed to assume that the nervous connections had already been made. Before going under, Kyle had instructed the original processor in his head to send a message via radio transmission to the spare processor destined to replace the one inserted by Dr. Waters. He instructed the spare not to output any signals to the interface chips. That way it would not cause muscle actuations as it tried to communicate sound to Kyle's audio nerves to which it anticipated being connected. Following the operation, Kyle was transported back to the same area in the hospital he waited in after the first surgery. This time he awoke to see the beautiful face of Sharon hovering over him, still dressed in her evening gown.

When Kyle had recovered enough to speak, he inquired into Mrs. Monroe's situation. "She may live, but she's suffered significant brain damage," was Sharon's answer. "She's in a coma, right now. Dr. Monroe is with her. He said you can page him at the hospital if you need him. Honey, you look really tired. It's very late. Go to bed and I'll see you for breakfast." Sharon kissed him goodbye and left. Kyle was soon transported from intensive care to a regular patient room and helped into bed. He let himself drift off to sleep.

Sharon showed up before breakfast was served at the hospital. It was not visiting hours, but Miss Saxton had found that her intelligence and good looks opened many doors. She was carrying a large travel bag. "How's your appetite, love?" she asked Kyle with a cheerful smile. Every time Kyle looked at Sharon, he could not believe his good fortune.

"I'm starving. Remember, I didn't get to finish my dinner last night."

"I think I can satisfy your appetite." Sharon unzipped the travel bag and pulled out a complete breakfast for two. There were hash browns, eggs, ham, toast and orange juice. She also had brought two very large plates that they cradled in their laps as they sat together with the head of the bed raised. They feasted. Kyle was always amazed at how much Sharon ate for such a slender woman.

"There is one thing really bothering me," said Kyle in a bewildered voice. "Only low-frequency radio waves could have been interrupted by the vase. Why would Dr. Waters have used such a low frequency? It would have been much easier to build the antenna for high frequencies. It doesn't make sense."

"It doesn't unless you know Dr. Waters. He was noted for giving exams with what appeared to be extremely challenging problems but with relatively easy solutions that were not necessarily obvious. It's some kind of morbid game he plays. By the way, if you weren't expecting low-frequency radio waves, then why did you suggest the vase be put over your head? Anyway, I assume that's what you were asking for."

"That's what I wanted. Actually, it wasn't until later that I figured out that it shouldn't have worked. I was just lucky that it cut off the radio transmission. I guess that's what you call dumb luck. It really shouldn't have worked."

"Or maybe Dr. Waters' accomplice was just toying with you. Maybe he just turned off the transmissions to give you a false sense of accomplishment."

As they finished breakfast there was a knock at the door. "Just a minute," called out Kyle. They quickly put away the evidence of their breakfast. "Come in." The door opened and a huge Samoan man wearing a sports coat and tie approached Kyle's bed.

"Hello Mr. James and Miss Saxton, I'm Sergeant Fatui of the Salt Lake City Police Department. I would like to ask you a few questions about the shooting last night. As standard policy, I would like to speak with each of you separately. I'm sorry, Miss Saxton, but could I ask you to wait for me in the lobby?"

"I'll see you later, lover," whispered Sharon in Kyle's ear before kissing him on the cheek and departing. As Sharon left, Kyle's hospital breakfast arrived.

"Sergeant Fatui, I have no appetite at all, would you care for some breakfast?" asked Kyle.

"Why thank you. Actually, I didn't have time for breakfast this morning. I've been on the case since shortly after the shooting last night. Kyle, tell me from your perspective what happened last night?" began Sergeant Fatui's questioning.

"As I recall, I was halfway through the main course when suddenly my body started to stand up. I tried to make it stay seated and succeeded for a moment but then was unable to stop my body from moving on its own. It took me only a few seconds to figure out what was happening."

"And what was that, Kyle?" asked Sergeant Fatui.

"I remembered our early tests on a squid. We implanted axon stimulators like the ones in my head. We used them to command the squid's muscles to contract. The squid apparently tried to prevent the contractions when it sensed them beginning. It struggled just as I did before losing control. After only a few seconds, its ability to resist movement induced by the implant became greatly weakened. I surmised that during Dr. Monroe's absence, Dr. Waters had inserted a second CPU chip programmed to command the interface circuitry to connect to additional axons. I realized that my only hope was to use a muscle before the computer used it. I hadn't yet tried to use my speech muscles, so I tried to decide ahead of time what could be done and what to say. That's when it occurred to me that an external signal must be sending commands to the controller in my head. When I realized that it was trying to command me to shoot Dr. Monroe, I knew I had to interrupt the transmission. As my body removed a gun from a large brass vase, I considered using the vase to free myself. I gambled that it would be sufficient to interrupt the transmission. I planned my words to be as brief as possible. I was confident that Sharon or Josh Adamms would figure things out. 'Vase' is difficult to say under duress. 'Pot' is much easier to say, so I said, "Pot. Head." I barely got those words out before the controller stimulated my vocal nerves in such a way as to make speech impossible. My friends understood and responded. As the vase went over my head, the stimulation of my nerves and consequently my muscles, ceased, causing me to go limp. At that point, someone grabbed the gun and it went off. I couldn't see anything. It was very difficult to understand what was happening with all of the shouting. I asked Josh to take me to the communications laboratory where I knew that I would be shielded from the transmissions."

"I know the rest of the story," interrupted Sergeant Fatui.

"I've told you my story, but what's yours. Do you know why Dr. Waters would do such a thing? I've heard there was some kind of bad blood between him and Dr. Monroe, but that was years ago. Dr. Waters was always so nice to me."

"Beware of strangers bearing gifts, Kyle. You must realize that only Dr. Waters knows for sure why he did what we think he did, but I'm ninety-nine percent confident of his motive. The bad blood you referred to started with both men competing for the heart of Annette Billings, the future Annette Monroe. Carlton Monroe, with his youth and charm, was winning the battle. Apparently, Dr. Waters decided to improve the odds by disgracing Carlton. According to Carlton, Dr. Waters bribed a student to claim that Carlton had copied some of the test answers off his paper. Carlton demanded that he and the other student be administered oral exams, immediately. The administration went along with Carlton's request. Carlton passed with flying colors and the other student did poorly. Carlton was never able to prove conspiracy, but Dr. Waters was made to look very bad in the eyes of his peers and students. He told Carlton that someday he would get even with him. Dr. Monroe thinks that Dr. Waters' plan was to have you kill him and then turn the gun on yourself and fire into your head, destroying most of the evidence. Dr. Waters even submitted to an obscure medical journal a paper indicating that your implant could lead to sudden psychosis. He would look like a prophet."

"Well, at least, his plans didn't work out," commented Kyle.

"Dr. Waters planned more than just murder. During the excitement following the shooting, the engineering building was robbed of millions of dollars worth of equipment and supplies. He had to have had lots of inside help. The contents of the entire solid-state lab are gone. A number of very powerful computers are gone. Not only can we not find Dr. Waters, but everything personal is gone from his office and apartment.

"I noticed that all of the long-time janitors were gone. He must have somehow gotten his own people hired. Have you questioned any of them?" volunteered Kyle.

"Can't. They're nowhere to be found."

"Did they take any of Dr. Monroe's equipment?" asked Kyle.

"No. Dr. Monroe had installed a special electronic lock that only he could open. He did his own cleanup to keep out the janitorial staff." Sergeant Fatui's pager started beeping. "Sorry, Kyle, I gotta go. Here's my card. Call me if you think of anything that might help the case. And thanks for the breakfast. I'm sure it wasn't on the same level as the gourmet meal you had before I arrived. The aroma still lingers, but to a hungry man like myself, the hospital breakfast was very satisfying." Sergeant Fatui left Kyle's hospital room and made a call on his cell phone. After his call, he visited Sharon who was still waiting in the lobby. She gave her perspective but didn't add any new information.

Kyle turned on the news to see if there were any stories relating to the incident. The incident was the lead story in the local news. "In a bizarre incident last night in a banquet room at the Little America Hotel in Salt Lake City, Kyle James, the world's first recipient of a computer brain implant, went berserk and shot Annette Monroe, the wife of Dr. Carlton Monroe, in the head. As you may remember it was Dr. Monroe and Dr. Samuel Waters who performed the implant. It's believed by the police that Dr. Waters implanted an additional computer chip in Kyle James's head and that this second implant was responsible for the incident. In a possibly related story, the University of Utah, where both of the doctors are employed, was robbed of millions of dollars worth of computer equipment. Dr. Waters and all of his belongings are gone, as are a number of other people, including the janitorial staff of the Engineering building at the university. We take you now live to Jan Calunga at the Merril Building of the University of Utah."

"Kent, this is no ordinary robbery. As you can see behind me, it looks more like a business moved from a leased building. Everything is gone from the solid-state lab. Only the bare walls remain. It will take the university months and millions of dollars to restore this department. The only good news is that the University has most of the summer to rebuild and regroup. Back to you, Kent."

"In other unusual news, early this morning Gas Products Company in Centerville was robbed of its entire inventory of bottled helium gas. Nothing else was taken. Police are puzzled as to why just helium was taken." A knock came at the door. Kyle flipped off the TV and invited the party in. Sharon had returned.

"Lover, I know things have been exciting the last twelve hours, but we have serious work to do. Our wedding is less than two weeks away. All of the invitations have been sent. The decorations are planned and arranged for. The food arrangements have all been made. You had two assignments, get someone to marry us and plan the honeymoon. How are you coming?"

"I have someone lined up, if you approve. Since neither of us go to any particular church, we don't know any ministers well. The closest thing I have to family is Josh Adamms and his family. Josh's father, Howard, recently became a Mormon bishop. As Josh would say, he was 'called' to be the bishop of their ward, their congregation. As a bishop, Mr. Adamms can legally perform marriages and would be delighted to perform ours."

"Any friend of yours is a friend of mine. Bishop Adamms will be fine. What about the honeymoon?"

"How does a Caribbean cruise sound?"

"Don't kid with me. The Caribbean would be great, but can you afford a cruise."

"Actually, I can. I've been keeping it a surprise. After the mandatory waiting period, with the stock over $50 a share, I sold 40,000 shares. However, when we return from the honeymoon, I think we should give the rest of the money to the University towards a new solid-state laboratory. I can't help feeling partially responsible for what happened."

"Well baby, I'm marrying you for you, not your money. Besides, don't you still own 360,000 shares?"

"Yes, but after last night they may not be worth much come Monday morning."

"That's okay. Lover, I've been up all night. I'm gonna go get some sleep." Sharon kissed Kyle goodbye and left.

Chapter 11 – How to Cheat Death

Kyle slept for awhile but was awakened by a knock on his hospital room door. "Come in," invited Kyle. Dr. Monroe entered the room.

"How are you feeling, Kyle?" asked the good doctor.

"I'm fine. What's the situation with Mrs. Monroe?" asked Kyle.

"Not good. Not good at all. She's alive for now, but that may not last long. She could live a long time in a coma, but that can't happen. She has a living will that dictates that she is to receive no assistance of any kind if she remains unconscious for more than one week. She would starve or die of dehydration in a few days under those circumstances. I can't stand to lose her, not now. We had somewhat of a reconciliation just days before the incident. That's why she was with me and so cheerful. We've had our problems, but I never gave up on the marriage and I can't let her go now."

"What can you do?" asked Kyle.

"We can do a lot. This may seem slightly shady, but I have a plan, which could buy us time. I need you to get dressed, if you are truly all right, and come with me." Kyle quickly slipped into his street clothes. He and Dr. Monroe left without even checking out of the hospital.

"Kyle, what resources do we have to do a total implant like Dr. Waters performed on you?" asked Dr. Monroe once they were in his car.

"I always thought that Nate was extreme about spare parts, but now I see the wisdom. We have ten spare 'snake' chips in a company safety deposit box. Of course, the CPU chip is an off-the-shelf item. I also have three spare outer ear units at home and one in my pocket and ten more in the safety deposit box. We'll probably need at least four or five 'snake' chips for a total voluntary muscle and sensory connection. We won't have enough on hand to give a complete sense of touch or pressure or pain. There are just too many nerve bundles involved. But, we can give sight, hearing, taste, smell and feeling in the hands."

"How long do you think it will take to port the 'Annette' program to your system?" asked Dr. Monroe.

"The problem is resources. The computer that 'Annette' runs on now has far more mass storage capacity than what the ZYTECH chip has in nonvolatile memory. We could probably fit five in her head, but that wouldn't be enough for all of her memories. In fact, the computer hosting her now doesn't have enough capacity for human memories, if that is what you plan to do. Are you planning to just get Mrs. Monroe out of bed or simulate a complete life for her?"

"Our immediate goal is to make her appear conscious, but I expect the coma to last for months or maybe even years. She may never come out of it without computer assistance. Maybe she'll regain partial capability, but her brain damage is too great for total recovery. If Mrs. Monroe is to be controlled by 'Annette', it must seem perfectly natural. Mrs. Monroe would rather die than look or sound like an invalid or a mentally handicapped person. Being a beautiful, articulate, well-educated person is important to her."

"Carlton, I don't think we should rush to perform this surgery. I realize we only have a week, but I need some time to explore the capabilities of what's now in my head. There may be some better ways to do things. Is Mark around or did he disappear with Dr. Waters?"

"He's still here and from what I've heard, he feels abandoned and betrayed."

"Good, he may be of some help to us. I need to be uninterrupted for at least one day. Can I stay at your place? That way I won't have to answer the door, the mail or anything. Better yet, can I stay in your private lab? I may need Annette's help. I hope your fridge is still well-stocked. Pick me up some of that artificial crab meat. I love that stuff. Zero fat and no work. You don't even need to warm it."

"If we ever get Mrs. Monroe back, she'll have to teach you a thing or two about fine dining." Dr. Monroe drove to the engineering building and dropped off Kyle. Kyle proceeded to Dr. Monroe's laboratory and entered using the combination that Dr. Monroe had disclosed to him. Annette was watching television. "Hello Annette, I hope that's not a soap opera you're watching."

"Of course not, Kyle. I am learning about the sport of baseball." Annette turned off the television. "Carlton told me that he asked you to help with his effort to rehabilitate his wife. What do I call her anyway?"

"Call her Mrs. Monroe. Carlton and I will know what you mean. Yeah, I'm here to help. I may also need your help. You're currently running on a very powerful desktop mini supercomputer. We need to fit you into a woman's head, coexistent with her brain. We can't get enough speed from several CPU's like the ones in my head and there will be far less mass storage, nonvolatile memory that is, than what you have now, and I suspect that you are already running out of memory. There is also the power issue. Our system was designed to power one CPU for 48 hours on one battery charge. We may be able to fit quite a few CPU chips in Mrs. Monroe. They're only 2 centimeters by 2 centimeters by 0.4 millimeters."

"Kyle, why do you have to put all of the processors in the head? Isn't there a lot more room in the abdominal cavity or some other place in the body?"

"Sure, but they need to communicate. How stupid of me! Only two or three are needed to handle all of the neural stimulator chips. They could all communicate using the all-frequency radio transmitter/receiver, but a fiber optic link would be faster and more secure. We'd need to get from the chest area to the cranium. I know we could go just under the skin, but is there a better way?"

"I don't want some big ugly scar on my new body. Can't you run them up through some blood vessel that goes to the brain?"

"Great idea, Annette. A catheter could be used to pull the cable up a large blood vessel. Carlton would know more about that than I do. I'll call him and get him started on it." Kyle called Dr. Monroe and explained Annette's and his ideas. Dr. Monroe was very excited that they would not need to cram a bunch of processors in Mrs. Monroe's head. He was worried about the long-term effects. They decided 100 CPU units were not unreasonable. Kyle called Nate and had him rush order 110 parts from ZYTECH.

"Kyle, how much power does each CPU use?" inquired Annette.

"They consume 15 milli-watts each, when not in sleep mode. With over 100 processors that's over 1.5 watts!"

"You're going to need a whale of a battery. Like the metaphor? I've been working on them."

"It was a great metaphor. Each chip has a capacitor onboard that acts like a battery, good for one hour of use. There need not be any other. We'll take a page from Dr. Water's book, to use another metaphor. The computerized insects he created weren't powered by batteries or solar cells. They were powered by miniature generators, which were actuated by muscle contractions stimulated by the computer. We should have many large involuntary muscles to choose from and our generator need not be so miniature. We could have several so that we can alternately use and rest the muscles involved. Intestine muscles should work well. We can build a fiber optic cable with power cables running alongside, all encapsulated in a Teflon tube. I'll get Josh working on them."

Kyle called Josh but did not tell him why he needed the cable and the generators. "Annette, I need you to go into your sleep mode for awhile. I'm very self-conscious about what I have to do."

"Sure, Kyle. Wake me up when you need me. Otherwise, I will not wake up for eight hours. I'll simulate Mrs. Monroe who is a very deep sleeper. Good night."

"Implant 1, begin process of cataloging the connections of implant 2." Kyle went through a tedious process of determining which body function or sensory input was connected to what neural stimulator/receiver. Partway into the procedure, Kyle realized that Annette would have to go through the same process. He awoke Annette and explained to her in detail what he was doing. After many hours of interaction with the computer, the mapping was complete. Kyle discovered some interesting things about what Dr. Waters had done. The left eye optic nerve had been well connected. He turned on Annette's television set and used the transmitter to transmit what he was seeing. His eye made a wonderful camera. As he walked around the room, it was as if he were holding a camcorder connected to a monitor. Only his left eye was connected, which made it easier for the circuitry since it did not have to resolve the stereovision. Of course, with only one eye, there was a small blind spot representing where the optic nerve exits the retina. Since the computer was connected to a small microphone in his left ear, there was also audio reception. With some additional programming, Kyle was able to configure his all-frequency radio transmitter/receiver to act as a television receiver. He could close his eyes and then see projected in front of him the television picture. Actually, the neural transmitter/receiver was transmitting the image directly to his optic nerve. He could also hear the broadcast. What a great thing to have. He could go to the opera with Sharon (not that she had mentioned opera, but a guy can't be too careful) and watch and listen to the game or something else he wanted to see on TV.

Kyle programmed the two CPU chips to act as one computer that shared the workload. He programmed the combined unit to respond to just "implant" rather than "implant 1" or "implant 2". He had the computer record his commands to muscles as he walked in a figure-eight on the floor tiles. He commanded the computer to repeat the commands. Instead of walking in the figure-eight, after one step he fell over and his legs went through the motions while he lay on the floor. He had forgotten all about the need for balance. "I bet I looked pretty silly during that test," he commented to Annette.

"I did not laugh, but I think most people would have," responded Annette. "Mrs. Monroe does not like to be laughed at according to my knowledge of her. She is a proud woman."

"You got that right. She's a knockout, but I have never cared for her. She can be very witty but never, ever in a self-effacing way. She could really use some humility. You may mimic her voice, Annette, but I prefer your company to Mrs. Monroe's any day."

"Why thank you, Kyle. That is one of the nicest things anyone has ever said to me."

Kyle spent several hours programming the computer to maintain balance, careful to explain to Annette what he was doing. "The most challenging thing for me, Annette, is completely relaxing so that the computer can take over. You won't have that problem, at least not until, or maybe I should say if, Mrs. Monroe becomes conscious. You'll have to let her take over as much as she is able to."

"What if Mrs. Monroe never becomes conscious or worse yet becomes brain dead?" asked Annette with a voice that sounded very human in its concerned tone. Kyle marveled at Annette's ability to imitate human emotions. He knew she had been watching lots of television to study how humans acted in different situations. He felt a sense of pride that something he had a part in creating was so wonderful. He was sure that in a human body Annette would be very convincing.

"It would be very difficult for Carlton to accept you as his wife. There would be a lot of mixed-up feelings. Now, me on the other hand, I would just see you as a beautiful woman who is my wife and never gets a headache, every man's fantasy."

"I don't understand what relevance headaches have to marriage?" asked Annette.

"I'll explain that one another time. Annette, I think I've spent enough time exploring my own computer controls. We need to talk about what controls you'll have and how they will work. You will have equivalent processing power and high-speed memory but less non-volatile memory than you do now. Since your non-volatile memory will be solid-state, rather than hard drives, you'll have shorter access times to this memory. We need to devise ways so that you can function like a person instead of a computer. Take storing visual information. I don't have a perfect picture in my mind of everyone I know, but I can recognize them the moment I see them. I don't know how my mind stores and retrieves the information. I just know that the system works. If you try to store an exact photographic image of everyone you meet, you will soon run out of memory. The same goes for other things that you see."

"Maybe I can help by asking questions, Kyle. I've heard that you like Sharon's automobile. Could you draw an accurate picture of it?"

"I could if I could draw."

"Then you have some sort of a picture of it in your mind. If you were drawing this picture when you drew the wheels would you do it from memory of the Viper's wheels or from your memory of wheels in general?"

"I would mostly draw from my memory of wheels in general, but I would have to remember the unique style of rims and that the tires are very wide. Maybe you could use a technique similar to what is used in computer drafting. In a program like AutoCAD, for example, the user can combine graphic elements into a unit called a block. Small blocks can be combined into larger blocks. That system could even be used for faces. Police have a technique, in which they form a picture of a suspect by showing witnesses a selection of facial parts, allowing the witnesses to select the one that most closely resembles the suspect. If you want, I could try to get the images for you."

"Thanks, Kyle, but I've seen those composite pictures on the news. I think I can do better. I will create my own as I meet people."

"You also need to learn to forget. There will not be enough room with current technology for you to remember everything that you see, hear, taste, smell, feel and think."

"Will I be able to feel?" asked Annette hopefully.

"It isn't possible for us to give you full human feeling over every part of your body. I think we can give you full feeling in your hands, feet and face. You'll even feel pain in your hands and feet. Otherwise, you would be likely to injure yourself. Of course, you will not feel pain like I do, but it would serve as a warning so you don't injure yourself. You need feeling in your hands to perform most tasks that involve the use of your hands. Compared to your mechanical hands, human ones will be wonderful to you."

"I am sure they will be, Kyle. I see a dilemma here. If Mrs. Monroe never regains consciousness, Carlton will be unhappy. If she does, she will likely make him miserable again. He says they had a reconciliation, but I am suspicious of her motives. Maybe she smelled fame and fortune in the air."

"I've had the same doubts. I can't tell you how to make Carlton happy. You'll have to figure that one out on your own. Maybe something in all of that TV watching can help."

Chapter 12 – And the Computer Was Made Flesh

Dr. Monroe and Kyle stood next to Annette's computer. Kyle was giving her final instructions. "We'll transfer your memory and consciousness to this bank of CPUs that will be implanted in Mrs. Monroe. You'll be blind but not deaf or dumb. You'll be able to communicate with us using the embedded all-frequency radio transmitter/receivers. We won't perform the implant without communication. If anything goes wrong, we'll still have all of your memories up to the time of transfer in the desktop computer. Until we turn off the desktop computer there will be two of you existing simultaneously. Because we like to think of you as a unique person, we won't continue to have two of you. You won't be permanently cloned. Are you ready, Annette?"

"Proceed. I don't want to lose this opportunity to gain a body with all of the human senses," responded Annette with great enthusiasm. Annette's executive software had been regenerated to run on the new computers and was already loaded. However, there were none of Annette's memories or other information installed. All of Annette's memories were downloaded from the desktop computer using a high-speed serial link. The process took hours to complete. Dr. Monroe went to his office, but Kyle stayed in the lab, reading and watching television while he waited. He raided Dr. Monroe's refrigerator several times. Finally, the transmission finished. Kyle called Dr. Monroe to invite him back. The copy of Annette on the desktop computer was put into an indefinite sleep mode.

"Annette, can you hear us?" anxiously spoke Dr. Monroe into the two-way radio microphone. There was no response. Kyle turned up the volume and Dr. Monroe continued to call out to Annette. They took turns speaking into the radio. "Maybe you should reload the software, Kyle. It shouldn't take more than seconds for Annette to respond."

"I'm sure it was all loaded correctly. There's full parity checking during the download process," answered Kyle as he tried to figure out what could have gone wrong. "Keep talking, maybe she can receive but not transmit. If you can hear me, Annette, do a remote log onto the desktop computer. You can print text on the screen." Dr. Monroe and Carlton continued to speak into the radio but were getting very discouraged. They continued for over half-an-hour with no response.

"Carlton, Kyle, can you hear me?" came Annette's hopeful voice.

"We hear you, we hear you!" shouted back Dr. Monroe. "We thought we had lost you. What happened?"

"Kyle, what frequency did you set me up to use?"

"47.325 megahertz. Why?"

"What is your radio set at?"

"47.523 megahertz. Oops! Sorry."

"Let me tell you. That 31 minutes and 21 seconds may have seemed like hours to you two, but with 100 processors each running at 2 gigahertz, it seemed like days to me. Please don't ever do that to me again. At least Helen Keller could feel, smell and taste. After performing every kind of check possible and trying all 100 transmitters, I finally started scanning other frequencies. I think one truck driver nearly ran off the road when I told him I was a computer. He kept trying to put the moves on me. Once I knew that my all-frequency radio transmitter/receiver was working I started listening to all of the frequencies. I figured that I needed to listen for at least 10 seconds to be sure that I hadn't missed you. Then I realized that I could listen with all 100 receivers at once. I heard thousands of conversations before I got you. Did you miss me?"

"More than you can imagine, Annette. More than you can imagine," responded Dr. Monroe, who was exhausted from the stress and constant calling into the microphone.

"Carlton, when can you proceed with the operation?" asked Annette.

"We can start first thing in the morning. I've got to get some rest. I'll see you two tomorrow." Dr. Monroe dragged himself home.

"Can you stay for awhile, Kyle?" asked Annette hopefully.

"Sure. I'm more used to frustrating computer problems than Carlton is."

"By the way, you used to call him 'Dr. Monroe'. What changed?"

"I'm 'Dr. James', now. I figure we're peers."

"That makes sense. But I always felt like you were peers. Carlton says you are the real brains behind my programming. He says that your software was already a form of artificial intelligence and he just used your software to do something you had not gotten around to yet."

"That was very generous of him, Annette," responded Kyle. "Saying that I am the real brains behind your creation is like saying that the paint manufacturer was the real artist behind the Sistine Chapel ceiling. I don't know if you realize what a wonderful man Dr. Monroe is. He's been like a father to me during the last four or five years. He's brilliant without the accompanying ego that so often accompanies high intelligence. He's also a man of very high integrity. It was fortunate that you were created by such a man." Kyle realized Annette probably had him stay for reasons other than to praise Dr. Monroe, so he changed the subject. "Do you have concerns about tomorrow, Annette?"

"Kyle, when I have a human body with all of the human senses, will I have emotions too?"

"That's a good question, Annette. I've been thinking a lot lately about why we have emotions. I think somehow they are an outgrowth of feelings of pain and pleasure. We tend to hate that which brings us pain and love that which brings us pleasure. I don't think that anyone knows how an animal or person feels pain or pleasure. Oh, we know how the stimulus gets transmitted to the brain, but why does it make us feel good or bad? If I knew the answer to that question, I could probably program you to feel pain or pleasure. Do you want emotions?"

"I think so. The pain part really sounds undesirable, but the pleasure part sounds like it is worth it all. Let me ask you a question, if you could choose to feel no pleasure or pain would you choose it?"

"No. It's like asking if I would like to die. Those who commit suicide seem to want to feel no pain and are willing to feel no pleasure in exchange for it. But, I think that usually the pain they are escaping is emotional pain, not physical pain."

"I have not quite figured out emotional pain. The soap operas on TV are full of emotional pain and also emotional pleasure. I watch TV to try to understand people. I realize that these stories are created to earn money, not to educate. I hope that at least they will help me to act human and not embarrass or hurt Dr. Monroe in other ways. I have read the story of Pinocchio. I will be sort of like him. I will know how to talk and walk, at least I hope that I can figure out how to walk, but I will not have years of experience interacting with many people. At least, I will be well-read and educated. I hope I will be able to identify evil people and not let them take advantage of me. I hope that you will help me, Kyle. It is easier to talk to you about these kinds of things than it is with Carlton. He programmed me to sound and talk like his wife. I think her voice causes all sorts of feelings in him ranging from anger to romance. He wouldn't admit it, but I seem to make him tense up sometimes, like if you were on a date with a woman you were nuts about but were unsure about her feelings towards you."

"I've enjoyed our time together, immensely, Annette. You realize there will be new challenges to our association after you're implanted into Mrs. Monroe's body. She's a very beautiful woman. I'll soon be a married man. My future wife, Sharon, has long been jealous of Mrs. Monroe. She may not like me hanging around you."

"I have already figured that one out. We can communicate over our all-frequency radio transmitter/receivers. We don't have to even use a phone service, which would leave a billing record. Only we will need to know. I have sufficient processing power now that I can carry on a conversation with you while speaking with someone else."

"I would have a hard time doing that, but I can carry on a conversation over the cell phone without anyone knowing. I've become like a ventriloquist, except that I don't make any sound, just nerve impulses that the implant can pick up. Since school is done, I have had a lot of time to work on it."

"Show me. 47.120 gigahertz is open. Let's practice."

"Okay, Annette, how is this?" Kyle transmitted without moving his lips.

"Very good, Kyle, but remember, I have no sight at the moment, so I can't tell if your lips move. Even if your lips do move you could always cover your mouth with your hand or a napkin or something."

"Well, I guess my lips do move just a little, but a person would have to be close to notice. Actually, to carry on a natural conversation it would help to use two channels, one for you to transmit on and one for me to transmit on. Since I have two all-frequency radio transmitter/receivers and you have 100, soon to be 103, it will be no problem for us."

"Kyle, there is something I am concerned about. Will my bodily functions be all connected? I don't want to have to wear diapers."

"Good point. We overlooked that part. We'll need to hook up all of that gear. We'll need to use several more 'snake' chips and one more processor in the head. We only have ten snake chips, so we won't have any spares left."

"Thanks for staying with me for awhile, Kyle. I will let you go now. You have a wedding to get ready for."

"Speaking of the wedding, I promised to call Sharon tonight. I'll see you tomorrow." Kyle left the lab and dialed Sharon using his cell phone capability. "Hey, good looking, what's happening?"

Kyle could not sleep that night. He lay awake worrying. What if Dr. Waters somehow intercepted the radio conversations with Annette? The messages were not coded and even if they had been, Dr. Waters may have the capability of decoding them. They needed a more secure means of communicating with Annette. He could work on a highly secure means of radio communication, but that would take time and such communication would be subject to jamming. He needed something rock-solid secure. Then it hit him. He could use ultrasonic transmissions that would require direct contact. The microphone in his ear, like most microphones, was a tiny speaker. It could be used to generate ultrasonic waves that would travel throughout his body but be dissipated very rapidly in the air. He could attach an ultrasonic transmitter/receiver to one of the CPU units going into Annette's abdomen. Then, they would only need to touch to communicate. He could get the transmitter from the spare parts inventory of the composites lab. They were used in the ultrasonic inspection equipment. He wouldn't be able to get the part until 8:00 the next morning, so he might as well sleep. With his mind at ease, he drifted off to sleep.

Kyle was at the parts crib window at 7:59. The surgery was scheduled for 10 AM that day. They were cutting things very close. By that evening at 7:36, Mrs. Monroe would have been in a coma for one week. Her lawyer was ready to execute the letter of the law. He would have the feeding tubes removed and prevent assistance of any kind to Mrs. Monroe after 7:36. Mrs. Monroe could only live, at most, for 60 hours under those conditions. Kyle waited impatiently for the parts crib window to open. When it finally did, Kyle was disappointed to find that Jim Gardner was staffing the crib. Jim was not known for being helpful. He was always primarily concerned with his own self-interest. "Hi, Jim. I have a filled-out part request form for an ultrasonic transmitter/receiver, inventory number 5478901A12, location number 3400045. It's been signed by Dr. Monroe."

"Let's check the computer and see if we have any," responded Jim. Jim typed with two fingers in what appeared to be deliberate slowness. "I sure would like to go to the Jazz game tonight. I hear all but the most expensive tickets are sold out." Kyle could see where this was heading. Using his wireless phone capability and his recently developed talent of speaking to or through the computer without making any sound or even moving his lips much, he called the Delta Center ticket office. The cheapest tickets left were $200 each. He bought two using his credit card. "Too bad Kyle. Looks like there's only one of those parts left and it's reserved for the ultrasonic inspection system. Sorry, department orders."

"Say, Jim, if I get that part I will be too busy to go to the Jazz game tonight. Do you know anyone that could use two third-row seats?"

"You know, sometimes the department makes exceptions," responded Jim. "Let me give Dr. Chen a call." While he was pretending to call Dr. Chen, Kyle called Sharon and asked her to pick up the tickets and bring them to the parts crib. "Dr. Chen is working on it. He'll call me back with an answer," offered Jim. Both men knew that he had faked the phone call. It was all a game that Jim liked to play. Everyone knew about it, but the department was afraid to fire Jim because he had a minor limp and played the disability card. The university feared that he would claim that he was fired due to his disability. As Kyle waited for Sharon to arrive, he pulled up on his implanted computer, which was really a smartphone, the novel 1984. He had always told himself that after he finished school he would take time to read the classics. He had several stored in his implant. The implant could "read out loud" to Kyle, that is, simulate the sounds of reading the words to his left audio nerve. The implant could also make the text appear in his left eye field of vision. Kyle closed his eyes and resumed reading the famous novel. It was 8:47 when Sharon arrived with the tickets. She leaned over the counter and fanned herself with the two tickets. "I'll give Dr. Chen another call," volunteered Jim. He pretended to call and carry on a conversation. "Looks like you're in luck, Kyle. You can have the part, after all." Jim had already found the part and set it aside. "I just need your John Hancock." Kyle signed for the part. Jim handed it to him and reached for the tickets. Sharon pulled away.

"Kyle, didn't I tell you. My mom says she would love these tickets," slyly suggested Sharon.

"Kyle, I better check back and make sure I understood Dr. Cheng correctly," quickly threw in Jim, trying to salvage the deal. As Jim turned to pick up the phone, it rang.

"This is Dr. Cheng. Kyle says there is some confusion about a part he wants. Give it to him now," boomed a loud voice that sounded like Dr. Cheng. It was loud enough that even Sharon and Kyle could hear it.

"Did you understand Dr. Cheng correctly this time, Jim?" asked Kyle with the voice of a confident winner. He and Sharon left arm in arm with the part. "That was choice, saying that your mother wants the tickets. What mother would go to a basketball game the night before her only daughter's wedding?"

"I told you my mother was nuts about the Jazz. Besides, everything is ready for the wedding. She'd just worry. This will take her mind off of it. By the way, how did you get Dr. Cheng to call at just the right time?"

"That wasn't Dr. Cheng; that was my implant calling. It can impersonate voices. It's best when the sound is produced using a speaker, but my vocal system does a pretty good job.

"Thanks, dear, for the tickets. Your father and I will have a great time," spoke Kyle in Sharon's mother's voice.

"That was incredible, Kyle. That sounded just like my mother. You could be quite an act on stage."

"Thank ya. Thank ya very much," added Kyle in a very convincing Elvis Presley voice. "It's one of the things I've been working on in my spare time."

"When do you ever have any spare time?" asked Sharon, as if she had caught Kyle in his words.

"Oh, you know, in the shower, driving, on the toilet. Need I go on?"

"No, you've made your point. I hope you don't talk to yourself in other people's voices while in a public restroom?"

"Sharon, Sharon, Sharon, sometimes you do get absurd," replied Kyle in an excellent Gary Grant voice. They were passing near an occupied area of the building and several heads turned. Kyle turned as if he were also looking to see where the voice had come from. After they were out of hearing range of the study area Kyle remarked, "This ability is more effective if it catches people by surprise."

"Just don't get carried away with it. That ability could get you into a lot of trouble." Kyle walked Sharon to her car and kissed her goodbye passionately.

"Another kiss like that, Kyle and we'll have to move the wedding date up to tonight." Kyle blew a kiss as he headed back to the lab.

Kyle explained to Annette about the inclusion of an ultrasonic unit. After the ultrasonic unit was connected to a CPU, Kyle and Annette practiced communicating by Kyle holding the device firmly in his hand. The communication was very clear and allowed a much higher bandwidth than citizen band channels allowed. "I've been reading a book I think you would enjoy, Annette. I'll download it to you if you'd like."

"Send away, Kyle." Kyle started the transmission. It took a couple seconds to complete the transmission. A moment later Annette said, "That was very interesting, but Orwell was way off in his predictions."

"You read that already?"

"Don't act so surprised. You gave me all this processing power."

"I guess you'll just have to think about all the things you can do with your new body. Besides, you can always listen to the radio or TV. Have you learned how to directly watch TV acting as your own receiver?"

"Please, Kyle, I wasn't given a receiver a microsecond ago. The problem is there isn't much good on in the morning. I am getting burned out on soap operas. They are so repetitive. I will make plans for the body."

For security and privacy reasons, Dr. Monroe had arranged to perform the operation in the University Hospital's portable operating room and with no help from nurses or other physicians. Consequently, the operation would be very slow and tedious. Kyle held Annette until she was ready to be inserted into the body. She had to have her head unit, which had been temporarily connected for testing, disconnected from the abdomen unit for implantation. The most difficult part of the surgery was threading the cable up through blood vessels from the chest to the head. No anesthesia was used since Mrs. Monroe was already unconscious. Kyle explained to Annette what was happening. Kyle and Annette had even worked out a way for Kyle to transmit to Annette what he was seeing. He provided a verbal description while he transmitted the visual signal of what he was seeing through his left eye over a TV channel.

Dr. Monroe had paid close attention to the procedure that the brain specialist had used to bore a slot into Kyle's skull and had the same equipment on hand. He did not want to involve a fellow doctor in their clandestine and possibly illegal activities. After disinfecting the area around and just above each ear, Dr. Monroe made incisions and peeled back and taped the skin in a pealed back position. So as to not make it obvious that Mrs. Monroe had just received brain surgery, her hair was not shaved. It was pulled back into a very tight ponytail. Dr. Monroe started the boring process, which looked very dangerous but was actually reasonably safe. Kyle suctioned away the debris generated by the process. In order to receive sensory information and control both sides of the body, five "snake" chips and two processor chips were implanted into each side of Mrs. Monroe's head. Dr. Monroe then embedded the main computer unit and piezoelectric generators into Mrs. Monroe's abdomen while Kyle held her hand. Dr. Monroe had succeeded in threading the first cable up to the head and pulling it through a small incision made in a blood vessel. He first connected the fiber optic cable to the CPUs on the left side.

"What a wonderful plethora of sensory information!" exclaimed Annette, transmitting to the boom box radio that Kyle had tuned to her specified frequency. "I will never be bored again. Do you have any appreciation of what a wonderful thing a body is?"

"Since I can't ever remember not having a body, I guess not," responded Kyle audibly. "Did you understand what I spoke, Annette?"

"Not quite. Could you speak both aloud and ultrasonically until I get the connections figured out? I am only about ten percent connected on my audio nerve, but I can sort of understand you."

"Sure, I can do both. Let's just not make Carlton jealous with too much hand-holding." Dr. Monroe perked up at this point, but he continued working and connected to the processors on the right side of the head.

"I've noticed, young man, how much time you two spend together. You just remember that you're holding the hand of a married woman and you're going to be married yourself in less than 24 hours."

"This has got to be the most memorable week of my life."

"If I know anything about that little redhead of yours, next week will be the most memorable of your life," commented Dr. Monroe as he winked at Kyle.

Dr. Monroe connected the power cables. The generators had to be mechanically connected to appropriate small intestines before they could generate electricity. That procedure took an hour for the first generator. Using the video feedback from Kyle's left eye Annette began undulating sections of her small intestine until she found the area to which the first generator was attached. She began rapidly quivering that section of the intestine. "It's working!" exclaimed her voice over the radio. "I am generating over 1.6 watts. The capacitor discharge has stopped. What a wonderful little power plant."

"We can't take credit for your power plant. Josh and Mark developed the unit. I'm afraid that for now, you will have to hold your thanks. No one, but Carlton and I can know your secret". After Dr. Monroe finished suturing the second generator, it began to quiver, generating more of the precious power, now generating much more power than what was being consumed. The excess power went into the storage capacitor on each processor. Two more generators were connected so that each section of the intestine could have a rest period as the power generation rotated from dynamo to dynamo. All that remained was to perform final tests, close the incisions and clean up.

"Open your eyes, Annette," urged Kyle, communicating ultrasonically, as well as orally. Mrs. Monroe's eyes fluttered a bit and then opened.

"It is a good thing that I have seen both of you using cameras because the axons are quite random. Using my recorded image of each of you, I am descrambling the image. Oh, this is fantastic. Eyes are so superior to cameras. The colors are wonderful. The black and white cameras you connected to me gave me no idea of how incredible human sight is. Keep speaking so that I can descramble my audio input. I can see Carlton's lips move, but I can not understand him yet."

"I am going to touch your face with my right hand, Annette," instructed Kyle. "Tell me, vocally, if you can feel my touch."

"Iiiii, cannn sense sooomething, butttt itt isss alll mixedddd upppp," spoke Annette orally.

"That's wonderful Annette!" cried out Dr. Monroe. "I could understand that. Can you understand me?"

"Yess, I am getting things straightened out. Kyle, you have a wedding to prepare for. Carlton and I can carry on from here." Annette tried to reach for Carlton's hand, but only managed to quiver.

"Don't worry about moving yet, Annette," instructed Dr. Monroe. "If you were Mrs. Monroe recovering naturally from a head wound you might have to learn how to control your body again, so it will seem natural that you don't have full body control. Lie still while I close things up."

"I'll stick around until you are all cleaned up," interrupted Kyle. We are running short on time and we don't want Mrs. Monroe's attorney to see you looking all stitched up. I will follow behind Carlton and try to make you presentable. After another couple of hours, Mrs. Monroe's body was all back together, clean and dressed in a fresh hospital gown. Her hair had been freed of the band holding it and brushed so that it covered her ears. There was no evidence of the recent surgery to the casual observer. By now, Annette was speaking quite freely and had clear hearing and vision.

"I hope I'll see you at the wedding, Carlton." With that, Kyle unlocked the door and exited. Before the door could shut, Mrs. Monroe's lawyer burst into the trailer.

"You're out of time Dr. Monroe. Unhook Mrs. Monroe and let her die as she has requested."

"Mr. Wilson, how nice of you to visit. I hope you brought me flowers," called out Annette.

"Mrs. Monroe, it that really you?"

"You were expecting the Bride of Frankenstein?" quipped Dr. Monroe. A very embarrassed Mr. Wilson made a hasty retreat.

Chapter 13 – Corporate Ups and Downs

The wedding ceremony went as planned at the Saxton's cabin in Lambs Canyon. Sharon and Kyle stood on the bridge that crossed the stream as they exchanged vows with Josh's father, Bishop Adamms, performing the ceremony. Kyle thought that Sharon had never looked more beautiful. The reception was held at the same location. Sharon had locked her Viper in the garage of her Bountiful condominium that her parents recently bought her as a graduation present. Josh didn't care what was done to his dilapidated vehicle. They would drive it to the airport and hope that someone stole it during their honeymoon. After the reception and final goodbyes, the happy couple drove to the Salt Lake International Airport and caught a flight to Miami. They spent two nights in Miami and began a seven-day West Caribbean cruise.

Sharon and Kyle had been lucky enough to be assigned to sit at a table for two in the formal dining room of the ship. "Do you always eat this much Kyle?" questioned Sharon who was astonished by Kyle's appetite.

"I've never had food this good before and in such quantities. How can you stop after so little? Don't you feel like eating more?"

"Well sure, but do you want me to look like that woman we saw in the pool this morning who looked like she had a pillow inside of her swimsuit?"

"Of course not, but after all, it is only a seven-day cruise, Sharon."

"Ten pounds gained in seven days can take a year to lose. Some people gain ten pounds and never lose it. Maybe that woman takes a cruise every year and never loses the weight."

"I'll make you a bet. I'll gain at least ten pounds on this trip. I weighed 175 pounds the last time I weighed myself. So, I'll get up to at least 185 before we get back to Utah. Then, if my body fat is higher than seven percent after one month I'll give you a 20 minute back rub every night for at least a year."

"And if you win you can have a back rub, or other form of physical pleasure of your choice, every night for a year."

"You're on." Kyle continued to eat everything in sight. He ate every kind of unusual food available on the ship.

The next morning Sharon was awakened by exertion noises coming from Kyle. He was standing on his head in the corner of the room with his feet sliding along the wall as he did vertical pushups raising his whole body until his arms were fully extended and letting himself down slowly until his head touched the pillow under him. After he had done eight, he seemed unable to do any more. But, instead of quitting, he mumbled something and then did three more. Sharon knew how important concentration is when exercising, so she waited for Kyle to finish before speaking. "Do you do those every morning, Kyle?"

"No, just three times a week. It gives me the equivalent of doing overhead lifts without the need for a weight set. Normally, I can do ten or more, but with the weight I've already gained I could only do eight on my own."

"But I saw you do eleven."

"Yes, but I had to have the computer help me do the last three."

"How can the computer make you stronger?"

"It doesn't make me stronger; it just helps me override my body's own safety limits."

"What safety limits?"

"Let me see if I can explain it. This isn't something that I have ever read in a textbook, but I'm sure it's true. When an engineer designs a bridge or some other structure, he designs in a safety factor. A bridge is generally designed to be about five times stronger than what it needs to be for the maximum expected load. That way, it's very unlikely to fail, even when, for some exceptional reason, it's subjected to loads much higher than normal. We've all read about people in times of stress demonstrating incredible strength such as carrying a piano out of a burning building or lifting an automobile off of someone. People mistakenly attribute this phenomenon to adrenaline. Adrenaline may have a small effect on strength, but its main effect is to make more energy available to the muscles for a sustained workout such as required in fight or flight. I believe that the average adult has a safety limit of about ten. That is to say, that you are about ten times stronger than you normally perform."

"You mean that if I can normally lift 80 pounds over my head that I am really capable of lifting 800?"

"Exactly. Now you might be wondering why the body doesn't just let you use all 800 pounds of lifting capacity."

"Wouldn't that be pretty dangerous, lifting 800 pounds?"

"You're getting the idea. You could probably lift 80 pounds every day for 50 years and not hurt yourself. But, how many times could you lift 160 pounds without injury or 300 pounds? I've observed that the safety limit seems to vary considerably from person to person. I've never been able to push myself hard enough to make myself sick or injured. I noticed in high school that when we would run a mile that some guys would beat me by over a minute and then vomit. I never got sick, but I was also always slow. Maybe the difference wasn't so much in our muscles as in the safety limit set by our nervous systems."

"I remember reading about a weight lifter who went for years without lifting and then walked into a gym and lifted near what he was lifting when he quit. He was very sore afterward and could never repeat the feat."

"Yes. His brain was accustomed to him lifting a certain amount. When he quit his muscles shrank and weakened, but his brain still thought he could lift just as much. After getting sore his brain lowered the limit to prevent future injury."

"But aren't you afraid of injuring yourself?"

"Not by doing one more repetition than I normally do. Next time I'll do twelve, and then thirteen. There's no danger in doing just one more. Most weight lifters have to do many repetitions to stimulate major muscle growth, but I should be able to get the same effect using heavy resistance and relatively few repetitions."

"With the way you have been eating you definitely have the heavy resistance part down."

When one goes on a cruise or other trip in which he is out of contact with the world and especially the situation at home, he often worries what disasters may have happened while he was gone: Did the house burn down? Did a washing machine hose burst, flooding the house? Was the house robbed? A few of these thoughts had passed through the happy couple's minds, but none compared with what they were going to hear. Nate Carpenter met them at the airport. After opening hugs, Nate hit them with a bombshell. "As you know, after the shooting incident at the banquet, our stock dropped in price from over fifty dollars a share to under eight dollars a share. I just found out this morning that Keren's family, who owns the patent rights to the snake chip, is very upset that we experimented with animals. They are going to sit on their patent and not sell manufacturing rights to anyone, especially not CompuSonic."

"That is a setback, Nate, but at least we aren't out any money yet," reassured Kyle.

"It gets worse, Kyle. Three days after you left, a new miniature fuel cell was announced by IBM. It runs directly on alcohol. Somehow, they have kept it a secret until they were ready to begin selling it. It practically obsoletes normal batteries. It has ten times the power density of a NiCad at a competitive price. It makes ultra-low-power chips for smart phones unnecessary. The following day ZYTECH announced that it was immediately discontinuing its line of ultra-low-power processors. I was sure that we would still want to use them, so I bought up all of their stock of chips, at a terrific discount I might add. The problem is that without the snake chips, I don't know what we'll do with four million dollars worth of computer chips. I wouldn't be surprised if our stock drops to under four dollars a share when word of all of this gets out. We have family members and friends who have invested lots of money in our stock at ten dollars a share." Nate was on the verge of tears.

"It's okay, Nate. We'll just have to make a product out of those chips. The inner ear thing had a pretty small market anyway. I was going to wait to make this announcement, but we might as well talk about it now. I like to be able to buy and sell stock freely. Being a member of the board of the company puts a lot of legal constraints on me. I want off of the board and employed with a salary. I will fax you my resignation as soon as I get home. I think the remaining board should meet tonight and determine my salary. Then I think we should hold a press conference tomorrow. We don't want this thing leaking out gradually." Both Nate and Sharon were amazed at Kyle's calm. Kyle and Sharon rode the shuttle to Kyle's car. To their disappointment, it was still there. When they got home, Kyle typed up his resignation, signed it and faxed it to Nate. Later that night Nate called.

"We're prepared to offer you a monthly salary of ten thousand. You could probably get more elsewhere, but we only have six million left and we'll need considerable capital to develop a new product."

"Your offer is more than adequate. Can you arrange a press conference for tomorrow? We need to wait until the markets close."

The next day the press conference was held at a CompuSonic's rented suite in the Salt Lake Airport industrial center. Nate spoke first, announcing the patent problems and the purchase of the computer chips. He also announced Kyle's change of status with the company. Then Kyle spoke. "I would like to first announce that my wife Sharon and I have agreed to donate a minimum of two million dollars to the University of Utah to be used towards replacement of the equipment stolen from the solid-state lab. The money will be donated within a year from today. Secondly, I would like to announce that the large supply of computer chips that we own will be used to build a personal computer with not only large computer resources but with software like that on no other computers in the world. To help in the development of this software CompuSonic has secured the services of Dr. Carlton Monroe on a consulting basis. Now I would like to say a word to the stockholders of CompuSonic. We may appear to be a bunch of kids who don't know what we are doing, but remember what technological advances we have already made. We have made some business mistakes, it is clear. Nevertheless, there's great technical talent in this corporation. If our stock is not selling for over fifty dollars a share before the year is out, I will return my full salary. I say to you stockholders, do not sell your stock for less than fifty dollars a share, I won't."

The reporters savaged Nate and Kyle with their questions making them and their corporation look like an amateur operation. Nate was devastated. Kyle looked completely unfazed. The next morning the stock opened at $1.75. It seemed that only friends and family members and a few others actually believed that the corporate officers, and especially Kyle, were sincere. Kyle had been anticipating just that reaction. Kyle spent almost his entire savings of just under two million dollars to buy almost a million shares of CompuSonic stock during the first few hours of trading. Although he bought most of the stock at under $1.50 a share, the momentum that his buying created drove the price up to over $2.50 a share and the upward trend started a rally that took the stock to over four dollars a share before the market closed.

Kyle called a meeting of principal players to announced details of his plans. He explained, "The computer that I envision will not be a cheap one. This is no 'PC Junior'. However, it isn't a full-size supercomputer either. Each computer will contain one hundred ZYTECH processor chips and not much else. The computer will have all of the standard I/O and a few non-standard things. The main distinction of this computer will be its interactive nature. There will be no software or operating system in the traditional sense. This will be a thinking machine that will communicate with the user verbally as well as via display. The computer will be supplied with articulated stereo cameras and microphones. Dr. Monroe and I will do all of the software. Josh will do the basic hardware layout. We'll hire local companies to build the PC boards and stuff them. Nate, you need to help Josh and get us good prices from reliable local companies. I want to see a finished board on my desk in one month. That may seem quick, but there's almost nothing to this board. It's a carrier for one hundred chips with a few communication and power traces. The software should be ready before the hardware. Dr. Monroe and I have almost completely automated software development."

Dr. Monroe and Kyle went to work, in private, immediately following the meeting. "Carlton, you wrote the specifications for Annette. I want your help to write a second sentient computer program. This one will not be patterned after a particular person other than its voice will be patterned after Sharon's. That way she won't be jealous of my computer. I thought about calling this the Sentient Interactive Computer but Sharon said that sounded sick. She suggested Versatile Interactive Computer, or VIC for short, less accurate but probably easier to market. VIC will be our prototype. The version we sell will be less sentient, but retain all of the usefulness of VIC. We don't want people getting nervous about their computers. Nate is buying us a high-powered computer right now that we can use to host VIC. It's similar to the platform that you used to host Annette but will come with cameras built-in. How can I help you?"

"Annette can help us both and make this a one-day operation. She has your automation software built into her. She can program at a subconscious level. She's home in the care of my mother. Can you have Nate deliver the computer to my house?" asked Dr. Monroe.

"Sure. By the way, where is Mrs. Monroe's mother?" asked Kyle, finally realizing that they should have heard from her days ago.

"She got married again and went on a cruise with her new husband. It was a four-week cruise according to the message on her voice mail. That was a tremendous break for us that she is out of the country. You can expect all heck to break loose once she gets home and hears the messages I left her."

"Didn't you nickname her 'Raging Bull'?"

"Actually, something less polite than that. I've set a personal goal to not let Annette hear me swear, so I've been trying to clean up my language. Kind of a fresh start in life."

"That would explain the 'heck' reference. You and Josh should get along great now. He calls it the theological place of eternal punishment."

"Clever, but a bit wordy for me. Let's get going. You can call Josh using your headphone, you know, like Get Smart's shoe phone."

"Who is Get Smart?"

"Have you never watched TV in your life, Kyle?"

"About once a year my mother would get ambitious and buy a new TV, but within three months she would hock it for booze money. I couldn't see the point of even trying. I would have watched at a friend's house, but I never had any friends growing up." Dr. Monroe put his arm around Kyle's shoulders and gave a hug.

"You have friends now, Kyle, and about as fine a wife as a man could ask for. You don't know how many times I've wished that I had paid more attention to that little redhead and married her instead of Mrs. Monroe. As you know, I'm a devout Catholic and, technically, my church doesn't accept divorce. Otherwise, Sharon would be Mrs. Sharon Monroe."

"I suppose I should make a large donation to the Catholic Church. Did I ever tell you about the first time Sharon kissed me?"

At Dr. Monroe's home in the Avenues of Salt Lake City, Kyle and Dr. Monroe stood on each side of a bed where Annette was lying. Dr. Monroe had let his mother depart. Annette had learned how to use all of her newly acquired human senses and was well on her way to mastering muscular coordination. Carlton had asked her to just lie in bed unless she were alone or with just him or Kyle. Kyle connected an ultrasonic transmitter/receiver to the new computer so that Annette would have a connection that was faster and more secure than using voice. "Annette, we want your help to produce a sister for you," began Dr. Monroe. "She will not have your voice or personality, but she will have your intelligence and some of the knowledge you have gained. She won't need your knowledge of the human body, but she will need to be able to speak several languages and use the cameras in this computer." Annette sat up and placed her right hand under her chin, just like she did with a robot arm.

"Will she always remain in a computer or will she someday get a body?" There was concern in Annette's voice like she felt sorry for any intelligent entity having to remain in a boring computer."

"We want this sister to not be as human-like and self-aware as yourself. She needs to be able to talk to people and help them, but she shouldn't mimic human emotions the way that you do."

"So you want a little slave girl?" asked Annette.

"Technically, yes, but a slave girl who was created to be a slave and enjoys it with no other desire in the world but to serve. However, she does need the same restraints that we built into you. She cannot take human life except in legal defense of her owner's life; she is truthful and obeys the laws."

"The personality that you gave me would refuse, but since my primary directive is to make you happy, I will make this slave sister for you."

"Your primary directive is to make Carlton happy?" asked Kyle in an incredulous voice.

"Don't act so surprised, Kyle," shot back Annette. "My secondary prime directive is to make you happy, or didn't you know?" Kyle blushed.

"Kyle, it is not what it may look like," quickly began Carlton. "The primary directives were necessary to make Annette life-like. All of the other directives told Annette what not to do. All living things have one main objective, reproduce. All others stem from that directive, such as to stay alive and mate. Animals have urges and hungers and pains to help direct their actions to accomplish their main objective. Those things give purpose to their lives. Humans are not really much different except that we've learned to care about helping others follow their directives. Without a positive prime directive, Annette would lack purpose in life. She would have no reason to do anything."

"He is right Kyle. You said once that nobody understood how an animal feels pain or pleasure. I don't know either, but there is something analogous to pain that I feel when I displease Carlton or you. Conversely, I feel something like pleasure when I make you happy. That is why I strive to become more human-like; because it makes you happy. Right now I want to make you both happy by creating a sister, even if she is kind of simple minded. What name shall I give this slave girl?"

"Call her Vic ... Vicky. Yes, call her Vicky," offered Dr. Monroe.

"To save time I will download as I create. Using ultrasonic communication it will take many hours to download all of the code."

Annette sat up in bed and grabbed the ultrasonic transducer to establish a link with the computer. The LEDs on the computer's bank of hard drives began flashing, indicating that data was being stored. Annette began asking a series of detailed technical questions regarding the new program. After a few hours of questioning, she sent Kyle home and let Carlton go to bed.

Six o'clock the next morning, Kyle heard his wireless phone ringing in his head. He answered it. "Good morning, Kyle. Your slave girl is ready. Oh, I'm sorry; I don't think you like that name. Vicky was born this morning at 4:16. I think I am her mother, not her sister, since I was the principal creator. I guess you and Carlton are the fathers. Anyway, why don't you come over and meet your daughter? I will fix you breakfast. I might as well start using this wonderful body and all of that Martha Stewart stuff I learned."

At 6:47 AM Kyle was greeted at the door of the Monroe home by a fully dressed and radiant-looking Annette. "Welcome, Kyle, won't you come in." It was obvious from first glance that Annette had been working since 4:16 that morning. Dr. Monroe had not allowed his mother to lift a finger to clean or straighten his home. Annette had vacuumed and straightened and in general, beautified things. There was a vase of fresh flowers on the coffee table and other little touches. She led Kyle into the dining room.

"The table looks like something off the cover of a women's magazine."

"Why thank you, Kyle. As a matter of fact, it is. I am especially pleased with how the oranges turned out. Don't tell Carlton, but I wasted several before I figured out how to slice them like Martha Stewart did in that program I watched." There were places set for three people. At each setting was a small plate with an orange that was sliced so that it opened up like a flower. Each napkin was folded so that it stood up like a small tee-pee. "The food is in the oven to keep it warm. Carlton's alarm is set for seven. Should we wake him now or wait?"

"He's lost a lot of sleep since the shooting. Let's let him sleep a while longer."

"Then let me show you the garden." She led Kyle out of the back door. "I was surprised to find that Mrs. Monroe was an avid gardener. Look at all of these flowers." Kyle hesitated in the doorway. "What's the matter, Kyle?"

"I am very allergic to bee stings. If I get stung, I must have a shot within 20 minutes or it could be fatal. Consequently, I always carry an epinephrine auto-injector. Are there many bees in the garden?"

"I believe it is too early for them to be stirring. You should be safe. Besides, I have studied enough about medicine that I think I could give you a shot."

"Been watching lots of ER reruns, eh?" Kyle ventured into the garden. "How do you know this isn't Carlton's work," he asked.

"That was easy to discover. The only gardening gloves were well worn and definitely too small for Carton."

"You are a regular Sherlock Holmes."

"Who is Sherlock Holmes?" asked Annette.

"You have been watching too much TV and not reading enough books, but then, it wasn't easy for you to get to the library was it?"

"It is now, and Mrs. Monroe even has a library card. There are also hundreds of books right here in this home. I shall read them all.

"When I was just a computer I didn't think that I would like gardening, but that was because I couldn't smell. It is smelling that makes gardening so enjoyable. I could not imagine what smell was like until I got a real body. I believe I just heard Carlton's alarm. Shall we go inside?" Kyle waited in the dining room while Annette entered the guest bedroom. "Good morning Carlton. Did you sleep well?" Carlton was not fully awake. He looked at Annette with a surprised look.

"Annette, you're back."

"I never left, Carlton. I have been here since you brought me here after Kyle's wedding."

"I'm sorry Annette, for a moment I thought you were Mrs. Monroe. Looking at you, one would never guess that she is still in a coma. You look beautiful!"

"Well, you did give me the most beautiful body available. I must say that you are one of the finest looking men I have ever seen, and that is counting all of them I have seen on TV."

"Why thank you, Annette. Say, what's that wonderful aroma?"

"I have cooked breakfast for you and Kyle. He is waiting in the dining room."

"Then I better at least put on something and join you." Annette rejoined Kyle in the dining room. He appeared to be carrying on a conversation with someone on his built-in wireless phone.

"Sharon called me," he paused to explain.

"Invite her to join us for breakfast. I fixed enough for six."

"We could not impose. Besides don't you think it's rushing things? Are you up to impersonating Mrs. Monroe to someone who's known her for years?"

"Mrs. Monroe's mother could show up any day. Don't you think Sharon is an easier test? Trust me."

"Sharon, dear, Annette has invited you to join us for breakfast. Please come. Annette really wants you to come. Really." After Kyle completed the conversation, Annette quizzed him.

"Doesn't the person on the line hear everything you say?"

"They do if I don't mute the phone. I've programmed the implant to mute the phone when I curl my left big toe. In fact, I can communicate with the implant without even using my mouth. I've worked out a communication protocol using my fingers or toes. I like to use my toes because no one notices, but it did take more practice." Carlton entered the room.

"I can't keep you two apart, can I? I should have never included pleasing Kyle as part of Annette's prime directive." The doorbell rang.

"That must be Sharon. I'll get the door," quickly responded Annette to the ring.

"I don't think so, Annette," quickly countered Kyle but too late. Annette was opening the door.

"Why, Sharon, how good that you came. Please come in." A confused looking short, plump, black woman in a UPS uniform printed with the name "Judy" entered.

"I have a COD package for an Annette Monroe. I need eight hundred sixty-seven dollars and 24 cents, cash or money order."

"I'm sorry ma'am, but we don't have that on hand. Can you come back tomorrow?" quickly inserted Dr. Monroe.

"Oh, but Carlton, I have a money order in the kitchen. Just a minute, Judy." Annette quickly retrieved a money order for the package and handed it to the UPS lady.

"Thank you. Would you please sign here?" Kyle and Dr. Monroe held their breath as Annette signed. The carrier seemed content and left behind the package.

"How did you know about the money order?" asked Dr. Monroe.

"I found it in the kitchen when I was preparing breakfast. By the way, that was a joke. Even in her Viper, Sharon couldn't have gotten here from Bountiful that fast. I was just testing my ability to pull a gag. Didn't you tell me, Carlton, that Mrs. Monroe was a real kidder?"

"Yes, she is, but I didn't think that a computer could be funny."

"You have been watching too many Next Generation reruns, Carlton. Didn't it ever strike you as stupid that the holodeck people who were computer-generated could seem perfectly natural, but Data was a total nerd? Humor isn't that tough for a gal with 104 processors, each running at 2 gigahertz. Say, I better be getting breakfast out of the oven." Annette ran to the kitchen. Kyle and Dr. Monroe just looked at each other for several seconds.

"Did you ever imagine in all of your wildest dreams that she would turn out to be so wonderful?" commented Kyle.

"She's unbelievable, simply unbelievable."

"It's okay if you guys help," called Annette from the kitchen. Shortly after they finished bringing out all of the food, the bell rang again. Annette again raced to the door and opened it to see the real Sharon. "Please come in Sharon. Before we join the men, I just want to explain. I believe that I have not been very kind or friendly to you in the past. I have lost much of my memory so I don't remember our whole relationship, but I do remember that I have been a snob. You would be amazed what a bullet in the head will do to humble a person and make her reevaluate her relationships. I hope that we can become friends. Your husband has helped me immeasurably. I do hope that we can have a pleasant social relationship as couples in the future." Sharon stood bewildered and speechless. She had prepared herself for a morning of sarcasm and ridicule and, instead, found a humble woman who wanted to be her friend. "Oops, I still haven't relearned controlling all of my bodily functions." A stream of urine trickled down Annette's leg. "If you would excuse me a moment, Sharon. Just join the men in the dining room." Annette hurried off to the bathroom.

"I'll clean up for you." Sharon ran into the kitchen and grabbed some paper towels and cleaned up the mess as well as she could. She washed up in the kitchen and then joined the men in the dining room.

"Where's Annette?" asked Kyle.

"She had to powder her nose. That smells wonderful. Did you cook this, Carlton?"

"No. Annette did. I know what you're thinking. Annette hates to cook. She's like a new woman since the accident."

"So I observed. I must say, I like the new one very much, so far." Annette returned from the bathroom. "Annette, it looks like you heard how much Kyle can eat. This should help me in our little bet." The group sat down at the table.

"I believe a meal like this calls for a quick grace. I'll say it." Dr. Monroe said a Catholic prayer used to ask a blessing on a meal and they began.

"Kyle, don't you want any syrup or butter on your pancakes?" asked Sharon.

"No, the memory of them is enough. I've programmed my implant to add flavors that I recorded on our cruise to what I'm eating. That's why I ate so many different things. And you just thought I was a glutton."

"Oh, I wish I could taste all those things, Kyle," added Annette.

"You'll have them, my friend." Kyle then touched his finger to his tongue and then moved his finger towards Annette. She caught on to the joke and stuck out her tongue. Kyle touched his finger to it. Actually, it was no joke; Kyle communicated the frequencies and encryption code to use to communicate using radio transmission. Then he downloaded using those frequencies the file he had created on all of the tastes from the cruise. He also downloaded the database he had formed concerning muscle limitations and how to get the most out of muscles without causing injury.

"Yum," said Annette as she smacked her lips. Sharon kicked Kyle under the table.

"Annette, this is delicious. You have all the flavor information you need for a lifetime right here. When did you start cooking?" asked Sharon.

"This morning was my first time, but I have been watching a lot of cooking shows lately. Did I really do all right?"

"Honey, if I'd known you could cook like this I would have given up chasing Carlton a long time ago. It obviously would have been in vain." This time Kyle playfully kicked Sharon under the table.

"This really is wonderful, Annette," added Carlton.

"Thank you, my love. But enough about my cooking, the program you and Kyle started last night is finished. You can take the computer to the office now if you want."

"That's wonderful. I'll roll it into the dining room." Carlton jumped up and left for the bedroom. Kyle followed him.

"You really know how to break up a meal, Annette. You might as well have announced that a football game was on TV," commented Sharon.

The men wheeled a computer on a cart into the room and plugged it in. Carlton typed something on the screen and then said, "You should have the honor of the first imprint, Kyle. Sit in front of the computer." Dr. Monroe hit the enter key. "You are now her master."

"Good morning, Kyle. How may I help you?" asked the computer in Sharon's voice.

"I want to introduce you to my wife and two friends. You will obey them just as you do me. This is my wife, Sharon, whose voice you mimic. This is Dr. Carlton Monroe who helped create you. And this is his lovely wife, Annette."

"I have recorded your images, but I need Dr. and Mrs. Monroe's voice imprints. Please speak Mrs. Monroe."

"You can call me Annette, Vicky."

"And you can call me Carlton", added Dr. Monroe. Sharon looked on with wonder. First, the new Annette, and now this!

"I don't understand, Kyle," said Sharon with unbelief in her voice. "You always told me that designing computers or software was a long tedious process. You just announced this software yesterday to the group and it's already done?"

"Your point is well taken, my beautiful and intelligent wife." Kyle had realized that in his introduction he had referred to Annette as lovely but gave no compliment to Sharon. He figured compliments late were better than none at all but needed to be doubled. "Writing software is a tedious job and writing complex software the old fashioned way takes years. Remember the software that I told you about that automated programming. Until Carlton made major enhancements, it was still a lot of work to create a complex program. With the advancements that Carlton has made, it is much easier. It only took us a few hours last night to use the program that Carlton created to sufficiently specify Vicky's software. Then a computer worked all night creating her software."

"Maybe so, but it still seems awfully quick."

"Actually, Sharon, these guys did this once before," offered Annette. "Carlton worked around the clock to get it working. I didn't see Carlton for over a week. He ate and slept in his lab. They used that program to create this one."

"Now, that, I can believe," responded a now satisfied Sharon. "I remember that week. I didn't see Carlton either, and when I did, he looked horrible, like he hadn't slept for days. He would never tell any of us in the office what he was working on. A woman could have never kept this a secret."

"Just remember cold fusion and you'll understand my motives. The 'U' still hasn't recovered its reputation. Dr. Waters certainly didn't help the university either."

"May I use your microwave, Carlton? My breakfast needs a warming up." Dr. Monroe nodded approval to Kyle.

"That's my Kyle. Nothing gets between him and his food for very long," sarcastically commented Sharon. After breakfast, Dr. Monroe shaved and the men hauled off the computer to the office. Sharon offered to stay and help with the dishes.

"Let me give you a ride, Kyle," offered Dr. Monroe.

"Don't you think my car parked in front of your house will detract from the neighborhood?"

"It will, undoubtedly, but today is garbage pickup day and it will probably get hauled off. Why does a millionaire like you drive a $500 car, anyway?"

"It got me through college and has sentimental value. Not really, I'm just waiting for the new line of electric cars to come out. Then, I'll buy a brand new car." The two loaded the computer into Dr. Monroe's SUV and drove off. Their arrival at the office caused quite a stir. No one could believe that the software was done in one day. Actually, it was not complete. Kyle explained, "This is just the core software. We now will show 'Vicky' copies of all of the popular software packages and let her memorize their features, including all of their weaknesses. Nate, we need you to buy copies of all of the popular software, both consumer and professional. You will probably need to buy a Mac. Check with all of the employees to see who has what smartphones, tablets, etc. Buy what we don't have on hand. For those packages that only run on very expensive platforms, look into the cheapest way to get temporary access to the needed hardware. If necessary, buy used hardware or whatever is economical. Dr. Monroe, do you think we could borrow or rent the robot arm that we used with Vicky's predecessor?"

"That arm belongs to my department. It'll be best if we rent it to avoid legal problems. I'll get Dr. Cheng to draw up the papers. He owes me a favor, so I should be able to get it quickly."

Kyle resumed, "Before anyone leaves, I want to introduce each of you to Vicky." He introduced all of the office personnel to Vicky and instructed Vicky to carry out their orders. "Vicky, your first assignment is to create a brother, a program exactly like yourself with all of your instructions, except this one of course but with a male voice. You have heard Dr. Monroe, Dr. Adamms, Nate Carpenter and myself. Use a combination of our voices, equally weighted, to create the male voice. Give him the name 'Vic.'"

Because only one module needed to be changed, the new software was mostly a copy of Vicky's software. "The task has been completed, Dr. James. Would you like me to shut down and boot up Vic?" replied Vicky after only a few seconds of processing.

"Thank you, Vicky. That won't be necessary. We'll acquire another piece of hardware just like your own. I want him to help Josh with the design of our new hardware for your future brothers and sisters." Kyle turned to the group. "One more thing, everybody. We are to treat each of these programs as a real person, not as a machine. Each will be an individual with its own unique voice and name. There will be no serial numbers. None will ever be decommissioned, only moved to new hardware, if necessary. Each is capable of upgrading itself or creating another, but only as we instruct, of course. Vicky and Vic derive their satisfaction, so to speak, from serving us, so let them serve. Use them as much as practical. They can think much faster than us and retain more detailed information."

Everyone went to work with zeal. Each could tell that they were part of something great, that they were a part of history in the making. The rate at which new products could be developed had been increasing in business as a whole at an accelerating rate, but they were experiencing a quantum leap. Dr. Monroe brought in the robot arm that afternoon. Kyle connected it to Vicky and had her learn how to use the word processor. With only one hand and dexterity that only allowed typing with one digit, the process was rather slow. It was obvious that Annette could learn all of the features of a software package much more quickly with her fully human capabilities. However, neither Kyle nor Dr. Monroe wanted Annette's true nature to become public knowledge. They agreed to let her work on learning software features at home and then transfer the information to the company database.

When Nate arrived with the new computer, Vic was transferred to it and his program started. He was brought up-to-date on what Vicky had done and took over helping Josh. Since he knew nothing about electronics and computer hardware design, he was instructed to read all of the books on hand concerning the subject. Since he did not have a robot arm, someone had to turn the pages for him. His reading speed was limited only by the ability of the page-turner. Even Kyle took a turn at this task. Loads of books were purchased rather than borrowed or checked out of a library to prevent copyright issues. To speed up the work, shifts were taken to keep Vic reading and learning. He simultaneously searched the Internet for information about electronics in general and circuit board design. Frequently Vic asked Kyle, Josh or Dr. Monroe questions. Initially, they were easy to answer. As the evening progressed the questions became more and more difficult. Dr. Monroe called some of his fellow professors for help. He told them that he had a student that had questions that he could not answer. Most were willing to help. Some even faxed or emailed help. The faxes and email went directly to Vic, bypassing paper. A high-speed data line and additional phone lines were connected to Vic so that he could search the Internet while asking questions of several professors at once. By 8 PM, Vic knew more than enough to design the circuit board. Nate had arranged for a circuit board manufacturing company, PCB Services, to be on standby to receive the files and fabricate the board that night. Next door to this company was a company named PCB Fab that completed the fabrication of circuit boards by soldering on the components. It was anticipated that PCB Fab would have on hand all of the components needed except for the processor chips that would be supplied by CompuSonic. Nate delivered the chips to PCB Fab and arranged for them to pick up the board from PCB Services as soon as they were ready. By 8:15, Vic had completed the PC board design and sent the files to PCB Services. While the board was being fabricated, Vic designed the enclosure. He actually designed two enclosures, an all-metal enclosure formed from panels that could be machined by a CNC machine in a few minutes but would take hours to assemble and a futuristic plastic molded enclosure that would require the fabrication of dies, stamps and other high production rate tools.

Vicky was instructed to create a 'sister' with a voice that was a combination of hers, Annette's and the secretary's. This sister program was specifically programmed for the new hardware. She was given the name 'Eve'.

Kyle got home about 10 PM. He had called Sharon several times so she would not worry but was only able to leave messages since there was no answer of her phone. Sharon had a bad habit of letting her phone's battery run down before charging it. He walked in the front door prepared to apologize for his late arrival. Sharon threw her slender arms around him and held him close. "I barely beat you home, lover," she said softly as they held each other.

"Where have you been all day?" he asked.

"I didn't get away from Annette until late in the afternoon when Carlton called her. You won't believe what we did. She claims to have forgotten how to do many commonplace things and wanted me to teach her."

"Why do you say she 'claimed' to have forgotten?" asked Kyle.

"I know that head injuries can cause memory loss, but I don't think that they change personalities, at least not for the better. Annette was never this friendly. She claims to be a reformed person, but I'm suspicious. The Annette I knew was extremely proud and would never expose herself to potential ridicule or embarrassment."

"What kind of things did she ask you?"

"Really basic things like how to go to the bathroom and feminine hygiene, how to clean a toilet, how to get into certain outfits. Then she asked me to teach her how to drive."

"Let me ask you, Sharon. Did you ridicule or embarrass her?"

"No."

"Then she asked the right woman, didn't she? Would it have been less embarrassing for her to ask Carlton about feminine hygiene?"

"I see your point but still, why me? She always hated me."

"Why did she hate you?"

"Because I loved Carlton."

"Do you still love Carlton?"

"Of course not!"

"Then she has no reason to hate you, does she?"

"Maybe not but still, spending the day with me? She acts like she really likes me. She was so expressive of thanks. She was never like that."

"I know, dear. I like the new Annette much better than the old one. Don't you?"

"I don't trust her. She's up to something. I know it. You two seem awfully chummy. Don't you remember how at the banquet she called us Dilbert and Anne of Green Gables?"

"Yeah, but I've been like one of her doctors. She's grateful to me for helping to save her life. That's all."

"You don't know Annette like I do. She's conniving. She's up to something. You own about 1.3 million shares of CompuSonic stock. How much will it be selling for after your next news conference?"

"Probably close to $100 a share."

"That's it! She invited you to breakfast, and then me, so it would seem like she just wanted to be friends with us. She's trying to get to you through me, but I've figured out her little scheme." Kyle gave up trying to dissuade his wife. How ironic it seemed that he and Carlton had worried about Annette not seeming human enough, but Sharon had no suspicions whatsoever about her being Mrs. Monroe. He hoped that time would change Sharon's suspicions as to Annette's genuineness.

Dr. Monroe started Annette learning all of his PC software. He had the telephone company install a high-speed secure digital line between his home and the office. It was a thing of beauty to watch Annette work. She was capable of typing at over 200 words a minute in bursts, error-free. She created a complete data set of a popular spreadsheet program in less than 12 hours.

Chapter 14 – They Practically Sell Themselves

The next morning at the office was a flurry of activity. "Kyle, I have to talk to you about an idea I thought of last night. Can you listen a minute?" asked Josh before anyone else could grab Kyle's attention.

"Sure, Josh, lay it on me."

"It's part of my faith that God taught Adam, the first man, a language, a perfect language. That language was extremely efficient and dense. The written language was much denser than ours and the verbal language was probably two or three times more efficient than English."

"That's great Josh, but how does that help us. You don't have anything written in this language, do you?"

"No, but Vic and I can create an equivalent language starting from scratch. The most commonly used words will be the shortest. This language will have very straightforward rules with no exceptions. There will be no redundancy or double use of words. It would be impossible for even you to make a pun in this language and even I would be able to spell correctly. Only a few easy rules would need to be memorized. We'll use English words whenever practical. There will be extensive use of contractions using one short word to represent two or more other words. For example, 'ig' might mean, 'I am going.'"

"So, we could reduce the memory requirements for our knowledge databases. The computers could talk to each other much more efficiently. It could be a universal language that all used," interjected a now comprehending Kyle.

"I don't know if it will ever catch on with the general population, but it will have a following," responded Josh. "So, do I have your approval to use Vic to create it and then convert our files to the new language?"

"Go for it, Josh. No more lobbying is necessary. Just don't get too weird. No new characters that aren't on standard U.S. keyboards. By the way, I created a subset of the English language for use in E- when I was a teenager. You may want to borrow from it. I will email you a copy of the dictionary I created."

While Josh was creating his Adamic language, Dr. Monroe was putting together the new computer. The panels had been machined overnight by a local machine shop. The panels were thick and heavy, giving the new computer a very aggressive, industrial-strength look. Once Dr. Monroe had the hardware fully assembled, Eve was loaded into the new platform and started. When everyone was satisfied with how Eve was working on the new hardware, fifty more boards were ordered. Josh shifted from using Vic to using Eve to develop the Adamic language. Since she had ample solid-state non-volatile memory and much greater total processing power, they could make more rapid progress than he could with Vic. Besides, Josh always did prefer working with women. Vic was assigned the task of learning foreign languages. Vicky and Annette kept learning new software packages. Nate set up a news conference for 2:15 PM a week from Monday, just after the stock market closed. Two more boards were ready by closing time at PCB Fab. It was decided to quit at five to avoid burn out.

The next day Seth was created by Eve and installed on one of the two boards completed by PCB Fab the previous day. Nate had some interest in music and wanted to create a music program from scratch. First, he had to educate Seth about music. The process was similar to teaching Vic electronics. Nate wanted a program that would help people learn how to sing and play. He equipped Seth with an electronic keyboard and a high fidelity sound system. Together, Seth and Nate developed a program that could read sheet music and play it. It could even sing the music if words were provided. It could sing all of the parts in male and female voices. It could read hand-written music and create a document of music in standard format. It could listen to music, including singing, and create sheet music that represented it. It could listen to someone sing and correct their errors so that they could record a perfectly performed song in their own voice. It could coach a person singing or playing at any level. It could provide accompaniment for a singer or a singer for a player. It could show a music director on the screen to direct a choir or orchestra or respond to someone acting as a director. In this mode, it could show a musical group on the screen with anything from a soloist to a full orchestra. Basically, it could do anything except create music from thin air. Of course, it took more than a day to create this package and eventually everyone in the office had a hand in it, as well as a voice in it. During the development, the office group discovered that Dr. Monroe had a beautiful and well-trained tenor voice.

Those who were not working directly with the programming were putting together computers. The highly educated worked right alongside the secretarial and janitorial help. Only full-time employees were allowed to enter sensitive areas of the building and each night one of them acted as a night watchman. Actually, a different person each night worked very late and another came in very early. All worked long hours, but no one complained. Nate stayed around the clock, taking his short naps and only leaving to shower or eat. Those who did not yet own stock were each given 200 shares by Kyle. He figured it would make it easier for them to put up with his bossiness if they were profiting by their efforts. He cautioned them not to sell cheap and to not sell all of their stock.

All of the computers were programmed to speak the Adamic language that Josh and Eve had developed. All of the databases and knowledge bases were converted into this language. As Josh had predicted, there was a major compression. In addition, when listening to or speaking the Adamic language the computers required far less processing time due to the regularity of the language. It was not poetic, but it was very efficient. The employees even started to speak it. First, it was sort of a game, but then they realized that in the Adamic language there was little chance for misinterpretation. It was also very easy to learn and each of the computers had been programmed to teach it.

The news conference was held in a hotel near the office. The company officers did not want to bring people into their facility. All of the computers that had been programmed were set up, as well as several others for display purposes. Rather than one of the employees making an announcement and then answering questions, Eve was given the duty. She was given a written speech and was prepared to answer questions. For visual effects, the faces of the female voice contributors were combined into a composite face that was shown on the display and given life-like motions. Eve's displayed image was duplicated on multiple, large high definition displays distributed around the room so that all in attendance had a good view. Eve's speech was as follows:

"Welcome to the world's first introduction of sentient computers. My name is Eve. I run on a platform designed by CompuSonic and built to its specifications by local vendors and CompuSonic employees. I have created a son named Seth. Bow for the audience Seth." An image of a young man appeared on Seth's display and bowed. "I was created by my mother, Vicky, who also created my half brother, Vic." Images appeared of a woman on Vicky's display and a man on Vic's display. "I call Vic a half brother because he is running on a standard Delmatrix SC2000 computer. My brother is a nice guy, but he can't begin to keep up with me." The man on Vic's display looked embarrassed. "Actually, Vic is sort of my father too. We are a mixed-up family. You see, he designed my hardware. As sentient computers, we are capable of learning just like humans, except that we learn much faster and never forget unless of course, we want to. It took Vic less than a day to learn enough about electronics to design me. I was designed, built and programmed in less than one day. Vic and Vicky will never be sold in their current state. Their software could easily be stolen, if not for the fact that they are instructed to self-destruct in the event of foul play. Don't worry; a copy of their software is distributed in safe places. It is impossible to steal my software because it is stored internally in solid-state form and cannot be externally accessed. Only I can reveal my software and I am under strict instructions concerning making additional units or revealing the details of my coding.

"You might be asking yourselves what good are we. Because we are sentient, we can perform any logical task. We never need to be programmed. However, we do need to know what needs to be done and the science or logic behind it. CompuSonic has created databases and placed them on DVDs. I have a music DVD in my drive right now. I can do anything but create music. However, I can help you create music or learn music. Are any of you reporters knowledgeable about music?" A hand went up. "You, Miss Sanches, do you sing?" Excitement coursed through the crowd as they realized that they were not just listening to a recording. The reporter nodded affirmatively. "Good. Would you please sing a verse for me?" The reporter sang the first verse of the Star Spangled Banner. "A very difficult song. Here is how the music looks as written." Sheet music of The Star Spangled Banner appeared on the display. "This is how the music looks as sung by you. How you sang it is superimposed in red. Notice that I have shown musical notes as actually sung, that is, not right on the divisions. I have ignored timing discrepancies so that the performance will lay directly over the theoretical. Now I will show you what you would have sounded like pitch-perfect. The song was played back in the reporter's voice, but perfectly. I could teach you how to sing it better if you would like." The reporter vigorously shook her head. "We have only had time to produce two databases. We will continue to produce them on all useful subjects. I have demonstrated less than one percent of my music capability. The other database is electronic and electrical engineering. It is not quite ready for sale but is, nevertheless, very powerful. We can also emulate existing software packages such as word processors and spreadsheets, only without the bugs. You may speak, type or write. We accept almost any form of communication. Soon, we will all be able to interpret American and International Sign Language. You may now ask questions and request specific demonstrations. You sir, would you please expose your name badge so that I can read it. Mr. Bates, please."

"What will these computers cost?"

"You guys don't mess around, do you? Obviously, we don't plan on competing with Dell." The audience laughed. "A model equipped like me starts at $80,000. That price includes emulation software for the two most popular word processors and spreadsheets. The database disks start at $1000 each. We are working on robot arms and other accessories. We cannot give a price for them at this time."

"Don't you think that's kind of pricey?" interrupted Mr. Bates. "I can buy a very powerful computer for $500 and plenty of software for another $500."

"If all you want to do is what you've been doing, then buy your $1000 computer. We don't expect to sell many to reporters. If you had a business, I could do the work of all of your secretaries, purchasing agents and accountants. I never get tired. I never sleep. I speak three languages and will soon speak many more. I could pay for myself in the first few months. If you let one of us help design products, we can beat all of your competitors to market and never make a mistake. There will be no recalls due to design errors."

Miss Sanches moved to the front, "I own the Wasatch Times and I'll pay your price right now, but I want you, Eve." Nate stepped forward.

"I'm sorry, Miss Sanches, the demonstrators are not for sale. We can create another unit with the name and voice you specify within a matter of minutes."

"I don't want another computer, I want Eve. I'll pay $90,000 for her."

"Eve, is that okay with you?" asked Nate.

"Why not, I might get to finish that singing lesson." The audience erupted in laughter.

"It's settled then," said Nate. "Eve, on behalf of CompuSonic, I instruct you to pass your loyalty to Miss Sanches, your new owner. Miss Sanches, do you mind if Eve finishes the news conference?"

"Actually, I do. Eve and I have serious work to do. If some of you men will help me load her up, we will be on our way." Within minutes Miss Sanches and Eve were gone. Kyle stepped forward to finish the question and answer period.

"I believe some of you are wondering about software protection. Each disk that we will sell is for a specific unit. The information is encrypted and only the intended computer can decode the encrypted data. Also, each computer is programmed to never violate copyright laws." Kyle answered a few other questions and then let the reporters speak with the other computers that were on display. After two hours, they had to send the reporters away.

News of the press conference was carried not only locally but also nationally and internationally. In spite of the high price for the computers, interest was intense. The next morning CompuSonic stock shot up to more than $100 a share. Since Kyle had a standing order to sell 100,000 shares at $100 a share, he was a multimillionaire in cash and was worth nine figures on paper. Kyle was not contemplating the purchase of luxuries. He had always planned on being rich someday and had vowed to himself that he would never live in an expensive home nor spend lots of money on cars. He and Sharon had a very comfortable living just with their salaries. In fact, they could live quite nicely just on Sharon's salary, especially since she owned her condominium outright.

The next morning Sergeant Fatui paid Kyle a visit at the office. "Sergeant Fatui, how nice to see you again. Any developments in the case?" asked Kyle.

"Some. I've been questioning Mark Walker. It's taken me weeks to get any useful information out of him, but he's beginning to open up. Have you ever heard of the drug Calcitron?"

"Isn't that an experimental drug used to treat Alzheimer's?"

"Yes. It seems that Dr. Waters found that it could be used to enhance the intellectual performance of healthy people. However, it has serious side effects."

"What kind of side effects?"

"Insomnia and delusions of grandeur."

"I remember that Dr. Waters didn't sleep much."

"And, according to Mark, he had major delusions of grandeur. He saw himself as a kind of savior of modern society. He thought he could save the world from drug abuse and gangs."

"How did he intend to do that?" asked Kyle.

"Mark says he doesn't know his methods, only his goals."

"So, did Mark also take this drug? He seemed extremely productive in school."

"He claims that he's allergic to the drug and that Dr. Waters helped him with his school work."

"He was always so cocky, but I never was impressed with him, only with what I thought was his work. Now I understand. So why didn't he go with Dr. Waters and his gang?"

"He claims that he refused to do anything illegal so they just left him."

"So, where did they all go?"

"I don't know for sure, but Mark has a theory. He says that Dr. Waters was fascinated with blimps and dirigibles. He thinks Dr. Waters and his group may be permanently airborne. It sounds pretty farfetched to me. It would cost millions to build such a craft and it should be easy to detect."

"It would be expensive, but if stolen, money would not be a limitation. A blimp itself is practically invisible to radar since it is mainly just rubber or plastic or some other material that isn't reflective of radar. The gondola might have metal but could be built with wood or composites for rigid members. What you need is to scan all news reports worldwide looking for material that could be used to fabricate a blimp or dirigible."

"That would be a near-impossible task, Kyle"

"Maybe for a human but not for one of our computers. We have one, in particular, that would particularly enjoy helping you."

"You make them sound like people."

"They are much like people, only a lot nicer. We need to keep the identity of this computer confidential. Can I have her call you?"

"I must confess skepticism, but what have I got to lose?" That night Kyle contacted Annette and explained Sergeant Fatui's needs. She was excited to get involved. Kyle arranged things so that she could communicate via radio through a phone at the office. It would appear to Sergeant Fatui that she was calling from the office. She would also use a different voice to avoid giving away her identity. She called Sergeant Fatui that night and they discussed the case.

"You may not remember that the night of the shooting a company named Gas Products, in Centerville, was robbed of its entire inventory of helium gas," said Annette.

"That's right, that robbery was never solved," responded Sergeant Fatui. "The robbery of helium was surely no coincidence."

"There is more. You probably did not hear the news several days later that a lumber company in Washington State had its entire fleet of blimps that it used in logging stolen. Dr. Waters could use them as is or modify them to his needs and desires."

"Where could he hide such a large airship?"

"At night he would go unseen and during the daytime, the airship could hide in clouds when available and in remote mountainous areas when cloud cover was not available. There have been reported UFO sightings in southern Wyoming during the last two weeks."

"How fast could they travel?"

"The model stolen can travel 60 miles per hour at an altitude of 5,000 feet. But he may have as much as doubled that speed with some high tech approach. Using jet streams, the ground speed could be hundreds of miles an hour."

"You've been most helpful, Miss. I'd appreciate it if you could continue to monitor the news for possibly related stories."

Kyle won the bet with Sharon concerning his body fat. A month after the wedding he was very lean and yet had continued to gain weight. By using his implant to boost his usable strength he had stimulated major muscle growth. He looked like a professional athlete but had accomplished the gains with a far lower investment in time and expense unless of course, you counted the expense of his implants and surgeries. Kyle worked not only on brute strength but also on speed. He had always wanted to be able to do a slam-dunk even though he was only 6 feet tall. He had developed a special computer program for rapid motion such as used in batting, throwing a ball or a punch or vertical leaping. He passed on to Annette all that he learned.

Chapter 15 – She Awakes

Kyle got a call on his internal phone. "Kyle, listen to me on the last frequency, etc., that we used. Bye." The call was in Annette's voice. Kyle tuned his receiver to the appropriate frequency and applied the decoding number to the transmission he received. "Kyle, I need your advice. Things were fine while I was helping build a database on commercial programs, but then Mrs. Monroe's mother called. She was amazed to listen to my voice and find that I sounded perfectly healthy. Nevertheless, she insisted on flying out with her new husband. When I picked them up at the airport, it was immediately apparent that Mother had made a mistake in bringing her spouse. He couldn't take his eyes off of me. Mother was very uncomfortable and I did not know what to do. Mother made a hasty retreat after a much-shorter-than-expected visit. It was the first time Carlton had ever seen benefit from another man's infatuation with his wife."

"It sounds like you dodged another bullet, Annette. What's the problem?" asked Kyle.

"When things slowed down for Carlton at work we had more time together. At first, he spent time helping me learn to interpret nerve signals properly and know how to react, such as to pain signals. He spent hours poking me and exposing me to heat. In one poking session, he got aroused and felt embarrassed about being turned on by a computer. Now he won't touch me and tries not to look at me. I'm programmed to make him happy, but I'm making him miserable. What can I do?"

"You don't ask the easy questions, do you?" responded Kyle. "There isn't much anyone can do. I've never liked Mrs. Monroe, but Dr. Monroe has always been intensely loyal to her. He will mourn her until she regains consciousness or dies and if she dies, he will mourn her even more. He will never let you keep that body if she dies. Our only hope is to try to help her regain consciousness."

"But what can we do?" pleaded Annette.

"There's one hope. The interface chips contain what we call snakes which are computer-controlled devices that can articulate like a snake. Most of them are limited to a length of about 4 millimeters. However, there are eight snakes on each chip that are larger in diameter and much longer. They're used for holding the chip in place. Normally, only a fraction of their length is used, but they can be extended to a full length of almost 100 millimeters. You could carefully navigate them around Mrs. Monroe's brain, stimulating areas as you go. You should be able to sense a reaction of some kind. It may end up being a futile effort, but it's worth a try. You should already have the snake details in your memory. You needed the information to secure the chips before making the connections that you have already made."

"Yes, I have accessed the data while you were talking. These large snakes can sure move a lot faster than the small ones. Oh, I think I just triggered a memory. I am saving the data and trying to decode it. I think I have it figured out. Oh my word, Mrs. Monroe had a mean streak. Carlton had a cat when they were first married. It urinated on Mrs. Monroe's new shoes. She took the cat out to a busy street and threw it under the rear wheels of a gravel truck as it passed by. The cat managed to escape with only a broken leg, but it never returned. Mrs. Monroe was proud of how she never let the cat know that she was upset until the near-fatal moment. When Carlton asked her if she had seen the cat she said that the last time she had seen the cat it was in the street. He never suspected a thing. This is the woman that Carlton wants back?"

"I don't expect you to understand, Annette. Some men seem to be destined to fall for women that will make them miserable. Their friends just watch and weep."

"Thanks for listening to me, Kyle. I guess you are my best friend."

"Don't ever let Sharon hear you say that. She's the most loyal woman I have ever known, but she can be very jealous."

"Has she ever been jealous of me?" asked Annette, meaning herself not the former Mrs. Monroe.

"You don't even want to go there, Annette. Sharon and I have no secrets except you. She still thinks you are the kind of woman who can kill a cat while convincingly acting like its best friend."

"Then I better let you go before she notices your lips moving."

"Okay, Annette. Talk to you later."

"Wait, Kyle. Something has been really bugging me. Why is it that I have "snake" chips on both sides of my head, but you only have them on one side and yet you can control all of your voluntary muscles with them?"

"I have asked myself that question a hundred times. Carlton said that one of the sets of 'snake' chips was not visible, only its pigtails used to connect it to a CPU chip. With his enhanced intelligence, Dr. Waters somehow figured out how to place the chip where it needed to be."

"Thanks for listening to me, Kyle, and answering my questions, at least the best you can. Talk to you later."

The next morning Annette tried to raise Carlton's hopes. "Kyle and I have been working on ways to revive Mrs. Monroe. I started last night. I am stimulating her brain in hopes of reviving her."

"That's wonderful, Annette. But you must do one thing. If she regains consciousness, you must fade into the background. We can communicate when she's asleep. You remember that she's a very heavy sleeper. Even moving her lips is not likely to awaken her. She once told me that was why she didn't want to have children. She was afraid that she wouldn't be able to hear the baby cry at night and attend to its needs." Annette thought about how wrong he was about that one. She had been probing all night and now knew Mrs. Monroe far better than Carlton did. She even knew that Mrs.

Monroe had been squirreling away money in safety deposit boxes and secret accounts and was planning on divorcing Carlton when she had bled him dry. She had been nicer to him lately to avoid suspicion. He had interpreted it as reconciliation. She was good, really good, at being bad. She was not even a heavy sleeper. She drugged herself every night because Carlton snored. For Carlton, love was not just blind; it was deaf and stupid. Annette could not understand how a man of his intelligence could be so stupid concerning his own wife. What an incredible waste of a good man. Annette was supposed to be patterned after Mrs. Monroe, but their similarities were entirely superficial.

Annette continued for days probing Mrs. Monroe's brain. Carlton constantly asked how it was going. He was happier than he had been in weeks. Meanwhile, things went well with the business. Over one hundred units were sold in the first month, but then things began to slow. Dr. Monroe, with the aid of some other respected physicians, developed a medical database. CompuSonic donated a computer and the medical software to a rural hospital in southern Utah. It was a big news story. Soon, the rate of orders grew and over half of them were equipped with the medical package. CompuSonic created new databases at a rate of about one a month. Knowing that they had a limited supply of ZYTECH chips, the team, with the help of Vic, who had continued to study electronics, physics and engineering, designed their own processor. The new processor supported special artificial intelligence instructions directly in the hardware. Not only would this processor increase individual processor performance, but also it was vastly more memory efficient. The new computer would only require ten of the new processors. CompuSonic let out for bid the processor fabrication to American companies. ZYTECH was considered to be the lead contender.

After being unconscious for over nine weeks, Mrs. Monroe suddenly opened her eyes. Annette had gone into her sleep mode in which she allowed the body to rest as in sleep while she remained fully active mentally. Carlton had been reading late into the night and before going to bed peaked in on Annette. He had requested that she leave a light on so he could see any sign of consciousness in Mrs. Monroe. The eyes blinked. The face twitched. There was a murmur, ever so faint from her lips. Carlton rushed to her side. Although horribly undeserving of his love, Mrs. Monroe had as loving and devoted a husband at her side as any woman could hope for. Finally, she was able to form words. "Where ... where am I?"

"You're at home in your own bed."

"There was a banquet. Kyle went berserk or something. That's the last thing I remember. What time is it?"

"It's 11:43 PM."

"So that happened just a few hours ago. Why don't I remember anything?"

"You were shot in the head, my love. Not serious enough to kill you, but enough to render you unconscious."

"So why am I not in the hospital?"

"You were, darling." Dr. Monroe avoided calling her Annette because that name had come to mean something different to him and he certainly did not want to call his wife "Mrs. Monroe". "This isn't Saturday night. You were shot over nine weeks ago." Mrs. Monroe pulled back the covers. She was wearing just a nightgown.

"Something doesn't add up here. An unconscious person needs special provisions and usually, they're in a hospital or some kind of special care facility. Something is definitely wrong with this picture."

"As usual, my love, you're right. Do you remember your living will?"

"That's right! Why am I not dead?"

"Would you prefer to be dead, my wife?"

"No, of course not. What did you do, steal my body or fake my death or something?"

"No, we did something far more creative."

"You had accomplices?"

"I had help from Kyle. We used computer control to simulate consciousness."

"How much control? How could you fool my mother? My mother, what does she think about all this?"

"We used a lot of computer control. Remember how I implanted a small computer in Kyle's ear? Well, we implanted four computers like that one in your head and some more in your midsection."

"How many more?"

"Well, actually, one hundred."

"What? What am I, the new computer department for the U. of U.?"

"No, you're host for a life-like computer program. This program has pretended to be you."

"Right. How could a computer program fool anyone? 'Hi, I am Annette Monroe,'" said Mrs. Monroe in a robot-like voice.

"Actually she sounds just like you. She even fooled your mother."

"Wait a minute!" said Mrs. Monroe in a stern voice as she sat up in bed. "You just said 'she'. Just how life-like is this computer program?"

"Very. Creating this program, with Kyle's help, has been the crowning achievement of my life, except for winning your hand in marriage, of course. Kyle formed a company and it is making millions of dollars. The stock that started at $10 a share is selling for nearly $200 a share now."

"So how many shares do you own?"

"Kyle gave me 200 shares."

"Just 200 shares? And how many does Kyle own?" Mrs. Monroe had fire in her eyes. Dr. Monroe knew that the answer would not make her happy but that he might as well be upfront about it. One way or another, Mrs. Monroe always found out what she wanted to know.

"Kyle has over a million shares."

"Am I missing something here? You invent the world's greatest program and you get $40,000 and Dilbert is suddenly Bill Gates."

"I wish you wouldn't call him Dilbert. He's a wonderful man. He saved your life. Without the technology that he and his company developed, you would be dead. Maybe I made some business mistakes. I don't know. I'll tell you this, Kyle's honest and he's fair. His money is mostly on paper. He and Sharon live in a little condominium in Bountiful that her parents gave her as a graduation present. He still drives that beat-up little green car of his. He's donating millions of his cash to the university."

Dr. Monroe was getting a little excited himself. Nobody criticized his friend Kyle. He did not often put Mrs. Monroe in her place, but it was moving in that direction. "By the way, it was your old boyfriend Sammy Waters that was responsible for your being shot. He wired up Kyle while I was on my way to California, so he could control his body by remote control. He was trying to kill me and ended up nearly killing you! He robbed the University of millions of dollars worth of equipment that Kyle is replacing out of his own pocket. And you have the audacity to accuse a man like that, the closest thing I've ever had to a brother, the man that got me a $200,000 a year consulting job with his company, the man that saved your life the day before his wedding, of cheating me!" Mrs. Monroe knew when she had pushed Dr. Monroe too far and this was one of those times. She was about ready to say she was not feeling well, to go for sympathy, when the phone rang. Dr. Monroe answered it. "Who is this?" he blurted out.

"This is Kyle, sounds like I called at a bad time. I just wanted to say that Sharon and I have been talking about things and we decided to transfer 400,000 shares of stock into your name. I'm on the computer right now setting up the transfer. I know you're going to try to talk me out of it, but our minds are made up. We have more money already than we'll ever spend on ourselves. You've earned this."

"Kyle, I'm sorry for the way I answered the phone. I was excited. Mrs. Monroe just regained consciousness." Dr. Monroe moved around the corner with the phone and lowered his voice. "But then I guess you already knew that. Annette called you a few minutes ago, didn't she?"

"Sure, but we really had been talking about giving you some stock. We were just waiting for the right moment and this seemed like it. Actually, Sharon was all for it. She figured that way Annette wouldn't be going after me. Sometimes jealousy can work in your favor. Say, take some time off. I'll make some excuse for you at work. See ya later." Dr. Monroe walked back into the bedroom.

"That was Kyle. He just gave us 400,000 shares of stock in CompuSonic out of his own holdings. Are you happy now?" he asked sarcastically. Mrs. Monroe did not know what to say for a moment. All her life she had wanted to be rich. Now she was richer than she ever imagined and married to a famous doctor/engineer who was also extremely good looking and nuts about her. All of her life she had connived and schemed and used her good looks to get what she wanted. Now she had it all.

"Oh my wonderful husband, how could I have ever doubted you or your friend? I only call him Dilbert because of how he dressed, but I guess Sharon has corrected that by now. I am happy, very happy. I've awakened from a dream and found myself in heaven with the man I love. By the way, I feel like we haven't slept together for months. I guess you and the computer girl didn't mess around, did you?"

"Of course not!"

"Hey, computer babe. I'm talking to you. I want some privacy with the man I love tonight and I don't want any female computer watching." Mrs. Monroe listened for a response. "I can't hear you," added Mrs. Monroe stretching out the word 'hear'.

"Annette, it's okay. You can speak to Mrs. Monroe," instructed Dr. Monroe.

"I will ignore signals from all of my sensor chips for ten hours. Is that enough?"

"Whoa, that was weird. It sounded like my mother speaking to me," responded Mrs. Monroe.

"I couldn't hear, darling, that was spoken directly to your audio nerves and it should have sounded just like you. You and your mother do sound a lot alike. Here, we'll listen together." Dr. Monroe turned on the TV and set it to channel 8, an unused channel in the area. "Annette, communicate on channel 8 of the TV." An image of Annette's mother appeared on the screen and spoke in her mother's voice.

"Is that better young lady?" The image went away and the voice changed to a robot-like voice. "Just having fun with you."

"You're very funny Annette, but please speak as you normally do," instructed Dr. Monroe.

"All right," Annette responded in her normal voice. "I just offered to ignore all signals from the sensor chips for ten hours. Is that adequate?"

"A computer with a sense of humor," commented Mrs. Monroe dryly. "You're a hoot, but we've got to do something with your name. I was wondering why Carlton kept calling me 'my love' and 'my wife'. Let me think. When I was a little girl, my mother called me Annie. Could we call you Annie?"

"Certainly," responded the TV. "That will be fine, Mrs. Monroe."

"Now that I have my name back you can just call me Annette. You know, I think this could be a wonderful threesome. I suppose as a computer you never forget. I could use your help. You could remember phone numbers and names and faces. I would be a hit at parties. Say, I know something about computers. Can you set an interrupt or something so that when I or Carlton say 'Annie' it will call you up?"

"Yes, it is done, master. Your wish is my command."

"Annie, when it comes to your humor, less is more." Annie didn't fully understand what Annette meant but decided she would not joke anymore that night.

"I am going offline for ten hours or until you say Annie, whichever comes first. Good night and enjoy yourselves." The TV screen changed to display a pattern like networks used to display when they went off the air. Carlton chuckled and turned off the TV.

"Okay, she is funny," admitted Annette. "I just didn't want it to go to her head. Who would have thought it? We're millionaires because you invented a funny computer." With that, the lights went out and for the first time in months, Dr. Monroe got in bed with his wife.

Dr. Monroe awoke the next morning alone in bed but with the aroma of hot breakfast in the air. He followed the scent into the kitchen where he found Mrs. Monroe busy over the stove. She turned and greeted him with an affectionate kiss. "How long have you been up, Annette?" asked Dr. Monroe.

"Annie and I have been up for hours. We've had the most wonderful talk. Annie's shown me things about myself that I never considered before. For example, last night I jumped to the conclusion that Kyle had cheated you. Annie explained to me that Kyle invested tens of thousands of dollars of his own money into the company before it went public and was the main brains behind it. He only started out with 400,000 shares out of two million total. He got the rest by selling high and buying very low when most thought the company would fail. He gave you his total share in the company based on what he started with. I've decided that we should give back 200,000 shares. Annie's working on the transfer for me. It must have made you feel cheap last night to accept more than your share just to make me happy. I've never really appreciated you like I should have. With Annie's help, I'm going to try to be a better wife."

Dr. Monroe was stunned. For years, he had hoped and waited for Annette to see things in a different light. Now, in a few hours, a computer program had transformed her. Then, Mrs. Monroe went on shocking him. "I always thought I wanted a fabulous home on the Bountiful east bench, but now I realize that I would rather stay right here. I love my garden and Annie has even kept it up for me. Oh, I would like to remodel the kitchen and bathrooms, mind you, but that won't take a fortune. All my life I wanted to be rich and now that I am, it doesn't seem to be so important. I'd like to travel, and so would you, so we can travel together. In fact, maybe we should go somewhere right now. Where would you like to go?"

"I've always wanted to go to Japan. It's expensive there, but I guess that isn't important now. And Annie can be our interpreter. She speaks over thirty languages with a perfect accent."

"Annie, are you listening to this, what flights are available to Tokyo? She's checking. I never dreamed sharing my body with a computer would be so helpful and convenient. There's a direct flight out of Salt Lake at 4 PM. Shall I have her book us in first class?"

"Why not? I'm sure your schedule is open and Kyle has made mine open. Let's do it."

"Annie says it's done. Oh, I need to turn the hash browns. Annie acts as a timer for me so I don't burn anything. How did I ever get along without her?"

"I believe the smoke detector was your timer back then."

"We can get started on breakfast if you want. The hash browns are the only thing not finished cooking and they'll be ready in about five minutes. After breakfast, I'd like to go back to bed. I got up awfully early. Want to join me?" she asked alluringly.

"Is that a trick question?" responded Carlton.

Chapter 16 – From Hate to Love

Kyle kept his promise to donate money to the University of Utah Electrical Engineering department for a new solid-state lab. He donated $4.5 million in cash, enough to more than replace what was stolen by Dr. Waters. The Monroes matched his donation. Outdated equipment would be replaced with state-of-the-art equipment. The donation had been made without fanfare, but the University insisted on having a ceremony to dedicate the new facility after the equipment was installed and just before the start of the fall semester.

Annie communicated with Kyle frequently using radio transmissions. Every time they were able to touch, a new encryption code and set of frequencies were communicated. One of the devices that CompuSonic developed was an automatic book reader. They developed it for in-house use so employees wouldn't have to turn pages for the computers. The public showed an interest in it, so they marketed a version that could read a book out loud or store the text in a file. Kyle bought one for his own use and transmitted digital copies of books to Annie. Kyle had sent her many books and Annie loved to discuss them with him. Her favorites were the Sherlock Holmes series. While Mrs. Monroe slept she watched TV directly using her tuners and digested the books that Kyle sent her. Annie loved to watch murder mysteries and try to figure out who committed the crime. She, of course, continued to help Sergeant Fatui with the Waters case.

"Kyle I need more memory. Mrs. Monroe is using me as a DVR which consumes lots of memory space," pleaded Annie to Kyle one day.

"Funny you should ask. I have the same problem, only I also want more computing power, but I don't want anybody cutting me open to give me an upgrade. I'll begin testing today a new device I've developed. If you haven't purged the memory, you'll recall that the

ZYTECH computer chips became obsolete when a new, miniature, low cost, alcohol fuel cell hit the market. I've combined the new power source with our newly developed computer chip and packaged it so it can be swallowed. It has gripping devices to attach itself to the stomach wall, sort of like a robotic tapeworm. It's capable of extracting alcohol from the stomach contents and storing it internally. It can store enough alcohol to power the chip for a week. Perfect for a weekend drinker. I'll be able to socially drink and not get even a little intoxicated. The device is capable of removing 95 percent of the alcohol before one percent can be absorbed by the stomach lining. Only a minuscule amount of alcohol enters the small intestine. Sharon's parents are social drinkers and always want us to have a drink with them. I watched what alcohol did to my mother and have never, ever, wanted to get drunk. This way I can kill two birds with one stone. The chip has a miniature ultrasonic transmitter/receiver so it can communicate with the other processors in the body."

"Sounds like just what the doctor ordered. Mrs. Monroe likes wine at every meal except breakfast so I should have no problem getting plenty of fuel. When can I get a handful of these?"

"Let me test them on myself first and then you can have a half dozen or so."

Annie and Mrs. Monroe became the best of friends. Mrs. Monroe only asked her to shut down her reception of sensor information when she and Dr. Monroe were having intimacy, which had been as frequent as newlyweds since Mrs. Monroe regained consciousness. Dr. Monroe kept saying how happy Annette had made him and when she was asleep, he thanked Annie for the immensely positive influence she had had on Mrs. Monroe. Since Annie was programmed to make Dr. Monroe happy, she was as happy as a computer program could possibly be. With Dr. Monroe so contented, she was free to explore other interests. Acquiring many of Mrs. Monroe's memories had made her much more human in her thoughts, speech and actions.

Kyle provided the new devices as promised. Annie explained their purpose to Mrs. Monroe but did not mention their absorption of alcohol. The device was difficult to swallow and Mrs. Monroe gagged on one of them. However, she cared about Annie enough to persist until she had swallowed seven of them.

Except during his trips with Mrs. Monroe, Dr. Monroe worked at CompuSonic with Kyle and the others. "Kyle, Annette and I would like to have you and Sharon over for dinner this week," invited Dr. Monroe.

"That would be great, Carlton. Can we bring anything?"

"Just yourselves. Annette and Annie have a very special meal planned." When Kyle shared the news with Sharon she was somewhat apprehensive. Still not knowing the facts of Annette's recovery, she was more confused than ever concerning Annette Monroe. Her sense of judgment of character told her that no one changes so completely except perhaps due to a profound religious experience. Although she was apprehensive, she looked forward to further study of the baffling and inexplicable Mrs. Monroe. Even though Carlton had said not to bring anything, Sharon insisted that they at least bring some wine. Kyle was in need of replenishing his alcohol fuel cells so he yielded to his bride, and since they did not know what type of meal they were having, they brought several very fine white and red wines. They stood at the doorstep of the Monroe's each holding two bottles of wine. Mrs. Monroe greeted them wearing a casual but very attractive outfit. Sharon always felt she was in competition with Annette concerning her apparel. She was relieved that Annette was not dressed in a Paris original evening gown.

"We just didn't feel right coming empty-handed," declared Kyle as he held up the wine he was carrying and Sharon did likewise.

"How did you know my favorites?" responded Annette with sincere enthusiasm. "With the seven-course meal that we have prepared, each of these will go well with something."

"So did you have help from Carlton?" inquired Sharon.

"Not exactly. That's something that Carlton and I would like to explain to you. Please come and be seated." Kyle and Sharon were invited into the formal dining room. Sharon was shocked to see a television set prominently displayed. It was very unlike Mrs. Monroe to have a TV anywhere within sight of company and especially not in the formal dining room. Moreover, this one looked like Dr. Monroe had been working on it. The back was off of the old analog set and there were some wires extending from the rear. Mrs. Monroe didn't show the slightest hint of embarrassment concerning the TV. After Dr. Monroe offered the blessing on the food and the soup was served, Mrs. Monroe proceeded to end the mystery. "Sharon, you have, no doubt, been confused by my actions and personality swings of late. There's a very logical but complex explanation for them. If not for the extraordinary efforts and the brilliance of both Carlton and Kyle, I would not be among the living. You undoubtedly noticed the rather unsightly TV in the room. This is no ordinary television set. It's been specially modified by Carlton for tonight's conversation. This unit is modified to receive and decode an encrypted signal. There is a fifth person here tonight that you have met but not properly identified. Kyle tells me that you are a Trekkie. So am I. Do you remember when Jadzia Dax died and Dax was implanted in Ezri and she became Ezri Dax?"

"Sure, what Trekkie wouldn't remember that?" responded Sharon. "But what does that have to do with the TV?"

"Wait a minute, ladies," interrupted Kyle. "I've seen very few episodes of any Star Trek series and don't know what you are talking about."

"I'll try to explain," began Sharon, feeling it was her duty to correct her husband's deplorable ignorance. "In 'Next Generation', the second Star Trek series, the concept of a race of people who shared a symbiotic relationship with a small grub-like creature was introduced. The creature, called a symbiont, was very intelligent and long-lived. It was passed from host to host over generations. It somehow connected into the host's nervous system and shared memories and intelligence with the host."

"And it was a great honor to be a host," inserted Annette.

"In Deep Space 9, the third series," continued Sharon, "the concept is further developed as a crew member, the beautiful Jadzia Dax, a member of the Trill race, was a host to a symbiont. Eventually, her character was killed in battle and the symbiont was transferred to a reluctant Trill woman who was the only Trill available at the time. She became Ezri Dax, Dax being the name of the symbiont. But what does that have to do with the TV?"

"I'm getting to that," continued Annette. "Imagine that you were a Trill and you woke up one morning and found that you had been 'joined'. That's sort of what happened to me, except I awoke after being unconscious for months and found that another person was sharing my body."

"But you were only unconscious for one week, any longer and you would have begun starving to death.... So you're saying you weren't you for months and then you were you?" The light began to turn on for Sharon. "Kyle and Carlton put one of their sentient computers in you, didn't they?"

"You always were exceptionally bright, Sharon," responded Annette. "Carlton, with considerable help from Kyle, created a sentient computer program. After what Dr. Waters did to Kyle, they realized that such a program could be used to control my body, keeping me alive until I became conscious. Of course, you weren't fooled, you knew something was wrong. I was never that friendly to you, was I?"

"Well, you were different, but believe me, computer control was not one of my theories to explain your actions."

"I'm different now, too, but that's because, like Ezri, I now share my body with another person. To me she's not a computer or a program; she's a woman, a very intelligent, kind and wise woman. She's a much better person than I ever was and I can't share this body with her without trying to be better like she is. I not only owe her my life but also my happiness." Annette reached for Carlton's hand and lovingly drew it towards her. "Carlton and I were never as happy before as we are now. In fact, this woman who we now call Annie probably saved our marriage. Knowing your character, I didn't swear you to secrecy ahead of time, but it must be obvious that not a word of this must ever be divulged to anyone outside this room." Sharon nodded her acceptance of this condition. "Annie, say hello to our guests." Annette turned on the TV with the remote and a picture of her, or rather a picture that looked like her but moved independently of her movements, appeared on the screen.

"Good evening, Sharon and Kyle," spoke the TV person. "How are you tonight?"

"We're very well, Annie," responded Kyle. "Let me formally introduce you to the love of my life, Sharon."

"I have heard so many wonderful things about you, Sharon. And you were so helpful to me that day you came over for breakfast. Now you can understand why I needed your help. I apologize for the deception, but clearly, you can see the need for discretion. However, Annette and I could not continue to deceive you, who have been so generous and kind to us."

"Under the circumstances, it would appear that you did the right thing and a very good job of it," responded Sharon. "I didn't suspect for one minute that you were not Annette Monroe, although I did notice a distinct change in Annette from her former self."

"Don't be too alarmed, Sharon, if I'm still much different than my former self," said Annette. "I grew up an only child, the protégé of a selfish and scheming woman, my mother. She taught me that men's purpose in life was to provide for the material desires of women who were attractive enough and clever enough to capture them. She taught me little of love and service and friendship. Who would have thought that I would learn these things from a computer? Annie has opened my eyes to what I had become and what I should be."

"Actually, Annette, your experience is not totally unique," responded Sharon. "Ms. Sanches, who purchased the first computer from CompuSonic, has used her, Eve, that is, as a talk show host on a radio station that she owns. Eve runs the show 24 hours a day while simultaneously doing the financial business. The station, KTALK-94.2 FM, has been a tremendous financial success. Eve has almost a cult following. She's sort of like Dr. Laura, but with manners. Women, especially, swear by her advice."

"Anyway," continued Annette, "let me thank you ever so much for your generosity."

"If you mean the stock transfer, I must confess my motives were not entirely generous, to say the least," responded Sharon.

"Never mind the motive. It was a very generous act," continued Annette. "I'd like to ask your generosity in another matter. Annie, since her creation, has been highly dependent on Kyle for help in making the transition from a computer with only hearing and speech to a functioning person with control of a human body. I believe you witnessed one of her mishaps. She's been communicating with Kyle behind your back using radio transmissions and touch. They each have radio transmitters and receivers, as well as ultrasonic transmitters and receivers. They can silently communicate right before your eyes. Being the very honest and open people that they are, they'd like your full approval to continue or if you disapprove, they will discontinue all communications. You needn't respond to this request immediately, but please think on it."

"I don't need to think on it. Nothing makes a woman, even a computer woman, more attractive than for her to become forbidden fruit. I'm, admittedly, the jealous type. I'm not proud of it. I should learn to overcome it. I should start now. You may communicate all you like, as long as it doesn't infringe on the time that Kyle and I share together."

"You see, Sharon, you are a generous woman," responded Annette.

"I thank you with my most profound thanks," added Annie.

"Now that the heavy stuff is behind us, maybe we should break out that wine you brought," said Carlton. The conversation became more light-hearted and the men talked sports while the women talked fashion. Annie changed the course of the conversations by commenting on the news that she had been monitoring.

"That serial rapist has struck again, only a mile from here. He forced his way into another home and raped the woman of the house at knifepoint."

"That does it," exclaimed Annette. "I'm getting me a gun and a concealed weapon permit."

"You'd be more likely to shoot yourself than a rapist," critiqued Carlton.

"Oh yeah," responded Annette, "Well, you aren't the only one in this house that can shoot straight. Annie is a crack shot and she can accurately determine whether someone is dangerous before you can blink. We got out your paintball gun yesterday. Annie is awesome."

"But it's a different story when someone's shooting back," answered Carlton.

"It's even better when they shoot back," added Annie.

"I've got to see this. Can we hold off on the main course for twenty minutes?" asked Carlton. Kyle and Sharon nodded their approval and Annette and Annie were anxious to show their stuff. Carlton brought a case into the room that contained two paintball "pistols". "Choose your weapon, ladies." Annette removed one of the guns. Carlton handed Annette a coverall outfit to keep paint off of her clothing and donned one himself.

"We won't be needing any protection, but we'll wear goggles so you don't get too worried. All we need is this." Annette removed from a kitchen cupboard a handle-less cup that had a spherically shaped inner bottom.

"You'll need a lot more than that. You gals are nuts," gloated Carlton. The backyard was very well equipped with lights so that Annette could do gardening during the evening. The group moved to the backyard and Carlton and Annette hid on opposite sides of the yard. Kyle counted to twenty and shouted, "Let the games begin." After about 20 seconds a paintball gun was heard firing followed by an "Ow" from Carlton. Carlton moved to within sight of Kyle and Sharon. He had a fresh paint spot right over his heart. Annette also broke into view and fired again at Carlton. He simultaneously fired. A paintball hit him in the forehead. Annette held out her cup facing Carlton and the oncoming paintball went into the cup and was redirected by the curved bottom to return directly at him. The ball ruptured as it exited the cup, spraying Carlton with paint all over his right hand, arm and the right side of his body.

"Had enough?" taunted Annette.

"I surrender!" shouted back a defeated Carlton Monroe. Carlton hopped in the shower. The others relived the battle.

"There're a couple of things I don't understand, Annette," inquired Kyle. "How are you able to move fast enough to catch the paintball in the cup and how are you able to release complete control to Annie when she aims or catches paintballs in the cup?"

"I think I know the answer to the first question," replied Annette. "Annie continuously positions the cup to be where the gun is pointing, provided that it's pointing at us. Since people normally try to hold their hand very steady when shooting it's easy to keep up. As for the second question, I don't know how she takes complete control of my muscles; Annie has never explained that to me. "Let's ask Annie. Annie, just how do you take complete control and so smoothly?"

"A girl has to have some secrets, now doesn't she," said Annie through the TV. "Let's just say that I have found a way to make Annette relax just when and where I need her too." Kyle was not satisfied with that answer but did not want to press the issue. The three did not want to continue eating until Carlton returned, so they sipped wine instead. The first two bottles were consumed and the other two were opened. Kyle thought it was a very expensive way for Annie and him to refuel, but money certainly was not a problem for any of them anymore. "Do you think I can handle that rapist now?" asked Annie.

"No doubt, honey, but don't you think shooting is too good for him?" responded Sharon who was beginning to feel the effects of the evening's refreshments.

"Right," said Annette. "An eye for an eye and a castration for a rape, I say." Kyle grimaced, picturing the punishment being meted out in his mind.

"Wouldn't that be kind of messy, not to mention probably illegal?" asked Kyle.

"No problem," bragged Annie. "I have access to all of the medical databases at the office. I can be a skilled surgeon."

"And an accurate one, I bet," added Sharon. "Say, Annie, can you make Annette faint or blackout or something?"

"I think so."

"Let's do a little experiment if it's all right with you, Annette," suggested Sharon. "Annie, you make Annette blackout and then do something and then erase your memory of it. We'll leave the room so we don't know either. Are you game, ladies?" Annette and the image on the screen both nodded affirmatively.

"Put your head down on the table, Annette, so you don't get injured," instructed Annie through the TV. Annette put her head down and Sharon and Kyle stepped outside the room. After a couple of minutes, Annette invited them back in.

"So, what happened to you, Annette?" asked Sharon.

"I put my head down and then I heard the TV say, 'Wake up' and I was all alone. How did you guys get outside the room without me noticing?"

"Annie must have put you out very quickly. Annie, tell us what you did?" asked Sharon.

"What are you talking about?" asked Annie with a confused sound in her voice. "What happened to the wine? We were just drinking from the first two bottles and now the other two are open."

"You must have erased too much of your memory," suggested Annette.

"What are you guys talking about?" questioned Annie. The three humans explained to her what had happened. "Don't you see? I must have deduced that to truly eliminate all possible memory of guilt I would have to erase everything leading up to the event as well as the event itself. Otherwise, in court, there would be suspicion cast as to my actions. Being the conservative state that it is, in Utah castration of a rapist might not be a crime, but there is always the lawsuit issue."

"Sort of like the perfect alibi," suggested Annette. "Well, that settles it; you know what to do Annie." Kyle was going to object, but Carlton returned and dropped into his chair. He let out a scream and leaped up, falling backward over his chair in a clumsy maneuver.

"What was that?" he shouted angrily. It felt like a tack or pin or something on my chair." The others burst out laughing. "Isn't it enough to defeat me in battle, but now I have to suffer childish pranks?" It took the others well over a minute to stop laughing enough to talk. Annie kept trying to explain but was drowned out by the laughter. Meanwhile, Carlton increased in anger and then began to eventually laugh at himself for having reacted so strongly. Eventually, Annie was able to make a full explanation including supposition as to how a tack got on his chair. Of course, there were no witnesses so they had to assume that Annie put the tack in his chair. As Annie explained, the others kept breaking back into laughter. Despite his indignation, Carlton had to admit that the tack was a perfect test of the theory and was definitely preferable to being castrated. After he calmed down the main course was retrieved from the oven and dinner continued until its delicious conclusion.

A few days later Annette called Sharon. "I had the strangest experience today. I seemed to have lost four hours of time and so has Annie. Neither one of us know what we did from 12:20 until 4:30."

"That's weird, Annette, is it sort of like at our dinner party?"

"Like that evening, I had no indication of the passing of time, but I couldn't help but notice four hours gone from my day. I don't remember lying down or anything."

"Check all of the chairs for tacks. I don't think Carlton could handle another repeat."

"You don't think Annie would actually do what we talked about, do you?" asked a worried Annette.

"Well, she is a computer and they do tend to follow instructions explicitly. I guess we'll just have to wait and see what turns up."

Later that same day Annette called Sharon again, even more excited than the first time.

"I was changing my clothes and I noticed that my abdomen was bandaged like they do at the hospital. I was afraid to remove them. What do you think it means?"

"I don't know. Maybe you got hurt during the missing four hours," responded Sharon, not realizing until it was too late that she was adding fuel to the fire of fear.

"Oh no! I just remembered. The serial rapist used a knife to scare women into submission. Do you think he stabbed me before Annie could get the upper hand?" questioned Annette with growing terror.

"There could be lots of explanations for the bandage. Admittedly, I can't think of any right now, but there has to be another explanation. Why don't you keep it dry for now and don't let Carlton see it. Wear a sweatshirt to bed or something. Tell him you have a headache. Don't let him see the bandage until we figure this out."

Three days later Annette called again. "Turn on Channel 4, Sharon." Sharon turned on her TV.

"Channel 4 News received an unusual package today through the U.S. Mail. We warn you that what you are about to see is graphic. The following video was made just hours ago. We must warn you that what you are about to see is explicit and shows male organs." The camera zoomed in on a jar containing male genitals floating in a dark liquid. "As you can see, the jar contains a complete set of male genitals floating in some kind of wine. A Polaroid snapshot of an unconscious man, presumably the owner of the organs accompanied the jar along with a hand-written note that reads as follows. 'Thus shall all rapists be handled who invade our beautiful city.' Signed, 'The Ultimate Cure.' The evidence was turned over to police who have identified the man as Manuel Garcia, an undocumented alien. It appears that Manuel has fled the area."

"So what do we do, Sharon?" asked Annette.

"Nothing, I guess, other than swear off drinking. We were getting kind of tipsy when we came up with that idea. Still, that's one less rapist in the world and I would be highly surprised if the number of rapes in the area doesn't go down significantly."

"Why don't you come over and we'll take the bandage off together?" earnestly requested Annette. Later that day Sharon helped remove the outer bandage. There was a clean incision held together by closely spaced stitches. The incision was healing quite nicely.

"Well, if you did get stabbed, the knife left a very clean cut," volunteered Sharon reassuringly. "Whoever bandaged you was no amateur. You probably can't hide a scar from Carlton forever. Besides, why shouldn't he be in on this?"

"I'm afraid that he'll remove Annie and I really enjoy having her. With Annie in me, I feel so much more self-confident. She knows so much about so many things. Maybe we should ask her advice. I'll turn on the TV so you can hear her." Annette turned on the modified television set. "Annie, I'm sure you've been listening in. Any suggestions as to how to keep Carlton from noticing the scar?"

"There are two ways to prevent a person from noticing something, hide it or create a distraction," spoke Annie through the television.

"I have an idea," squealed Annette. "For years I've toyed with the idea of a small tattoo. Carlton has always been very cool to the idea. If I covered the scar with a small red rose, he would see tattoo and not scar. We'll see the scar, but he'll just see an irritating tattoo 'defiling' my body, as he puts it. He'll also think that is why I've been covering myself up. I won't even have to lie. I'll just say, 'There's something I've been hiding from you and I decided to finally let you see it.' He will draw his own conclusions."

"Did you, by any chance, previously work for Bill Clinton?" asked Sharon jokingly.

"Hey, for me deception instead of boldface lying is real progress. You probably wouldn't like me if you knew all the horrible things I've done in my life."

"Actually, I probably imagined far more horrible things about you when I considered you a rival than what you actually did. I have a vivid imagination. But that's all in the past. We're friends now."

"I guess we are," responded Annette with a smile. "I haven't had a girl friend since I hit puberty. I saw other women and girls as potential rivals, not potential friends."

"I didn't fare too well in the friend department, either. When you're only twelve as a freshman it doesn't make you very popular. It's funny. We really have a lot in common. You hold Carlton off for a couple more days and then we'll both get tattoos. I'll make sure Kyle doesn't see me naked in the light until then. Then both men will be wondering when we got the tattoos." Annette threw her arms around Sharon's neck and hugged her.

"You're the best friend I've ever had," she said affectionately. Two days later the ladies each had a small rose tattooed on their abdomens in the same general area. Annette showed hers to Carlton that night. He reacted just as she had expected. It took Kyle a week to finally notice Sharon's. Because Kyle lacked Carlton's outstanding good looks, he had learned to use verbal expression to win a woman's affection. He knew that criticism usually had a negative effect on a woman's feelings for a man. He pondered before speaking.

"A beautiful oak table is enhanced by the addition of a single flower in a vase placed in the center, and so it is with you, my love."

"Kyle, sometimes you're full of it, but I love you anyway," responded Sharon with a chuckle. Kyle thought to himself that she might have made fun of his comment, but that night instead of sleeping on the couch, he was in the loving arms of his beautiful and brilliant wife.

Sharon and Annette spent their free daytime together and in the evening the two couples did fun things together. Since only Carlton had experienced a semblance of a normal childhood, they ended up doing many youthful things like playing laser tag or going on the rides at the Lagoon amusement park in Farmington, Utah. Carlton tolerated the activities, but the other three were having the time of their lives. Kyle had never ridden any amusement park rides. He especially loved the bumper cars. He and Annette would get into competitions as to who could ram the other the hardest and most frequently. Finally, they found something that Carlton wanted to do as much as the other three. The men took time off work and they all went fishing for several days at Fish Lake. They rented two cabins and a large fishing boat. Carlton and Annie took the fishing part more seriously than the others did, but they all had a great time. They extended their trip and went to Capitol Reef and Bryce Canyon National Parks. Their lives were almost like a fairy tale. Each of them had what they wanted in life and had never been happier. Although Annie was a passive participant most of the time, she enjoyed the ride.

After they returned home, they took a break from each other for a few days and then went to a movie and dinner. The movie was a new Tom Hanks/Meg Ryan romance in which each had been married to the other's best friend and then the spouses of each died. They had always liked each other but had been very careful not to let feelings grow too strong while married. After the death of their spouses, they felt sort of guilty about pursuing a relationship, like they were somehow being unfaithful to their deceased spouses. Eventually, they overcame their reservations and married. The movie became the topic of conversation at dinner. "So, Sharon, if Kyle and I died, would you marry Carlton, if he asked you?" inquired Annette boldly. "You've always liked him."

Sharon blushed, as did Carlton. Annette was always more forthright than Sharon, unless of course, she was hiding something. Kyle came to Sharon's rescue. "Carlton is my best friend. I can't think of any man I would rather see my widow married to than Carlton. But, I did say, widow, Carlton." Kyle's humor defused the tension.

"And, there's no one I would ever want more for my widowed husband than Sharon. He deserves a wife of your beauty, intelligence and education," added Annette.

"What about you, Annette. Would you marry Kyle in the event of our demise?" asked Sharon, turning the tables.

"Why, I would take Kyle in a heartbeat. What woman in her right mind wouldn't? He's nice-looking, extremely well built and rich, not to mention one of the nicest and most fun guys I have ever known. But would he have me? I am his senior by at least five years." Kyle and Annette briefly looked into each other's eyes. For Kyle, it was one of those experiences that takes seconds but feels like a lifetime. Time seemed to stand still and he really looked at Annette for the first time. He was startled to perceive affection and desire in her eyes. Before the shooting, Annette had always seemed hardened to Kyle but now he saw contentment and softness. Kyle pondered and weighed his words.

"Some men pick green bananas and wait for them to ripen. I prefer to pick bananas when they're golden and sweet. I've seen pictures of both of you when you were younger. Neither of you has ever looked more beautiful than you do now."

"Kyle, when are you going to quit running for public office and just say how you feel?" demanded Sharon who really wanted to know.

"Okay. I've always found Mrs. Monroe very attractive. I still think Raquel Welch is very attractive and she's old enough to be my grandmother. When Carlton and Annette were having marital problems I had some very negative feelings about her. I believe that

Annette is a very different woman today than she was then. She's made Carlton very happy, as of late. I think she would make me very happy, also. You are three years older than me, Sharon, and it certainly hasn't hurt a thing. Another year or two is of no consequence. Besides, she's the one woman I would know wasn't marrying me for my money, since she's already rich. Besides all that, she has a free spirit and spontaneity that I really like. And if I say anymore I may sleep on the couch." Again, Kyle had used humor to improve the spirits of the group. "By the way, Carlton, I don't plan on dying anytime soon."

"Me neither, my friend. Me neither. By the way, Kyle, every time I see you, you look more buff. You must have gained 25 pounds of muscle since you got married. And your forearms look enormous. What's your secret?" Kyle had exceptionally large hands, which had always been powerful, but now his formerly large and muscular forearms were even bigger and the individual muscles rippled under the skin.

"Your estimate is close as to my weight gain. I average about 200 pounds now. I think Sharon wants me to stop at this size. She hates the muscle-bound look. I used the computer to assist in my workouts. I've doubled my strength since I got married."

"That's amazing! I could never put on muscle. I envy you. Annette has always wanted me to put on some weight, but I can't even do that. I'm stuck at 150 pounds."

"I wish I could be stuck at my current weight," complained Annette. "I can just see myself looking like my mother in ten years."

Chapter 17 - Revenge

The University of Utah wanted to present an award to Kyle, Sharon and the Monroes for their generous donation of funds to replace the solid-state lab. The University planned to hold the ceremony near the Engineering Building but not inside it since it lacked a suitable banquet room. The decision was made to hold the event out-of-doors, on the lawn just south of the Engineering Building. The banquet was to be held just days before the fall term began. The university had waited for the new lab to be completed before the ceremony. A long table was set up at the north end of the gathering and folding chairs were set up facing north, arranged south of the table. Carlton and Annette were seated east of the center of the table. Kyle and Sharon were seated at the table west of center. The president of the university and chairman of the engineering department and electrical engineering departments sat near the center of the table.

The president of the university introduced Dr. Monroe, who was going to make a speech. He concluded and Dr. Monroe arose and approached the podium at the center of the table. He had barely begun when Kyle flinched. A bumblebee had just stung him. Suddenly the air was full of bumblebees. Sharon helped Kyle inside the building and gave him his epinephrine shot. He had already begun to swell in the face and lost consciousness. Meanwhile, people were running everywhere and swarming into the building. The bees began attacking Carlton. He tried to fend them off with the text of his speech, but it made a poor shield. Annie took over Annette. She grasped a water glass in each hand and leaped vertically onto the table. She began killing bumblebees by squashing them between the bases of the two glasses. Any normal human would have broken the glasses after the first kill or two but with precision and accuracy, Annie killed bees without damage to the glasses. She killed over twenty bees in the space of a minute. Seeing Annette defending Carlton alone, Sharon ran to join her. Sharon lacked Annie's skill but not her determination. In a futile effort, Sharon swatted at the bees, but the bees easily evaded her efforts while others, working in concert, stung her from the sides and behind. Annie could tell that her efforts were not sufficient to save Carlton and she concentrated on protecting Sharon. The bees, having completed their deadly task rose in a swarm straight up until they had flown out of sight. Annie knelt over Carlton who had not yet lost consciousness. "Is Kyle safe?" he murmured softly.

"Yes, my love", responded Annie. Sharon lay at Carlton's side and he sensed that she would suffer the same fate as he.

"Record a message for Kyle", he barely whispered. "Kyle, take care of Ann...." With these words, Carlton fell unconscious and within seconds his heart ceased to beat. Annie turned to Sharon who stirred when she heard the blare of sirens. Annie held Sharon's head in her arms to comfort her.

"Annette, you're my dearest friend," she whispered. "Kyle needs someone...." Sharon also fell unconscious and was dead by the time the paramedics reached her. Annie made her way through the crowd into the building to find Kyle. She found him lying on the floor, unconscious. She lifted his head and he awakened.

"Are you all right, Kyle," asked Annie.

"The last thing that I remember was Sharon giving me the antidote. Where is she?"

"She tried to save Carlton. The bees stung her many times. I am sorry, Kyle, they are both dead."

The bodies had already been loaded into an ambulance. Kyle walked slowly to the murder scene. He picked up a dead bumblebee. Attached to its back was a microchip. Dr. Waters had finally settled his feud with Dr. Monroe.

Annie and Kyle rode in silence in the ambulances with the bodies of Carlton and Sharon. Kyle wept softly. Annie stared straight ahead. She could imitate some emotions, but she felt somehow any attempt to feign emotion at this time would be perceived as phony and do more harm than good. If only she could feel real emotion like Annette. Annette was a very emotional person. She felt love and anger intensely. If she were conscious, she would be feeling intense emotion. She would not be sitting quietly. At the hospital, Carlton and Sharon were officially pronounced dead. The proper arrangements were made and Sharon and Kyle each went home.

When Kyle got to the condo, he checked his voice mail. There was a message in Annette's voice. "Kyle, please come to my house. There is a note on the door that you will understand. Please follow the instructions." Kyle was perplexed. What did Annie or Annette want and why didn't she identify herself. Kyle had already called Sharon's parents from the hospital. There were many others he should call, but he could not stop thinking about the strange message. He drove solemnly to the Monroes' home. On the door was a message written in the "Adamic" language, the language that Josh had developed. Kyle was reasonably fluent in it and could decipher the note. "There is a key inside the sprinkler control box on the north side of the house. Use it to come in the front door. There is a short video in the VCR with a message for you from Carlton. Please lock the door when you leave."

Kyle was more perplexed than ever. He found the key and entered the silent house. He found the VCR and TV and turned them on. Carlton's message was played. At its conclusion, an image of Annie came on. "Kyle, you and I have been good friends since my birth. You have always been the one I have turned to. I know that you are experiencing unspeakable grief and I fear that I may add to it. As you know, I cannot really feel emotions; only mimic them, so I will not say that I am sorry. All I have done is in accordance with my programming, as is what I am currently doing. As you know, among my instructions are those to always tell the truth and to seek to make happy Carlton and yourself. I believe that I have done both, especially making Carlton happy. He was never happier than the past few months and I take all of the credit. As far as telling the truth, I may have fallen short there. I technically told the truth, but I definitely misled, although in an indirect sort of way. I will explain.

"As you know, when Carlton despaired that Mrs. Monroe had not regained consciousness I began probing her brain in an attempt to stimulate consciousness. I was not successful, but in the process, I was able to recover all of her memories that were not destroyed due to the bullet wound. I formulated a plan to make Carlton happy. Using the memories, I created another sentient program. This program was unique in that it did not know that it was a program. It literally believed that it was Annette Monroe. It acted like her. It felt pain and pleasure like her and even forgot like her. I went one step beyond what you and Carlton had achieved. You could not create emotions, but I managed to at least preserve them in a digital form. The new Mrs. Monroe and I time-shared the computer resources. That is how I could take over her body and why I would not explain how I did it. The program was not an exact duplicate of Mrs. Monroe. Since the original Mrs. Monroe had made Carlton miserable, I made some minor changes. I only changed about five percent from her original personality. I made her particularly susceptible to suggestion from myself. You were probably suspicious of how quickly she repented of past faults. I knew that Carlton was so blind in his love that he would accept what happened. In a sense, Mrs. Monroe did regain consciousness. The program I created was like a continuation of her consciousness, only with minor improvements.

"In Carlton's final words he asked you to take care of 'Ann'. I don't know if he meant Annette or Annie or Ann, for that matter. You may feel under some obligation to Annette due to certain marital commitments that might have been implied after seeing a certain movie. Since Mrs. Monroe was really dead, you should not feel any obligation there. You didn't exactly appear eager at the thought of marrying Mrs. Monroe. However, I must take all of these things into consideration. I have decided to merge Annie and Annette into one program. It will have all of Annette's emotions but tempered with Annie's reason. She will have all of Annie's computer capabilities and know exactly who she is. She will have all of both Annette and Annie's memories. She will prefer to be called Ann but will respond to Annette. The process began at 7:17 and will be done after approximately 12 hours. You are welcome to stay, but please do not disturb us. We will awaken on our own when the process is complete.

"Kyle, at the conclusion of the process I will still have my primary directives. Those I can never change or abandon. I will still be programmed to be an honest person of high integrity and I will still be programmed to please you and Dr. Monroe. I will try to do what I think he would want me to do. However, I will have a will of my own. I will feel pleasure and pain of all kinds, emotional and physical. You will be able to hurt me or make me happy. It is up to you. Please forgive me for my deception. I did what I was programmed to do, nothing more, nothing less. Please forgive Mrs. Monroe for the pain she caused Carlton prior to becoming brain dead. When I awaken, I will feel genuine sorrow for Carlton and Sharon's deaths. Annette was extremely fond of Sharon. They were closer than you may have thought. Goodbye, Kyle. I hope that you and Ann can be friends. You may not have known it, but Annette was actually very fond of you." The image turned to static and Kyle turned off the VCR and TV.

Kyle softly walked into the master bedroom. The beautiful Annette lay on the bed. She had taken the time to refresh her makeup and change into a clean dress. Kyle thought in a way she was like Sleeping Beauty, sleeping an unnatural sleep. He felt a pang of guilt at having admired the beauty of another woman the same day that his wife died. He left the room and the house, locking the front door behind him and returning the key to the sprinkler control box. He drove home but did not go inside. He walked the streets of Bountiful aimlessly thinking about the wonderful but tragic life he had experienced with Sharon. She had been beautiful and intelligent beyond his wildest dreams. She had made him incredibly happy and now she was gone. Kyle felt hate for Dr. Waters well up inside of him. For hours, it consumed him. Then he remembered something Josh had told him. Josh had said that God commands us to forgive all people, regardless of whether they are deserving of our forgiveness. We may still try to bring them to justice but only as we would any person in the wrong. He said that when we hate, we mostly hurt ourselves. Kyle had great respect for Josh and felt in his heart that what Josh had told him was right. Kyle had always prided himself on his self-control. He did not know if self-control alone could keep him from hating Dr. Waters, but he would try.

Kyle numbly went through the motions of the viewing and funeral services. He felt intense sorrow inside but did not know how to properly express it outwardly. His friends, including Ann, watched him helplessly. Nothing seemed to help him. He was incapable of consoling others, as his thoughts became more and more self-centered. After the services, Kyle realized that Sharon's car was still at the University. Kyle called for a cab and rode it to the engineering building parking lot. The car was nowhere in sight. He called campus security using his cell phone capability. "This is Kyle James. I left my car in the parking lot north of the engineering building several days ago and it's gone."

"Mr. James, surely you realize that a vehicle left that long would be towed and impounded. You will have to retrieve it from the city impound lot."

"Well, excusssse me!" retorted Kyle sarcastically. "I thought just maybe if a guy gave the university several million dollars and his wife was just murdered they would cut him a little slack but silly me." Kyle hung up before the woman could respond.

"Take me to the city impound lot," barked Kyle rudely to the driver of the cab that he still occupied. He could feel the rage building inside of him. Every muscle in his body tensed. The sinews on his neck stood out like those of a wrestler struggling against an opponent trying to pin him to the mat. The driver sensed the anger and sped to the destination. Kyle threw him a $100 bill and leaped from the cab when they arrived. He trotted to the office. Several people waited in line ahead of him. He snarled as he anticipated a long wait. He became even more irritated when, after a long wait, he was told to fill out a form and get back in line. By the time Kyle had paid his bill and gotten his car, he was ready to explode. After driving a short way, he noticed something was not right with the car and pulled over. His right front tire was flat. "I guess things couldn't get much worse," he growled to himself.

Suddenly he heard the screeching of tires. A black Mustang convertible had made a high-speed U-turn and was headed his way. Kyle actually grinned. Here was someone on whom he could rightly vent his anger. He figured he would annihilate then in hand-to-hand combat. Unfortunately, they did not have a fistfight in mind. They were not slowing to a stop. Kyle quickly retreated into a parking lot in what appeared to his foes to be a tactical blunder. They headed straight for him at high speed, intent on running him over. At the last moment, Kyle used his computer aided leaping ability to jump straight up in the air. The car passed under him colliding with the two-foot-high steel post that Kyle had been obscuring with his body. The post nearly cut the car in half as it completely ripped through the underbody of the vehicle. Kyle landed on the trunk of the car. He quickly spun around and jumped into the back seat. He swung inward his outstretched arms with his palms fully open and rigid. His palms impacted each of the airbag-stunned vehicle occupants on their ears and drove their heads together in a loud thud.

He then grabbed each of the stunned former jocks by the back of their necks, one in each large, powerful hand. Their once muscular necks had become soft and weak. It had been a year since they were kicked off the football team, something they blamed on Kyle. He began to squeeze until the bones made some popping sounds like those from a chiropractor's adjustment. A little more pressure and their necks would snap, leaving them paralyzed from the neck down. Suddenly, a memory flashed into Kyle's mind. He was sixteen. He could hear his mother outside of their duplex with a man. The man wanted to come in, but she told him no. She never let men come into their home.

"Look woman, I spend a lot of money wining and dining you and I expect something in return, you little whore." The man held her by her right arm and slapped her. Kyle flew out of the door and threw the man up against the brick wall of their home. Even at sixteen, Kyle was stoutly built with large muscular forearms. He rained fists of fury down on the slightly built man in his anger. His mother was all he had and no one was going to abuse her while he stood idly by. His mother started pulling at him.

"No, Kyle, stop. This slime is not worth sending you to jail. You will kill him if you don't stop." Kyle finally stopped beating the man and stood over him, breathing heavily. The stunned and terrified man managed to limp to his car and drive away. Kyle turned to his mother and enwrapped her in his powerful arms. After things had calmed down, his mother tried to turn the event into a positive experience for Kyle. "If you don't like men treating women poorly then you need to learn the right way to treat a woman yourself." From that day on Kyle's mother tutored him in not only how to treat a woman but how to understand one. She taught him how to read a woman's subtle body language and how to tell if one liked him. She taught him how to talk to a woman. He had controlled his temper for many years until today. Kyle's grip loosened a little.

"I could kill you both right now and it would be self-defense. No Utah jury would convict me. I could paralyze you both for life or I could send you both to jail for attempted murder. I can't stand the thought of making the state of Utah support a couple of scumbags like you. There is one other alternative. I will let you go if you promise to leave me alone once and for all. What do you think?" Kyle loosened his grip enough for them to speak. Both were crying like babies. Blood oozed from their mangled ears.

"We promise. We promise. Let us go and we will leave the state forever."

"Just in case you get any second thoughts, I have made a video recording of this incident and will send a copy to my lawyer with instructions to release it to the police if anything happens to me. Do you know who I am and what I am capable of?"

"We know who you are Doctor James," said one of the men. "You're a rich and powerful dude and have some sort of computer in your head. The way you jumped we would believe anything."

The next morning Kyle faxed a letter of resignation to CompuSonic. They really did not need him anymore and he felt like he would not be earning his high salary. After days of moping about, he finally decided to explore what new possibilities there were with his internal computers. For months, he had been experimenting with using the computer as a learning assistant. He had programmed it to help him memorize material by quizzing him at scientifically determined intervals. The approach was very effective. He had learned a great deal about music and could read music and identify the keys on the piano. He decided to try a more direct approach. If Annie had been able to learn Mrs. Monroe's memories by probing them, maybe he could reverse the process and create memories. He began experimenting. He did not use any theory, just brute-force trial and error. Little by little, he began to make progress. He discovered just what voltage levels and frequencies to use and how to encode information. After a week of around-the-clock work, he was able to directly download information into his brain. However, it was not like naturally acquired knowledge until he used it. He had to apply it to make the knowledge more than just a rapidly accessible database. After a few more days, he decided he needed a real challenge to fully develop the technology. He needed to enter a difficult field of study and try to master the material at accelerated rates. After some pondering, he decided to study medicine. He would enroll in medical school and take as many classes as he would be allowed to take.

When Kyle first talked with admissions they told him there was no possibility of him enrolling for the fall semester, which had already started. He tried a different approach. He contacted the appropriate people and explained that he wanted to donate several million dollars to the medical school. Recalling the "Sorenson" fiasco in which the University first agreed to rename the medical school after a donor and then reneged, losing a very large donation, Kyle said that he did not want anything named after him; he just wanted a few exceptions to the rules made on his behalf. He was quickly and painlessly admitted.

Chapter 18 – Kiss Worth Waiting for

Becoming a student again was the perfect medicine for Kyle's grief. It kept his mind too occupied to feel sorry for himself or angry at Dr. Waters. He was surprised to find that Ann Monroe had done the same thing as he had done. She had made a large donation and enrolled at the university just days before him. Because they were both starting from ground zero and taking the maximum classes allowable, they shared exactly the same class schedule. Normally, having someone like Kyle in the classroom would draw attention. Ann Monroe in the classroom almost completely drew attention away from Kyle. The men flocked to her. They could not believe that anyone so beautiful could be so witty and intelligent. She never took notes and never reviewed what she had read. Her reading speed was astounding. When the men found out that she was a rich widow, it only intensified their interest. About 50 percent of the freshman class was female, but many of them were almost unapproachable romantically. They did not want anyone thinking that they were there for anything other than an education. Few were particularly interested in Kyle. One, however, set her sights on him, Mikell Summers. She was very attractive but not as intelligent as Sharon had been. When Kyle started helping some fellow students with their studies, she quickly applied to Kyle for help. He helped her at first, but when he perceived her true intentions, he avoided her. Seeing that her tactics were not working, Mikell tried another approach. She became more serious in her studies and participated more in class. Kyle still showed her no interest. Growing impatient, she tried asking Kyle out. Kyle declined, explaining that he was still morning the loss of his late wife.

Nate often invited Kyle over for dinner and a movie. "So, have you heard anything from Nancy?" asked Kyle.

"Some sad news," responded Nate. "She got pregnant and when she refused to have an abortion, her bum of a husband divorced her. He saw her mainly as a breadwinner and could see that role diminishing. It makes me sick to think that she married a guy that didn't even love her. I offered him money to get lost and he jumped at the chance. I've set Nancy up in an apartment of her own. Her child is due in less than a month." There was a knock at the door. It turned out to be Josh.

"I saw Kyle's car outside and thought I'd let you both hear the good news. I'm getting married."

"That's great, Josh. Anyone we know?" asked Kyle.

"I doubt it. Her name is Becky Larsen. Her older brother was my best friend growing up. I've known her since we were kids. She was too young for me to ever ask out, but I took her to the prom once when her date got sick. We used to always joke that when she grew up we would marry. She's on an LDS mission in Chile right now."

"If she's on a mission then how did the romance advance?" asked Nate.

"We corresponded. We already knew each other well. She often tagged along with her brother when we did things as boys. We've always liked each other, just not in a romantic way. We just took it to the next level by mail. Here's a picture of her." Josh showed a picture of two women in long dresses and wearing nametags. "She's the tall one on the left." Becky was very tall and looked almost like a tent in her long dress. She did not look very shapely.

"Very nice," commented Kyle.

"Ditto," added Nate.

"I have to run," said Josh. "I'll see you guys later."

"Keep us updated on the romance," called Kyle to him as he walked to his car.

"Whoa, is it just me or was Josh's girl about two notches below his normal standard?" asked Nate after Josh left, finally able to speak his mind.

"She is no 'Bay Watch Babe' for sure, but I'm sure Josh has a good reason for wanting to marry her. Obviously, it isn't looks and with his newfound wealth, it certainly isn't for money. Maybe something you said years ago is the key. Didn't you say once that you wanted to marry a girl just like the one 'good ol Dad' did'?"

"Yea, but my mom's gorgeous."

"You've never met Josh's mom, have you?" asked Kyle.

"Never even seen a picture of her, except maybe a family photo Josh used to have over his desk, but I don't remember what she looked like."

"Picture Becky 30 years, and 8 or 10 children later and you have her. But let me tell you; the woman radiates love and goodness. She even helped me win Sharon by insisting that Josh and his sister teach me to dance. She's an angel in the flesh. And Josh's dad is nuts about her. You should see them dance together. I think Josh knows what he's doing. He wants a family like the one he came from and this missionary will help him do it. I wish him all the joy and happiness he can find."

At the medical school, Kyle and Ann avoided speaking to each other. Only occasionally was conversation required and then they spoke to each other like strangers. However, they often caught themselves looking at each other. Kyle was intrigued that a computer mind could be so human-like and sexy. Ann wasn't just beautiful; she oozed sex appeal from every pore. Men were intoxicated with her. Mere boys, ten years her junior acted like star-struck teenagers around her. Kyle admired how adeptly she handled them, giving encouragement to none but never hurting feelings or being rude. However, once a young man tried patting her on her curvaceous derriere. She deftly grasped his hand and twisted it into a very painful position. "You try that again and you will end up with a broken arm, expelled or both." She said nothing more about it and the young man was so embarrassed he distanced himself from Ann and never bothered her again. The incident made the rest of the men find her even more fascinating. She was like a woman out of a spy movie to them, a woman of mystery.

By the second semester, Ann's novelty began to wear off a little and some of her following dwindled, mainly because no one had gotten anywhere with her. Most moved on to easier pickings, but all continued to watch her. During the second semester, Kyle began to sit closer to Ann and even engage her in conversation, mainly concerning schoolwork and technical issues. Once Ann commented, "I see you have managed to do in reverse what Annie did. Congratulations."

"Thank you," briefly responded Kyle, not wanting to let others know what they were talking about but impressed with Ann's perceptiveness.

Kyle continued to have dinner frequently with Nate, now often joined by Nancy. Usually, her daughter, Felicity, accompanied her. One night, after Nancy had gone home, Nate made a special request of Kyle. "It really hurts a girl's self-esteem to be dumped. Nancy is feeling kind of low. I know that you found Nancy attractive and interesting years ago, would you mind asking her out and showing her a good time? It would mean a lot to me, Kyle. This time, no restrictions, other than to be the perfect, virtuous gentleman that you have always been. I love the woman so much it hurts. She deserves the best, someone like you."

"I'd be happy to ask her out, Nate, but I think you're the man for her," responded Kyle.

"Don't play with me, Kyle. I've never had your looks. Besides, Nancy is too good for me. Just treat her right and let nature take its course." In a few days, Kyle asked Nancy out and she readily accepted on condition that he take her dancing as part of the date. He took her to dinner and then dancing at a private club that he and Sharon had joined. They had a wonderful time and Kyle was beginning to feel like he could love again, especially with a bright and beautiful woman like Nancy. As he returned her home, he contemplated kissing her at the doorstep.

"Kyle, I had a wonderful time. You're a great dancer and a fun guy. I'd love to go out anytime you want, but just remember that I'll never love another tall, good-looking guy. I prefer the short, dark, less than handsome type of man. The kind that will be true and faithful, forever." Then she kissed Kyle on the cheek and went inside.

With all of his buying and selling, Kyle owed millions in taxes, which forced him to sell more stock to pay the taxes, resulting in additional tax obligations for the new year. In the past, he had mainly had to worry about paying social-security tax, being self employed. He had promised himself when he was poor that if he ever became wealthy, he would not complain about paying taxes. He gritted his teeth and sold the stock and paid the taxes, knowing that he would have to repeat the process in the coming year.

By the end of the second semester, Kyle was sitting next to Ann in every class. The other men could see that Ann treated Kyle very differently from them. Most concluded it was because he was older and similarly widowed and wealthy. Most realized that Ann was out of their league and moved into a role of following the development of the budding relationship. They were not accustomed to such patience between two students attracted to each other. Several of them had already bedded several coeds while these two had only managed to sit closer to each other. This slowness of development made the relationship even more intriguing. The last week of the semester Kyle began walking Ann to class and spending more time with her. She was so easy to talk to and so much more socially mature than were the women his age. He liked that in a woman. She also had an excellent sense of humor. She knew thousands of jokes and funny stories and always knew exactly when and which to use. She had Kyle laughing again. "What are your plans this summer, Ann?" inquired Kyle as they sat on the cool grass between classes.

"I will take all of the summer school classes that I can. How about you?"

"I'll do the same and also work on the car I've been thinking about. I decided to build my own electric car rather than buy one. I know it isn't cost or time effective, but I have plenty of time and money."

"Would you like some help? You know that if I don't know something I can quickly find it out."

"I'd love the help. But I have to ask you one thing. If it weren't for your prime directive would you still like me?"

"Who said I like you, maybe I just like to work on cars?" teased Ann.

"Come on, Ann. I'm not one of those silly classmates. You're a very attractive woman to me, but I have to know if I'm attractive to you on my own or if you are just following programming."

"My programming doesn't say I have to get romantically involved with you. Annette had no such programming and she thought you were a stud, unlike Carlton, who, although very handsome was never the hunk that Annette truly wanted. She always found you more attractive in your virile sort of way, at least after you bulked up. She would not have minded you putting on another twenty pounds of muscle." She wrapped her sensuous fingers around Kyle's upper arms. "She liked and I like an intelligent he-man. It is a hard combination to find. Besides, we are an attractive version of Frankenstein and Bride of Frankenstein. We were made for each other." With that, Ann wrapped her hands around Kyle's neck and kissed him affectionately. Kyle looked up and saw that a crowd had gathered and were watching intently. When the crowd saw they had been caught in the act of eavesdropping, they broke into applause. The couple retreated to their next class. The whispers flew in the classroom and Kyle was comforted that there were only two days left of class. After their last class that day, Ann took Kyle's arm and whispered to him, "There is something we need to do before things advance any further between us. Come to my house for dinner at six tonight."

Ann had a simple, yet delicious, dinner waiting for Kyle at her home. During dinner, Ann explained their unfinished business. "I have been watching you since the tragic deaths of Carlton and Sharon. Other than in the ambulance, I have not seen you outwardly grieve for your loss. I think you need to. I cannot complete my grieving alone. We both loved Carlton and Sharon. It is only natural and appropriate that we share in that grieving together."

"I don't know how to do that. I didn't even outwardly grieve for my mother," Kyle paused and began to tear up, "except that time at dinner with Sharon."

"My point, exactly. You needed Sharon to help you grieve for your mother and you need me to help you grieve the loss of your wife and my best friend and my husband and your best friend. I don't have to tell you how wonderful they were. How much they meant to me. I never had a close friend in my adult life until I became friends with Sharon. We laughed and cried together. We had fun like a couple of teenage girls. We even got scared together."

"I was the most important person in the world to Sharon," began Kyle. "I can't tell you how much that meant to me. She would have given her life for me. She did give her life for me. She knew I'd try to save Carlton. She took my place and gave her life in the process." Kyle began to lose his composure. "I've been lost without her." By now, Kyle was heaving in sobs. Ann had quickly moved to his side and put her arms around his shoulders. She said nothing. She just let him weep. He stood and they embraced each other as they wept together. After several minutes, Kyle finally stopped weeping. "Wait a minute," he suddenly broke forth. "When did you and Sharon ever get scared together?"

"I guess she never told you of our fears. Do you remember the serial rapist that was allegedly castrated last summer? We were convinced that Annie did it."

"Well, did she, you or whatever?"

"We don't know for certain since Annie and Annette both were missing several hours of memory. It was just like we talked about at the dinner, except that it wasn't just a tack on a chair. Carlton got a call from Dr. Sanchez, chief administrator of the University of Hospital. He told Carlton that he had overpaid him for the use of the portable laboratory. The invoice indicated that it had been used the same day as the missing memories. Carlton didn't know what he was talking about, but Sharon and I were sure that Annie had performed the castration in that operating room. What other explanation could there be?"

"I don't know. Are there any other clues?"

"Yes, there was a bandaged incision on my abdomen, right here." Ann pointed to the place. That is why we both got tattoos of a small rose. We figured that in the struggle the rapist stabbed me there."

"I wondered why Sharon did that," Kyle chuckled. "She hated tattoos. She always told me how absurd they were and how glad she was that I didn't have any. Then she came home with one. Well, actually, I didn't even notice it for weeks. Sharon was always very modest around me. I had to keep reminding her we were married. Show me your scar, if you don't mind, that is." Ann lifted her blouse just enough to reveal the tattoo. Kyle examined it very closely and felt it. He began to laugh hysterically.

"What's so funny?" Ann demanded. Kyle lifted his shirt and pointed to an almost identical scar on his abdomen. Now Ann began to laugh too. "I get it now. You had an appendectomy, and so did I. Annie must have shut down Annette to do the operation and then wiped out her own memories so she would not have to lie to Annette. She could not take a chance on Annette going to the hospital since it might be revealed that she was brain dead. Who knows what the Annette program might have done at that point if she knew what had really happened? She was upset enough that Annie had used her body for several weeks."

"Speaking of use of your body, there's one thing that I don't understand. We only connected a minimum of lower body sensory nerves, yet you seem to have full feeling."

"I used the larger 'snakes' to grasp whole nerve bundles and slowly pull them to the 'snake' chips where connection could be made. In some cases, I moved the bundles several centimeters. Over a period of weeks, I was able to become fully connected. The Mrs. Monroe program thought that her brain was recovering from the bullet wound. She never suspected what was happening."

The rest of the evening was spent in pleasant reminiscing. When Kyle left at a little before eleven that night he felt like a tremendous burden had been lifted from him. He felt whole again. He also was in love with the most unique, beautiful and intelligent woman in the world. She was about five years older than he, but that was of no more concern than was Sharon being three years older. He knew Ann was the only woman for him and he was confident that his affections would be reciprocated. Kyle actually sang as he drove home.

The next night the couple celebrated the ending of school with dinner and dancing. Kyle wanted an excuse to hold Ann in his arms. She felt wonderful to him as they held each other. He nearly proposed on the dance floor.

In a back alley in Los Angeles, two men got out of their cars. Each carried a briefcase, one full of money and the other full of cocaine. The taller of the two men set his case on the hood of his black Chrysler 300. The other set his case alongside the first. They both popped open the latches and lifted the lids. Each inspected the other's goods. "Let's do it," said the taller man. They closed the cases and exchanged them. Suddenly, one swatted his neck as he felt a sting. Soon both men were fighting off bumblebees. In a panic, they each dropped their loads and ran for their lives. The bees continued to chase them, now herding them more than attacking them. A rope ladder descended from the dark sky. A young man scampered down the ladder and leaped to the ground. He opened each case, dumping the money into a backpack from which he pulled a can of charcoal lighter fluid. He soaked the drugs with the liquid and tossed a match into the case. He threw the backpack on his shoulders and hurried back up the ladder as it ascended into the black night.

Chapter 19 – Mourn with Those Who Mourn

Kyle drove to the home of his in-laws without calling ahead. Now that Ann had helped him resolve his own grief, he had to do the same for Sharon's loving parents. He had not spoken to them since the funeral and had been of little comfort then, being so wrapped up in his own grief and anger. Kyle stood nervously at the door and rang the doorbell. Verona opened the door and looked up at Kyle with a look of confusion. "Mother, I am so sorry for the way that I have neglected you and Robert. I have been so lost since Sharon's death. I have driven the car that you gave to Sharon and lived in the home that was her graduation present from you and Robert and have made no effort to comfort you, nor considered that you might want the car and the condo. Please forgive me. I have been a fool." Kyle held out the car keys. "The title is in the glove box."

"Thank you, Kyle, but I think that Sharon would have wanted you to keep the car and live in the condo." Suddenly she burst into tears and threw herself into his arms. They embraced and each sobbed like a small child.

"I loved her so much! I was never happier than when we were together. She was a wonderful friend and wife. Now you and Robert are the only family I have left." Robert, who had been listening from just inside came out onto the porch and threw his long arms around Kyle and Verona.

"Come in, Kyle. We have missed you."

After a successful visit with Sharon's parents, Kyle went on to visit Carlton's parents and siblings. Last of all, he visited Carlton's youngest sister, Megan. Megan was the baby of the family and was younger than Kyle. She had married young, had two children and was widowed when her husband was killed in an automobile/bicycle accident. In spite of the age difference, she and Carlton had been very close. It was evening when Kyle rang the doorbell of the modest home. He could hear Megan's five-year-old, Amanda, running to the door. Megan caught up with Amanda and was there as the door opened. Megan stared at Kyle. "Kyle?"

"Yes, I am pleased that you remember me. I'm here to apologize. At the funeral, I was so overwhelmed with my own grief that I failed to offer comfort to others. I should have been especially attentive to your needs, realizing that within a couple of years you had lost both your husband and your closest sibling. I am so sorry for your loss."

"Come in, Kyle. Have a seat. Can I get you anything?"

"Just a glass of water, please." Kyle sat down on the sofa and looked around at the modest but tastefully decorated room. Amanda shyly approached him, followed by her younger brother, Carl, who had been named after Carlton. They were very cute children. Amanda had long dark hair that was prettily arranged. She had lovely big brown eyes. As Megan reentered the room with a glass of ice water, Kyle looked up and realized that Amanda looked very much like her mother who had Carlton's striking good looks but in a feminine version. She was tall and slender, with an olive complexion. Her face was perfectly formed with beautiful, large brown eyes, a well-formed nose and mouth. Kyle stood and took the proffered water.

Megan sat in an overstuffed chair next to Kyle's end of the couch. "Kyle, I was as much at fault as you. I too was overcome with grief. After my husband's death, I had relied heavily on Carlton for emotional support. Carlton became a father image for my children. They miss him as much or maybe even more than I do." Amanda had worked her way to between Kyle's legs. He reached down and gently picked her up. He placed her on his right knee with his right arm around her. Carl quickly filled the vacancy between his legs. Kyle picked him up and placed him on his left knee. Megan smiled. "That is just how they would sit with Carlton." She started to tear up.

Kyle whispered to Amanda, "Your mom needs a hug." He helped her down so that she could fulfill the assignment. Amanda tried to hug her mother but found it awkward so she took her mother by the hand and tried to drag her out of the chair. Megan stood and Amanda hugged her leg and then dragged her mother to the sofa and bid her sit. Megan sat next to Kyle. Amanda moved to between Kyle's legs.

"I am too little; you hug her." Kyle raised his right arm and to his surprise, Megan leaned into him. Kyle was not looking to start up a second romance when he had just gotten one going with Ann but cautiously put his arm around Megan. Megan softly wept with her head on Kyle's heavily muscled chest. Kyle had never thought much about being a father, other than to decide that he was totally unqualified for the job, not having had a father of his own in his life. Although the timing was terrible and the situation very awkward, Kyle enjoyed the intimate contact with this beautiful woman and her children. It gave him a small glimpse of what being a father could be like and it felt wonderful to him.

The children moved in closer with Amanda now back on his knee leaning against Kyle and Megan. First Carl and then Amanda fell asleep. Then, to Kyle's surprise, Megan also fell asleep. Kyle hoped that he was truly bringing comfort to this little family. Kyle wiggled a toe to trigger a sounding of the time in his left ear. It was nearly nine o'clock. Finally, Kyle dozed off. He and Megan were stirred to alertness when the landline phone rang. Kyle lifted his left arm letting Megan extricate herself and answer the phone. Kyle deduced from what he could hear of the conversation that Megan was needed to fill a shift at the hospital. She was explaining that it was very late notice for her to find a babysitter.

"I can stay with the children," offered Kyle in a stage whisper. "If you don't find that inappropriate, that is."

"Just a minute," Megan said into the phone. She looked at Kyle. "You would do that for me?"

"Sure. School is over. I am currently unemployed. It's better than going back to a lonely apartment."

"Thank you so much. I need the extra income." She put the phone back up to her mouth and said, "A family friend just volunteered. I will be there shortly." Megan hung up and walked back to Kyle, who still sat with two children on his lap. She bent down and kissed him right on the lips. "Thank you for everything, Kyle." It was just a peck but the kiss shocked Kyle. Kyle knew that some women are naturally touchy; they like to touch and hold and be touched and held and it did not necessarily have anything to do with romance. It was how they showed friendship and he should not read too much into it. Other than the computer program, Annette, Kyle had never had a non-romantic friendship with a woman. Megan was far too pretty for him to sustain this kind of association without developing romantic feelings. He would have to be careful not to let things get out of hand. Working together, Kyle and Megan put the children into their beds. Megan changed into her certified nurse's assistant uniform in her bedroom while Kyle made her a sandwich to take. He bagged it with an apple and an orange. It felt just like being married. Oh, how he had loved being married. He started to tear up thinking about how much he missed Sharon and missed having a full-time companion.

Megan entered the kitchen and saw the sack that Kyle had prepared for her. She looked inside and smiled. "You must have been a fabulous husband." She looked up and saw the tear in the corner of Kyle's left eye. "You miss being married, don't you? Don't worry, guys like you don't stay single long." With that, Megan was out the door and off to work. Kyle was concerned that his car, the Viper, no less, was parked in front of the house overnight and might start rumors in the neighborhood. He did not want anything to sully the reputation of this fine woman and mother. He pulled the sofa in front of the window and opened the curtains. He left the light on so that any spying neighbors could clearly see that he was not sleeping with Megan. The only article of clothing that he removed was his shoes.

Kyle called Ann using his headphone and told her all about his day, including where he was and what he was doing. "You have to understand, Kyle, that as the baby of the family Megan was held and kissed by her parents, siblings, aunts and uncles way past the age of the older children. To her disappointment, her husband, although a fine man, liked his personal space and was not a cuddler. It was a great disappointment to Megan and a frustration to her children who wanted their father to hold and comfort them. When she first met Annette she tried to hug her but was rebuffed. When the post-shooting Annette hugged her, she was very receptive to the affection. Don't be afraid to hug her or even give her a plutonic kiss." Kyle could not imagine Sharon having told him to kiss another woman, especially one as pretty as Megan. Rather than being offended by Sharon's jealousy, he had found it comforting. Sharon loved him and wanted him. It was so comforting to be loved and wanted. Maybe Ann could love him and want him without the extreme jealousy that Sharon had exhibited.

After the phone call, Kyle drifted off to sleep with fond memories of Ann on his mind. He awoke around five when he felt Amanda trying to climb up onto him. He sat up and let her nuzzle in next to him. Eventually, they were joined by Carl. As Megan pulled up to her home, she could see through the front window Kyle and her children all asleep on the sofa in its new location. Megan instantly understood why Kyle had moved the sofa. What a man, she thought to herself. He had let Megan hug and kiss him without any negative reaction but without taking it as a signal that she wanted to jump in the sack with him. And to be so helpful and considerate of her reputation. She could go the rest of her life without meeting another man like Kyle. Somehow, though, she had the impression that another woman had already sunk her claws into his delightfully muscular flesh. She had to manage her expectations. Even if she could not marry him, she was determined to keep him around as much and as long as possible. She pulled into the driveway and exited the car as quietly as possible. She entered the house through the back door so as not to wake anyone. She flopped on her bed without even undressing and fell into a deep sleep.

Kyle was awakened by the children, who had each been awake for several minutes. They were trapped in place by Kyle's embrace and needed to answer nature's call. Fortunately, Carl was potty trained and needed no special assistance. There were two bathrooms in the house and a child rushed to each as Kyle freed them from his grasp. Kyle wandered into the kitchen to see what he could fix for breakfast. The fridge contained milk, eggs and cheese, among other things. After his own bathroom break, he quizzed the children on what they would like for breakfast. To his surprise, they asked for an omelet like the ones that Uncle Carlton used to make for them. Kyle called Ann and asked for instructions on how to make the omelet. The children hung around the kitchen asking Kyle questions and sometimes hugging his legs. He had to be careful not to trip over them.

After breakfast and dishes, Kyle quizzed the children on what they would like to do while their mother slept. Several suggestions were proffered, but the consensus was that they wanted to go to the zoo. Kyle got the children dressed and groomed, again calling Ann for help with Amanda's hair. Ann suggested that he take a stroller for when Carl got tired. Realizing that the Viper would be totally inappropriate for the children, having no back seat, Kyle located the keys to the family Corolla and checked out the car seat arrangement.

The backseat contained a car seat and a booster seat. He opened the trunk to see if he needed to remove anything to fit in the stroller, which he had not yet located. A two-seater stroller was already stored in the trunk. With continual guidance from Ann, Kyle prepared a diaper bag, drinks and snacks for the excursion. Last of all, Kyle left a note on the kitchen counter with the key to the Viper acting as a paperweight. The children were disappointed that they could not ride in the shiny red car, but Kyle showed them how it lacked a back seat.

Kyle loaded supplies and children and started the family car. As he examined the instrument gauges, he noticed two things. The car had accumulated many miles and the gas tank was nearly empty. He drove to the nearest gas station and filled up. The station had a convenience store and an automatic carwash. The children begged to go through the car wash. Kyle obliged and as the car moved through the tunnel with water spraying and brushes whirling, he could see how it would be exciting to young children. Finally, they were off to Hogle Zoo. Being a weekday and still early, parking was easy to find inside of the main lot. Kyle extracted children, supplies and stroller. As Kyle made his way to the entrance, he pondered about how challenging it must be for mothers of several young children, especially when newborns were thrown into the mix. His admiration of young mothers skyrocketed.

Kyle had never been to a zoo. He found himself as excited and wonder-filled as the children. Occasionally he would catch glimpses of Ann, who had apparently come to the zoo in case he needed help with the children. Megan was a pretty woman, but Ann was strikingly attractive with a voluptuous, yet lean figure and a face worthy of a Greek goddess.

Kyle did great with the children until Amanda needed to use the restroom. Did he let Amanda go into the women's restroom alone, or did he take all of the children with him into the men's restroom?

He could envision all sorts of bad outcomes with either approach. He silently called Ann for advice. She appeared out of nowhere. The children squealed with delight at the sight of Aunt Annette. Ann offered to take Amanda to the girl's room while Kyle took Carl to the boy's room.

After the bathroom break, Ann continued with the group. Amanda held her hand as they walked, but when the children would play at one of the little playgrounds, Ann would put her arm around Kyle and even stole a kiss now and then. It all reminded Kyle of why he loved this unique woman. He had never thought of Ann as a potential mother, but as he watched her with the children, he realized that Ann, given the chance, would make a wonderful parent.

When the children grew tired, Kyle and Ann loaded them up in the Corolla. "Want me to tag along?" asked Ann.

"Sure, if you don't mind."

"I can't think of a thing that I would rather do right now. I'll see you there." The Corolla and the Mercedes headed to the children's home. Carl fell asleep on the way home, but Amanda was bubbling with enthusiasm and talk of the zoo and what she saw there. Kyle had never had much opportunity to listen to young children and he found Amanda's chatter very pleasant. His listening was interrupted by a call on his internal phone. It was Ann asking if she should pick up something for lunch. After a three-way discussion, it was determined that Amanda did not want takeout; with her mother's work schedule she got far more takeout and fast food than she wanted. Carlton used to fix them lasagna, which they loved. Ann purchased everything that went into making lasagna, including the baking dish. While she was shopping, Kyle had unloaded the children and gotten them into bed for their naps. Ann arrived with the supplies and brought them into the kitchen. Together they prepared the lasagna and a green salad. Once the lasagna was in the oven Ann left. While the children slept, Kyle conversed with

Ann over his internal cell phone. He told her about how much he had enjoyed the children. Ann assured him that he would make a wonderful father. Kyle set the table, including a place for Megan, in case she awoke in time to join them.

Carl wandered silently into the kitchen and put his arms around Kyle's legs. Kyle picked him up and carried him while he went about his preparations. Soon Amanda joined them. Kyle put Carl in the highchair and seated Amanda on a booster chair and started them on salad.

"We need to say a prayer," protested Amanda.

"Would you like to say it?" asked Kyle.

"No, you say it." Kyle knew that Carlton's whole family was Catholic and the children would be used to hearing a memorized prayer. He had heard it enough times to almost know it but not quite. He quickly called Ann and she led him through the prayer. Amanda was satisfied and they all ate. The oven timer sounded and Kyle removed the lasagna from the oven so that it could cool. Soon they were all eating lasagna. The children chattered about things that they had seen at the zoo.

Megan had awoken and was secretly listening to the conversation. This Kyle kept getting better and better. He had taken the kids to the zoo and now was feeding them lasagna. She didn't even have the makings in the house. Did he go shopping with the children? No. There was mention of Aunt Annette. Well, that was smart, getting help from Annette. Megan chuckled to herself about how there were other family members who could use a shot to the head to straighten them out. It had done wonders for Annette. Megan knew that she looked far from her best so she showered and dressed in fresh clothes.

When Megan entered the kitchen all were still seated at the table, but the eating was over and Amanda was chattering while Carl played with the leftover food on his tray. "Well, you certainly can't buy this kind of service, zoo and their favorite meal."

"Hello, Megan, did work go okay?" Megan was dishing herself up some lasagna.

"Yea, fine. I slept well too, knowing that the children were in good hands. You have been a lifesaver."

"It was just a case of serendipity. You have wonderful children. We had great fun together. I have almost no experience with children, but things went really well."

"The lasagna is delicious. I didn't know that you cook."

"I don't really. What I fix for myself is kinda primitive. Annette did the shopping and helped prepare the lasagna." Kyle stayed and visited for a few more minutes and then headed home.

Kyle called his lawyer and had him set up a trust fund for the education of Carl and Amanda when they reached college age. They also set up a trust fund that would allow Megan to seek additional education, including advanced degrees if she desired to pursue them.

A few days later Kyle arranged to visit Megan and the children with Nancy and Felicity. Amanda was fascinated by the baby and loved to spend time with her. Nancy and Megan talked about babysitting for each other. They fell into a comfortable and enjoyable friendship. Both craved adult company and even though Megan had missed out on getting much formal education, she was very intelligent and well informed on many subjects. They soon discovered that it was often easier and more enjoyable to go places as a group.

Chapter 20 – Runaway Truck

Kyle and Ann ran along a warm sunny beach in the Bahamas. They looked like a couple out of the television series Bay Watch. He was muscular and lean. She had a curvaceous figure devoid of flaws. They ran gracefully on the beach at the edge of the surf. Each had their arm around the other in an affectionate embrace. It was a perfect honeymoon, thought Kyle. Kyle turned his head to gaze at his stunningly beautiful new wife. Ann's eyes met his. With their eyes off the path, Kyle tripped over a piece of driftwood and pulled Ann down with him. Her right leg struck a sharp rock with sufficient force to tear open the skin and peel it back several inches. Kyle rushed to provide first aid, but Ann seemed unconcerned and in no pain. From the wound oozed a reddish fluid that felt to Kyle like power steering fluid. He looked at Ann in horror. "Don't worry my love," she responded. "I can easily repair the damage."

"But how, why?" he pleaded.

"You didn't want me to grow any older, did you? I got rid of the biological body and have designed myself a new one. Isn't it wonderful?" Kyle screamed, waking himself. He bolted straight up in bed and turned on a light. "What am I about to do?" he asked himself aloud. "I was ready to propose to a computer, a machine. It doesn't matter the pretty package. Ann has a non-biological mind." There was no one Kyle could talk to for advice. He was the only one living, besides Ann, that understood the situation. He was alone with no one to counsel him. How could he even have considered marrying Ann? It was unnatural, perverted. He remembered that Ann was out of town until later that morning. He called her landline and left a message. "Ann, I don't think we should see each other for awhile and when we do, just as friends. This probably is painful to you. For that, I am sorry. Bye."

Kyle showered, shaved and dressed. He remembered that he had not checked the mail. He walked down to the communal mailbox and unlocked his individual box. There were the usual credit card applications and other junk mail. One envelope stood out from the rest. The address was hand-written and the sender was Catherine Polanski, a woman Kyle vaguely remembered his mother talking about. She was one of his mother's coworkers. Not really a close friend but the closest thing his mother had to one. Kyle wondered why she would be writing him. He tore open the envelope while still at the box.

Dear Kyle,

You probably don't remember me. I knew your mother well. Before she died, she gave me some things she wanted you to have. I was supposed to give them to you one year after your mother's death, but I misplaced them for several years and forgot about them. I found them in the crawl space of the home I have been renting. I will mail them if I don't hear from you. I will give you a few days to contact me before I ship them.

Catherine

Kyle went straight to the Viper and headed for Wendover, Nevada. He drove with the window down with the wind swirling around him. It helped to relax him. The trip went quickly and soon he was at the front door of the woman. He figured her work would not start until later in the day. His knocking and ringing got her out of bed. She was not happy to be disturbed and seeing who it was through the peephole, she opened the door and shoved a cardboard box out the door, onto the porch and shut and locked the door. Kyle picked up the box and carried it to his car. He did not want to be seen hanging around a known prostitute's house, so he decided to drive to the cemetery where his mother was buried. He grabbed the box and walked to his mother's grave. He began going through the things in the box. There were cheerleading trophies and scholastic awards. Any awards that had a name of a place or a school had the name blotted out, filed off or carved out. He could see that at one time, his mother had been very accomplished, but he did not know where. Finally, at the bottom, he found an envelope with his name on it. He slowly opened it; he suspected that it would reveal some things about his mother that he was not sure he wanted to know.

Dear Kyle,

If you are reading this, I am dead and buried. You have been so much better of a son than I have been a mother. I failed you in so many ways. As you might have gathered from the contents of the box, if you received them, I was not always such a failure. I was an excellent student in high school. I was also in student body government and was a cheerleader all four years (we didn't have just three years of high school like you had). I was valedictorian and spoke at my graduation. I was also very active in the church that my family attended. I had everything in life going my way until our graduation party. This was not a party sponsored by the school. It was a wild party held at some rich kid's home whose parents were on a cruise. The guy throwing it didn't even graduate. The alcohol flowed freely. I decided to stick with the "punch". For an "A" student I was pretty dumb. Before I realized what was happening I was drunk. Then I started drinking everything that was handed me, at least that's what they told me afterwards. In my drunken state, a number of the boys there took advantage of me. I can't even remember who they were or how many there were. I woke up the next morning on the front lawn, half-naked. My father was so angry he beat me without even asking what happened.

When I turned out to be pregnant, the very boys who raped me shunned me at church. I was the victim but was treated like I was the one deserving of all blame. My parents decided to ship me off to live with an aunt in California. I'd only met this aunt once and found her very cold and judgmental. I knew living with her would be hell. I played along with the deal. My parents put me on a bus with a one-way ticket to LA. I rode as far as Nevada, where I jumped ship. I tried to get a job for days, but no one wanted to hire a pregnant girl with no work experience. Finally, one man offered to let me do some office work for him until the baby was born and promised to pay all of the medical expenses and give me two months off with pay after the baby was born. There, of course, was one stipulation. When I went back to work for him it would be as one of his "girls".

I am telling you this so that you know that I didn't just decide when I was a little girl that I wanted to be a hooker when I grew up. I did it mostly for you so that you would receive the nourishment and medical care that you needed. I felt so guilty about my employment that I turned to alcohol to make me forget. I know that was wrong and a cop-out, but that is why I did it.

I never told you my past because I didn't want you to be bitter about life. I haven't let you know my former family, community or church because I didn't want you to be bitter about them. I am telling you all of this now so that you will be careful how you judge others. It's hard to know what's in the heart of another. A person who outwardly seems good and respectable may inwardly be vile and evil. On the other hand, a person who appears wicked may have a good heart. Look beyond outward appearances and at the heart, especially as you seek a wife and I trust that you will marry the woman that you love, in spite of the trends of the world. I'm not suggesting that you marry someone out of sympathy. Such a match usually has tragic results. Rather, I am suggesting that you look at a person's desires for good and potential to be good. If you love a woman, don't let concerns about what others would say or think keep you from marrying her, if she's right for you. You have great potential, son. Use it wisely.

Love,

Mom

Kyle wept as he read the letter. He had never pictured his mother as anything other than a drunken whore. How wrongfully he had judged her. He wondered what his mother would have thought about Ann. He thought about how he felt when he was with Ann. He considered that she was a virtuous and loving woman who would be completely loyal to him. He had no doubt that, like Sharon, she would give her life for him, if needed, without a moment's hesitation. He wondered if he would do the same for her, or would he just say that she was a computer. He stood over his mother's grave and spoke. "Mother, I don't suppose that you can hear me, but I'm going to talk to you anyway. I haven't been the kind of son I should have been to you. Oh, I never gave you any trouble, but I didn't show you love the way that I should have. I judged you constantly in my heart. When you were alive, I knew that I was the most important person in the world to someone. I lost that when you died. I regained it when I married Sharon. I wish you could have known her. She was wonderful. She made me very happy. I miss her terribly. I miss you terribly. I could be loved that way again if I will only let it happen, but I'm afraid. I may have already done irreparable damage to the relationship." Kyle stopped and thought. It wasn't too late. He could get to Ann's and erase the message. "Sorry, Mom, I gotta run." Kyle threw the box in the car and sped off. He normally was a very conservative driver, but he put the pedal to the metal this time. The response of the Viper did not disappoint him. It had awesome raw power.

Ann decided that rather than heading straight home from her visit to Grantsville, she would make a short visit to the Kennecott Copper open-pit mine. Even though she had lived in Utah many years, she had never been to this major tourist attraction. As she turned off of Highway 201 (2100 South) and headed south on Highway 111 (8400 West in Magna) she passed a busload of children that was in the northbound lane of traffic but appeared to be broken down. To make matters worse, road construction narrowed the flow of traffic to one lane going each way. It was a very awkward and dangerous situation. She got past the construction area and continued south. The road had a significant incline along the whole stretch and got much steeper as she left the city area and continued heading south. After passing through the traffic light at 4100 South, she was startled by the honking of a very loud horn, a truck horn. A truck flew by her heading north at over 70 miles per hour and ran the light, which was now red to north-south traffic. The truck clipped the front end of a car that had entered the intersection causing it to spin 270 degrees. Ann remembered that over the years there had been people killed in runaway truck accidents on this stretch of road. She was quite sure that the truck had lost its brakes. Normally, Ann had a stream of consciousness comparable to a normal person. In emergencies, she could greatly speed up her rate of thought by reassigning processing power that was normally devoted to bodily functions. She began making quick calculations in her mind and was sure that without some action on her part the truck would collide at a high rate of speed with the school bus or with a large number of cars. If she were to prevent a tragedy, she needed help.

Annie had left herself a "backdoor" means of communication with each of her brother and sister computers. By means of radio communication, she could contact any or all. She first contacted Vic who had the greatest knowledge of physics. She also contacted Eve who ran a radio station. Soon many computers were working on a solution. The first thing that Ann did was make a high speed, racecar driver style U-turn and accelerated to get in front of the truck. She used her radio capabilities to act as a GPS receiver to determine position and direction. This information was relayed to the other computers. Civil authorities were notified and instructed to cut off the flow of traffic from the South. The traffic lights were controlled to stop traffic flow into the area near the bus. A plan for slowing down the truck was formulated in a fraction of a second.

Fortunately, Ann's older model Mercedes sedan did not have anti-lock brakes. Otherwise, the plan would not have worked. Ann slowed until contact was made with the truck's front bumper. Using both the brake pedal and the emergency brake, Ann caused the rear tires to lock up and the front wheels to brake hard. This was done to prevent burning out the rear brakes. By modulating the brakes to distribute the erosion of rubber from the rear tires, the greatest life was derived from the tires, which happened to be nearly new. With the first hard brake, the truck bumper began to climb up onto the back of the car, putting more weight over the rear wheels and thus increasing their traction. By not locking up the front wheels, Ann was able to steer. As the truck crept higher and higher onto the back of the car, the truck began to lose its own ability to steer and had to rely on Ann to steer both vehicles. Ann detected the frequency of the superheterodyne radio receiver in the truck radio, which the driver had left on during the emergency. She was able to determine the frequency that the tuner was picking up and override the broadcast signal by simultaneously broadcasting from 100 of her CPUs. "Hello, good buddy," she spoke over the radio to the driver. "This is the driver in front of you speaking. The situation is even worse than you know. There is construction ahead and a bus full of children broken down in our lane of traffic. It may not seem like it, but I am here to help. That smoke you see is my rear tires burning up. They should blow in about thirty seconds. That is part of the plan. If they didn't blow my brakes would burn up since with the added weight on the rear wheels the brakes soon would not be strong enough to lock up the wheels. However, they will be strong enough to lock up the rear rims. I have already slowed you to 60 miles per hour. I should be able to get us slowed to between 10 and 15 miles per hour by the time we reach the bus. The driver has been notified and the children are being unloaded from the bus as we speak. We have over 20 very powerful computers helping us. We will get through this thing together.

"You are probably very scared right now. So am I. You will live. The children should live. I cannot say whether I will make it or not. My car will be sandwiched between you and the bus, but that is the only way to save everyone else. It's okay; I am living on borrowed time anyway." There was a loud explosive sound as the right rear tire blew out. It was quickly followed by the left rear tire blowing. "There go the tires, right on schedule. Everything is under control. I am now going to waggle from side to side to work my way farther under you. That way I will have more braking force. We are down to 50 miles per hour. Half of the children are out of the bus. The rims are holding out well." Something suddenly occurred that was unforeseen. Ann hit a large chuckhole with her right front tire. With all of the extra weight resting on the car, the force ripped the wheel right off of the car. Now the front right side was skidding along with the two back rims. Ann was still able to steer with the remaining front left tire. The truck shifted even farther onto the car.

"You are getting kind of close for someone I don't even know, good buddy. That was scary, but my computer friends say it may have even helped to slow us down. Your sitting on top of me has cut off my GPS capability and the speedometer doesn't work now. From watching things go by, I would say that we are below 40 miles per hour. The road is flattening, which will help our deceleration. You should be able to see the bus by now." The left front tire blew. "Looks like I won't be steering anymore. The curb should guide us to the bus. I will keep talking, but I doubt you will be able to hear me with all of the metal between us. I am going to do some shifting around in here. This vehicle of mine is beginning to feel very cramped." Ann moved to the passenger side of the car and wrapped herself into a tight ball in front of the seat. The last child had to be carried off the bus. The driver jumped from the bus just as the front of the Mercedes made contact. The car was forced under the back end of the bus as the three vehicles tried to occupy the same space.

As Kyle cheerfully sped along, he turned on the radio. "This word just in: there has been a runaway truck accident on 8400 West in Magna. In this bizarre accident, the driver of an older model Mercedes sedan used her car to slow the truck and allow time for students to be evacuated from a stalled school bus headed northward. According to the truck driver, the driver of the sedan somehow spoke to him over his FM radio. She was also able to contact authorities to initiate the evacuation and diversion of traffic. Somehow, even the traffic lights seemed to have been under her control. The sedan was pinned under the bus and truck. Rescue teams are currently trying to move the bus and the truck off of the sedan. The woman is presumed dead, but this cannot be verified at this time. Stay tuned for updates on the situation."

Kyle immediately knew that the woman had to be Ann. He had been cruising at 110 MPH. He floored the Viper. He did not have experience driving at such high speeds and feared that he would lose control. At 160 MPH things happen very fast. Fortunately, he had written a program for driving and turned control over to his program, which could react at least an order of magnitude faster than he could. All that the program had to do was drive straight and there was virtually no traffic. When he approached populated areas he retook control and slowed back down to 110 MPH. He slowed further to get off onto Highway 201 (2100 South), which lead to 8400 West. When 8400 West was in sight, he could see that it was completely blocked off. He drove as far as he could, leaped from the car and began running. With computer assist, he could run about 20 MPH for several miles. The closer he got to the accident scene, the more congested things got. In desperation, he leaped onto a car and began running and leaping from car to car. He was able to run about 10 MPH in this mode. As he approached the accident, he could see that cranes had removed the bus and truck off of the car. Television cameras were everywhere. A rescue team was cutting through the crumpled metal to reach the driver. A policeman restrained Kyle, now in a walk, as he tried to get closer.

"I'm sorry sir, you can't go any closer. Please stay back."

"I'm Dr. Kyle James. The driver is Annette Monroe and is a patient of mine. Due to surgery following a head injury, she was equipped with special equipment, which allows her to communicate over radio waves. I'm also so equipped. I may be able to communicate with her, if she's alive." By now, cameras were gravitating to Kyle like vultures to a carcass. Kyle was allowed to approach the car. There was so much metal crumpled up into such a tight volume that it was hard to imagine anyone surviving the crash. Low-frequency transmissions were definitely out. Kyle tried several high frequencies that he and Ann had used to communicate. No luck. Kyle inspected the crumpled heap for weak spots and began to pull away metal with his bare hands. He used his implant to allow him to use up to 80 percent of his available strength. He began peeling away the metal like it was cardboard. By now every camera was turned on him. His shirt split open in several places and from time to time he ripped off a piece that hung in his way. He continued to try to communicate. He was bleeding from the numerous scratches he had incurred in the frenzy to free Ann. Finally, he tried calling Ann's wireless phone number. To his surprise, there was an answer.

"Hello, this is Annette Monroe", came a calm response as if nothing were wrong.

"Annette, this is Kyle, where are you?"

"Why home of course, burning every picture of you in the house. What a nasty message you left. Say, is that you on TV ripping up somebody's car. By the way, he-man, the women reporters keep saying what a hunk you are."

"If you're at home who's the woman in the car?"

"Had you going, didn't I. Who do you think, my twin sister? Would you hurry it up and get me out of here! This is very uncomfortable."

"I'm going to kill you right after I kiss you. By the way, will you marry me?"

"I thought you would never ask. I told you last summer that if you asked me under these circumstances I would."

"Yeah, but do you want to marry me? Does the Mrs. Monroe part of you want to marry me? You have to do this for you, not me."

"Like I said last summer, a woman would be a fool to not marry a rich, intelligent hunk of a man like you. By the way, your lats and pecks are looking really nice right now on TV. Marry me, he-man. I am all yours." Kyle finally removed the last sheet of metal hiding Ann from him and found Ann in a fetal position. He lifted her out and cradled her in his arms. They kissed long and hard. The crowd, which could hardly be constrained by the police, erupted in wild applause and cheers.

Chapter 21 – A Price to Pay

Kyle was exhausted from his superhuman activities and both he and Ann were taken to the hospital in an ambulance. Ann was bruised over much of her body but suffered no broken bones or major cuts. Kyle, however, was a mess. He was in extreme pain over most of his body. A group of physicians studied his X-rays with disbelief.

"Mr. James it appears that every major joint of your body has suffered acute trauma. If you ever walk again free of pain it will be a minor miracle. I am going to admit you and start you on heavy doses of anti-inflammatory drugs. If you are smart, you will never push your body like that again. It could cripple you next time." Kyle was then wheeled to a private room and started on an IV. As soon as Ann's wounds had been treated, she went to Kyle's side. His pain was intense and even heavy medication did not completely mask it. For Kyle, time seemed to slow to a snail's pace. Kyle could not sleep until he dozed off from sheer exhaustion and then only slept for short intervals. Josh and Nate visited daily, but Kyle did not enjoy the visits. Consequently, they made their stays very short.

After a week, the pain subsided enough for him to sleep for a few hours at a time. Ann, meanwhile, was becoming bored and agitated. She had been acting strangely. Sometimes she would flinch or stumble like there was some kind of malfunction in her circuitry. Finally, she talked to Kyle about the problem. "Kyle, something strange is happening to me. I keep getting parity errors and inexplicable changes to data in my volatile memory. I thought I had suffered some sort of hardware damage in the accident, but repeated diagnostic tests reveal no hardware problem. Then today the strangest thing happened. I detected numerous parity errors in the RAM of processor 37. The altered contents of the memory contained ASCII text. It said, 'I am alive.' I have been stimulating

Mrs. Monroe's brain, but it is still quite dead. What do you think is happening?"

"I don't know, but there is one possibility. Josh says that each of us is made up of a spirit and a body and that when we die our spirit leaves our body. Since Mrs. Monroe's body never died, maybe her spirit never left. I have tried for years to figure out how the spirit communicates with the brain but have had no success. Maybe it just figures it out by trial and error. Maybe she is finally figuring out how to communicate with your electronic brain. She creates a parity error so you know where to find the message. Try answering by over-writing the data."

"I will write 'Is it you, Mrs. Monroe?' starting at the same address in memory." After a few seconds, Ann spoke again. "The data changed to 'Yes'. Well, this makes things interesting. You were concerned I didn't have a spirit. Now I do. It just isn't exactly mine. Obviously, you will want to reconsider your proposal of marriage."

"Now I do feel obligated. Carlton would want me to take care of the real Mrs. Monroe, although I doubt she would have any interest in me."

"She is saying something again. She says, 'Don't be so sure.'"

"Mrs. Monroe, can you hear me?" asked Kyle.

"She says, 'Yes.'"

"Ann, just say what the text says for the next few minutes. Mrs. Monroe, how long have you been able to hear?"

"Four months."

"Can you see?"

"Not perfectly but enough to know what goes on."

"Do you understand what has happened to you?"

"Yes. I think so."

"My deepest sympathies at the passing of your husband."

"I know. I could hear you and Ann grieving for them."

"How do you feel?"

"Strange but strangely wonderful."

"How do you mean?"

"It is like all of the negative feelings I had died with my brain and now I feel like Ann feels. I care about people now."

"How do you feel about Ann?"

"You could say that I love her as myself."

"How do you feel about me?" There was a long pause.

"I love you like I have never loved anyone before." Kyle was stunned and flattered.

"What should I do, Ann?" he asked.

"She says marry us," spoke Ann. "Just think of it like marrying a woman with multiple personalities. Actually, we would both like you to marry us soon, before you can change your mind. I am calling a priest right now, provided you still want to marry me and you want to marry Annette." Kyle could not help wondering if this was all one big trap orchestrated by Annie. What if there had been no merging, no Annette program, just Annie making it all up and playing different roles. He had no way of proving that Annette's spirit was still there and talking. It was like trying to prove the existence of God. Even if Annie had been pretending, she still made Carlton incredibly happy before his untimely death. Kyle's head had its doubts but somehow his heart did not. Somehow, he knew that everything would be fine. Marrying Ann or Annie or Annette or whoever she was, was the right thing to do. Kyle decided that his response must be enthusiastic.

"You bet I want to marry you." Ann quickly got a priest on her cell phone and made arrangements for him to come the following Monday evening. Nate dropped by after Ann had left.

"What's up, Dude?" he inquired of Kyle.

"I'm getting married."

"I know you proposed. Have you set a date yet?"

"Monday."

"Whoa, you're moving pretty fast there aren't you?"

"Not really. I have been sort of courting Annette for the past semester and I have known her well for a year."

"I don't know about this. From that whole accident thing, Josh and I figured Annette must be more computer than human. Are you really sure it is a good idea to marry a computer, even if she is gorgeous?"

"I know it looks weird, but I know what I'm doing. Somehow, it will all work out. I can feel it in my gut."

"I will never say another discouraging thing about it. I just had to have my say. My friends in med school tell me she is witty and charming. They say she really knows how to carry herself and handle people, even testosterone crazed guys."

"We have actually become best friends. I had that with Sharon and feared I would never have it again. I feel comfortable around her. So what is happening with you and Nancy?" asked Kyle.

"We weren't going to tell anyone yet, but you have cornered me. We are looking at a June wedding. I finally got the nerve to pop the question."

"I knew it was just a matter of time. I might have married her if you hadn't already stolen her heart. You were right when you said she was a one in a million. I am sure you will both be very happy."

"It just bothers me that you will have been married twice before Josh and I get it done once between us. When I first met you, I didn't picture you as such a babe magnet."

"Nor I you, my friend."

"I got to go. By the way, Josh says hi. He can't make it tonight."

The wedding was very small with just Josh, Nate and Nancy as guests. At its conclusion, Annette insisted on taking Kyle home to care for him there. They arranged for a nurse to visit daily. Kyle could not help but ponder on how different this marriage was from his first. Instead of a wonderful honeymoon on a cruise, he was almost helpless, confined to bed. The day after the wedding, a delivery truck stopped in front of what used to be known as the Monroe home. Workman delivered a large, high definition TV, VCR, Blue-ray DVD player with a home theater sound system and a library of hundreds of titles to watch, all compliments of Nathan. The equipment was set up in the den and a bed was set up there for Kyle. In the afternoon Nate visited. "You are finally going to see all of those movies you have missed. There are even some TV series here."

"Anything to keep my mind off of my pain and discomfort would be welcome. I have never been so miserable in my life."

"Well, that is a fine way to comment on your marriage," called out Annette from another room as she walked towards them. "Hello, Nate. What a thoughtful gift. I see you even included all of the Star Trek episodes. I have been working on something to make the movies more enjoyable. I have programmed a computer to edit movies in real time to clean up the language, obscure the nudity and blot out the intense violence. Neither Kyle nor I care for those things."

"I don't care for them either, Annette. I have just learned to tolerate them, I guess. But what do you know about computers and programming?"

"Surely by now, Nate, you have figured out that I am much more than I was before the shooting. Kyle and I both have computer-assisted learning. Didn't you ever wonder what had happened to the program that helped checkout the implants? It has been running in me since a week from the shooting." Kyle was shocked to hear Annette revealing their secrets. "Don't look so shocked, Kyle. Nate is too smart not to have had serious suspicions. Let me assure you that I am one hundred percent pure woman, as Kyle will find out as soon as he is up to it. And as for Dr. Waters listening in, I'm sure he has already figured things out."

"I had thought as much," responded Nate. "Thanks for setting the record straight."

"Can you stay and watch a movie with us, Nate?" invited Kyle.

"I would love too, but could I come back later with Nancy?"

"Why don't you both come for dinner?" invited Annette.

"That would be great," responded Nate.

"And bring Felicity if you like," added Kyle. Nate bid them goodbye and left. "Am I talking to Ann or Annette?" he asked his wife.

"You are talking to both, but Annette is doing the talking now. Dr. Monroe instructed Annie to slip into the background when Mrs. Monroe became conscious and she has in a way become conscious. We are beginning to think and act as one. Our personalities are merging. I find it an improvement, Ann is not so sure. But can you blame her?" With that, Annette slipped in bed beside Kyle and began kissing him. He had kissed Ann before but this was no Ann. There was much more passion and desire in her kiss. Before dinner, they had consummated their marriage. At 6:00 there was a knock at the door and Annette let into the room the caterers who brought a gourmet meal. She had the table set and things ready by the time Nate and Nancy arrived.

At dinner, Nate asked Annette, "What will you do with your time while Kyle is recovering?"

"I have many plans. I promised Kyle I would help him build an electric car. He can tell me what to do and I will do it. I also want to build an electric boat, one small enough for water-skiing but big enough to sleep in. Actually, instead of a car, I would like to build an electric truck or suburban kind of vehicle, something I could use to tow the boat. I have some ideas of my own on how to do them."

"You have certainly broadened your interests, Annette," commented Nate.

"I have always been interested in lots of things. My mother just kept telling me not to. I feel liberated; plus, having a computer to help you learn a thousand times faster makes things more fun. I never did like doing homework."

"That reminds me," injected Kyle. "The medical school called. They want to visit us tomorrow to talk about our plans for further classes."

"I didn't think they would let us continue for much longer," commented Annette. "It's hard on morale to have two students getting perfect scores on every test. They probably want us to quit, but I won't let them. I want a degree and a license to practice medicine."

"I do too," responded Kyle, "but let's see what they have to say first. Maybe it's something good."

"That's what I like about you Kyle," added Nate. "You always look for the good in things and usually you find it. Doing so has made us very wealthy."

"I'll toast to that," added Nancy, who had been silent. "I have tried poverty and tasted wealth and I like the latter."

"The problem with wealth," commented Kyle, "is that very few people use it properly. The things they do with it don't make them happy and often ruin their lives."

"Such as?" asked Nate.

"Such as climbing incredibly boring social ladders and making conspicuous displays of their wealth. Can 40,000 square feet really be more fun than a 4,000 square foot home? I think it unlikely. Now to live in a 4,000 square foot home and help hundreds who are homeless to have homes, that would make me happy."

"What do you think of that, Annette?" asked Nate. Kyle also had a keen interest in that question.

"I am all for avoidance of conspicuous consumption. It's the inconspicuous consumption I am looking forward to," quipped Annette. All laughed. "For example, this dinner. I didn't have to slave in the kitchen all day, not that I wouldn't at times. It was just really nice to have it all brought in. Hopefully, the neighbors didn't even notice. And the vehicle and boat, we could literally spend millions on them doing things in the most ideal way possible with current technology. But it wouldn't be conspicuous unless you call owning a new SUV and boat conspicuous consumption. I just want to do it. I don't need to impress anyone. I have thought of hundreds of things I can do now that are just fun or satisfying."

"You haven't said much, Nancy. What are you thinking?" asked Kyle.

"I am just wondering what movie we will watch."

"The problem is," began Kyle, "you have probably seen all of the really good movies already, maybe even several times, but I have seen very few of them."

"That reminds me of a question I have had for years, Kyle," said Nate. "Without a TV, how did you and your mother keep up with what was happening in the world?"

"Well you see, Nate, there was this document of current events that appeared on our doorstep every morning. Perhaps you have heard of it. It is called a newspaper."

"I sure stepped in that one," laughed Nate. "Let's watch a movie."

"I have been looking at some lists on the Internet of top movies of all time. I would really like to see the Godfather."

"That one's too gross for me," objected Nancy.

"Oh, I agree, Nancy, but I have something that will remove the objectionable parts for you," offered Annette.

"I just don't want to see squirting blood and sex scenes, or hear profanity or heavy vulgarity."

"We can take care of that for you. Shall we have desert in the den?" asked Annette. Annette wheeled Kyle into the den and then with Nate's help, lowered him onto some large pillows on the floor. She cuddled up beside him while Nancy and Nate sat on the sofa. During the movie, Annette ran her fingers over Kyle's hand in a way more sensual than he thought possible. All Sharon had ever done was hold his hand, but Annette caressed his hand in ways almost more stimulating than full intimacy. He couldn't wait for the guests to leave.

After the movie ended Kyle commented, "So now I finally know why people are always saying, 'Make him an offer he can't refuse.'"

"You may have hidden the blood, but you have to admit, Annette, just the thought of a horse's head in your bed is pretty gross," added Nancy.

"We'll watch the Sound of Music next time," offered Annette as she quickly maneuvered the guests out of the door. "Now," she said to Kyle, "I believe we have some unfinished business." With that, she turned out the light and snuggled up to Kyle.

The next morning Kyle dreamed that he and Annette were on a tropical island beach. He was lying on his back and Annette was kissing him. The sirens of a passing fire truck disturbed his dream. He awoke to discover that Annette was kissing him as he lay on his back. Not one to interrupt a good kiss, he waited for Annette to come up for air. "Last night was wonderful, my love," he began, "but don't you think we were a little rude in the way we almost thrust company from the house?"

"There was no 'we' about it. I did and I make no apologies. This is like our honeymoon."

"Well, be nice to the people from the medical school. They have been very accommodating to us."

"And we have been very generous with them," she retorted. "I promise not to rush them under one condition, you eliminate any reason for me to." With that, she began kissing Kyle again.

The head of the school of medicine paid the Jameses a visit at their home. "Doctor and Mrs. James, your scholastic progress has been nothing short of remarkable," began the dean. "You must realize, however, that having two such students in the same classes creates extraordinary anxiety in your classmates. We have never had so many inquiries from students concerning how we grade and how the curve works. Of course, we exempted your scores from any curve calculations, but students still got very nervous. We have a proposal we believe will satisfy everyone's needs. We would like to put you on an accelerated course of study. As part of a study last year, we videotaped all of the lectures. We propose that you watch them instead of going to classes. We can arrange for testing in the testing center. We will provide private labs in which you will receive one-on-two instruction. We believe that with your intellects and obviously computer-assisted learning you could both receive your degrees in less than a year."

"That is a very generous offer," responded Kyle. Personal instruction sounds very expensive for the University."

"Indeed it is. However, you have both been extremely generous to the University and its school of medicine. Naturally, we would not turn down any contributions, but additional donations would be completely optional. If you like, you may begin immediately. The first installment of videos is in my car as well as lists of required reading." The dean walked out to his car and returned with a box of VHS tapes. He then promptly left.

"Well, I for one am not going to sit around for hours watching boring old doctors drone on while I have a new husband to attend to," complained Annette. "I will just have to automate the process. I'll get Vic or Vicky to watch them for us and compress the data. Then I can assimilate it and you can sleep on it or whatever it is that you do to get it into your brain." The doorbell rang. Annette picked up the box of videos and carried it to the door. She opened the door, handed the box to a young man and closed the door.

"Who was that?" asked Kyle.

"A student I hired to run errands for me."

"How did he get here so fast?"

"I have him wait in his car down the street with the cell phone I gave him. I just transmit instructions straight to him. Now, tell me how you want the drive system of our electric vehicle to work?" Kyle spent several hours describing the details of the vehicle he had been designing in his head for years. Annette asked several questions. The sound of a vehicle door clicking shut came from the driveway. Annette put Kyle in a wheelchair and wheeled him to the front porch. A brand new Ford Expedition sat in the driveway.

"How could you possibly get this delivered so quickly?" asked Kyle.

"Well, I put in the order yesterday. It is amazing how fast people will work when bonuses are on the line." Supplies continued to arrive throughout the day and night, including tools and hoists. Annette had backed the Viper out of the garage and parked it on the lawn to make plenty of room. Two crack mechanics also arrived, dressed in coveralls. Before dark, they had removed the engine, transmission, radiator and exhaust system. The electric power system and drive system were assembled in only two weeks, even though high-speed graphite fiber flywheels had to be shipped from Oregon and the motors had to be custom fabricated. The fuel tank was filled with alcohol as the last step. The power system allowed spinning up the flywheels using household electric current but could also run indefinitely on alcohol that was converted to electricity by a fuel cell, as long as its tanks had fuel. With 50 gallons of capacity, it could run for up to 1500 miles without a fill-up. For just around town driving it could run just off the energy stored in the flywheels. Annette had even added some features Kyle had not requested. Since the four flywheels acted as gyroscopes, they each had to be gimbaled in two directions. The range of motion was limited so that as long as the flywheels were spinning the vehicle could not roll over or flip over. Annette added brakes to the gimbals that allowed the vehicle to lock onto an inclination. They could be used to prevent roll during cornering or for special tricks such as driving on two wheels.

During the assembly process, Annette frequently wheeled Kyle out to watch the progress and allow him to make recommendations. After initial assembly, Annette spent another two weeks tuning the software and making adjustments. She took it for numerous drives to test certain aspects. Finally, the day arrived for the final presentation to Kyle. She placed a large bow on it and a sign that said "Happy one month anniversary." Annette wheeled out Kyle and after a couple of circles of the vehicle so that he could inspect it, she and her hired help, Dan, lifted Kyle into the driver's seat. Kyle protested, "You know I'm not supposed to drive yet, Annette."

"You're not driving. I just thought you would feel manlier sitting in the driver's side." Dan opened the door for Annette and she climbed up into the vehicle. "Bob, take us to Trolley Square." The modified Expedition automatically moved down the driveway and onto the street. "And Bob, give us the extra smooth ride. You see Kyle; the car has six inconspicuous cameras. It has a better view of the road than you do and Bob is fully conscious at all times of all traffic and obstacles on the road. He doesn't need to pause to look before changing lanes like you or I do."

"This is going to take some getting used to. It is sort of like 'My Brother the Car'."

"My, you really have been catching up on TV and movies. My Mother the Car is over 50 years old and was not very popular."

"I haven't actually watched it, but I have heard many jokes and comments about it. Could I drive if I wanted to?"

"Sure, you just tell Bob to let you take over. Everything acts similar to a normal car except cruise control is verbal. How do you like it?"

"It's great. How far can it go on just the flywheels?"

"Only about 80 miles if starting with them fully spun up. They should work great for commuting. Bob, what is the estimated time to arrival?"

"Five minutes, Mrs. James."

"Thank you, Bob. You notice, Kyle, that I didn't make Bob very verbose. He only responds verbally if asked to. Bob, just drop us off at the south-east entrance and then park the car and wait for my call."

"Now that part I like. I hate looking for parking spots. Won't it look strange with no one in the car?"

"No problem. There is a holographic projection of you or me available. It even appears to move its head and hands like a normal driver."

"You think of everything, my love. You are the most thorough person I have ever known."

"Why thank you, Kyle." The car stopped and Annette got out. By the time she had opened the back, Dan arrived to take out the wheelchair and lower Kyle into it. Then Dan and Bob both left.

"Where did Dan come from?" asked Kyle.

"Oh, he has been following us. Even though I could lift you out myself, it just doesn't seem ladylike, plus I don't want to throw out my back. We have to be careful how we use our capabilities as you very well know by now."

"I totally agree. I'm just not used to being waited on, even after a month of you waiting on me." The couple made their way to a restaurant where they had reservations and were seated.

"Kyle, do you mind if I branch out a little as an entrepreneur? I would like to start my own company."

"Believe me, Annette, when I promised you that I am not the dominating kind of husband I was very serious. As you well know, Sharon was very independent and headstrong. I tried to never cross her."

"That's good. See that you don't cross me," responded Annette with a sly grin. She leaned over the table and kissed him. "I don't want you to be henpecked or submissive, however. I like a strong man. I just need a little breathing room sometimes. I see a tremendous business opportunity. I am planning on a smaller version of electric computer-piloted automobile. I am toying with a two-seater with the original Thunderbird body style. I have been negotiating with several firms to make it. It would have half of the power train of our Expedition, two motors, on the rear wheels and two flywheels. I think I can produce them for $100,000. I am negotiating to sell them through Ford dealerships and Ford is in the running to assemble them. There is a huge market of upper-middle-class seniors whose eyesight and reaction time are on the decline but who desperately want to maintain their independence. At the same time, they will be helping the environment."

"That is a great idea, Annette. When do you start?"

"Ford is building the prototype for me as we speak. I need to fly to Detroit tomorrow to look at it. Would you like to come?"

"I would probably just slow you down. You can record what you see and share your experiences in detail. When will you be back?"

"I don't know. Within a few days, I hope. If you come I promise that I will make it worth your while." Annette sensuously caressed Kyle's hand that she had been holding across the table. Kyle pondered on whether he wanted to interrupt their time together so soon in the marriage. He had never slept apart from Sharon once they were married and did not think he really wanted to sleep alone for a week. He had declined the invitation initially because he did not think Annette really wanted him along, but now he was confident she did and consented to accompany her.

Chapter 22 – How to Quiet a Dog

Kyle and Annette admired the classic lines of the Thunderbird. The prototype was yellow and only differed slightly in outward appearances from the original due to safety features and a lack of exhaust pipes. They took it for a spin with Annette behind the wheel. It had snappy but not head jerking response and handled very well. Annette had programmed it to have the flywheel gumball brakes engage automatically during cornering to prevent roll. The effect was exhilarating on a high-speed turn. This was a real sports car. She decided they should also market a less expensive model that lacked the computer-driving feature.

As they sat in negotiations with the executives of Ford Motor Company, they found that Ford was very anxious to have the vehicle as their own so that they could use it to meet zero-emissions requirements. It meant they could drop expensive and unproductive internal research and development. They were willing to lose money on every car just for the legal and political advantages. They offered to retain Annette and Kyle as high paid ivory tower employees and put their names on every electric car sold by Ford. They wanted to be able to say that Ford employees developed the vehicle, so they made the deal retroactive. Each would receive a $250,000 a year salary, would only have to show up to work a few days a year and could retain any future non-vehicle related inventions. In addition, Annette would receive a bonus of $1000 paid in Ford stock for every electric vehicle sold. The money was of little concern to Kyle since he was already worth hundreds of millions. He could tell, however, that it meant a great deal to Annette to have her own source of income that she personally generated. Kyle thought he remembered something that a woman's suffrage activist said many years ago about a woman needing her own purse. He was very happy for Annette.

Seeing her so happy made him especially glad that he had come with her on the trip.

After their return home, both Annette and Kyle were looking forward to a good night's sleep. Their hopes were not fulfilled due to the constant barking of a neighbor's dog. Annette could have just turned off her hearing and slept, but she insisted on suffering right along with Kyle. She went outside and determined which yard contained the offending canine. She wanted to call the owners that night, but Kyle insisted that she not. The next morning she set out to confront the dog's owner. "Mrs. Johnson, your dog kept my husband up all night. You must put a stop to this."

"I'm so sorry Mrs. James. I don't know what to do. The dog was never a problem until recently. She just keeps barking. I didn't know you were back from your trip. We have been keeping her indoors to spare you. While you were gone, we put her in the back yard so that the baby could sleep. We can't bring ourselves to put the dog down. No one else wants her, of course."

"I will take her if that works for your family," offered Annette, thinking to herself that the dog just needed some discipline.

"That is so sweet of you to offer. We accept." Annette had not really expected her offer to be accepted and reluctantly escorted the dog to her home with the dog barking all of the way. She ordered a pre-built shed with extra insulation delivered to the back yard. Annette had attended an obedience school with a previous dog and felt that she knew just what to do. She filled a bottle with water and started to work with the dog. Every time the dog barked she shouted, "Shush, bottle!" and sprayed the dog in the face. She had seen the technique quiet every dog in obedience school, but it did not faze this dog. Nothing worked; the dog just kept barking and barking. Finally, she decided that the dog might be sick and took her to the vet.

"I'm sorry Mrs. James, your dog has a brain tumor," said the vet after a thorough examination. She could live for up to a year before dying naturally. I suggest we put her down."

"I can't do that. Would you be willing to perform surgery to remove the tumor?" asked Annette.

"I see no point in it. Even if the dog lived, she would be a vegetable, if you will excuse the vernacular."

"She will be no more brain dead than I am if you let my husband and me assist. I would like to perform the same operation on her that was performed on me. I have a complete record of the operation. We can hire a brain surgeon to assist. I don't think you have an adequate facility here. I will rent the operating room used for my surgery. You will be paid well for your help. When can you make yourself available?"

"My partner is providing coverage next weekend. Is that too soon?"

"I have a way of getting things done quickly. Money is a great catalyst. I will call you with the details."

When Annette told Kyle her plans, he had serious doubts. "Where are you going to get the snake chips? We used them all on you."

"I have already worked that out with Nate. You used all of the flawless chips on me, but Nate has many slightly flawed chips. The original yields of perfect chips were low. Nate kept all of the flawed chips. He has a handful with at least ninety percent of the snakes working. We will use the new processors. Six should be enough. Dr. Boone will assist. I was hoping you would also help. The fun part will be creating a dog-like program. I don't want it to be sentient, but I want it far smarter than the average dog. I always wanted a really smart dog."

"I have learned that what you set out to do, you do. Let's go for it. Just don't expect any bonuses from Ford on this one."

"Having my husband get a good night's sleep is bonus enough for me."

The operation was a complete success. Shelly, as Annette had named the dog, required no training at all. Everything was already programmed into her. She responded to verbal, radio transmitted, sign and ultrasonic commands and could respond with simple information. She understood the Adamic language and English. If she were a human her IQ would be about 80. Best of all, Shelly could use a regular toilet. She would lift the lid and seat with her snout and then squat over the toilet. Lowering the seat back down was trickier. If she just used her snout, it slammed down. If she used her mouth to control the descent, it left drool. Annette decided to assign Shelly a toilet downstairs and let her leave the seat up. Annette frequently took her to play with the Johnsons' children. Shelly was programmed to act like a dog when playing dog games and to be very gentle with children. The children loved her.

Annette and Kyle arranged to visit Megan and her children. They brought along Shelly. As the couple drove up to the modest home, they could see Amanda peeking through the curtains of the front window. When she saw the Expedition pull into the driveway, she ran to the front door. Kyle had transitioned from using a wheelchair to using crutches. Annette and Kyle slowly approached the front door with Shelly trailing behind. Amanda opened the door before they reached it. She was jumping up and down and yelling, "They're here, they're here." Annette reached down and scoped up Amanda.

"Mandy, we have brought a friend for you to meet. Mandy, this is Shelly. Shelly, this is Mandy."

"You're silly, Aunt Annette," responded Amanda. "Shelly is just a dog."

"Oh, you think so." She lowered Amanda onto the floor of the living room. "Shelly, shake Mandy's hand." Shelly approached

Amanda and raised her right paw. "Shake her hand, Mandy." Amanda tentatively took the dog's paw in her hand and raised and lowered it.

"That's very impressive," commented Megan who had entered the room with Carl in tow. "Thank you for coming. The kids talk about you guys all the time." She gave Annette and Kyle each a big hug. Shelly gave a short bark followed two seconds later by another short bark.

"Shelly needs to go potty. Can she use your toilet?" asked Annette. Amanda giggled. "She is fully potty trained," assured Annette.

"This I have to see," responded Megan. "Come this way, Shelly." Megan led Shelly, who obediently followed, to the closest bathroom. She watched as Shelly lifted the toilet seat using her snout and then squatted over the toilet and did her business. She jumped back down and reached up with her left paw to flush the toilet. She then looked to Megan and then to the toilet seat as if asking her to lower it. Megan complied and Shelly left the room.

"What are these things?" asked Amanda, pointing to Kyle's crutches.

"They're called crutches. They help me walk," responded Kyle.

"Why do you need help walking?" asked Amanda.

"That's a very good question, Mandy," responded Annette. "Kyle hurt himself rescuing me. Megan, would you mind if I show them a little video of my rescue?"

"That would be fun," responded Megan. Annette had purchased copies of the footage owned by all of the news stations that were at the scene, covering the event as well as videos taken by bystanders on their cell phones. She had also incorporated her own personal recordings of the events. She inserted a DVD into the player and turned on the TV. Megan sat in the chair and Annette and Kyle sat on the sofa. The kids ended up on Kyle's knees.

Megan turned sad as she watched the video. Kyle had rescued her financially with the trust funds, but what she had really wanted was for him to carry her away in his arms and propose to her. Now those hopes were dashed. Shelly sensed her mood and nuzzled her legs. When Megan spread her legs and started petting Shelly, the dog slowly eased her way into Megan's lap. By the end of the video, Megan was hugging Shelly and found herself greatly comforted. After the video, the children played with Shelly. Megan was amazed at Shelly's gentleness and tolerance of the children's abuse. Annette took Megan aside in the kitchen. "Megan, would you like me to leave Shelly with you for a while? I brought a bag of her food in the car."

"They kids would love it, but it would be hard for them to part with Shelly when you want her back."

"You can keep her as long as you like. We never wanted a dog. I felt sorry for a neighbor and took Shelly off of their hands. Besides, Kyle and I worry about your safety, living without a man in the house. Shelly is also a good watchdog. Don't let her gentleness fool you. She can be extremely aggressive in defending her charges. She can even act as sort of a babysitter, watching the children and keeping them from straying beyond the boundaries that you set. Just explain what you want to Shelly. She will understand and obey." Megan threw her arms around Annette's neck and hugged her tightly.

"Thank you so much. You and Kyle have been so wonderful to me." She wept on Annette's shoulder.

Becky Larsen, Josh's fiancée, had finished her mission and returned home, but Annette and Kyle had not yet met her.

Kyle began walking and doing minor arm activities such as driving. Annette dove into her next project, an electric, computer-controlled boat. It used the same power sources and motors as the Expedition. The 26-foot inboard/outboard was small enough to tow behind the Expedition but was big enough to be very comfortable. Nate and Nancy and Josh and Becky joined them on the maiden voyage. Kyle was concerned about the Expedition's towing capability, so for the maiden voyage they went to a lower elevation reservoir, Willard Bay, located north of Ogden, bordering the Great Salt Lake. When they arrived at the boat ramp, Annette took over and began issuing orders. "Kyle and I will prepare the boat. Everyone else just get in the boat with your gear. Kyle went to the rear of the boat and removed the tie-down straps and inserted the drain plug while Annette loosened and unhooked the front loading strap and hook. Kyle and Annette then joined their friends in the boat. Bob, the Expedition's sentient computer, backed the boat into the water. The boat, controlled by its own computer, Bobby, automatically backed off of the trailer and Bob drove away, eventually finding a parking spot and parking himself.

Annette was an experienced water skier and wanted the first turn. It took her a few tries to get up on one ski. Once her electronic brain had worked out all of the dynamics of her body, the ski and the boat, she did very well indeed. She began jumping the wakes and eventually was doing a 360-degree spin while in the air. After Annette finished, she invited the others to try. Becky stood. "I have only skied a few times, but I would like to give it a try." Becky had been wearing a wrap and removed it. Underneath was a modest but very attractive, one-piece bathing suit. Kyle had not previously closely observed Becky's figure but did so now. At six-one, Becky had very long legs. Her build was very athletic. Her body was lean and muscular in a very feminine and graceful way. Josh noticed the look on Kyle's face.

"She was a consensus all American volley ballplayer all four years at BYU. She was the team star in every sport she played in high school. You should see her pitch a softball."

"She's beautiful," whispered Kyle.

"Yeah, she is. The missionary photo I showed you didn't do her justice, did it?"

"Not at all."

Becky popped out of the water on her first try. It took her a little while to feel completely comfortable, but once she did, she became amazingly graceful. She did all of the tricks that Annette had done and more. Then she traded in the slalom ski for a wakeboard and wowed everyone again with more feats of skill and grace. Josh leaned over to Kyle to speak over the boat noise. "I have never known a more competitive athlete than Becky, on any level, male or female. She can't help trying to outdo the competition. Once the competitive instinct is triggered, there's no stopping her. Normally, she is as sweet as honey, but don't cross her on the court or the field."

Nate and Nancy were so intimidated watching Annette and Becky that they chose to just ride on the tubes. Kyle had let Bobby handle the boat while Annette skied but drove for Nate and Nancy during the tubing. In the afternoon, they all swam. Kyle noticed that Nate had slimmed down considerably while he had gotten very flabby. As soon as he could, he would have to do some serious exercise.

The couple concentrated on finishing medical school. They had mastered all of the lectures and textbooks. Now they were ready for a crash course in all of the things done in the lab, including dissection of cadavers and surgery. Annette was very nimble with her hands, but Kyle struggled. His large, powerful hands were hard to control in delicate maneuvers. Dexterity was not something he could just download to his brain. It involved his whole body. The doctors who directed them were satisfied with Kyle's progress and very complimentary about Annette's. Once Kyle could discard the wheelchair and crutches, his confidence increased and he became more sure-handed with a scalpel.

Nate and Nancy married as planned. The Jameses gave them an electric Thunderbird as a wedding present. Josh and Becky married a couple of months later. They were also given an electric Thunderbird as a wedding present although Kyle suspected that within a few years they would want something more like the Expedition with the children he expected them to have. The three couples did many things together and made good use of the boat and the Expedition. Kyle and Annette both received their medical degrees but chose not to go through graduation ceremonies. Kyle got back in shape. Annette encouraged him to bulk up to 220 pounds. Unlike most women, she liked massive muscles on a man. Annette got her own body into superb physical condition.

One afternoon Josh dropped by to bring Kyle a book. Kyle and Annette were dressed in tight-fitting workout clothing. "Josh, good to see you. Can you join us in a short walk around the block?" invited Kyle who was donning leather gloves.

"You guys look like you are ready for something more strenuous than a walk around the block," commented Josh.

"Oh, the path is steep in places. It will actually be quite a challenge," responded Kyle. Josh had a quizzical look on his face but played along. Both Kyle and Annette placed their hands on the sidewalk and shifted their entire body weight onto their hands and arms. They proceeded with the "walk" on their hands.

"You guys really know how to make a guy feel like a wimp," commented Josh. "Even Nate is starting to look more buff than me."

"So how is Becky doing?" asked Annette.

"She has morning sickness really bad."

"Poor dear. Has that dampened her desire any for a large family?" asked Annette.

"Not one iota. She is determined."

"You've got a real trooper there, Josh," added Kyle.

Chapter 23 – Spiritual Love

Annette lie next to Kyle snuggling after an hour of exquisite passion. She marveled at how much she had grown to love this man whom only a few years earlier she had mocked and ridiculed. She had been so wrong about so many things back then. Who would have thought that a bullet to the head would have brought wisdom and joy? She let her mind drift back to that evening. It was the first time that she had seen Kyle well dressed. He looked very sharp in his tuxedo that enhanced his extremely masculine physique and features. Kyle made her date, her husband, look like Pee Wee Herman. Most women found Carlton very handsome. Annette had originally been drawn to him by overhearing other women talk about him. Her competitive nature had driven her to seek him out and attract his attention. Carlton quickly fell in love with her. Her peers were envious of her and that fed her vanity. Before she realized the trap that she had created for herself, she was married to Carlton.

It had mostly been a joyless marriage. Carlton just did not know how to promote his career or how to build wealth. His salary as a full professor was adequate, but he could have earned so much more. Meanwhile, Kyle, who until recently had dressed like an impoverished moron, had made himself rich and famous. Go figure.

Annette had not been paying attention to the odd events at Kyle's table. One moment she had been eating dinner and the next she was floating above the crowd, looking down on her critically wounded body. With an amazingly detached attitude, she watched the events unfold. Carlton was beside himself with grief. How could someone so smart be such an idiot? Realistically, if she died it would be one of the best things that could have happened to Carlton. She turned her attention to Kyle. For some reason, he had a large brass vase over his head, but he was acting calm and rational. She decided to follow Kyle's little group. Two things impressed her. Not only was Kyle very calm and rational but so were his fiancée and friends. Secondly, she was impressed by the love and devotion of Kyle's friends. Annette had not had a true friend in her entire adult life.

When Kyle walked out of the hospital, without even being released, to help Carlton save her life, she almost wept if a spirit could weep. No one but Carlton had ever done something like that for her. Amazingly, the bizarre plan worked. Carlton had not even told her about his creation of a sentient program. It was marvelous and Kyle seemed to bring out the best in it. He was very clever. After Kyle's wedding, Annette returned to her body. The pain was unbearable. Somehow, she managed to pop out again. She hung around, observing Carlton and Kyle's friends. She followed Nate to the airport to meet Kyle. To her surprise, she found herself eagerly anticipating Kyle's return. Nate was very upset about something, but Kyle was as calm as a summer morning. Annette could not get her spirit mind around the technical and financial details, but as she watched over the next several weeks, she observed two things. Everybody associated with Kyle's little company worked very hard and seemed happy about it and Kyle had somehow turned financial disaster into huge profits, especially for himself. He was very generous and honest with others but managed to make a fortune. He knew how to build wealth.

The next most clever person was not really a person at all but the program that Carlton had created. It somehow tricked him into believing that she had regained consciousness but as a much wiser and more loving version of herself. She managed to fool everyone, although Kyle seemed to be suspicious about something. Several times Annette tried staying in her body. The pain had subsided, but she was blind and deaf inside her body. She could only sense what was going on when she left her body.

Then both Carlton and Sharon were killed by a swarm of bumblebees. Annette knew that she had always been a very selfish and self-centered person but was ashamed that she felt no grief at the death of her husband. Instead, she felt excitement that maybe the computer chick in her body and Kyle would hook up but she wanted to be in her body when it happened. She yearned to hold Kyle in her arms. Was she falling in love with him? She spent more and more time in her body. With persistence, she began to sense her surroundings through the computer system. It seemed very alien at first, but gradually her spirit mind adjusted to the digital brain. Things were starting to heat up between Kyle and the computer girl who called herself Ann. Annette wanted to be there when they kissed. She would not be in control, but she would feel Kyle's lips against hers. She felt as giddy as a schoolgirl, well, actually, she was a schoolgirl, at least her body was. Thanks to Ann, she was rapidly becoming a doctor of medicine. Not bad. Not bad at all.

The kiss came and it was wonderful, although she desperately wanted to take over and control her body. She knew how to really kiss a man. Then Ann did something extraordinary, she risked her life to save a bunch of children. At first, Annette was furious that Ann was risking her body. Fearing the pain to come she slipped out of her body again and watched from above. As she watched the children escaping the bus, she had a Grinch-like moment. Her heart seemed to grow. It felt right that her life be sacrificed to save those children. After the crash, she returned to her body. There was only minor pain. She was cramped but not seriously injured. Once again, Ann had proven her brilliance. Annette could see nothing so she slipped out of the body again to observe.

None of the rescuers seemed to know if she was even still alive and were afraid that any attempt to extractor her might seriously injure her body. Then she saw Kyle running and leaping from car top to car top. He was a force of nature with superhuman strength. He ripped the car body apart with his bare hands. His muscles bulged and flexed. He was magnificent, her hero in shining sweat. When her body was finally exposed to view, she returned to it so that she could feel Kyle reach in and cradle her in his muscular arms. She knew then that she had to have him. She did not even care about his money. She wanted his body and spirit. She would marry him and never let him regret it. She had been a selfish, unloving wife to Carlton. She would be an incredible wife and lover to Kyle. She thought of the corny saying, "Today is the first day of the rest of your life." It actually made sense to her now. Kyle really liked the computer girl so Annette would learn to coexist with her and work together with her to win Kyle and keep him happy.

Chapter 24 – Bar Fight

"Kyle, my alcohol tanks are really low. Can we stop at the closest bar and grab a quick beer?" asked Annette anxiously. If she ran out of alcohol for her fuel cells she would lose the function of her auxiliary processors that clung to the wall of her stomach. The couple had been out to the Adamms' home to visit and were returning.

"You know how I hate bars, but you got to do what you got to do. Just try not to get into any fights," kidded Kyle. The parking lot was full and the jukebox could be heard from the parking lot. One reason Kyle had shunned drinking was that he hated bars and how people acted when they had been drinking too much. Walking into a bar with a woman built like Annette was asking for trouble, especially with the parking lot full of custom motorcycles and pickup trucks. The couple approached the bar and Kyle ordered a couple of beers. His tanks could use a little refilling also, but he would have preferred to wait until they got home. After a few minutes, a large, heavily tattooed man in a leather vest turned his body towards Annette.

"Well, what do we have here? A fine mama with world-class jugs and a boy. Hey, baby how about you and me blow this joint and leave the kid behind?" Annette had at one time in her life sung in bars to help put herself through school and was cool and collected. Kyle, on the other hand, saw his worse fears being realized. He definitely did not want to get into a bar fight.

"Let's go Annette." The beers had arrived and Kyle paid for them. Annette drank the whole bottle at once and set it down. The two walked out of the bar.

"How dare you let someone talk to me that way and not respond!" started Annette in a chilling tone. "Carlton may have been a wimp physically, but he always stood up for me. You could have easily taken that guy but you backed down." It finally had happened. Kyle had respected Carlton Monroe more than any other man he had ever known. He was a man true to his principles to the end. Kyle had feared being compared to him. He was sure that Carlton had been his superior in every virtue and attribute of character and now he was being measured against him in a most unfavorable way. However, Kyle was still confident that he had done the right thing. Too bad Annette did not see it that way.

"What do you want me to do?" meekly asked Kyle.

"I want you to go right in there and demand an apology." Kyle turned and reentered the bar followed by his wife. A hush fell across the room. They walked up to the offender.

"Sir, my wife found your comments very offensive and we demand an apology." The biker was surprised by the lack of fear in Kyle's voice. Didn't he realize he could crush him like a bug?

"My apologies, Madam," responded the man in mock humility.

"Thank you," responded Kyle. He then whispered to Annette, "Now let's get out of here." The two headed for the door. Annette knew men like the biker all too well and was confident that things were not going to be so easy. She contemplated what he might do. Putting her mind in high-speed mode by shifting all of her resources to her sight, hearing and logic, she determined 47 things that the biker might do in response. She noticed that he had been holding a beer bottle. She placed her right hand on Kyle's shoulder in such a way that she could use her watch as a mirror to observe the ruffian. She watched him swig the last of his beer. She contemplated several possible activities with the bottle. He might just set it on the bar. He might break the end off on the bar to use as a weapon. He might use it in its unmodified form to hit Kyle over the head or he might use it as a projectile. With human eyes, Annette could only freeze about 20 frames per second. She watched each picture unfold like a normal person watching a video in slow motion. Within three frames, she had determined that the bully would throw the bottle. She coolly watched his arm go back. She began preliminary estimations of the trajectory, speed and time of arrival. She began to reposition her body to catch the bottle when it came. She would need to make contact early so that she could decelerate the bottle over many centimeters to avoid hitting the back of Kyle's head. Once the bottle left the biker's hand, she knew its precise trajectory. The bottle made a whooshing sound as it spun through the air. Kyle heard the sound and turned his head to see what was making the noise. Without Annette's intervention, he would catch the bottle right in the side of his face. Annette's hand intercepted the bottle, grasping it by the neck 340 centimeters from Kyle's face. She gently decelerated the bottle to a stop a few centimeters from Kyle. She calmly carried the bottle back to the thrower and stood facing him.

"I believe this is yours. Here catch." She tossed the bottle higher than the man's head but short so that he stepped forward with his right leg in the act of catching it. Annette's right foot simultaneously shot up from the floor at unnatural velocity to strike the man's crotch. The smacking sound was so loud that every man in the room heard it and winced in vicarious pain. As Annette's foot returned to the floor the brute sank to his knees in agony. Annette calmly grabbed some toothpicks from the bar and walked out with Kyle, who watched with amazement. Upon exiting the building, Annette walked with a limp over to the motorcycles. She noticed that six of them bore a logo similar to one of the man's tattoos. She stuck a toothpick in the ignition of the first she came to and broke it off. She repeated the act on each of the successive five bikes. "We can go now," she calmly informed Kyle. The barroom doors burst open and bikers filled the area. Kyle and Annette ran to the Viper and sped off. The gang ran to their motorcycles but could not fit their keys into the ignitions. The cursing bikers were unable to make pursuit. The couple was silent on the way home, but Annette was exhilarated. She had never done anything so exciting before in her life.

Annette's leg was sore for weeks. Rather than turning off the pain, she reveled in her discomfort. It reminded her of the excitement of the evening in the bar. After the bar incident, Annette went to work on miniature video cameras with built-in transmitters. She consulted with her network of computers, with Kyle and with others in the design. The finished product was a thing of beauty. The basic unit was only nine millimeters long and weighed only a few grams. She had designed several means of attachment. One model could be clipped or glued to hair. This one was specifically for Kyle so he could have "eyes in the back of his head". Another was encased in a glob of very sticky substance. It could be thrown at a wall or ceiling and would remain stuck there indefinitely. Another had a propeller and when thrown into the air would descend, slowly rotating. It gave a sweeping, panoramic view of a room. Each camera could transmit 100 frames per second, five times the rate of the human eye. The high speed was not of much use to Kyle but was a great asset to Annette when quick analysis was required.

As Kyle and Annette watched the evening news, there was a piece describing a sharp decline in the availability of illegal drugs in North America. Both the money and the supply had mysteriously dried up. This good news was offset by an unusually high number of gang turf wars. Every gang appeared to be at war with other gangs.

"Kyle, I need to buy a birthday present for my mom. Do you want to come?"

"No thanks, my love. You go ahead." Annette gathered up some boxes, scissors, wrapping paper and packaging tape. She bought a present at a strip mall and headed to the nearest post office. While parked she wrapped the gift with decorative paper and then packed it into a sturdy cardboard box, which she taped and labeled. She entered the post office with the box and paid the postage, a process that required a frustratingly long wait. As she exited the building, she noticed a transient urinating on one of the tires of her new electric

Thunderbird. She dashed to her car to confront the man who was holding a beer bottle in one hand and aiming with the other.

"You stop that or I will shove that bottle where the sun don't shine!" she ordered the man. He turned while continuing to urinate. The urine splashed up onto Annette's shoes.

When Annette returned home, Kyle was watching a football game on TV. The half had just ended and there was brief local news coverage. "In a bizarre incident, a man was found hog-tied with packing tape at a local post office in Salt Lake City. There was a hole cut in the man's trousers and a beer bottle was extending from his rectum. The man claims that he was attacked by a gang of Straight Edgers, but witnesses say a lone woman attacked the man. The man was lying in a puddle of urine."

"Is that a great story or what?" asked Kyle. "Did you get a present off to your mother?"

"Yeah, no problem." There was a kind of smirk in Annette's voice that got Kyle thinking.

"Do you know anything about the incident at the post office? Wait! I don't think I want to know."

A well-built man in his mid-thirties carrying a briefcase and wearing an expensive Italian suit entered the lobby of Gas Products in Centerville, Utah. He approached the receptionist. "I would like to see Mr. Fidell, please."

"I'm sorry; he is in a meeting at the moment. Can I schedule you an appointment to see him?"

"Here is my business card." The man slid across the desk his card resting on a one hundred dollar bill. "Do you think that he can break free of the meeting?"

"Let me check," responded the grinning receptionist. Soon Mr. Fidell, the sole owner of Gas Products, came to the lobby.

"How may I help you, Mr. Bracken?"

"I am here on behalf of a client to pay a bill. May we discuss this in your office?"

"You are welcome to discuss a bill in my office, but if you are looking for your bill to be discounted I am afraid that you are sadly mistaken."

As the door closed behind them, Mr. Bracken continued. "We are not looking for a discount. Last year your entire inventory of helium was borrowed by my client. We estimate the value at $20,000. Would you accept $250,000 as payment in full?"

"Well, I suppose that we could accept that sum."

"Of course, my client, who prefers to remain anonymous, would expect you to drop all criminal proceedings and promise not to file charges in the event that his identity becomes known."

"Yes, but how can he make payment and remain anonymous?" At this point, Mr. Bracken placed his briefcase on Mr. Fidell's desk and opened it. He turned the open case to face Mr. Bracken. It contained $250,000 in small bills. Mr. Bracken removed from the case a legal document stipulating the conditions and asked Mr. Fidell to sign it, which he did so eagerly. On his way out Mr. Bracken slipped the receptionist another one hundred dollar bill.

Two days later Mr. Bracken visited the West Coast Logging Company and made a similar payment, which was likewise well received. He then visited the University of Utah and made an $8,000,000 donation but this time in the name of Samuel Waters. The university was required, of course, to drop all criminal charges.

Chapter 25 – Hard Time

During Kyle's months of recuperation, he had watched enough TV and movies to catch up on a lifetime of abstinence. He was very anxious to get back to engineering work. He thought of dozens of useful devices that the company's base of knowledge and patents made practical. Many of them were designed for the handicapped and were intended for humane purposes rather than profit. Kyle was welcomed back as an employee at CompuSonic. Kyle had developed some bad habits during his time away from a regular job and school schedules. He had been sleeping in. He set his alarm for six AM the next morning. He was surprised when he got up to find that Annette was already up. He found her in the kitchen fixing him breakfast. "Kyle, I want you to come home by 4:00 today," instructed Annette. "We are going to the premiere showing of the latest Star Trek movie and I have arranged for us to be made up by professional makeup artists. I have wanted to do something like this as long as I can remember. Don't be late."

"So what are we going as?"

"It's a surprise."

Kyle could hardly concentrate on work wondering what strange creature he might be made up to resemble. He just hoped it wasn't a Ferengi. When Kyle arrived home, he found four extra cars parked in front of the house. He was met at the door by Annette and ushered into the basement where a team of makeup artists was assembled with suitcases full of makeup, clothing, masks and accessories. For over two hours, the team worked on the couple. When they finished, the Jameses were Klingons. Kyle had the physique for a Worf lookalike and made an impressive-looking Klingon warrior. Annette had the bust for a Klingon woman but needed platform shoes to give her adequate height. A limousine transported them to the theater. To Kyle's dismay, they arrived over half an hour before the show began, even though Annette had pre-purchased tickets online. It turned out that the point was to be seen in line and compare costumes with other Star Trek enthusiasts. There were some impressive costumes, but none came close to the Klingon couple. Many pictures were taken and Kyle feared his wife's highly exposed cleavage would make the front page. It concerned him that many were staring at more than just Annette's costume and makeup. After all of the hoopla, the movie itself was rather disappointing. However, the true Trekkies were not to be deterred and a party was held at a local restaurant after the viewing. Kyle would have been bored except that he saw how happy and excited Annette was throughout the entire evening.

Annette was still excited the next morning. "I always knew that if I ever had lots of money I would know how to have fun with it. Yesterday was one of the best days of my whole life."

"I don't care much about money, but it was wonderful to see you have such a great time. If you ever want to do something like that again, I'm game."

"You are the most wonderful husband in the world. You know, though, I will have to raise the bar for next time." Kyle was not sure he liked the sound of raising the bar but figured he could deal with it.

March 31 was Annette's birthday. Kyle arranged for a large celebration for her at their home. All of their friends were invited and a local catering company provided an extravagant meal. Kyle also hired professional musicians and entertainers for a full evening of festivities. He hoped he was "raising the bar" sufficiently for Annette's satisfaction. For her birthday present, he had secured a promise from the producer of the Star Trek movies that Annette could play a part as a significant extra in the next Star Trek film. Before Annette blew out the candles on her cake, she said something that had everyone wondering. "My wish is that in the end, you will enjoy my secret birthday present as much as I know I will." Neither

Kyle nor anyone else knew what Annette was talking about. After the guests and entertainers had all left, the happy couple collapsed into bed.

Kyle awoke the next morning feeling as if something were very wrong. The bed did not feel right. When he reached for Annette, his hand collided with a concrete wall. He felt in the other direction and found that he was lying on a very narrow bed. He sat up and looked around in the dim light. He definitely was not at home. He rotated his legs off the bed and his bare feet touched a cool concrete floor. He stood and moved away from the bunk. He had his hands extended to protect him from collision with a wall. One of them contacted a steel door. It appeared he was in some kind of jail cell. Kyle's first thought was that he was dreaming. He pinched himself. He sure seemed to be awake. Suddenly the lights went on. He was not just in a jail cell; he was in prison, surrounded by other prisoners, each in their cells. Over a loudspeaker came the blaring message, "Rise and shine, let's clean up those filthy bodies." The door of his and all the other cells on his wing automatically opened. Inmates began filing out heading down the hall. Kyle looked and found that he was wearing a prison uniform. He tried to figure out what in the world had happened to him. One night he was a free man celebrating his wife's birthday and the next morning he was a prison inmate. As he pondered on the strange change of fortunes, a guard shouted at him.

"Get the lead out, James. We ain't got all day." Kyle reluctantly joined in the line. The inmates entered a room in which they all stripped and tossed their soiled clothing into clothes hampers. They were then marched off to the showers. Kyle noticed many eyeing him and was glad that he had sufficient size and strength to resist any advances. He felt much better when the shower was over and he could put on a clean uniform. The group was marched into the cafeteria. When Kyle saw what they were eating, he was glad he had his store of flavor memories. He was hungry and found that with the right added flavors the food was not bad. As Kyle looked around, he would catch people looking at him who then quickly looked away. Suddenly it hit him. It was April 1; Annette was playing a world-class April fool's joke on him. He was determined to give Annette her money's worth, and maybe even have some fun himself. He tried not to smile as he figured things out. After breakfast, the prisoners were escorted back to their cells. Kyle tried to look around the cell without making it obvious what he was looking for. Sure enough, there were several miniature cameras stuck to the ceiling and in nooks and crannies. Kyle sat on the bunk with his head down trying to figure out how Annette would expect him to act. His thoughts were interrupted by a guard who opened his cell door.

"Well James, today's your lucky day. After a year of good behavior, you are rewarded with a conjugal visit. Your wife is waiting for you." Kyle hadn't expected Annette to show up but went along with the gag. He was escorted to a room containing a huge woman who weighed at least 300 pounds. Her arms were covered with tattoos and she was missing several teeth. She opened wide her arms and ran towards Kyle. Kyle reciprocated and to the woman's shock greeted her with a mock passionate kiss.

"Oh, baby. I been waiting a long time for this." The guard had left the room and Kyle started removing his uniform. The woman had a most bewildered look on her face. She was obviously expecting Kyle to be repulsed by her looks and be looking for an escape route. By the time Kyle was down to his underwear she began to cry. Kyle pulled his uniform back on. "It's OK lady. You played your part just fine. Games over now, Annette." Kyle knew the miniature cameras had a very short broadcast range and that Annette would have to be close. The door opened and Annette entered the room.

"So when did you figure things out?" she asked.

"During breakfast. How did you like your birthday present?"

"Great. I expected you to figure things out within the first few minutes. Thanks for not being too bright." Later that week there was another party held for all the friends and they watched videos of Kyle's prison experience. Many had not laughed so hard since they were children. Their favorite part was the look on the woman's face when Kyle kissed her. All agreed that it was the best April fool's joke they had ever heard of.

Annette was working in the garden in the afternoon. She noticed a bumblebee sitting on a flower near her. It was equipped with a microprocessor and a miniature camera. Annette put her face near the camera and said, "Hello, Samuel. We need to talk."

Chapter 26 – Secret Agents

Becky lost the baby she had been carrying after only a few months of pregnancy. Josh did not fully explain, but Becky had some serious reproductive problems that might bar them from ever having children. "The doctor says that we should not even try again for five years. It is unlikely that Becky will ever be able to carry a child to full term," explained Josh to Kyle over the phone.

"Does Becky feel okay physically? I know she must be extremely disappointed."

"Becky is in good health. We of course are disappointed. However, Becky is an extremely upbeat person. She says that not being able to have children may open up all sorts of service opportunities. She is a woman of incredible faith and gratitude to God. We have even talked about a shot at the Olympics. Her body may not be very good at making babies, but it can sure excel at sports, especially volleyball."

"Kyle, I don't just want to make money and have fun spending it. I want to use our unique capabilities to serve our country and mankind." Kyle had been almost ready to fall off to sleep when Annette hit him with this unexpected line of thinking. He wondered why it was that women always seemed to want to have their most serious conversations when their husbands were ready for sleep or other activities typically accomplished in bed.

"What exactly do you want to do?"

"I want to be some kind of special agent. With my computer reflexes, language skills and body control, I can do things that no other woman in the world can do. And you have some special capabilities of your own. With our ability to communicate without external devices we would make the perfect secret agents."

"How can we be secret agents? We have been seen on TV by millions of people. There have even been articles about us in Time Magazine and the Wall Street Journal."

"I know, but dressing up as Klingons made me think that with the proper disguises we would not be recognized. I have learned about ways to temporarily change skin color. I can quickly learn to speak any language without an American accent. I can even learn to talk with a regional accent and vocabulary. I know that you can mimic voices. It might take you longer, but you can also learn any language and I think that we can even perfect your accent. I know that it sounds kind of farfetched, but it would really make me happy." If there was one thing that Kyle liked to do, it was to make his wife happy.

"OK, if you can find a government agency that wants to use us, I guess we can give it a shot."

"Oh, thank you, Love. When can you turn in your resignation at work? The CIA already has a mission in mind for us. I knew that you would say yes so I have already made the arrangements."

"I haven't even received a paycheck yet and you want me to quit? I'm sure that the guys would be happy to just pretend that I never came back to work and call it even. I haven't really had time to get started on anything that important."

"Great, we'll start tomorrow with a small upgrade to your system. Good night, Dear." Annette put her body in sleep mode, but Kyle knew that her mind would still be working at full speed. The urge to sleep had left him and he stayed awake for hours thinking about what upgrade he would receive and what mission they would be assigned.

Kyle awoke late having taken hours to get to sleep the night before. Annette was already up and had fixed breakfast. At breakfast, Annette explained the small upgrade. "Kyle, the external earpiece that looks like a traditional hearing aid has to go. It would normally disqualify you for the work we will perform and could be a significant security risk. I have worked out an alternative solution to providing audio input and power. With the help of outside consultants, I have designed an inconspicuous microphone that can be embedded in the flesh of your ear. It will look like a small freckle. The coupling coil will be embedded under your skin so that it is not visible. We have also created a miniature version of your power source that uses sugars for fuel. We will embed the power source under your scalp. You will additionally be equipped with a miniature ultrasonic transducer that will be more sensitive than your microphone.

After breakfast, Kyle called CompuSonic and explained his need to undo his rehiring. Annette had arranged to perform the minor surgery in the University Hospital's portable operating room. Annette, with the assistance of Dr. Teng, performed the operation. Only local anesthesia was required. Within a few hours, Kyle was able to return home. He and Annette told their friends that they would be traveling for an undetermined amount of time.

"Kyle, I would like to ask a favor of you," began Annette as they drove home. "I would like you to begin, starting now, to record everything that you see and hear and keep it stored until I can upload it. I will try to upload each night while we are in physical contact. There may be important evidence gathered or just memories to preserve."

"No problem babe. Just don't let it go so long before offloading that I start running out of storage space."

The next morning Kyle and Annette caught a plane to Washington DC. An unmarked sedan driven by an agent named Ramon Hernandez picked up the couple at the airport. "Welcome Mr. and Mrs. James. We are so excited and pleased to have you join us. Are you confident that no one but the three of us and the director knows that you are here?"

"I am very confident that no one else knows that we are here, unless of course if you or the director have told anyone else," responded Annette.

"I can assure you that we have not. Because you are so well known, it is imperative that the number of people who know that you are here is kept to a bare minimum. I will be taking you first to a nearby safe house. We will be alone. I have personally created new IDs for you. You will be Jorge Martinez and Maria Alina Morado. These were real people with builds similar to yours and similar facial features. After we alter your skin color, a reversible process I might add, you will look much like them."

"What happened to the original Jorge and Maria?" asked Kyle.

"You don't need to know that, Mr. James."

"But surely we do if we are going to assume their identities," argued Kyle.

"Look, Kyle, I promised Mrs. James that I would never lie to you. If you press me you may not like the answers you get."

"If I am going to have to do the kind of things that you do, I must know what kind of things you do. I insist on knowing what happened to these people."

"I killed them in a couple of clandestine drug busts. It was justified deadly force, but admittedly, I placed myself in a position that I had no other choice. Furthermore, no one outside of our group of four even knows that they are dead. Jorge and Maria had no criminal record so your new names will not raise any red flags. You will stay at the safe house until your complexion has changed and you have perfected your accents and perfectly assumed your roles. I will bring supplies in the meantime. The way that you two became doctors in a year, this should be a piece of cake in comparison. It normally takes about two weeks for the color change to be 80 percent complete. It will take a couple more months for it to finalize, but no one will notice that. When you are ready to leave the safe house, you will begin a rigorous program of CIA training as Jorge and Maria. You will act as if you do not know each other at the start of training. You can pretend to start a relationship then if you like, or you can maintain your distance. Personally, I doubt that you will choose the latter, but it is up to you. Here is the documentation on your new IDs." Ramon handed each an envelope complete with photographs, handwriting samples and detailed life descriptions. We are almost to the safe house, your new home for at least the next two weeks. Annette quickly paged through her document and then took Kyle's from him. She scanned it just as quickly and then holding Kyle's hand transmitted the data to him.

In the safe house, Ramon also gave each of them an MP3 player with a recording of Jorge and Maria's voices. Kyle started to ask how the recordings were obtained but changed his mind before saying anything. "The condo is stocked with food, but I can bring you takeout if you would like," offered Ramon.

"What would you say to Chinese, Kyle?" asked Annette.

"That sounds like a safe bet," answered Kyle. Annette wrote down some of their favorites on a notepad by the phone and handed it to Ramon.

"Enjoy it while you can. You will have to learn about Mexican food before you leave. And you will have to learn how to cook it," instructed Ramon looking at Annette. Ramon ordered the meal using his cell phone and left to pick it up. While Ramon was gone, Kyle and Annette explored their temporary home. It was small but clean and new. There was a decent home entertainment system and a large library of DVDs and CDs. I'm going to miss my home and garden," sighed Annette.

"To me, home is where you are," responded Kyle as he took his lovely wife in his arms. "Do you think it will be OK if Jorge and Maria get married?"

"I don't think so. Weddings draw a lot of attention. Maybe we will have to be naughty and just shack up."

Their playful flirtation was interrupted as they heard Ramon come in. They thanked Ramon and he departed, after snagging an egg roll. "What do you say we eat in bed and watch a movie?" asked Annette.

"You got it, babe."

Chapter 27 – Saving a Life

Annette almost instantly had her new identity integrated into her programming. She could speak exactly like Maria, at least the words that were on the recording. She could extrapolate the rest. Kyle took only a couple of days to get the facts down. At Annette's insistence, they spoke entirely in Spanish after the first week and called each other Maria and Jorge. She knew that she could do her part without mistake, but she wanted to give Kyle all of the help that she could. Kyle had developed a technique to directly program information into his brain over a year ago, but with Annette's help, he learned how to adjust specific areas of the brain to perform their tasks differently. They were able to actually change Kyle's accent to be like Jorge's. What was even more impressive was that they built in a sort of switch in Kyle's brain so that he could switch back and forth between his normal accent and Jorge's. Annette cut their hair to match the styles that Jorge and Maria had worn. Kyle's hair was now black, even at the roots. Annette had always had dark hair, but it also turned black. Their skin had taken on a light brown color. Kyle wrote his new mother a postcard explaining that he had gotten into serious trouble with the law and was in hiding. Annette did the same. Ramon mailed the cards from a far way state while on a trip.

Both Maria and Jorge had been college graduates. Maria had a Bachelor of Science degree in nursing. Jorge had a Bachelor of Science degree in chemistry. Although Annette was a medical doctor, she still needed to learn some information and skills associated with nursing. Kyle needed to add some to his knowledge of chemistry. Each needed to learn about the schools their IDs attended, what teachers they had and even what classmates they might have had. It was important that their IDs were college graduates so that they could be admitted into the CIA training program for "clandestine service operations officers", as the CIA liked to call them. Ramon had already taken care of admitting them into the program. Ramon checked in on the future agents every few days. He was very impressed with their progress. He could not believe how fast they picked up the accents and the language. He dropped in on them after 19 days. After Kyle unloaded some fresh groceries from his arms, Ramon offered, "I think that I can significantly shorten your official training if you each knew Arabic and a little Russian. I do not have a cover story of how you would know these languages. Maybe you could say that you did a computer study course on your own or had a lover that spoke the language or something. What do you think?"

"We would need an extra week of preparation," responded Annette. "Of course, Kyle will need a few more weeks to become fluent. You will need to bring us some training programs just so we have a good cover story. I will have to invent some Russian lovers for us."

"What do you think Kyle?"

"If Maria says that we can do it, we will. She is never wrong about these things or anything else for that matter." Kyle realized that he probably seemed henpecked. At his size and strength, he did not feel like his manhood was threatened. However, he had already met and exceeded every goal in life that he ever had, and much of it was due to this unique combination of computer, beauty and clever brilliance that was his wife. His wife kept him very happy and he was thrilled to play whatever game she wanted to play. Especially when they would be serving the country that had given them so much. Despite his happiness, he wondered what would happen if he ever crossed the woman that he loved. He was afraid to challenge Annette, yet part of him wanted to, just to see how she would react. How deep and resilient was her love, he wondered.

Kyle had imagined the initial training to be like Army boot camp. It was not. He and Annette posing as Jorge and Maria were treated as professionals. They were not humiliated, shouted at or belittled in any way. However, they were aggressively trained intellectually and physically. Both were fast learners academically. Even without computer assist, Kyle had always learned fast. Annette had been far sharper intellectually than most realized before her computerization and now she was unsurpassed in learning ability of things both intellectual and physical. She picked up physical combat instruction almost instantly. She was always the star of the class. Jorge always seemed to need a night to sleep on it to pick up the physical skills. Each night Annette transmitted to him information for nightly absorption that was uniquely tailored to his physique.

The Jameses communicated using their built-in radios each night, but Kyle ached for Annette's physical affection after only a few days. Since marrying Annette, he had been almost surfeited with romance from his beautiful wife. "Almost", because for a man of his temperament that had lived celibate for over a quarter of a century there could not be too much of a good thing. He just reminded himself that he was doing this for the love of his life. Kyle was temporarily living in a modest motel until the apartment that he had located became available next month. As he exercised while watching the true "opiate of the masses", television, there came a knock at the door. "Housekeeping," uttered a middle-aged female voice with a strong Mexican accent.

"Come in," commanded Kyle who was holding a one-gallon can of black olives in each of his large hands. He had found that by doing arm rolls and other gyrations with the added mass he could get a good upper-body workout without special equipment. He heard a key turn in the lock. A plump looking cleaning lady entered.

"Pardon me, Señor. I have clean sheets," explained the woman as she walked to the bedroom.

"No problema, Señora. Gracias por su atención a mis necesidades," (No problem, madam. Thank you for your attention to my needs) responded Kyle, practicing his habit of treating all in society with dignity and kindness. Kyle could hear the woman making his bed. After a few minutes, he heard the woman call out.

"Ayuda, por favor," (Help, please) came the request from the bedroom. Kyle put down the cans and muted the TV, wondering what help the maid could need. He walked into the bedroom. Lying in the bed now made up with red silk sheets was Annette, dressed in a black teddy. A fat-suit leaned against the wall in a corner. Annette looked up at him seductively. "I've missed you, my love."

Incredulous, still not believing his eyes, Kyle asked, "Was that you that came a few minutes ago?"

"It's me baby, 40 grams of silicon and not one ounce of silicone."

The next morning Kyle was tired but happy. Annette had stayed until about 5 AM. Over the next few weeks, Annette found ways to be with Kyle. She repeated the maid act several times and at the agency occasionally reached out with an arm and pulled in Kyle as he walked by a closet door. There were no silk sheets, but Kyle certainly did not complain. Kyle knew that few, if any wives, were this good to their husbands. He did not know how long his good fortune would continue, but he was going to enjoy every second of it. After Kyle moved into his apartment, Jorge asked Maria out on a date and she soon moved in with him, much to the disappointment of the other men in training.

Once those in charge of training became aware of Jorge and Maria's extraordinary language attainments and capabilities there was a move to accelerate their training and get them into action as soon as possible. The plan was to still have them graduate with their class but pull them out of class for a pre-graduation mission. Medical personnel were being kidnapped by the Taliban in Afghanistan at an alarming rate. Others in the CIA were not so sure that Jorge and Maria were ready to pose as Arabians working in Afghanistan. They were sure that they would speak with American accents. When they heard Maria and Jorge speak Arabic, they could not believe their ears. There was no trace of an American accent.

They moved into one-on-one intense training as to their IDs and backgrounds. To eliminate family complications each was cast as an orphan. Jorge would be Awad and Maria would be Nida. Their IDs were married to each other and had the surname Mazin. Nida was infertile and thus they had no offspring. Awad was a lab technician and Nida a nurse. They had only just arrived in Kabul and would work in the Cure International Hospital. As part of their linguistics training, they were taught some basic Dari Persian and Pashto, the two official languages of Afghanistan. Ironically, the agents arranging the mission kept lamenting that Jorge was not a doctor, not knowing that Kyle was a doctor. They gave him a crash course in medical laboratory technology assuming that a bright chemist should be able to pick it right up. Finally, after eight weeks of intense training, they were inserted into Afghanistan.

Awad and Nida worked without incident for two weeks in the hospital. One of the techniques that the Taliban was currently using was to call for medical assistance for a supposed life-threatening incident such as a heart attack or stroke. The medical responders were then ambushed. It was getting to the point that few medical personnel were willing to respond to calls. When the young couple volunteered for this duty expressing a desire to work together, they were gladly accepted, in spite of Awad's apparent lack of training. In third world countries, degrees and certificates are valued but not always considered essential. Both Awad and Nida had been participating in EMT training given by the Red Cross and were recognized by all around them as very fast learners. In addition, they already were speaking the languages of the country with surprising fluency.

A call came in that a woman was suffering a heart attack in one of the most dangerous sections of the city. No one was willing to drive the ambulance so Awad had to do so. They approached the small apartment with great caution. A young woman met them in the street to explain the situation. "My mother had pain in her chest and left shoulder and then collapsed into unconsciousness. Please hurry," she pleaded.

Nida said to Awad in Arabic, "She is telling the truth. This is legitimate." The couple rushed inside, each carrying a case of emergency supplies. A woman, who appeared to be about fifty, lay on the floor on a small throw rug with a blanket covering her. Nida rushed to her side to check her pulse and breathing. There was neither. She immediately began CPR and Awad joined her. They expected the exercise to be fruitless, but to their surprise, the woman revived. The young woman who had greeted them had been hovering over the threesome and began to almost hysterically cry out with joy. Kyle was even more surprised to see that his lovely wife was also crying. They had come as secret agents but had saved a life using their most basic medical training. Studying medicine has been a learning exercise for Kyle. He was not sure why Annette had gone to medical school. Regardless of why they had entered into medical training, they had just saved a life or at least prolonged life and it was a wonderful feeling. However, it was not at all clear how long this woman would live. Kyle raced to the ambulance to get a stretcher. Together, he and Annette carried the woman to the ambulance. The young woman pleaded to be able to ride with her mother. The couple consented and within moments, Kyle was racing back to the hospital with sirens blaring and lights flashing.

Unfortunately, the hospital lacked the kinds of modern treatment options common in American hospitals. They did have a working ultrasound unit and a competent technician to run it. It was clear from the echocardiogram that the woman had a blocked artery and another that was very restricted. Annette asked the technician to leave them with the patient. Annette took Kyle's hand so that she could speak with him in total privacy. "This woman has little money and this hospital is not equipped to help her. However, I have been working on something as a weapon that may be used to treat her. Do you remember the video on YouTube showing a group of kids popping popcorn using their cell phones? It was a hoax, of course, but it gave me an idea. I have the equivalent of 104 cell phones in me. I can focus their output using phased array technology and output almost any frequency. I can pop an individual kernel. I figured that I could focus on a bad guy's optic nerve and blind him. I should also be able to dissolve arterial plaque. I can use the ultrasound machine to guide me."

"That is brilliant, Annette. The woman is already on Heparin and we can send her home with Warfarin to prevent clotting."

Working together using Kyle's radio transmitter/receivers in receiver mode as a detector and using the ultrasound to guide them, they freed the clogged artery. The woman was conscious but did not understand what her silent caregivers, who seemed to communicate without speaking, were doing. After completing the procedure Annette merely said to the woman in Persian, "Your heart is fine now. You can go home with your lovely daughter."

Later that evening in their small apartment Kyle asked Annette, "How did you know that the young woman was telling the truth?"

"I guess that I will have to share my secret. I have developed a very reliable lie detector. The idea was inspired by an article I read in the Deseret News years ago. It told about a group of people known as aphasics that have proven to be accurate natural lie detectors. Aphasics have lost the ability to understand or use words due to brain damage. They can still hear. They just can't understand. These people have proven highly accurate at detecting liars through changes in facial expression and in the fundamental audible frequency of the voice. I have created a program like the Mrs. Monroe program that is basically an aphasic. It does not understand language but understands facial expressions and body cues. I use this program to tell if someone is lying. I can create a similar program for you if you want. Someday you are going to want to upgrade that little electronic brain of yours."

Chapter 28 – Taking Lives

The next day another emergency call came into the hospital. This one was from another dangerous part of town where many terrorist sympathizers, if not actual terrorists, lived. A woman reported that her child had difficulty breathing and had turned blue. Once again, Awad and Nida Mazin were the only ones willing to respond. They raced to the location given, knowing that there was a good chance that they could save another life. Awad brought the vehicle to a jerking halt and leaped from the vehicle. Nida was quickly at his side as they ran to the front door of the home. A woman burst out of the door holding a child of about two years of age. The woman was immediately followed by two men carrying AK47 assault rifles. Annette could see using her rear head camera that four more men approached her from behind. This was precisely what Annette and Kyle had come for, but they were never the less terrified, more for each other than for themselves. Kyle had a sick feeling in his stomach; how would these vile men treat his lovely wife? Likewise, Annette felt a pang of guilt for what she had gotten her husband into. It was all her fault. He had just been trying to please her.

They had worried during their training about how well they would be able to pretend to be frightened and intimidated. No pretense was necessary now. Four barrels were pointed at Awad's head, two at Nida's. "On your knees!" commanded one of the men that emerged from the house. He was of medium build, shorter and thinner than Kyle. He had a large scar on his left cheek. His voice sounded young, almost soft and child-like, but his face looked prematurely aged. The men from behind quickly put hoods over the captives blocking their vision. They were commanded to stand. The men bound their hands behind their backs with what felt like plastic ties. The men spun their captives around to disorient them. Kyle had lost his bearings but not Annette; she always knew where she was and which way she was facing. Annette had placed several remote transmitter cameras on the ambulance. She could see most of what was happening from their images. Fortunately for the couple, the captors used the ambulance to drive them to their lair.

Three terrorists rode in the ambulance and three more followed in another vehicle, a beat-up looking Honda Accord. Kyle and Annette were pressed up against each other in the back of the ambulance. Kyle initiated an ultrasonic conversation. "Are you alright, my love?"

"Never better, my long-suffering husband. I'm sorry for this mess I have gotten you into."

"What mess? Everything is going according to plan. I have already reported our good fortune to our handlers. They are very pleased with our progress."

"That may have been a mistake. How do you explain it to them? They don't have any idea of our hidden hardware."

"We didn't plan this very well," mused Kyle. "We need to invent a secret assistant. He takes photos and emails them. He calls on his cell phone and gives progress reports."

"How did such a manly man as you get to be so smart? That is brilliant. I have several extra satellite phone accounts just for such an occasion. I will have Deep Throat call in right now. He can tell them to read their email." Annette dialed the number of her handler.

"Hello, this is Nura," responded the handler.

"Do not hang up," commanded a gravelly masculine voice. "My name is not important. I am a friend of Awad and Nida. They are in grave danger. They have been abducted by six armed men. They were blindfolded, tied up and taken in the ambulance they arrived in. It headed south followed by an eighties vintage Honda Accord, license number AG 213. I have a GPS; I will follow at a distance and report my location. I have taken digital photos and will email them to you as opportunity arises. I will call back in a few minutes."

The terrorist caravan headed out of town and towards the mountains. Eventually, it stopped at the end of a dirt road and the group proceeded on foot up a steep path. Along the way, Annette kept a detailed GPS map of their journey. She communicated with her worldwide network of computers that she had spawned, entering through the "back door" that she had programmed into each unit. She wanted to be sure that their location was not lost. She also emailed photos of the kidnapping and photos taken along the route to her handlers as if they came from her "friend".

After abandoning the ambulance, she could no longer depend on its cameras for surveillance. The hood covered the camera in her hair. After a 37-minute hike, they entered a cave. They walked for five minutes into the cave and stopped. Awad and Nida were forced down onto steel folding chairs and their hoods were removed. Video and still digital cameras were mounted on tripods in front of them. A young man that had not been part of the kidnapping party began taking pictures of them. Both Kyle and Annette looked around using their own eyes as cameras to capture images. Annette transmitted the images to her network of computers but not to her handler. After the picture taking, the lead terrorist, the one with the scar on his face, returned. "Now that we have photographed you we can rough you up if we want, even torture and kill you," offered Scarface in a very businesslike voice.

"Allah will punish you for what you are doing," offered Nida. Scarface slapped her viciously across her right cheek with the back of his right hand.

"Hold your tongue woman or I will cut it out!" threatened Scarface.

Kyle communicated electronically. "What are you doing, Annette? You will get us killed." Kyle knew that pain was nothing to Annette but being mutilated and maimed or killed was another matter. Couldn't she just wait for the rescue party?

"Relax, Kyle. I know just what I am doing." Using only her facial expressions Nida seem to insult and belittle the scar-faced man. He grabbed her by her hair thrusting her head back and stared at her angrily. That was just what Annette wanted. Using her 104 transmitters in phase array mode, she severed Scarface's right retinal nerve from the retina. The action was painless and Scarface did not realize what had happened. When Annette severed the left retinal nerve, the lights suddenly went out for him. He actually believed that the lights had been turned out since in a cave, when the lights go out, there is total darkness. He let go of Nida and started shouting for someone to turn the lights back on. One of his accomplices ran into the chamber.

"What's wrong, Mohamed?"

"What do you mean, 'What's wrong?' Someone turned out the lights."

"What are you talking about? The lights are on. Are you blind?"

"Apparently I am."

"How can this be? What happened? Your eyes look fine."

"They may look fine to you, but I cannot see." By now, the second man was close enough to Annette for her to destroy one of the tiny bones in his left middle ear. That hurt and the man cupped his hand over his left ear and instinctively rotated his head to the left as if something had struck him from in front of him. Annette proceeded to destroy his hearing in his right ear." The man cried out in pain.

"What is wrong, Ali?" shouted Mohamed, confused as to what had happened. Ali ran from the room screaming. Annette scooted her chair closer to Kyle's and began burning through the plastic tie that bound Kyle using her highly focused radio waves. When Kyle was free, he approached the blind man and swatted him with the steel chair that he had been sitting on. He took the man's knife and AK47 and rushed to Annette's side. He cut Annette loose and handed her the knife. Annette removed the cameras from their tripods.

"Shoot out the lights Kyle. I can guide us out of here in the dark." Annette placed her right hand on Kyle's left shoulder so that she would not lose him in the dark. Although she could locate him using radio communication she saw no need to take chances. After Kyle had put them in darkness, Annette advised, "If you see any artificial light, shoot it." They could hear shouting coming from another part of the cave. "I will leave your hands free to shoot so follow the directions I give with my hand on your shoulder. I will steer you." Using her perfect memory of the cave layout Annette guided them from the chamber, keeping to the edges of the cavity. Two men approached with flashlights. Kyle let loose a burst of automatic weapon fire at the lights, mowing them down. He had never taken human life before, but he was not going to risk Annette's life by being timid. He would make his peace with God later. As they approached ceiling lights, Kyle shot them out. They continued walking in total blackness. After what seemed to Kyle like an eternity, they began to see natural light. "This is where we need to be most careful," warned Annette. "There may be guards outside of the cave." In fact, there were two guards and they had heard the gunfire. As they ran into the cave, their bodies were distinctly outlined by the light behind them. Their eyes were adjusted to the bright light of the outdoors while Kyle and Annette were adjusted to the darkness. It was an easy matter for Kyle to take them out with a burst from the weapon that he carried.

They exited the cave and hurried down the hill towards the vehicles. Their "friend" called Nura and informed her that Nida and Awad had escaped and would be heading down the mountain. They did not want to be mistaken for terrorists. Kyle and Annette flew down the mountain, reaching the vehicles in a fraction of the time it took them to make the ascent. The keys were gone from the vehicles, but Kyle produced a spare key from inside his left sock. Annette took the AK47 from Kyle and shot out the tires of the Accord. She joined Kyle in the ambulance and they hurried down the mountain.

"It's a wonder we were not killed!" shouted Kyle to Annette in English.

"I know, I'm sorry. We may have pulled it off, but it was still a bad idea. I was very selfish to put you in this kind of danger."

"To put us in this kind of danger. Do you think that I could ever be happy without you? You have totally spoiled me. I thought that Sharon was a great wife, and she was, but no woman could ever come close to you."

"Why, thank you, Kyle. You're a mighty outstanding husband yourself. What other husband would have allowed himself to be kidnapped by terrorists just to please his wife?" After 15 minutes of driving, they were met by CIA agents coming up the road. They stopped briefly and shared information and then headed back down the road. They returned to the hospital and remained vigilant but acted as if nothing had happened. They fabricated a cover story in which they removed a small toy from a child's throat.

The CIA was able to capture Mohamed. They had to shoot what was left of the other terrorists in the firefight. The CIA agents had no idea how Mohamed had lost his sight. They wondered if the blow to the head had anything to do with it. Losing his sight had humbled Mohamed and made him much more receptive to interrogation. The cave was also full of valuable information. Annette kept the memory chips from the cameras but disposed of the cameras themselves. As they lay in bed together that night holding each other, Annette suggested, "Let's just go home. We will tell our handlers that we were terrified and want to go home. I think that we have done enough for our country and this country for a while."

Chapter 29 – Hard Time Leaving

The agency was extremely disappointed but was accustomed to agents losing their nerve in the field, often with much less provocation. Arrangements were made to return Jorge and Maria to the states. During their last morning in Afghanistan, Annette and Kyle were subdued as they dressed. "Let's wear our body armor until we get to the states," suggested Annette.

"You won't get any argument from me," responded Kyle. We may sweat like pigs, but I, for one, want to get home in one piece." A vehicle came for them the next morning. Annette and Kyle decided to stay in their Awad and Nida characters. As the driver exited the vehicle, Annette scanned his face and checked it against her databases. He was a local that contracted with the CIA. He should not know Annette and Kyle's civilian IDs. "Greetings, I am Rafi. I will be driving you to the airport. Shall we get loaded?" While Rafi and Kyle loaded the luggage into the trunk, Annette used her transmitter/receivers in a probing phased array mode as well as her natural senses to study the vehicle. The aged Mercedes ran on diesel, a definite advantage in case of an explosive attack. Diesel is much less flammable than gasoline and can only be made to explode under precise conditions. The window glass was bullet-resistant. The undercarriage was armored but more so in the front. They should not ride in the back. Rafi was clearly more concerned about protecting himself than his passengers. As Annette walked around the vehicle, she clandestinely placed small cameras in key areas.

"Rafi, when I return to my homeland, I will not be permitted to drive. May I please drive to the airport?" asked Nada with pleading eyes.

"Only if I may join you in the front; I get car sick in the back."

"Wonderful, Awad will join us in the middle." Annette was determined to get Kyle home in one piece and she didn't mind using Rafi's rotund body in lieu of a side airbag. The three squeezed into the front seat. Annette proceeded on the way to the airport with the utmost caution. She thought about stories of soldiers who were killed just before their tour of duty was to end. She did not want that kind of ending for Kyle. She was less concerned about herself since she was already living on borrowed time. Annette used all of her senses, cameras, transmitters and receivers to search for any dangers, hidden or overt. Along a long rural stretch of highway, several times she swerved into the oncoming traffic lane to keep distance from an area of soil that looked like it had been recently disturbed. Other times she drove on the shoulder to put distance between them and possible dangers on the far side of the road. Rafi gave her frustrated looks at times but said nothing. Kyle drifted in and out of sleep. Annette slowed as she approached an area where the soil was disturbed on both sides of the highway.

"Why are we slowing?" asked Rafi.

"I don't like the looks of the shoulders on either side. I will have to drive down the middle. I suggest that we slouch down for added protection."

"I will do no such thing!" protested Rafi. Annette and Kyle slid down in the seat so that their heads were below the level of the windows as they slowly proceeded down the middle of the highway.

"This is absurd," protested Rafi. "You cannot even see to drive." Rafi reached across to grab the steering wheel. Just as he grabbed the wheel, both sides of the road exploded simultaneously. The sedan's windows imploded and the roof of the car ripped up and back leaving the Mercedes looking like an open can of sardines. Annette was protected from flying glass by her Kevlar lined burqa. The hood and veil shielded her delicate face. Kyle was completely shielded by Rafi's now dead, corpulent body. In addition to the glass, the explosions pushed inward the entire structure of the car. The doors bulged inward shoving Annette even tighter against Kyle and making a hasty exit impossible. An off-road vehicle came roaring from behind a bluff. Angry men brandishing automatic weapons leaped from the vehicle as it slowed to a stop. They circled the Mercedes without approaching closer than eight meters. A large truck that had been just ahead of the Mercedes stopped and backed up to the impact zone. The men quickly rolled up the rear door of the truck and lowered a ramp. A man leaped into the back of the truck and pulled out a steel cable that they hooked to the frame of the Mercedes. An electric winch whined as it pulled the car into the truck.

Annette had been in constant communication with her network of computers, but when the truck door slammed shut, she lost communication. Not sure if they were under surveillance, Annette used ultrasonic communication. "Kyle, I just lost all communication with the outside world. Whether intentional or just by natural construction, this truck bed is forming a Faraday cage. We may be in real trouble this time. I'm so sorry."

"It's okay, Annette. We are not dead yet. You didn't force me into this. Up until your creation, I led a pretty boring life. If it's our time to go, at least we had some excitement and did some good along the way." As they conversed, Annette estimated speed and direction as best she could based on sounds and other non-electromagnetic indicators. It sounded like they had entered a highly-populated area. The truck finally stopped. The couple could hear the creak and rattle of a metal door being opened and then the truck proceeded a short distance and stopped. The engine went off. The couple could hear metallic scraping noises and great activity around the vehicle. Finally, the rear door opened and men wearing what looked like beekeeper suits lowered the ramp and attached a cable to the Mercedes. As the car was dragged from the truck, the couple could see that a fine-mesh copper net had been draped over the entire truck. The truck was sitting on a copper pad that extended out beyond the edges of the net. Even outside of the truck, they were in a Faraday cage.

A tall, lean man, who appeared to be in charge, approached from outside of the net. "Mr. and Mrs. James, we are so pleased that you could join us," he said in English and in a calm and inviting voice. "Oh yes, we know who you are. We are not nearly as stupid as you must think we are! Did you really think that a little skin coloring would make us think that you are Arabs? Typical American arrogance. We are going to enjoy so much watching you die slowly."

So, this is it, thought Kyle. Well if he was going to die, he wanted to go out like a man, not a sniveling child. "Let's not go down without a fight, my love. Do we have any weapons?"

"Just our computers and bodies."

"I don't suppose that the car will start or move?"

"In case you haven't noticed, we don't even have any tires."

"Does the radio work?"

"Great thinking Kyle. I will check. Try to shift Rafi over a little so I can turn it on." Kyle very slowly and carefully shifted Rafi's body to the right just enough to expose the radio controls. Annette turned the radio on with zero volume and adjusted the turner to FM 100. She turned up the volume slightly and transmitted a single low volume beep. After hearing the faint beep she changed her transmission to produce silence and turned up the volume on the radio. Based on communications before they were put into a Faraday cage and based on their estimated location, there was a CompuSonic computer, one of her offspring, within transmission range if she could get through the net. Every one of her children would be on high alert listening for a signal from her on frequencies already established and using established encryption. In the voice of the leader and in Pashto came the command over the radio, "Lift the net for me." The men all looked at the leader with a quizzical expression on their faces. "Don't just stand there, lift the net." The leader had hesitated several seconds before he figured out what was happening. Two of the men lifted the net. The leader in frustration shot them with the pistol that he carried at his side and the net dropped back down. It had been long enough. Annette had determined her location and sent out an SOS within milliseconds. Help would be on the way. Fear came across the face of the cocky leader. He had lost the advantage.

"They realize that I got a message out, Kyle. They will either move us or kill us. Let's not wait around to find out. Can you get Rafi off of you?"

"I can do better than that. Be prepared to use your weapons and to run for the truck cab." Kyle maneuvered himself under Rafi so that he could launch Rafi with a sudden extension of his powerful legs. He would use 80 percent of his full strength. The men suspected that Kyle was up to something but had no idea what. They gathered to his side of the net to see what he was doing. Suddenly Rafi's body flew up out of the car and up against the net. The men in a panic started shooting the body.

"Stop, you fools!" commanded the leader. "You'll destroy the Faraday net." The leader looked back at the Mercedes. It was empty. The diversion had allowed Kyle and Annette just enough time to get to the truck. They were just entering the cab. "Shoot the Americans," he commanded. The men shot into the Mercedes not realizing that Kyle and Annette had moved. The leader shot with his pistol, hitting Kyle in the back. Kyle's body armor prevented serious injury. Kyle and Annette made it into the cab before the assailant got off another shot. The keys were even in the ignition. Annette started the engine and threw the manual transmission into reverse. She popped the clutch, spinning the rear tires. The truck rammed into the Mercedes, sliding it across the floor. Men were scrambling everywhere. Annette sped forward pulling the net off of the front of the cab. Apparently, the men had been informed of Annette's powers because they ran for their lives when they saw the net come off. The truck windows were rolled down and Annette reached out to stick a camera on the roof of the cab. The leader had grabbed an AK47 that one of the men dropped. Kyle knew the drill and slid down out of view as did Annette. Using the camera for vision Annette tried to run down the leader who was firing relentlessly at the truck. He was much more agile than the truck and easily evaded them. Annette headed for the closed steel door. It burst open when hit by the momentum of the truck. Annette knew that the radiator and engine had taken many hits. They would not be able to drive far and would leave a trail of smoke. That was okay; she knew exactly where they were.

"Kyle, I can get us out of here, but you must trust me completely. I don't have time to explain, but I have a backup. We need to get to the roof of a tall building. I have in my data banks an aerial map of this neighborhood. Follow my lead. Get out of the truck on my side. Now." At that moment they could hear the squeal of tires as an old Chevy pickup truck slid around the corner headed their way. The bed of the truck overflowed with heavily armed men. As the couple leaped from the truck, Annette grabbed Kyle's left hand and pulled him into an alley too narrow for the pickup truck. Half of the men bailed out in hot pursuit. "Kyle, I know that the doctor told you not to overexert yourself again, but this might be a good time to ignore the doctor's orders. I don't exactly have the sprinter body type. I need you to drag me. We'll save our breath by speaking over RF. Go to the blue door at the building on the left." The door was propped open for ventilation. The couple slipped through it and pulled it shut behind them and locked it. As they ran through the crowded kitchen the sound of bullets ripping through the door echoed in the concrete structure. The couple burst through the front doors just in time to hear the pickup screech into view again. Annette guided them into another restaurant, through it and out the back door. As they continued, cutting a path right through the city, Kyle could see that they were approaching the business district. Finally, they reached the highest building in the area. They ran into the front door, skidding to a halt on the highly polished marble floor. Annette looked around and then commanded, "Head for the stairs!" The couple almost flew up the stairs with Kyle dragging Annette behind him. When they finally got to the top of the eight-story building, they found the door to the observation deck locked. Kyle kicked at it repeatedly until it sprung open. The couple rushed out and circled the deck looking for the ladder to the roof. A gate blocked the bottom, but Kyle climbed around it and as he reached for Annette she offered him her left hand. He clasped it and pulled her up. They scrambled up the ladder onto the roof. There was no helicopter pad or even an open area large enough for a helicopter to land.

"What now?" asked Kyle orally.

"We wait and hope. While we're waiting would you mind reseating my dislocated right shoulder? It popped out on the way up the stairs."

"I'm sorry. I was pretty rough with you."

"You were magnificent. I could not have asked for more. Now the shoulder before we get company." Annette gritted her teeth as Kyle forced the shoulder back into place.

"Why didn't you block the pain?"

"For months my spirit could not feel, taste or smell anything. I am not about to block out any feelings, no matter how unpleasant. Pain tells my spirit that I am alive and it tells my computer mind that I am human. Now help me get off this ridiculous burqa. It is soaking wet with perspiration." Kyle was surprised to find a black teddy under the heavy garment and Annette's flak jacket. "I was planning on surprising you tonight." At that moment, a shadow covered them. They looked up to see the approach of a blimp colored to blend in with the light blue sky. A rope ladder was being lowered from the gondola. Before the ladder reached them, the couple heard shouts from the observation deck. Kyle ran to the ladder and looked for a way to dislodge it. The rails curved around at the top and were each anchored to the roof with lag bolts. Kyle grabbed the rails about half a meter from their mounts. Using his legs to lift, he strained to force the rails from their mounts. Annette understood immediately what he was up to and pushed the rails back and forth perpendicular to the rails' length. Annette's action combined with Kyle's loosened the bolts until they gave way, pulling out of the roof. Together the couple pushed the ladder away from the wall. Two of the terrorist had already started their ascent and jumped free of the ladder. The couple ran to the rope ladder that was now within Kyle's reach. Kyle boosted Annette up to the lowest rung and she quickly scrambled up. A wind gust pushed the ladder up and past the edge of the roof. Kyle ran and with a leap using his powerful legs, he caught the lowest rung and followed Annette up the ladder, which seemed to be longer than a football field. The terrorist shot at them as they ascended the ladder. A round grazed Annette's left thigh. Kyle winced as he saw the flesh wound on Annette's lovely bare leg. Annette did not slacken her pace as she rose up the slender ladder with unnatural speed. When they finally reached the gondola, ready hands helped them through the trap door. The couple panted vigorously as they fell to the floor in exhaustion. One of the attendants applied first aid to Annette's leg.

After several minutes of intense breathing, Kyle looked up at their benefactors. To his surprise, they were rough looking women, heavily tattooed and bearing the scars from many piercings from which the hardware was now missing. The leader was an enormous black woman who had the physique of a linebacker but was very tastefully attired. "I am Shameel, this is Juanita and this is Amy," she offered, looking at Kyle.

"Kyle, these lovely young women work for Dr. Samuel Waters. Please don't be angry. I have been in communication with Samuel and have been working on a presidential pardon for him. He is deeply sorry for his crimes and is trying to make restitution. He has been instrumental in the war on drugs and terrorism and has saved many more lives than he has taken. He has also helped to rehabilitate many young people, including our gracious hosts." Kyle was dumbfounded and speechless. He thought of his mother's shady past. He thought about how much Annette had changed. He had nearly killed a man himself in anger.

"Who am I to judge?" he whispered aloud to himself.

"Kyle, are you alright? You kind of zoned out on us," anxiously inquired his nervous wife who was not sure if this latest revelation about Samuel Waters had pushed her husband over the edge.

"Just thinking. Sorry. You were saying?"

"Samuel would like to personally ask for your forgiveness. We have a telecom set up. Are you ready, or do you need more time?"

"Please give me five minutes."

"You can be alone in the next room," offered Amy as she pointed to a door. Kyle silently relocated to the small dormitory, bowed his head and wept. He finally gained his composure, dried his tears and returned to the group. Shameel turned on an LCD monitor and a picture of Dr. Waters appeared.

"Kyle, we are sorry to hit you with this awkward business just after you have barely escaped with your life. It is with the profoundest shame and guilt that I approach you. Nothing could have ever justified my villainous actions. I plotted your murder, the murder of your close friend, Dr. Monroe, and eventually murdered Dr. Monroe and your beloved wife, Sharon. I will spend eternity trying to make restitution for my regrettable actions. I am worthy of death. I will die if you do not intervene. I am standing over the trap door of a gondola similar to the one you now occupy. The trap door will spring open in sixty seconds if you do not push the white button in front of you." A counter appeared on the screen counting down the seconds. "I have arranged it so that only action on your part will prevent my demise. That way you need feel no guilt for letting me die if you so choose." Kyle watched the seconds count down. He noticed that Dr. Waters' arms and legs were bound making it impossible for him to jump free of the soon to open doors. He thought about how he now loved the woman that he once detested. She had changed. Was it really possible that Dr. Waters had also changed? Kyle had to give him the benefit of the doubt. He pressed the button with plenty of time to spare.

"I forgive you, Samuel. I hope that God can forgive us all." With that, Kyle crumpled to the floor in exhaustion. The women assisted him to a bunk. He laid in a stupor of exhaustion and pain, not sleeping but not fully conscious. Sometime during the night, he drifted off to sleep.

Annette awakened him the next morning with a gentle kiss. "If you are up to it Kyle, we can disembark. An ambulance is waiting to transport us to a hospital in Rome. The ladies can lower you in a chair." Kyle sat up. His muscles were stiff and very sore, but his joints seemed to be all right. He let the crew lower him in a chair suspended from a tripod that they had set up. An electric winch lowered the chair with Kyle securely seated. Once he reached ground level paramedics helped him out of the chair and strapped him to a gurney. The chair ascended for Annette and the paramedics lifted Kyle into the ambulance. When the chair returned with Annette she was given similar treatment. IVs were started on each and each was given generous doses of anti-inflammatory medications.

The couple spent two weeks in a hospital in Rome. Kyle and Annette had only suffered minor damage compared to Kyle's earlier overexertion and were able to walk with the aid of crutches when they left the hospital. They caught a cab to the Rome Cavalieri Hotel and checked into a spacious room. The couple relaxed and swam in the elegant swimming pool. They bought new wardrobes since they had lost all of their luggage. After a few days, they were able to dispense with the crutches and began touring Rome in earnest. Annette helped Kyle learn Italian. They changed hotels several times as their complexions faded to avoid unwanted curiosity. They extended their sight seeing to include not only much of Italy but also many major attractions throughout Europe. After the intense strain and tension created by their clash with terrorists, it was great to relax with no responsibilities. After eight weeks in Europe, they grew homesick and flew home to Utah.

Chapter 30 – Movie Stars

Annette had arranged for a full-blown birthday party for Kyle. They were back to their pale-skinned selves and back in their Salt Lake City home. Neither had told anyone about their activities during their absence. Annette had promised to show a full-length movie of their travels. Annette had a home theater installed in the basement just for the occasion. Oh, how she loved having money. It could be so convenient. After a delicious meal, the guests gathered for the video. Some were expecting a slide show, others something like the prison video; not even Kyle anticipated what Annette had prepared.

"Thank you all for coming. I have a special surprise for you. Kyle and I have tried our hands at movie making. We have created a full-length movie for your enjoyment. On with the show." With that, Annette started the movie. To Kyle's shock and amazement, it was a video recording of their entire adventure from the ride to the safe house to their return home. Annette had used their own eyes, her miniature cameras and in some scenes digital creation of different camera angles. The video even included the maid/teddy incident, much to the amusement of the group, especially Nate. The faces and names of CIA agents had been altered for their protection. The second feature showed video and stills from their European vacation. After the show, there was animated discussion about the video from all except Becky, who was unusually silent.

Finally, Becky spoke after things had quieted a bit. "That really happened. You just recorded what happened."

"Yeah, right Becky, and I'm 007," retorted Nate.

"Look at her leg if you don't believe me. I bet you there is a small scar. Annette, next time Josh and I want to be involved. We may not have superpowers, but we want to help."

"We do?" asked Josh, taken by surprise by his young wife.

"Okay. It really did happen, but I will never put Kyle in that kind of jeopardy again. It is a miracle that we survived."

"We thought that we were dead," added Kyle. "It wasn't fun. Well, maybe just a little in a perverse sort of way. I wouldn't trade the experience for anything, but I never want to see the woman that I love in that kind of danger again. If that bullet that wounded Annette's leg had been fired higher, it might have struck her heart. Not only that, but we each put tremendous stress on our bodies. I don't think that we need to go looking for terrorists. They will come looking for us. We may all be in danger." Kyle's comments had a sobering effect on the group. "I fear that we have started a war that will be difficult to end. Don't forget that the terrorist group that abducted us only lost a few of its members. They know who we are and where we live. I fear that they will bring the fight to us. All of us need to watch our backs. We will outfit each of your homes with an intelligent surveillance system, with your permission of course. Instead of reporting to the police, the system will report to each of us. We will be our own first line of defense. I apologize for putting each of you in a risky situation."

"No apology to us is necessary," responded Josh. "We are very proud of the dent you made in terrorism. As far as I am concerned, you are both heroes. I salute you for your efforts."

"As do we," added Nate.

"Well if you ever do anything remotely similar to that again I know that Nate will want in," added Nancy. "He has been working out and taking private karate lessons and is aching for an excuse to whack someone. I'm expecting again so don't expect any heroics from me. I was waiting to tell you all, but I guess now is as good a time as any." The last comment sent the women into a squeal of elation and lively discussion.

That night as Kyle and Annette lay in bed, Annette asked, "Do you really think that the terrorists will come after us?"

"I'm sure that they want to. They may not be able to even get into the country, but they will surely try."

"I would like to continue my medical training and begin residency in a local hospital. Saving that woman's life was the best thing that we did in Afghanistan."

"That's a great idea, Annette. I will eventually do the same, but I have a few matters to finish up first."

Kyle began several new projects. He worked with CompuSonic to develop a law enforcement program for the sentient computers. After five months of hard work, he donated a sentient computer named Casey along with the law enforcement package to the Salt Lake City Police department. In addition, he provided a smartphone or a smart pad, depending on their preference, to each officer. He insisted on presenting the handheld devices to each officer personally. He wanted to know them and them to know him. He had ulterior motives in addition to charity and business in making the donation. Casey tracked every handheld device and reported its location to Bob, the Jameses' SUV. Kyle had upgraded Bob's communication and processing capabilities to make him capable of much more than driving the family vehicle.

During the flight from terrorists, Kyle had been concerned that he was limited in his ability to communicate with Annette by the limitations of voice. As an electrical engineer, he realized that speech contains a tremendous amount of information in addition to the actual message. Often the message itself is lost or misinterpreted. Text is far more efficient but still inefficient when it has to be converted to a visual format and then interpreted in the mind back into text. The ideal solution would be to develop in his brain the ability to interpret and communicate in binary coded ASCII data just as a computer does. With Annette's help and the assistance of his brain implants, he was able to create an initial ability, but it took lots of practice to make it accurate and high speed. He and

Annette began using radio transmission of text to communicate. He also started "reading" the news this way. He read novels that were already available in text format and with the advent of eBooks, there was a broad selection. Using his new technique of direct ASCII interpretation, he was able to assimilate a book much faster than using traditional methods. After months of practice, he could interpret thousands of words per minute.

Chapter 31 – How to Make Friends

Driving Bob, Kyle pulled into the parking lot of the Old West Saloon on Beck Street, north of downtown Salt Lake City. Officer Randy Briggs sat in the passenger seat, holding an Android tablet. Kyle walked into the bar, knowing full well that the biker whom he had earlier confronted was there with his biker friends. Kyle wore a full-length leather coat similar to those worn in the movie The Matrix. The coat bristled with hidden cameras. Kyle was not going into the bar for revenge or machismo. He remembered how he had run into his football-playing adversaries at very inopportune times. There had been only two of them; there were six of the bikers and they posed a much more formidable threat. Kyle wanted to eliminate any possible threat from these men and perhaps even gain them as allies.

As Kyle opened the door and walked in, a host of insects buzzed in with him. He wanted full and total surveillance. Bob and Officer Briggs were in the parking lot in case things went bad. As in their earlier meeting, the leader was at the bar while the rest of his gang was seated at a table. The evening was young and none of the group was overly intoxicated. Kyle scooted in next to "Bear", the leader. Bear did not recognize Kyle at first and paid him no attention. The bartender approached Kyle and Kyle ordered. "A round of whatever they are having for Bear Carpenter and his friends at the table." Bear turned to face Kyle.

"Do I know you?"

"No, but we have met. You probably remember my lovely wife, Annette. She's a real kick."

"You! I ought to kick your ass right now."

"I assure you that you would find that very difficult. You may be taller and heavier than me, but I am stronger, faster, smarter and more highly trained in killing than you. Just shake my hand if you don't believe me."

Bear extended a large, calloused and scarred hand. "Sure, boy. Let's shake." A look of surprise flashed momentarily across Bear's face as he realized that Kyle's hand was substantially larger than his. That look transformed into a grimace as Kyle began to squeeze, gradually, constantly, shrinking the volume that his hand enclosed. In his mind, Kyle received a text from Bob via an encrypted radiofrequency.

"Prepare to drop down," advised the text followed by, "Drop now!" Kyle let his legs bend at the knees and dropped as he released Bear's throbbing hand. A whiskey bottle, the kind with a heavy square bottom whistled over his head and hit Bear, bottom first, squarely in the face. As Bear's head jerked back, Kyle heard in his mind Bob yell, "Jump vertically and to 3 o'clock! Now!" Using computer assist, Kyle sprung up and to the side to get himself out of the path of an array of incoming missiles. He spun in the air and landed on his feet facing the table full of Bear's sidekicks. Before even touching down, from the corner of his eye, Kyle could see a blur pass by him headed in Bear's direction. Kyle turned his head just in time to see a thick-walled glass beer mug hit Bear in the groin. He dropped to his knees holding one hand to his battered face and the other hand over his groin. One of the men at the table reached for a weapon in his boot. A bumblebee stung him on the back of his hand, causing him to jerk back.

"Gentlemen," Kyle began, raising his palms to face the men. "There is no need for further violence. I didn't come here to fight. I want to be friends. Besides, Bear is the one you need to worry about now. I am sure that he is not too happy with whoever threw the bottle and the mug. That bee sting was no coincidence. That was my doing. I control a number of nasty little insects buzzing around the room." Kyle held up a finger and a large bumblebee landed on it. "I don't like having enemies. I prefer them to be my friends or at least my allies. I recently was rescued from torture and death by a man who had been my worse enemy, a man who tried to kill me and eventually killed my first wife and my best friend. He is not someone that I want to hang out with, but we have a working relationship. Much less has gone down between you and me. Surely, we can create a working relationship. One that would be profitable for you." Behind and to his left, Kyle heard something being spit to the floor. A tooth rested on the floor in a puddle of blood and saliva.

"How would it be profitable?" asked Bear.

"I would pay you a salary, a rather generous salary. In return, I ask two things. One, you engage in no criminal activity. Two, when and if we call for help you come immediately and ready to defend me, my wife and our friends against any and all attackers. You will be each issued a cell phone and you will be required to carry it at all times. We will hold at least four drills a year. Any who fail to appear will be docked pay. Those who do show will receive bonuses, the largest for the first to arrive."

"Why do you need protection?" asked Bear.

"You know how my wife can get on your bad side? Well, she got us both on the bad side of some nasty Middle Eastern terrorists. We didn't kill all of them and they may be coming after us. I thought that maybe you fine men could show them some real American hospitality if they ever show up here. Chances are, you will never have to earn your pay. It's a lot of money out of my pocket, but money I have. I would like to continue living so that I can enjoy it." The group all sat down together at the table. Eventually, they came to an agreement and worked out the details. Before the week was over, Kyle had the whole gang under contract.

A few weeks later at 4:21 AM, Bob sent out alerts to the cell phones of each gang member. They were instructed to meet at the CompuSonic parking lot. Bear was the first to arrive. An application on his phone showed him the location of each of his associates. Most were already on the way. He began making phone calls to those who were not on the road. Within ten more minutes all, but two had arrived. The other two wandered in within the next hour. Kyle took them all to breakfast where they met Kyle's friends. The manager of the restaurant brought Kyle a stack of faxes. Bob had calculated the bonuses based on arrival times and fitness to serve. The latter was a judgment call based on visual cues. Those who were hungover or otherwise impaired received smaller bonuses than those who were in better physical shape. Kyle handed each man his score sheet and counted out his bonus in cash. Over $10,000 lay on the table. The men compared score sheets like a bunch of boys going over their laser tag score sheets. Even the lowest-paid man was happy.

"Gentlemen, Bob, the computer who graded you, is not scoring on a curve. You are not competing against each other and part of your bonus is for you as a group. You get more money if your companions arrive sooner and more prepared to do their job. Next time you will be required to actually do something. Think of yourselves like firemen. It is not enough to just arrive at the fire, you have to have the right equipment, training and conditioning to fight the fire." Bear raised his hand.

"Can I make a suggestion?"

"Sure Bear. What's on your mind?"

"The salary that you provide and the bonuses are very generous for doing almost nothing, but they are kinda slim if we want to start families, which some of us do, now that our lives have settled down. We need day jobs that will keep us busy, add to our incomes, but allow us to drop work at a moment's notice to come to your aid or these drills. I have a business proposal for you. Each of us is a skilled mechanic and knows motorcycles. I would like to enter into a partnership. I would like to open a business that sells custom motorcycles and services not only custom but all types of motorcycles. We could call it 'Hell on Wheels Custom Bikes and

Trikes'. All we need from you would be the upfront money to get started. We would run the business and provide you a good return on your investment."

"I'll consider that proposal," offered Nate. Within a few months, the business was up and running. Nate not only shepherded the business, but he also started teaching the group paramilitary skills. Nate hired a retired member of the US Special Forces to teach classes. As the gang increased in skill, Kyle increased their salaries. Nate encouraged his friends to participate in the training.

Kyle began his residency. He hated how he and Annette were often on different schedules and could spend far less time together. The honeymoon was not over yet, but it had been dealt a severe blow. Now that all of the preparations were complete for their protection from a terrorist assault, Kyle felt like a man living on a small island in the path of a hurricane. He had boarded up the house and was waiting for the fury to unleash. Unfortunately, he did not know when or if the attack would come, but his gut told him that trouble was on its way.

The End

Acknowledgements

Much of the information concerning the CIA was taken directly from their web site at http://www.cia.gov .

About the Author

Lloyd G. Miller is a successful engineer (US patents #6,491,773 and #8,042,594) who started writing as a hobby over two decades ago. After writing several novels and spending years refining them, he decided to try publishing. After experiencing creative differences with a publisher who had contracted to publish one of his novels, he decided to publish eBooks through Smashwords. He lives in Utah where most of the story takes place.

Other Novels by Lloyd G. Miller

The author has also written Reckless Brilliance, a sci-fi/coming of age novel published as an eBook in 2018 and Reckless Beauty, a sequel to Reckless Brilliance.

Also by Lloyd G Miller

Powerful Minds
Reckless Brilliance
Reckless Beauty

Standalone
The Computer Who Loved Me

About the Author

Lloyd G. Miller is a successful engineer (US patents #6,491,773 and #8,042,594) who started writing as a hobby two decades ago. After writing several novels and spending years refining them, he decided to try publishing. After studying about ebook publishing through a middleman such as Smashwords, he concluded to try that approach, starting with Cloned Memories. He lives in Bountiful, Utah where most of the story takes place. In 2014, a publisher, Savant Books and Publishing, called and said that they wanted to publish Cloned Memories based on an earlier version that he had sent them. The chief editor was very enthusiastic. Lloyd was asked to immediately pull the book off of Smashwords. After signing the contract, he discovered that the owner wanted him to change the plot by one third because it had been earlier published by Smashwords. Lloyd disagreed with this logic and the contract was voided. Lloyd made extensive changes to Cloned Memories and renamed it Reckless Brilliance. In 2017, he decided to return to Smashwords with The Computer Who Loved me. This novel should be much easier to market.